To Hell on a Fast Horse

THE COMPLETE LOU PROPHET, BOUNTY HUNTER SERIES

TO HELL ON A FAST HORSE

A WESTERN DUO

PETER BRANDVOLD

FIVE STAR

A part of Gale, Cengage Learning

GALE
CENGAGE Learning·

Farmington Hills, Mich • San Francisco • New York • Waterville, Maine
Meriden, Conn • Mason, Ohio • Chicago

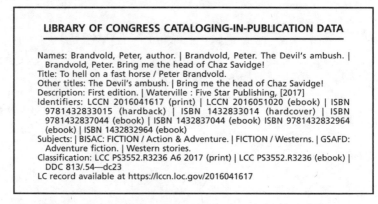

LIBRARY OF CONGRESS CATALOGING-IN-PUBLICATION DATA

Names: Brandvold, Peter, author. | Brandvold, Peter. The Devil's ambush. | Brandvold, Peter. Bring me the head of Chaz Savidge!
Title: To hell on a fast horse / Peter Brandvold.
Other titles: The Devil's ambush. | Bring me the head of Chaz Savidge!
Description: First edition. | Waterville : Five Star Publishing, [2017]
Identifiers: LCCN 2016041617 (print) | LCCN 2016051020 (ebook) | ISBN 9781432833015 (hardback) | ISBN 1432833014 (hardcover) | ISBN 9781432837044 (ebook) | ISBN 1432837044 (ebook) ISBN 9781432832964 (ebook) | ISBN 1432832964 (ebook)
Subjects: | BISAC: FICTION / Action & Adventure. | FICTION / Westerns. | GSAFD: Adventure fiction. | Western stories.
Classification: LCC PS3552.R3236 A6 2017 (print) | LCC PS3552.R3236 (ebook) | DDC 813/.54—dc23
LC record available at https://lccn.loc.gov/2016041617

First Edition. First Printing: March 2017
Find us on Facebook— https://www.facebook.com/FiveStarCengage
Visit our website— http://www.gale.cengage.com/fivestar/
Contact Five Star™ Publishing at FiveStar@cengage.com

Printed in the United States of America
1 2 3 4 5 6 7 21 20 19 18 17

CONTENTS

★ ★ ★ ★ ★

THE DEVIL'S AMBUSH

★ ★ ★ ★

CHAPTER ONE

Lou Prophet reined Mean and Ugly to a halt along a dusty trail somewhere on the devil's backside of southeastern Colorado Territory, between hell and high water, though if there was a drop of the wet stuff out here, Prophet hadn't seen it after two days of hard riding. He swabbed sweat from his sunburned forehead with a grimy shirtsleeve and popped the cork from the mouth of his hide-wrapped canteen.

Mean gave a snort, twitched an ear, and glanced back over his right wither at his rider, the lineback dun's wide, mud-brown right eye cast with a question.

"Sorry, pard. You had all you're gonna get for a while," Prophet said. "If it don't rain soon, neither one of us is gonna be drinkin' again until we find a spring."

He glanced at the sky. Cobalt blue with only a few clouds hanging just above the southern horizon, somewhere over the vast New Mexico Territory. He glanced over his right shoulder and saw the Front Range of the Rocky Mountains jutting against the horizon like a badly uneven saw blade, a couple of the longest teeth touched with wax.

No clouds in that direction, either.

He was surprised that there was still snow this late in the year up there. His mouth watered as he thought of cool, gurgling streams tumbling down those verdant slopes through fragrant spruce forests and beaver meadows.

The bounty hunter would rather be up there than out here

on this parched plain. But he'd been summoned out here. Now he took a sip of the tepid, brackish water, returned the cork to the flask, and hung the canteen from his saddle horn. He fished a scrap of lined notepaper out of the breast pocket of his pullover shirt, which he wore beneath a brown leather vest, and unfolded the paper, soggy with the sweat his dried-out body still managed to ooze out his pores.

In a woman's flowing hand, in blue-black ink, it read:

Mr. Prophet,

On September First, please ride to the old Ramsay Creek Cavalry Outpost on Ramsay Creek in Brush County, eastern Colorado Territory. Take the Soldier Creek Trail west from Colorado Springs. A rider will meet you at the outpost with news regarding your friend, Miss Louisa Bonaventure.

The only signature was three X's.

Prophet scowled down at the paper, which fluttered in the hot, dry breeze, the sweat in the paper drying even as he held the note in his hand. Concern and curiosity plucked at him, causing the muscles between his shoulder blades to twitch uncomfortably.

He carefully folded the note and returned it to his pocket. He didn't know why he was so careful with the paper, which had come from a small, lined notepad you could purchase in any mercantile. He'd already memorized what the note said. He'd recited it to himself over the three days he'd been riding through this vast country from Colorado Springs, where the note had been slipped under his hotel room door.

Still, since it alluded to Louisa, he felt proprietary toward the note—maybe because he didn't have his partner and sometime-lover here to be proprietary to in person.

He smiled at that. Whenever he acted proprietary to Louisa herself, he got an earful. He'd welcome that earful now, however. He was worried about the girl. Damned worried. Did someone have her? Was she dead, and was the writer of the note wanting to tell him about it?

Had she been kidnapped?

Or was someone using Louisa's name to bait him into a trap?

"Ah, shit," Prophet said, looking around carefully for any sign of an ambush. He glanced behind him again. There was no movement along the horse trail that rose and fell and meandered and disappeared for long stretches as it dwindled off into the distance, as though swallowed by the distantly looming and majestic Pikes Peak. The land was all shades of brown, relieved only by the cream color of buttes and the deep blue of the arching sky.

No movement back there. If someone was trailing him, they were damned good at trailing. If they were that good at trailing so that he, a veteran man-tracker himself, couldn't detect him, then the tracker was likely a damned good bushwhacker, too.

Prophet didn't have to remind himself to be careful, but as he touched spurs to Mean and Ugly's ribs and started off along the trail, he did anyway.

"Go easy, hoss," he muttered, continuing to look around. "Ole Scratch ain't ready for you. Er . . . well, maybe *he's* ready for *you*, but *you* ain't ready for *him*. You'll shovel his coal in good time, but you ain't done stompin' with your tail up on this side of the sod yet."

Again, Mean and Ugly twitched an incredulous ear and glanced at him over his right wither. The horse blew.

"Hobble your lips, Mean."

Mean shook his head, rattling the bit in his teeth, and continued walking down a grade and around the shoulder of one of the many hogbacks out here. As they climbed into some scrubby hills peppered with clay-colored boulders and twisted

11

cedars and junipers, Prophet stopped the lineback dun once again.

He stared ahead, frowning.

They were almost to Ramsay Creek. The cavalry outpost would be a quarter of a mile or so ahead and to the north, on the left side of the trail. Prophet knew the outpost from having holed up there a couple of years ago. It had been abandoned even back then, and it had afforded good cover from the pack of young Kiowa he'd run into and who'd chased him, whooping, hollering, and laughing and waving war clubs.

He hadn't been sure if they were just funning with him, wanting to scare the shit out of the white-eyes because they were bored and simply out looking for a white-eyes to scare, or if they really meant to lift his hair. He hadn't taken a chance on them not intending the latter, so he'd hightailed it to the outpost along Ramsay Creek, which consisted of a half-dozen or so still-standing adobe brick, brush-roofed shacks, and snapped off a magazine of Winchester loads at the braves slithering around the surrounding rocky buttes and arroyos.

Prophet had thought that one of his slugs might have pinked one of the Kiowa. That had sobered the natives right fast and they'd slipped quietly back, like coyotes with buckshot-peppered behinds, into the southern badlands along the Arkansas River. He'd neither seen nor heard from them again, though it had been a nervous night he'd spent there at the ghostly old outpost, which some settlers in the country claimed was haunted by the ghosts of cavalry soldiers who'd been killed there during an Arapaho attack twenty-five years earlier.

Prophet could have sworn he'd spied a couple of blue-clad soldiers dancing together to the strains he heard of a loose-stringed, scratchy-sounding fiddle. He never told anybody about that, and he'd long since put it out of his mind though, obviously, not completely because he was remembering those two soldiers now. He could see them as though he'd seen them only the night before, and he could hear the squawks of a fiddle though it had to have merely been a trick of the wind stealing through the rocks and brush that hot summer night.

Not a fiddle. And the two soldier-ghosts had not been dancing together the way soldiers often did when no women were available.

Nope. The Kiowa had merely rattled him. He wished he could have blamed those ghost soldiers and that fiddle on too much tangle-leg, but he hadn't had so much as dipped his tongue in any who-hit-John since he'd pulled out of Julesburg two days before.

"Ah, hell," Prophet complained as he swung down from Mean and Ugly's back. "Why did I have to go and remember that?"

The horse looked at him through a dubious left eye.

"Remember what, you ask?" Prophet said, accustomed to having conversations with the hammerhead. "Them two soldiers. Now, why in the hell did I have to remember that? Not only do I got Louisa to worry about, but now I'm gonna be worried about them two blue-bellies showin' up again just as soon as the sun goes down. And believe me, Mean, when the sun goes down out here, it goes all the way down. I mean, it sinks all the way down to the bottom of the dadgum universe so's you don't think you're ever gonna see it again, and that's a bonded fact."

Prophet was reaching under the stocky dun's belly to unbuckle the latigo. "What I'm sayin' is—it gets dark out here. Well, you were here. You remember."

He slipped the bridle bit from Mean's teeth, so the horse could forage, and held the horse's snout steady while he said, "Mean—you an' I never talked about this, but . . . did you see 'em? Them soldiers, I mean? Did you hear that fiddle?"

The horse stretched his neck out so he could try biting off one of the bone buttons from the V-neck of Prophet's soggy cream pullover.

"Ah, shit," Prophet said, releasing Mean's snout. "I don't know why I ever try talkin' to you. You never take nothin' serious. If you had seen them two soldiers, or heard that fiddle, you woulda been so scared you'd have pulled your picket pin and you'd still be runnin' straight north. Likely be all the way to the North Pole by now!"

Prophet chuckled as he doffed his hat and carefully poured an inch of water into it from the canteen. He set the hat down in front of Mean and Ugly and while the horse slurped up the little bit of water, Prophet lifted the lanyard of his ten-gauge, sawed-off Richards coach gun from over his head and right shoulder and hung the shotgun from his saddle horn. The ten-gauge cannon was savagely helpful for work in close quarters, but the bounty hunter anticipated no such work out here.

He slipped his Winchester '73 from its scabbard, ran an appreciative hand down the barrel and walnut forestock, and pumped a cartridge into the action. By the time he'd off-cocked the hammer, the horse had finished the water and was snorting and bobbing his battle-scarred head, demanding more.

"You'll just have to wait and hope the well at the outpost has water in it," Prophet told him. "If not, we'll both be chewin' leather."

The horse whickered and shook his head.

"Fuss all you want, pard," Prophet said, leaving the horse's bridle reins hanging, knowing the horse would stay with its reins until Prophet whistled for it. "Just stay put." He glanced around, squinting one eye beneath the brim of his salt-stained, funnel-brimmed Stetson that had once been tan but was now bleached to Confederate gray, which was fitting. "Let me know if you smell Injuns on the wind."

Prophet pulled his hat brim down low on his forehead and walked through the brush between two low buttes. To his left was a twisting, gravel streambed as bone-dry as the rest of this country, with a couple of bleached cows' skulls, half-buried in the sand scalloped by previous floodwaters, mocking him.

Prophet made his way through the rocky buttes. The sun beat down, and an occasional hot breeze scratched the creosote and Spanish bayonet branches together. That must have been what he'd heard that night.

So, if that's what he'd heard—what had he seen?

He shrugged the niggling thoughts away, concentrating instead on the task at hand. He wanted to approach the outpost without being seen—at least, without being seen before he saw whomever had summoned him here and had learned what in hell they wanted to tell him about the blond-headed Vengeance Queen herself, Louisa Bonaventure.

He moved through the brushy hills, narrowly avoiding two rattlesnakes, hearing a hawk hunting unseen in the deep blue sky, for a good twenty minutes. Then he hunkered down behind a boulder sheathed in scrub brush and sage.

Below, in a clearing amongst the buttes, sat the scattered adobe brick shacks of the old outpost though a few weren't so much standing as leaning, part or all of their brush roofs having fallen inside the wind- and sun-blasted walls. There were a half-dozen other log shacks around the perimeter, but they'd long since fallen to one side, or their roofs had collapsed. In typical army fashion, they hadn't been built well. Probably not enough stone or straw in the mud. Only three or four of the shacks appeared to still be hospitable, though likely hospitable only to black widows and diamondbacks.

It was eerily quiet down there.

The breeze lifted a plume of dust that tried desperately to form a devil and failed. It bounced around a few tumbleweeds and threatened to scrape a few of the other many tumbleweeds away from the walls of the shacks, where they hunkered like frightened children.

Prophet raked a thumb down his unshaven jaw, making a scratching sound.

"I don't like this," he told himself aloud. "I don't like this one damn bit."

Then a horse whinnied. It wasn't Mean who whinnied. It was a horse somewhere down there in the hollow but hidden back in the brush and rocks on the other side of the outpost.

Someone else was here.

Why didn't he show himself?

Prophet was starting to like this even less. He hadn't enjoyed the night he'd spent here several years ago and now, like a fool, he'd come back for more.

Now, as he started down the slope toward the ruins, the breeze started sounding like the scratching of an old fiddle . . .

CHAPTER TWO

Prophet stayed behind cover as he made his way down the rocky slope of the bluff. He moved crouching, the Winchester in both his gloved hands. He looked around and he sniffed the breeze like a dog, because he'd learned that sometimes even a man could smell trouble before he saw or heard it.

At the base of the bluff, he stared out across the hollow in which the outpost sat, the shabby buildings looking especially fragile and insignificant amidst the surrounding high buttes and overarching sky. Occasionally the breeze kicked up a dust devil or two and moaned as it blew amongst the ruins.

Scrub and prickly pear had grown up around the outpost yard, and he meandered amongst that and the rocks that had tumbled down from the bluffs as he made his way toward the old post commander's headquarters, which was still fronted by a sagging brush gallery. A well stood off to the right, near the base of a low, brushy, and rocky southern slope. He hoped the well held water, but at the moment he had other matters on his mind—namely, the question of whether or not he was walking into an ambush.

He stepped past a gnarled post oak and pressed his shoulder up against a wall of the post commander's headquarters. A window lay to his right now, as he faced the direction from which he'd come. He stepped to the window, which was a dark cavity without shutters and certainly without the waxed paper that might have covered it sometime in the past.

He peered into the deep shadows relieved by amber-yellow light pushing in through windows on the hovel's opposite side. Nothing moved. The air pushing out of the window smelled like mouse and bird shit and the dankness of the old mud comprising the walls.

Prophet moved toward the front of the shack. He stopped beside the second of the two windows on this side of the building and again peered inside, seeing and hearing nothing and smelling only mud and wood rot and animal droppings.

Carefully, he moved to the front of the shack. From the corner, he stared out at the parade ground that was almost blindingly bright. Nothing much grew out there. The southern butte rose about a hundred yards beyond. To its right, a well-worn, two-track wagon trail twisted through a crease between that butte and the slightly higher, steeper one beside it.

Prophet scoured the grounds before him and to both sides and the bluffs rising in those directions, as well. The invisible bugs creeping up and down his spine and around behind his ears told him someone else was here. The bugs and the horse's whinny, that was.

Someone else was here, all right. Who? And were they friend or foe?

Prophet ducked under the rail of the gallery fronting the post commander's office and stepped up onto the sagging stoop. The old wood creaked precariously beneath his boots. A cracked clay *olla* hung from the brush roof. It was covered with dirt and cobwebs as was the rope from which it dangled.

He looked into the front window left of the door and then he stepped quickly through the door, which, like the windows, was an empty cavity. Every bit of extra wood in the place, save for the gallery, had likely been scavenged long ago. The bounty hunter pressed his back to the wall to the left of the door and extended the rifle straight out from his right hip, squinting into the shadows that lay heavy in the derelict place. The only remaining furnishing was an old sheet iron stove against the adobe brick wall straight ahead of him. The stove was badly rusted and covered in grit.

The front room, where the commanding officer's adjutant probably had his desk, was all dirt and old leaves. Prophet stepped quickly through the door flanking the stove and into the room that was probably the officer's official digs. Nothing here but the same grime in the main room. There was another office, probably for the second in command.

Empty.

Prophet walked back out to the main room. He was just ducking his six-foot-four-inch frame back out through the front door, when a thud sounded behind him and to his right. Heart hiccupping, he swung around, clicking the Winchester's hammer back to full cock.

He eased the tension on his trigger finger, letting the rifle sag in his hand. The liver-colored cat that had just leaped through the window meowed at him, arched his or her back, and then meowed again as it sauntered forward, copper eyes glowing in the dim room.

"Damn, cat—you likely spooked two, three years off my allotment," said the bounty hunter, resting the rifle barrel on his right shoulder.

The cat folded its body around his right boot, trilling.

"You're right friendly," Prophet said. "I got a feelin' folks who pass through here from time to time feed you. That right, Puss?"

The cat purred as it arched its back and stuck its tail nearly straight up in the air. It looked up at Prophet with its copper eyes and meowed again, beseeching.

Sure enough—the cat was tame. Probably lived out here. He remembered other cats prowling around the outpost, when he was through here last and got to watch the ghostly do-si-doers. This cat was probably offspring of that pack. Folks probably passed through here regularly on account of the well and that's how the cat got so friendly.

Prophet turned back to the door. "Anyone else here, Kitty?"

He stood in the doorway, looking around. He turned his head to stare off to the left and froze. A man's silhouette faced him from the far front corner of a dilapidated cabin whose gallery roof was sagging at a forty-five-degree angle over its crumbling wooden floor. The man was staring at Prophet through that gap beneath the gallery roof. He stood there for only about two seconds while Prophet stared back at him, and then the *hombre* disappeared behind the cabin's far side.

"Well, now," Prophet said under his breath, moving slowly out onto the gallery, "who in hell are you?"

He stepped off the end of the gallery. Looking around cautiously, in case other men were moving around him to take a shot at him, he strode through the rocks and brush toward the cabin. He circled a scrubby *piñon* and approached the cabin's front corner. He scrutinized the place carefully, pricking his ears to listen.

Nothing.

His heart was beating insistently in his chest and apprehension caused those bugs to skitter faster along his spine.

He looked behind him. There was only the cat sitting on the gallery of the building he'd just left, casually washing its face with a paw.

The cat had the life. Wasn't worried about a damned thing. Prophet envied the furry critter.

The bounty hunter walked slowly around the front of the collapsed gallery roof and stared down the far side of the cabin. Nothing but sunlit tumbleweeds, clumps of blond brush, and rocks. Prophet walked quietly down the side of the cabin, moving on the balls of his boots to keep his spurs from chinging. He was striding through the shade along the back wall, skirting an empty rain barrel, when he stopped suddenly.

He'd heard something behind him. Either heard it or sensed something. He wasn't sure. But he swung around and raised his rifle to his shoulder, slowing ratcheting the hammer back to full cock.

He definitely heard something now. The slight crunch of gravel beneath a boot.

Prophet licked his lips, raised the rifle higher, and aimed toward the corner of the cabin.

He waited, aiming, his heart thudding, sweat dribbling down his back. There was one more crunch of a boot on gravel and then a man stepped out around the corner of the cabin. He held a cocked pistol straight out from his shoulder and she— yes, it was a woman—was squinting one almond-shaped hazel eye beneath the brim of her cream Stetson, aiming down the Peacemaker's silver-chased barrel.

Blond hair spilled across her shoulders, which were clad in a green and white calico shirt.

Prophet kept his rifle aimed at her. She kept her cocked pistol aimed at Prophet. They stood there stubbornly aiming at each other, as though neither could quite believe what they were seeing, and then Prophet depressed the Winchester's hammer and lowered his weapon to his side.

"Ah, shit."

"My sentiments, exactly," Louisa Bonaventure said, wrinkling a pretty nostril at him as she depressed the hammer of her Colt and lowered the gun to her side. She wore a snooty frown on her high-cheek-boned face with saucy lips and bold, shrewd eyes. She wore a long, chocolate-brown leather skirt and brown stockmen's boots. She had a shell belt and two cross-draw holsters cinched at her narrow waist.

Her full bosom pushed out from behind the loose-fitting blouse, forever taunting him.

Prophet tried to hide the relief he felt at seeing her alive, but was unable to conceal the fact that he wasn't overly happy to see her again, as their last parting had been on bad terms. Their partings usually were. He wasn't ready to suffer her superior, condescending company again so soon after she'd called him a "Rebel carouser and general no-account scalawag who drank too much and broke wind too loudly in camp . . . when he was in camp, that was, and was not frequenting fallen women in the crudest settlements on the western frontier—settlements," she added, "in which he fit right in."

"What the hell are you doin' here?" Prophet raked out, scowling down at the infamous Vengeance Queen, whose pretty head came up only to his shoulder.

"I was about to ask you the same question," she said in her snobby tone, staring up at him as though he were a ragged bear who'd just stepped out of her parlor.

Prophet stared at her. And then he looked around, the hair once again pricking along the back of his thick neck.

"What's your note say?"

Louisa stared up at him and then she swung around and stepped out away from him, looking around and raising her pistol, once more cocking the pretty piece. She unholstered the other one, cocked and raised it, as well.

"You got one, too."

"Uh-huh."

"Mine told me you likely had your neck in another sling and needed my assistance. Why I rode down here to rescue you . . . again . . . when I was having a very nice, comfortable time in Denver, taking in the opera and other cultural events that would only leave you hang-jawed and cross-eyed, I have no idea."

Prophet had walked to the other end of the cabin and stared

out at the sun-blasted yard that was just as eerily still and silent as before. Louisa was looking out from the cabin's opposite side, sliding her revolvers this way and that.

"Yeah, well, I was havin' a nice time with the pretty doxies in Colorado Springs, too, and was just fixin' to head up to Cripple Creek, where I've heard they're even better." Prophet was backing toward her. "Let's see it."

"See what, you cad?"

"Your note."

Keeping her back to him, Louisa pulled her note out of her shirt pocket and gave it to him. He shook it open.

"Do you need me to read it to you?"

Ignoring her, Prophet read the note:

In a woman's flowing hand, in blue-black ink, it read:

Miss Bonaventure,

Please ride to the old Ramsay Creek Cavalry Outpost on Ramsay Creek in Brush County, eastern Colorado Territory. Take the Arkansas River Trail south from Denver. A rider will meet you at the outpost with news regarding your friend, Mr. Prophet.

Three X's were the only signature.

Prophet handed the note back to Louisa. "Same as the one I got. Only yours is in a different hand, looks like."

Louisa returned the note to her shirt pocket and then unholstered her second Colt again.

"So someone wanted us both out here at the same time. Just what I get for riding to your rescue. Live and learn. Next time, I'm going to stay and enjoy another performance of *Romeo and Juliet.* Mr. Edgar Carr and Sonja Baldwin were in top form three nights ago. Now I'm out here in the middle of God-forsaken nowhere on account of you, and someone's probably drawing a bead on my pretty head."

"Yeah, well, I came down here for you, too—though don't ask me why—and that same person or persons is likely doin' the same thing to me."

"It isn't any consolation, Lou."

"Let's spread out and scour the place. I'll take the southern buttes, you take the northern buttes. We'll meet back at the post commander's headquarters in an hour—if we're both still alive, that is."

"Lou?"

Prophet glanced at her.

"Be careful, you big ape."

He drew her to him, tipped her head back, and kissed her plump lips. "You, too, darlin'."

Releasing her, he tramped away around the shack.

CHAPTER THREE

When Prophet finished scouring the southern buttes, he headed back to the post headquarters. Halfway across what had once been the parade ground, he whistled for Mean and Ugly. The horse came galloping, dragging its reins.

As the horse pranced up to the well, having smelled the water, Prophet saw Louisa walk into the canyon through a crease between the rocky bluffs to the north. She was trailing her brown-and-white pinto, which she called simply "Horse."

That was Louisa's way. Like many cowboys, she saw no reason to get close enough to her mount to give it a name. To her and many drovers, a horse was a means of getting around— nothing more, nothing less.

Secretly, Prophet called the pinto "Peaches," chuckling to himself when he did. It was just the kind of name the unsentimental Vengeance Queen wouldn't have named it had she been inclined to name it anything at all.

The well was nothing more than mortared stone coping over a hole in the ground. It had a stout wooden cover, one whose boards had been replaced by some unknown handyman over the years. The well was obviously valued by everyone traveling the Old Arkansas River Trail between Sullyville, in western Kansas, to Pueblo, which sat at the foot of the Front Range to the west. There were many relatively fresh tracks leading into the old parade ground and marking the area around the well, including the week-old tracks of what Prophet assumed was a stagecoach.

Prophet removed the cover, dropped the bucket, which was attached to a rope, into the well, heard it splash and gurgle, and then heaved it up. He set the bucket down on the ground, doffed his hat, slurped water cupped in his hands, and then splashed himself with the refreshing goodness. Finally, he dunked his head up to his neck, and blew.

He pulled his head out of the bucket, water streaming down his face, and shook his head. The eager Mean and Ugly whinnied, nudged Prophet aside with his long snout, and sank his lips in the bucket.

"Damn, that feels good!" Prophet intoned, letting the water drip down his chest and back, cooling and refreshing him. "Bone-chillin' cold, too—just like I remember it. Them soldier boys dug 'em a deep well."

Louisa slipped her pinto's bit. "Don't let your guard down over some cold water. Someone called us out here for a reason. I'm assuming you didn't come across anyone to the south. I saw no one to the north, but there's a reason why we're here, Lou, and I have a feeling we're going to find out what that reason is soon."

"Ah, shit, I'm just enjoying some water, Louisa. Do you mind if I enjoy myself for two minutes?"

"Two minutes—hah! You live to enjoy yourself, Lou."

"You got a point there." Prophet looked around as the water already began to dry on his face. "Nothin' wrong with a man enjoyin' himself. That's why we're put here, after all. But don't worry, Miss Bonnyventure, I know we ain't here to pay our respects to no belle of the ball. That don't mean we're necessarily on death's doorstep, though."

"No? Then how do you account for the lie we were both told?"

Louisa had pulled the water bucket away from Mean and Ugly and dropped it into the well. Now she was grunting and flushing prettily beneath her hat brim as she fetched it up out of the cool darkness below.

"I can't," Prophet said, scooping his hat off the ground and running an elbow around the inside of the brim, soaking up the sweat from the band. "But I got a feelin' that if whoever called us out here wanted us dead, he'd have tipped his hand by now. He . . . or they . . . would have been waitin' here to bushwhack us."

"Possibly." Louisa looked around, concern showing in her pretty, refined features with her clear hazel eyes, straight, fine nose, and delicate, dimpled chin. Her skin was tanned a dark olive, with a light peppering of freckles across her cheeks, but it was still smooth despite all the traveling she'd done, hunting down bad men beneath a harsh, frontier sun. The tan made the hazel in her eyes stand out.

Her religious-like zeal for hunting men—especially those who harmed women and children, like those who'd wiped out her family, leaving her alone alive to hunt the killers and kill them one by one, hard and bloody—often shone in those pretty hazel orbs, lending them an off-putting sharpness that contrasted bizarrely with her otherwise sweet schoolgirl face.

"Possibly," she said again, quietly, as the dry breeze blew her sun-bleached blond hair around her shoulders.

Prophet slipped Mean's saddle and blanket from the horse's back, and set them on the ground by the well.

"What are you doing?" Louisa asked him.

"Figure we're gonna be here a while."

"Don't need to be." Louisa ran a toe of her boot along the ground in front of her. "We could just ride out of here."

Prophet removed a hackamore from a saddlebag pouch. "You really wanna do that?"

She shrugged and looked off. "No point in us sticking around when we know we were lured here by a lie. For what will most likely turn out to be nefarious reasons."

"What kind of reasons?"

Louisa rolled her eyes. "Never mind."

"Wasn't really a lie," Prophet said as he slid the hackamore over Mean's ears. "The notes just said someone wanted to talk to us about the other." He grinned. "I for one would like to hear what they have to say about you."

"It's hogwash and you know it."

"Yeah, I know it." Prophet sighed and stared to the south from over Mean's back. "But, yeah—okay, what the hell. Let's pull our picket pins. I was havin' a fine ole time in the Springs."

"I'll bet you were."

Prophet looked at her. Louisa was leading the watered pinto back toward the post commander's headquarters. "What're you doin'?"

"Gonna picket my horse out of sight. No use leavin' him out here where someone could shoot him and leave me afoot."

"I thought you wanted to go back to Denver and continue enjoyin' them opera shows."

Louisa gave him a droll glance over her shoulder.

Prophet chuckled and led Mean after Louisa and the pinto. "Yeah, I'm right curious, my ownself."

Prophet pulled the quirley down and blew smoke at the headquarters' low ceiling, watching the blue smoke flatten out against the herringbone-pattern rafters that were coated in dirt and cobwebs in which dead flies and leaves hung suspended.

"So that's the story of how my pal Jeff Diddle stole the old planter's prized Thoroughbred and got himself hitched to that sweet little Belle Pinkett, who didn't turn out so sweet, after all, seein' as how she got poor ole Jeff thrown in the Dalton hoosegow." Prophet chuckled as he stared at the burning end of his loosely rolled cigarette. "My Lord—that was a time ago. Why, that was before the damn Yankees—"

"Lou, his name was not really 'Diddle,' " Louisa interrupted him in disgust.

Prophet looked at the woman sitting on her saddle near the front window right of the door. Prophet himself lay back against the eastern wall, leaning against his own saddle, legs stretched before him on the grimy floor, boots crossed. The ten-gauge Richards lay across his thighs, freshly cleaned and oiled, both bores loaded and ready to go. "His name sure as hell was Diddle. Jeffrey Diddle."

"You made that up to try and shock me, though nothing you could say or do could ever again shock me."

"Louisa, I swear on a whole stack of family Bibles."

"What would you have to lose? You already sold your soul to . . ." Louisa let her voice trail off as she turned to look out the window over her right shoulder.

She turned full around and then grabbed her own carbine and pressed her shoulder against the wall, to the right of the window. "Someone's coming."

Prophet blew out another drag, mashed the quirley on the floor, set the Richards aside, and grabbed his Winchester. He crabbed over to the window on his side of the door, and, doffing his hat, edged a look around the frame. He saw the movement about the same time he heard the clattering of what could only be a wagon.

A mule was just coming into view along the main trail snaking through the crease between the buttes. Now the wagon the mule was pulling came into view, as well. It was a small wagon with an old, gray-bearded man sitting in the driver's box, mule-eared boots propped against the dash.

A yellow dog sat on the blanket-covered seat beside the old

man. As the mule headed for the well, Prophet saw that the wagon was full of lumpy sacks and mining paraphernalia, including pans, picks, shovels, and sluice boxes. The wagon had been painted orange at one time, but the orange had faded to a dull copper. One of the wheels was relatively new, and it sported red spokes.

The old man drew up to the well and punched the brake home. While he clambered down from the driver's boot, the dog leaped down and immediately began sniffing the yard around the well. The mongrel had obviously picked up the scent of Prophet, Louisa, and their horses.

"Shit," Prophet muttered. The dog would find them. The old man was probably harmless, but someone could have put him on the scout for a few pinches of gold dust.

"What the hell you smell, Skeeter?" the old man asked the dog, who was running zigzags in the yard between the well and the post headquarters. The old man studied Prophet and Louisa's hideout suspiciously, his eyes small and dark in his craggy, leathery face beneath the brim of his low-crowned straw sombrero. He was dark enough to have some Indian blood, but something told Prophet he was just an old desert rat wizened by the sun.

The dog continued to follow its nose toward the cabin.

Prophet looked over at Louisa, and shrugged. What could they do?

But then the dog turned on a dime and went running off into the brush to the west. Shortly, a cat hissed loudly. The dog yipped and ran back to the wagon, snorting and shaking its head as though it had gotten its snout scratched. Pouring out water for the dog and the mule, the old man laughed.

"Someday, Skeeter, you'll learn to leave them cats alone."

When the old man had watered his animals and himself, and filled a couple of canteens and canvas water sacks, he gazed once more toward the post commander's headquarters, shading his eyes against the glare as the sun dropped in the west. He lifted his hat, sleeved sweat from his forehead, muttered something that Prophet couldn't hear from this distance, and then climbed back into the wagon.

As the mule swung the wagon around and headed back out to the trail between the buttes, the old man glanced once more over his shoulder. And then he and the mule and dog were gone.

Prophet and Louisa shared a glance and a shrug.

As they continued to sit in the headquarters shack, waiting, the sun dropped lower in the west. Now Prophet felt like pulling his picket pin. The idea of getting caught here at the outpost after dark held little appeal. His memory of the two cavalry ghosts was still fresh in his mind. He was about to suggest to Louisa that they pull foot, but then a horse whinnied out toward the main trail.

Hooves thudded. Two riders were approaching.

Prophet looked at Louisa. She returned the look but said nothing as she turned to edge a look out the window, caressing her carbine's hammer with her thumb.

The visitors turned out to be two saddle tramps who paid no attention to the post headquarters building, and didn't even look around the outpost overmuch. That didn't mean they weren't on the scout, but Prophet doubted it. The two tramps chuckled as they jeered each other the way bored saddle tramps do; then they mounted up and road off with nary a look behind them.

"Shit," Prophet said when they'd drifted out of sight.

"What?"

"Night's comin' on."

"Yeah, we'll likely get some action soon."

That wasn't what he meant. Suddenly, he was more concerned about the ghosts that haunted this place than he was about the person or persons who'd lured them here.

He shouldn't have been.

CHAPTER FOUR

The sun fell behind the western ridges that turned darker and darker until they disappeared against the velvet sky dusted with stars. The night grew eerily quiet. A very slight breeze rustled around the old outpost, but mostly the silence was like that at the bottom of a deep well.

Prophet and Louisa munched hard tack and jerky and sipped water from their canteens. Prophet walked into the northern bluffs to check on their horses, then returned to the cabin to find Louisa sitting on the front gallery, her carbine across her thighs.

Another breeze rose, moaning across the southern bluffs. Prophet remembered that fiddle he'd heard a few years ago—or thought he'd heard—and felt cold fingers walk up and down his spine, giving him a shudder.

"Don't much care for this place at night," he said, stepping into the shack's deep shadow off the east front corner.

He'd been talking mostly to himself, as he was wont to do, but Louisa said, "You've been here before?"

"A few years back."

"You spent the night?"

Quietly, looking around, he told her about that night.

Louisa chuckled as she stared at him sidelong.

"What's so damn funny?" Prophet asked, annoyed, wishing he hadn't told her, but he'd never told anyone before and he felt the need to get it off his chest.

"You."

"What about me?"

"Are all southerners superstitious?"

"Ah, shit." Prophet shrugged a shoulder, adjusting the position of the Richards hanging down his back by its leather bandolier. "I'm gonna stroll around. If someone's lurkin' out there I'd just as soon find them before they find us."

"I only asked if all southerners were superstitious!"

"Just the ones who've watched a pair of ghost soldiers dancing cheek-to-cheek to a scratchy ole fiddle for way longer than he cared to, Miss Sassy-Britches!"

Prophet strode off to the east. Behind him, Louisa whispered, "Lou, get back here!"

"You done wore out your company!"

"Come on, Lou. I hate to admit it, but now you got *me* feelin' spooky!"

"Good!"

Prophet smiled devilishly as he meandered around ruined cabins and clumps of scrub brush. The girl needed to feel spooky. She was too damned cool and sassy for her own good. Maybe some fear would humble her a little, cause her to think twice before she jeered at him for spilling his guts for something he was embarrassed enough about in the first place.

"Snotty britches, is what that girl is," Prophet muttered. "I'll be happy to get shed of her again. Really oughta just get shed of her once and for all."

The girl got way too much enjoyment out of mocking him.

When he'd walked north and east, skirting the perimeter of the old outpost, he climbed a rocky bluff at the outpost's far eastern end. He took a long, slow look around, listening intently. There were no sounds out here at all. Not even the scuttling of a breeze amongst the brush. Not even a night bird or a mouse.

He stared out across the parade ground. There was enough

starlight that he thought he could see the vague outline of the post commander's headquarters, where Louisa was no doubt feeling damned chagrined over mocking his story about the dancing ghost soldiers. As Prophet thought about that, he chuckled despite himself.

It was a damned crazy story. Was it true? Or was Louisa right—was he just so indoctrinated by hillbilly hoodoo that his brain had conjured those two soldiers and that fiddle music one night when he was alone out here amongst these ruins, feeling spooky and primed for feeling even spookier?

He sat down in a niche amongst some boulders and gnarled junipers, and rolled a smoke. He scratched a match to life, and, cupping the flame in his palm, lit the quirley, blowing the smoke straight down so there was less chance of anyone smelling it.

He wouldn't have lit the smoke out here if he'd thought someone was actually going to show. He was starting to doubt it. If someone were going to show, why wouldn't they have shown by now? Besides, he'd scouted the outpost thoroughly and he'd spied no sign of anyone.

He was starting to think those notes had been a joke, and that he and Louisa were wasting their time out here. Someone was kicked back in a saloon somewhere, having a good laugh at their expense.

Now, he just wished the stars would hurry up and wheel through their courses and that the sun would show itself in the east, so he and Louisa could haul their freight the hell out of here.

He'd just taken another drag off the cigarette when he lifted his head sharply and frowned straight out ahead of him.

He'd heard something.

He heard it again—the thud of a shod hoof kicking a rock.

Then the clomping of several sets of hooves rose quickly. Riders were moving into the canyon from Prophet's left and about two hundred yards ahead. Their shadows jostled in the darkness, starlight winking off what were probably bits, bridle chains, and saddle trimmings, possibly spurs.

"Shit!"

Prophet tossed down his quirley, gave it a quick stamping out, grabbed his Winchester, and began moving as quickly as he could in the darkness down the side of the bluff. He looked up to see the riders moving in the direction of the post commander's headquarters. He could hear men's voices now and the blowing of the horses and the occasional hoof kicking more stones.

Reaching the bottom of the bluff, Prophet began jogging straight across the parade ground. There were a few boulders that had rolled down from the surrounding bluffs. He swung around the obstacles. The men's voices grew louder. He couldn't hear them clearly above the thudding of his own boots and the rasping of his breath.

He stopped, drawing a quiet breath through his mouth.

The voices rose more clearly. He could hear Louisa's voice now, as well.

"Miss Louisa Bonaventure?" one of the riders asked.

Prophet moved ahead more slowly, quietly, wanting to hear above the thudding of his heart and the faint crunching of gravel beneath his boots.

"Who wants to know?" The night was so quiet that Prophet could hear Louisa as clearly as if she were only a few yards away.

"Where's Prophet?"

"Who wants to know?" Louisa asked again.

One of the other men chuckled.

Prophet ground his teeth together. He didn't like the sound of that. He didn't like the sound of any of it. There had to be ten riders up there, maybe a few more, a few less. It didn't matter. Prophet and the Vengeance Queen were outnumbered.

Prophet increased his pace as he headed toward the shack.

"What do you think you're doin' out here?" asked the man who'd spoken before—the group's leader, most likely.

"Who wants to know?" was Louisa's mocking response to that question, as well.

Oh, shit, Prophet thought. *Oh, shit!* He quickened his pace even more.

"Who wants to know?" asked the man who'd been doing most of the talking. "I'll tell you who wants to know. The sons o' bitches who're gonna burn down your purty ass, Miss Bonaventure!"

Prophet broke into a dead run.

He tripped over a prickly pear, fell, and rolled.

"Burn down this, you smelly sons of bitches!" Louisa wailed, and Prophet heard the metallic rasp of a Winchester being cocked loudly.

A horse whinnied.

Prophet heaved himself to his feet as flames lapped in the darkness.

"Louisa!" he shouted, running.

Again, he tripped, rolled, and gained a knee. He raised the Winchester and began firing at the flames lapping from the guns of the riders clumped in front of the post commander's building. He triggered the rifle as fast as he could, pumping the cocking lever. Empty cartridge casings arced over his right shoulder to clink onto the gravel behind him.

Men shouted, cursed, and horses whinnied.

Prophet's rifle jammed. *"Goddamnit!"* he bellowed.

He could hear the squawking of tack as the riders turned their horses hard toward him. Rifles began lapping flames toward the bounty hunter, who, down on one knee, tossed away the Winchester, threw himself to his right, rolled, and lay belly flat against the ground.

He gritted his teeth as hot lead tore into the ground around him, some way too close for comfort, spraying him with gravel.

As Louisa continued to return fire, Prophet heard one of the shooters yelp.

"Eldon's hit!" one of the others yelled.

Yet another shouted, "They got us in a whipsaw! Let's go, boys!"

The group turned nearly as one and began galloping off to Prophet's left. One more rifle flashed. Prophet rose, extended his Colt straight out from his right shoulder, and triggered several shots at the jostling shadows. He didn't think he hit any of the ambushers. He was too worried about Louisa for straight shooting.

The riders' jostling shadows disappeared into the crease between the buttes, and the hoof thuds dwindled quickly to silence.

"Louisa!"

Prophet holstered his six-shooter, picked up his rifle, and ran.

Shortly, he saw her shadow sprawled on the shack's front gallery. She was on her back, arms thrown out to both sides, one leg bent under the other one. She'd lost her hat, and her blond hair shone like liquid gold in the starlight, splayed out around her head and shoulders.

Prophet leaped onto the gallery and dropped to a knee.

"Louisa?"

He placed a hand on her chest. He couldn't tell if she was breathing. His hand immediately became wet with a warm, oily substance he didn't want to believe was blood.

"Louisa?" he said, more urgently, picking her up and cradling her against him, jostling her. "Louisa, goddamnit, you say somethin'. Let me know you're still alive. Goddamn it, Louisa!"

She groaned, turning her head slightly. Her eyelids fluttered.

"Lou," she said, almost too softly for Prophet to hear. "Go . . . after . . . them. . . ."

"And leave you here? Forget it. How bad you hit?"

He looked at her closely, pressing his hand against the blood glistening in the starlight. It was coming from a wound just above her stomach and slightly left. He set her down on the gallery floor and ran his hands over her, finding another bloody patch on her upper right leg. She had what appeared a bullet burn across the left side of her neck.

Again, almost too softly for Prophet to hear, she said through a groan, "Nooo, Lou . . . I'm dead. Leave me. Go after . . . those bushwhacking curs and . . . kill them for me." She coughed, winced against the agony of her wounds, and tossed her head from side to side, gritting her teeth. "Oh, Lou!"

"Louisa, you hold on, you understand!"

He ran into the shack and returned to the gallery with his saddlebags and canteen.

Behind him, she said, "Lou . . . it *hurts!*"

Prophet's heart hammered so hard that it made his ribs ache. Worry ravaged him. He couldn't lose her. Not now. Not ever. If he hadn't gotten his stupid feelings hurt when she'd laughed at his story about the ghosts, and he hadn't tucked his tail between his legs and stormed off to that eastern butte . . .

No point in thinking about that now.

Louisa.

He rummaged around in a saddlebag pouch until he hauled out a pair of winter balbriggans. Quickly, he used his bowie knife to tear the long underwear into strips. He balled up one strip, lifted Louisa's shirt and chemise, and shoved the wadded strip into the wound from which blood was pumping. Her life was pumping out of her. He had to keep it inside her.

He couldn't lose this girl. What a fool he'd been to think he'd ever want to!

She by turns sobbed and gritted her teeth, growling and kicking like a wounded mountain lion, as he tied a long strip of the cloth around her waist and knotted it taut over the wound he'd stoppered with the wadded strip. Louisa groaned and writhed, grinding her heels into the gallery's rotten floor.

"Hold still, goddamnit!"

He grabbed another strip of the torn longhandles. Louisa grabbed his forearm, digging her fingers in. "I'm giving up the ghost, Lou. Go after them and kill them."

"Shut the hell up, now—I'm tryin' to keep you from bleeding to death."

"I'm cold."

"I'll get you warm in a minute."

"I'm . . . really cold."

"Louisa!" Prophet clamped her lower jaw between the index finger and thumb of his right hand and stared down at her eyes, which were beginning to roll back into her head. "You don't die on me, Louisa!" He shook her head. "You stay right here—you understand? You fight it! Fight it, goddamn you!"

". . . so . . . cold. . . . Kill them for me, Lou . . . whoever they are. . . ."

Her body fell slack against the gallery floor. When he released her jaw, her head turned to one side, and she lay still.

"Louisa!" he cried. "Don't you dare pull foot on me!"

He lowered his head to her chest. His own heart was beating so loudly in his ears that he couldn't hear hers.

Or . . . maybe there was nothing to hear.

"Goddamnit, Louisa Bonnyventure—if you die on me out here, I'll tan your ass!"

CHAPTER FIVE

Prophet drew a deep breath, held it, and lowered an ear to the girl's chest. Her heart made a soft hiccupping sound—a slow, shallow beat. He lifted one of her hands to his cheek. It was cool. Not cold but cool.

He squeezed her hand between his own, rubbed it brusquely, did the same to the other one, and then slid his saddlebags beneath her head for a pillow. He retrieved her blanket roll from the shack, and spread it over her. Seeing her lying slack against the floor, eyes closed, hair in disarray around her head and shoulders, made him sick and weak with grief.

"Don't die now, you hear, girl?" he urged her quietly, rising, glowering down at her, silently urging her heart to keep beating. "Don't you pull your picket pin. You wait for me. We'll do it together."

He leaped off the porch and jogged off into the northern buttes to retrieve their horses. A half hour later he had both mounts saddled. He eased Louisa up onto Mean and Ugly's back, and then Prophet heaved himself up behind her. Wrapped in her blanket roll, the girl leaned slack against him. He took up the reins and held Louisa on the saddle before him, sandwiched between his arms.

He glanced at Louisa's pinto, whose bridle reins he'd tied to Louisa's saddle horn, and clucked as he touched his spurs to Mean's flanks. Both horses whinnied and headed out, the pinto following the lineback dun. Prophet headed for the main trail and the crease between the southern buttes. He knew there were settlements to the south, along the Arkansas River. He'd head for one of them—the first one the trail led him to. He hoped like hell he'd find a sawbones there.

Of course, the trail could very well lead him into another bushwhack, but it was a chance he had to take. The trail would take him by the most direct route possible to a settlement. If he was hit again by the ambushers who had not finished their job— well, then he and Louisa would die together, but he'd be damned if he wouldn't take at least a couple of those yellow-livered dogs along for the ride.

The ambushers . . .

Somehow, though they'd managed to sink two bullets into Louisa, they hadn't seemed up to the task. They'd been rattled badly when one of their own number had taken a bullet. Amateurs. Now why in the hell would amateurs be after Lou and Louisa on a dark summer's night way out here at the Ramsay Creek Cavalry Outpost, far from any town he was aware of?

As Mean made his way through the buttes, Prophet glanced toward the east. A slight lightening against the horizon there. The false dawn would be upon them soon. Good. He could increase his pace a little. Not by much, because Louisa couldn't take much more jostling than she was already having to take, but a little. The need to reach a settlement and a doctor was a physical urgency inside him, screaming at him, drawing every muscle in his back taut as piano wire.

Occasionally as he rode, he touched his hand to Louisa's cheek, gauging her temperature. She was cool and pasty but not yet cold. Sometimes he stopped Mean and lowered an ear to the girl's side, checking to see if her heart was still beating. A couple of times he broke out in a cold sweat, unable to hear it, but then he heaved a sigh of guarded relief when he detected the faint hiccups from beneath her breastbone.

Occasionally, she'd groan or mutter very softly, unintelligibly, against his neck, and those noises, too, were hopeful signs that she had not drifted off to the next world without him.

Dawn became a pearl wash in the east. The paleness spread, blotting out the stars and the darkness, and then the sun rose—a giant, molten yellow ball climbing over low western buttes the tawny dun color of a mule deer's winter coat. Meadowlarks piped from bending weed tips. A coyote loped off through the brush and followed a winding trail up a sandstone escarpment that peeked up out of the prairie like a half-submerged ship.

The sun revealed the tracks of several shod horses on the trail beneath Prophet. The bushwhackers' tracks. Prophet's heart quickened at the prospect of running into them. He'd have enjoyed nothing more under less dire circumstances. He didn't want to run into them again now. At least, not yet. Not until he had Louisa to a sawbones.

The riders were heading in the same direction as he and the Vengeance Queen, but Prophet had no intention of swerving off the only trail out here to avoid them. The trail would likely lead to one of the several settlements along the Arkansas, and, he hoped—even prayed—a doctor.

From his saddle, he made out eight separate sets of tracks.

Midmorning, Prophet reined Mean and Ugly to a stop in the trail that meandered through the rolling, sage-covered hills, and held a hand to his hat brim, shading his eyes.

A horse stood about a hundred feet off the trail, in the shade of a low, shelving escarpment. The horse was saddled, but the saddle and bedroll were hanging down its side.

Since it wasn't far from the main trail, Prophet booted Mean into the sage. A man was sprawled in the bromegrass and sage about twelve feet from the horse, only the man's boots in the shade. He was curled on his side, facing away from Prophet. Prophet could see the man's shoulders moving as he breathed.

Prophet ground his teeth, fury burning through him, as he stared down at the man—one of the bushwhackers, for sure. One who'd taken a bullet thrown by Louisa. The bounty hunter slipped his Colt from its holster, clicked the hammer back, and fired.

The slug plumed dirt and tore up brush six inches from the wounded ambusher's head. The man's horse jerked away from the blast. The man screamed and rolled onto his back, lifting bloody hands to his bearded face as though to shield himself from another round. Louisa jerked a little, and whimpered, then fell slack against Prophet's chest once more.

"No—wait! Help me!" the bushwhacker pleaded.

He wore a shabby three-piece suit and a gun belt with two holsters. He had no hat. He was thick-bodied with a considerable paunch, broad-shouldered, and hawk-nosed. His dark-brown hair was so thin that his domelike skull shone through it, but it hung long in back. His pain-wracked eyes stared up at Prophet with fear and beseeching. His face behind the gray-laced beard was sunburned, craggy. Blood oozed from a hole in his side, just above his cartridge belt. He was breathing hard.

He studied Prophet, eyes dancing around in their sockets. Recognition shone in them. Tears rolled down the man's cheeks.

"Oh, hell . . ."

"Hell is here—you got that right," Prophet said, glaring at the middle-aged bushwhacker over the barrel of his smoking Colt. "Who're you?"

The man said, "Plea . . . please help me. I'm hurt bad."

Prophet steadied the Colt and narrowed an eye as he planted a bead on the man's forehead. "I asked you a question."

"I'm Eldon Wayne!" The man sobbed as his hands quivered in front of his face. He stared at Prophet over his fingertips.

"I know you're one of those yellow-livered dogs who bushwhacked my girl here last night, Eldon Wayne. I wanna know who those others were, where they're from."

"I can't tell you that!"

"They left you here, Eldon."

"They didn't realize I dropped behind. I called out but they must not have heard me. I must've passed out, and my horse wandered off the trail." Wayne glanced around expectantly, hopefully. "They'll likely be back soon . . . lookin' fer me."

Prophet gritted his teeth with urgency. He didn't have time for this; he needed to get Louisa to a sawbones, but he was desperate to know who'd shot her. "Who are they, Eldon? Where they from?"

"Please—I can't tell you that!" Wayne sobbed.

Prophet lowered the Colt's barrel slightly, fired. The bullet slammed through the inside of the man's right thigh. His leg jerked. Blood gushed from the ragged hole in his broadcloth trouser leg. Wayne yelped and rolled onto his side, clutching his quivering leg with both hands.

"Ohhh . . . you've killed me, you son of a bitch!"

"No, I haven't, but I'm about to . . . less'n you tell me where them other dirty dogs is from."

Wayne ground his forehead into the gravel and sobbed. Spittle bubbled over his lower lip. His shoulders jerked, and his wounded leg quivered like a leaf in the wind.

"Eldon!" Prophet intoned, losing patience.

"Box Elder Ford!" Wayne screamed, his breath blowing gravel out beneath his chin. "Box Elder Ford, you bastard. *Box Elder Ford!*"

He rolled onto his back and once again cast Prophet a helpless, beseeching look. "Now, you help me. Don't let me die alone out here."

Prophet wanted to know why they'd ambushed them but there was no time. Now he knew where to find his and Louisa's attackers, at least. The answer to *why* would come in good time.

Prophet glanced at Louisa leaning slack against him, her hat hanging down off her right shoulder by its chin thong. Another wave of fury boiled up from the bounty hunter's core. He extended the Colt out and down, and clicked the hammer back once more.

"No!" Wayne cried.

Prophet's bullet blew a quarter-sized hole through his forehead. Wayne's head bounced like a rubber ball, fell back against the ground in a large pool of liver-colored blood and white skull and brains, and then turned to one side. Wayne's eyes were half-open, opaque with instant death. He shivered as though deeply chilled.

He was still shivering as Prophet reined Mean around and booted the horse back to the main trail, Louisa's pinto following from about thirty yards back, warily twitching its ears at the dead man.

Prophet continued along the trail for another fifteen minutes. Wanting to give Louisa a break from the jostling, he stopped, dismounted, and eased the girl into the shade of a boulder. While Mean and the pinto grazed together along the trail, Prophet uncorked his canteen and dropped to a knee beside his partner.

"Louisa?"

Her head rested back against the boulder, turned slightly to one side. Her cheeks were papery. He could see the faint blueness of veins beneath her skin. He still couldn't tell just from looking at her if she was breathing.

Panic wracked him.

"Louisa?" he said, squeezing her right arm and giving her a little jerk.

The girl's eyelids fluttered briefly. That was the only movement she made. She didn't make any sounds.

"Louisa, I'd like you to drink a little water," Prophet said, holding the canteen up to her lips, which were slightly parted.

She didn't move or say anything.

Prophet left her leaning there against the rock, giving her a rest, and watered the horses from his hat. He took a sip himself from the canteen, and then mounted up once more, with Louisa before him on the saddle. He moved out, worry sitting like an anvil on his shoulders, a rusty knife of anxiety stabbing his belly.

He rode for nearly an hour, dropping into a broad, shallow valley at the bottom of which, he knew from having been through this part of the territory several times in the past, the Arkansas River twisted. He came to a fork in the trail. A post stood in the middle of the fork bearing two badly weathered, arrow-shaped wooden signs. The arrow announcing LAS ANIMAS pointed toward the trail's left tine.

The arrow announcing BOX ELDER FORD pointed toward the trail's right tine.

Prophet studied the two-track trail. The riders, seven now in number, having lost Eldon Wayne a few miles back, had taken the tine toward Box Elder Ford.

Prophet did, as well.

CHAPTER SIX

Prophet had been through Box Elder Ford before.

It had grown up some since the last time Prophet was through here, but it still didn't amount to much—only about four blocks of shabby wood-frame and mud-brick buildings, with log cabins and adobe huts dotting the surrounding hills, which were lush down here near the Arkansas.

The river, wide and brown and sheathed in cottonwoods, box elders, and willows, twisted between buttes to the south. The river was too shallow this time of the year for hauling gold down from and freight up to the mountain mining camps via flatboats, but Prophet knew it was rollicking in the springtime.

Now in August, the river meandered between broad, sandy banks and around sandbars, glittering in the harsh summer light. A couple of boys in overalls were fishing with long cane poles from one of the sandbars as Prophet rode down into the town, looking around the broad main street lined with gaudy false fronts.

The town was mostly quiet on this hot early afternoon, but as Prophet rode along the street, looking desperately for a sawbone's shingle, a couple of men in bowler hats stepped out of a saloon on the street's right side. They stared at Prophet dully, one with spectacles glinting in the sunlight.

Prophet rode with his jaws set hard, both apprehension and barely bridled rage burning along his spine. The tracks of the seven bushwhackers had disappeared in the well-churned dust

48

of the street, indistinguishable from the other traffic.

"Sawbones!" Prophet yelled at the bowler-hatted gents—local shopkeepers, likely.

As the batwings swung back into place behind them, they both stopped with starts, scrutinizing Prophet and the girl lying slack against him. They glanced at each other quickly, quickly turned away, and began striding down the boardwalk, back in the direction from which Prophet had come.

"You yellow-livered sonso'bitches," Prophet raked out as they hurried away.

He rode on. The local marshal's office was a block-like stone building with a high front porch sitting above barred windows on the lower story, and with a brush-roofed gallery. A young, blond-headed young man stood atop the steps in a black suit with a boiled white shirt and billowy red neckerchief. A five-pointed star was pinned to the lapel of his suit coat. He was a tall kid, but his clothes hung on his long-boned, sparely tallowed frame.

As Prophet rode up to the stone building, the young marshal tried to look appropriately steely-eyed, thumbs hooked behind his cartridge belt, which glistened with polished brass. He wore a walnut-gripped Remington in a cracked leather holster on his right thigh.

He poked his broad-brimmed slouch hat back off his forehead as he said in a tone that was intended to match the hardness of his eyes, "What you got there, stranger?"

"I got a wounded young lady here, as you can likely see, sonny, so if you'd direct me to a sawbones, I'll be on my way. Pronto!" To Prophet, everyone in town was his enemy, and they would be until he'd singled out those devil's seven.

A softness in the young man's mortar shone when he frowned as though indignant—maybe his feelings were a little hurt at the stranger's obvious lack of respect for the badge on the kid's lapel. He canted his head over his left shoulder and said, "Doc Whitfield's down one block and east, by the river. I don't care for your tone, though. Hey, mister!" the kid scolded as Prophet rode off, the pinto following dutifully from about fifteen feet behind Mean and Ugly.

Prophet looked around as he turned the corner and started toward the river. He wondered where the seven were who'd bushwhacked Louisa. Were they still in town or had they ridden on? Eldon Wayne had said "Box Elder Ford" as though Prophet would be able to find them there, but could he take the word of a bushwhacker—one who'd been dying from possibly his, Prophet's, own bullet?

Prophet saw a neat, wood-frame house along the right side of the street that was little more than a two-track trail out here between the town and the river. There was a lot of green grass and sage around the house. The house, painted lime green with dark-red trim, was set back in a spare grove of cottonwoods and box elders, with what appeared a few fruit trees out back.

There was a chicken coop, a hog pen, and a stable and small corral back there, as well. Prophet saw a man in shirt and suspenders tossing food to a small flock of cream-colored chickens that converged on it loudly, fighting amongst themselves and squawking. As Prophet rode into the yard, the man swung toward him—a man much younger than Prophet was expecting. Most of the pill-rollers he'd known were old and gray and given to wry witticisms and gallows humor due to the innate darkness of their trade.

The young man's round spectacles glinted in the sun.

As Prophet rode toward him, the young man set the bucket down and began walking toward Prophet. Limping, rather. He was half-dragging his right foot. Prophet hadn't seen a boy until the young man crouched through the rails of the hog pen, where he'd obviously been working. He couldn't have been much over ten, if that. He was dressed in a white shirt, vest, and knickers, with a ragged straw sombrero on his straw-blond head. His face was round and tanned by the sun. The sombrero's chin thong bounced against his chest.

Tentatively, he walked beside the limping man, shading his eyes with a gloved hand as he stared toward Prophet.

"What happened?" the man asked as Prophet approached on Mean and Ugly.

"You Whitfield?"

"That's right."

"*Doctor* Whitfield?"

"Yes."

While holding Louisa on the saddle with one hand, Prophet swung down from Mean's back. He eased the girl into his arms, and turned to the young doctor and the boy. "She took two bullets, Doc. She needs help bad."

Whitfield turned to the boy. Apparently, he didn't need to say anything. As though he knew the drill, the boy grunted and ran for the house, clamping his sombrero down tight on his head with one hand.

"Follow me," said the doctor as the screen door on the side of the house slapped closed behind the boy.

Whitfield limped to the door and winced as he climbed the three, mortared stone steps and entered the house. Prophet followed him into a mudroom where coats and jackets hung from pegs.

Whitfield canted his head to Prophet's right. "In there. I have two beds for patients back there."

Prophet carried Louisa through a low, curtained doorway and into what appeared a lean-to addition of the house. There were two beds—one to the left of the door, one to the right. Both were outfitted with white sheets and pillows with crisp, white covers. The walls were papered in red and black velvet with gilt flower trimmings, and there was a large, gold-framed daguerreotype of a woman, her hair in a neat bun atop her head, on the far wall over a bureau and between two red-curtained windows.

Prophet gentled Louisa into the cot left of the door. She didn't groan or sigh or grunt or even squirm around. She was as still and quiet as death. Her eyelids were like thin paper, the blueness of veins showing faintly through the skin. The doctor's limping shuffle sounded behind Prophet, and then Whitfield came in carrying several towels over one arm, and wearing a stethoscope around his neck.

Without looking at Prophet, he set the towels on a table near Louisa's bed and said with businesslike crispness, "You'll need to leave the room. I'll tend to her and let you know how she's doing as soon as I know."

Prophet detected a faint note of disdain in the man's voice. He probably tended quite a few gunshot wounds out here and had built up a reasonable disgust for the folks who get involved in such shenanigans.

"Listen," Prophet said. "You gotta know—this girl means everything to me, Doc."

Whitfield glanced at the holstered Peacemaker thonged on Prophet's thigh. "Are you threatening me?"

Prophet didn't know what to say to that. He supposed he was, in a way.

"Every moment you stand here, sir, with that big gun in your holster, is a moment I could be working to save her life."

"You got it."

Prophet glanced at Louisa as he backed toward the door. Worry hammered at him, making his ears ring. Reluctantly, he pushed through the door and stopped. The boy was heading toward him with a smoking iron pan filled with utensils, including a scissors and scalpel, in his two small hands.

"Excuse me," the boy said.

Prophet held the curtain open for him, and the boy slipped through into the hospital room.

Prophet pushed through the screen door and out into the sunlit yard. The chickens clucked as they fed. A breeze had come up and was kicking dust around. Mean and the pinto stood side by side, regarding Prophet as though sensing his worry. The pinto whickered and turned to Mean as though to confer.

Mean turned his head away, a dark, customarily surly light entering the horse's gaze.

Prophet walked over and stripped the tack off both horses, leaving it in the yard where it fell. There was a well between the house and the chicken coop and hog pen, with a pitched, shake-shingled roof over it. Prophet winched up a bucket of water and set it down beside the well, for the horses who'd followed him over. The pinto dipped its head to drink but Mean, in typical bullying fashion, nudged the pinto aside and dipped his own snout into the bucket.

The pinto shook its head and loosed an angry whinny, which Mean ignored as the dun loudly slurped water.

"Don't worry—you'll get your turn, Peaches," Prophet said, smiling despite his worry about Louisa. He wondered what she'd say if she knew he'd dubbed her otherwise nameless horse with such a sissy name. Likely, she'd merely roll her eyes and call him a fool to name a horse anything but "Horse."

It wasn't that she was cold-hearted, Prophet knew, though she tended to act that way. The reason she hadn't named the horse was because her heart was so large she didn't want it getting broken if she should lose the mount.

"Ah, shit!" Prophet cuffed his hat off his head, letting it drop to the dirt at his boots. His knees buckled, and he knelt there near Mean and Ugly, grabbing fistfuls of his hair and tugging, trying to distract himself from his own heart, which had a large, rusty bowie knife of grief sticking straight out of it.

He'd been wrong to threaten the doctor. But that's how desperate he was for Louisa to survive. He'd have given his own life to see the surly, beautiful, blond-haired, hazel-eyed Vengeance Queen come walking out of that house right now, fit as a fiddle. He'd run to her and squeeze her and throw her high in the air and catch her, and grind his lips against hers.

He'd paw her up and sniff her all over, savoring the feel and smell of her.

Oh, Christ—why had he left her alone?

If he'd been there with his Richards, he could have saved her.

"You're a goddamn fool, Prophet!" he castigated himself, raking his knuckles across his scalp. "You're a goddamn, cork-headed fool. Now you've gone and killed her, and what're you gonna do without that girl runnin' drag on your raggedy ass?"

Louisa Bonaventure was the only grace note in his otherwise coarse and crude existence.

He fisted tears from his cheeks. Mean had lowered his head toward him, sniffing him as though trying to figure out what the trouble was. The pinto eyed Prophet from a little farther back, warily.

"Ah, shit—don't worry, Mean, Peaches. I ain't totally loco. Not yet."

Prophet heaved himself to his feet and sat on the edge of the well, letting the peaked roof shade him. He dug in his shirt pocket for his makings sack and started building a smoke. He hated the rawness he felt in his chest. He'd been wounded several times over the years—back during the War of Northern Aggression and several times on the frontier. He'd had the shit nearly literally kicked out of both ends.

And he'd just as soon have to endure that torture all over again than be dealt the kind of agony he'd been dealt here now.

It made him want to cut out his own heart and chuck it into the well with a plop.

Mean turned his head, and whickered warily.

Prophet followed the horse's gaze toward the main trail. A rider was just then swinging off the trail and into the doctor's yard. Prophet recognized the shabby suit, billowy red neckerchief, and tan slouch hat of the young marshal.

"Hell," he said.

He was in no mood to deal with the law.

The young man rode up to him, his chestnut kicking up dust and giving it to the breeze. The pinto whinnied. Mean whickered. The lawman's horse whinnied in return. His badge glinted in the brassy afternoon light. He halted his horse near the well and studied the bounty hunter blandly for a time, pensively.

Then he looked off, looked back at Prophet, and said, "How's she doin'?"

"Don't know yet. Doc's with her."

The young man nodded. He was leaning forward against his saddle horn. "Got a name?"

Prophet scowled at him. He didn't feel like telling the man his name. For all he knew, he was one of those from this town who'd shot Louisa. He didn't trust lawmen any more than he trusted any other man. But there was no point in making trouble until he knew for sure he was making it with the right folks.

"Prophet. I'm a bounty hunter. So's Louisa." Prophet set a boot on a knee, and blew smoke into the breeze. Sweat trickled down his cheeks. "There were eight of 'em that bushwhacked us."

"Why'd they bushwhack you?"

"That's what I was hopin' you could tell me. They're from here. At least, they rode back this way last night. Left one of their pards lyin' wounded up near Ramsay Creek. Said his name was Wayne. Eldon Wayne."

"Eldon Wayne," said the lawman as though he knew the name. "Was he alive when you left him?"

"Nope. I drilled a round through the bastard's head." Prophet touched his index finger to his forehead. "Right here."

The young lawman stared at him.

Prophet stared back at him—angry and defiant.

"He was one of those who bushwhacked my partner. I take that right personal."

"I understand." The young lawman flicked some windblown grit from his lips. "I'll send someone out for him."

"He live here?"

The young lawman stared at Prophet until his stare became a glare. "Mr. Prophet, you're not the one askin' the questions. I'm the one askin' the questions. I'm the law in this here town." He touched the star on his coat. "I am town marshal Roscoe Deets, and I'll ask the questions. Is that clear?"

Prophet rose, rage burning hot in his cheeks. He rolled the quirley to one corner of his mouth and lowered his hands to his sides, raking a thumb against the holster on his right thigh.

"Look, sonny, I don't give a good goddamn about that peach tin on your coat lapel. Eight men from your town, or from hereabouts, ambushed my partner and me last night. There's seven o' them cowardly devils on the lurk somewhere around here. Before I blew Wayne's wick, he told me they were all from your fine little dung heap of a town. When I find 'em, I'm gonna kill every last one of the gutless sonso'bitches. If you think you're gonna stop me, you got another think comin'. And you'd best go home right now and tell your purty young wife to iron your burial suit." Prophet had seen the gold band on Deets's finger.

Prophet drew air into his lungs and let it out his nose.

Young Roscoe Deets glared down at him. Deets's cheeks were bright red, his eyes small and round in the shade beneath his hat brim. Finally, unexpectedly, the young marshal jerked his horse around and spurred him into a gallop toward the main trail. When he hit the trail, he turned the chestnut hard again, and galloped back into town.

Prophet stared after him in surprise. He rolled the quirley from one side of his mouth to the other.

"Now, what have we here?" he muttered.

CHAPTER SEVEN

Marshal Roscoe Deets checked the chestnut down to a dead stop on a narrow cross street with a two-story frame house on the right side of the street and a mercantile warehouse on the left. The house was his own and Lupita's. Roscoe had built it himself just after he and Lupita married last fall. He'd knocked down an old trapper's cabin that had occupied the lot, and he'd planted rose bushes and a couple of cottonwoods. He hadn't yet gotten around to painting the house, but he planned on it soon.

He was about fifty yards from the main street, Hazelton. Dust whipped up around him, powdering him. He blinked against it.

The chestnut snorted and shook his head.

Deets pulled his hat off his head and batted it in frustration against his thigh. He cursed loudly and then looked around, wondering if anyone had heard, his cheeks flushing with embarrassment.

The house's front door opened and Deets's wife, Lupita, stepped out onto the porch. She was a short, busty, full-hipped half-Mexican girl—simple, kind, and eminently loving and devoted to Deets. An earthy girl five years younger than Deets, she'd grown up on a remote horse ranch with her old Mexican father and her brother. Lupita's rich, curly, dark-brown hair fell to her slender shoulders.

"Roscoe?" Lupita said, frowning. "Roscoe, what is it?"

"Lupita," Deets said in surprise. "Please . . . go back inside." He'd stopped here instinctively in front of his home, a place of safety. He'd been a fool to do so and to let Lupita see him in the state he was in.

"You better come in, too. You do not look so good, *mi amor.*"

"Me?" Deets laughed without humor and brushed his coat sleeve across his mouth. His knees were still tingling. He'd damned near tangled with Lou Prophet, the notorious bounty hunter. "Me?" He laughed again and sucked a deep breath, trying to steady himself. "Ah, hell, no—I'm just fine. Nothin' a couple belts won't cure."

He laughed again, his nerves firing like six-shooters beneath his skin.

Prophet had been ready to shoot him. If Deets had slid his hand toward one of his own six-shooters, he'd be dead now. As dead as Eldon Wayne lying dead out in the bluffs around Ramsay Creek.

Wayne, dead. Killed by Lou Prophet. And now Prophet was here in Box Elder Ford with his equally famous partner, Louisa Bonaventure, otherwise known as the Vengeance Queen.

Why?

What was this all about?

Why had Eldon Wayne and seven others bushwhacked the two bounty hunters up by Ramsay Creek? And why in hell hadn't the town marshal of Box Elder Ford known about such a scheme beforehand?

"Roscoe?" Lupita said, coming down the steps in her red dress trimmed with white lace, holding the hem above her ankles.

As usual when she was home, she was barefoot. Deets often laughed and said it was harder keeping his young wife shod than it was a broomtail bronc. Her dress was a low-cut little number, outlining her firm, round breasts beautifully. It was the first dress Roscoe had bought her after they were married and he'd earned his first paycheck as town marshal of Box Elder Ford, Colorado Territory. That was just after he'd lost his nerve. The red frock was a little dressy for everyday wear, but Lupita knew that Deets liked the way it flattered her figure, so she wore it often.

"Roscoe, please don't . . ."

Deets turned his horse into the yard that he had not surrounded with a picket fence yet, though he intended to do that, as well. A white picket fence. He stopped near Lupita, who stood at the bottom of the porch steps, arms crossed on her breasts, looking worried. She wore a thin, gold-washed necklace with a small, gold cross hanging an inch above her deep, tan cleavage.

"Not to worry, Lupita," Roscoe said. "I don't know why I said that. I'm done with that. I'll never take another drink again—you know I won't. I just run into a little problem, and I reckon it rankled me more than I expected. But I'm gonna get to the bottom of it now."

"What problem, Roscoe? I don't understand."

"I don't understand it, neither. But I'm gonna understand it soon." Deets winced. "Ah, hell—I'm sorry I worried you, Lupita. There's nothin' to worry about. You go on back in the house. I'll stop back soon for some cookies and afternoon coffee, just like I always do."

He offered a weak smile.

She returned it, lifting her chin. She was a stalwart girl, and her toughness, coupled with a kind heart, not to mention her lush figure, had been what had drawn Deets to her in the first place way back when she was still living out on that wild horse ranch in the Jasper Buttes.

"All right," she said. "You go on now and solve your marshaling problems. I will have the cookies and coffee ready by the time you get back. I have your socks boiling, so I'd best get back to work, too."

Deets leaned down over his left stirrup. Lupita rose up on her tiptoes, and they kissed.

"Later, Lupita."

"Later, my love."

Lupita smiled brightly, knowing how her smile always buoyed her often-troubled husband. Deets pinched his hat brim to her and swung the chestnut back into the street.

When he'd turned away from her, he clenched his fists and hardened his jaws. Damn his nerves! They'd turned him into a coward. Ironically, it had happened just before he'd pinned the cheap tin badge to his chest, taking the luster out of it for him. He'd wanted the job so badly, but what he'd had to do to acquire it had soured it.

When Deets came to Hazelton, he turned left and rode down the middle of the street, nearly vacant this time of the hot afternoon. There was one wagon parked before the mercantile, and a couple of horseback riders were walking their horses through town—two Double H Connected men. Roscoe knew, by face if not by name, most folks in the town and surrounding county. Miss McQueen's red-wheeled leather chaise was parked in front of Johnson's Millinery & Accessories.

As Deets passed in front of the millinery, which sat on the street's south side, Goose Johnson himself was standing in the open doorway in his white apron and bowler hat, smoking a cigarette. Deets could hear Johnson's wife and Mrs. McQueen talking in the shadows behind him.

Johnson stared at Deets without expression. The lanky man had a dark look in his eyes. Curious about that, Deets swung the chestnut toward the millinery. As he did, Johnson flicked his cigarette into the street and then turned back into the store, closing the door behind him.

Deets stopped the chestnut, which he'd named Kiowa back when he was still a drover for Old Chester McCrae on the other side of the Jasper Buttes. That was back when he'd still had his nerve. (Losing his nerve had become a dark milestone in his still-young life.)

Deets studied the closed door. Johnson had not wanted to talk to him. Deets looked at the half-smoked cigarette smoldering in the well-churned dirt and horseshit of the street.

He looked around. He could see a gaunt, mustached face in the window of the barber and bathhouse shop behind him. Quickly, the face disappeared. The face had been obscured by the reflection of the sun off the dark window, but that would have been the barber, Melvin Bly. He was acting damned odd, as well.

Deets continued to look around the nearly silent street. A few chickens were pecking out front of the Occidental Feed Barn. That was the only movement now aside from a couple of breeze-jostled tumbleweeds. The wind was picking up, moaning between the tall buildings around him, rattling a couple of shingle chains.

It was a hot day. But Deets had a cold, dark feeling deep in his twenty-six-year-old bones. An old man kind of cold.

What was going on?

He booted Kiowa on up the street. He turned at the next cross street and stopped in front of a sprawling shack of gray boards and shake shingles, with a brush-roofed gallery out front. This was Eldon Wayne's place. Wayne did everything from fixing leaky roofs to hauling wash water for the old ladies in town, and from cutting and hauling firewood to shoveling snow in the winter.

He was a big man with a bullish personality, and he'd often worked as a bouncer in the town's three saloons on Saturday nights when the boys from the Double H Connected were in town. He'd worked as a night deputy for the previous town marshal, Bill Wilkinson, whose name Deets wished like hell he could scour from his brain.

Wayne *had been* a big man, according to the bounty hunter, Prophet. Now he was lying dead somewhere out near Ramsay Creek.

A saddled piebald gelding stood in the shaggy front yard littered with junk of all kinds—ancient washtubs, rain barrels, hay rakes, a mound of long saw blades, several small wagons with missing wheels. There was even a pile of wagon wheels around which the bunchgrass had grown thick. The front porch of the shack, supported on stone pylons, had spikes driven into it. All manner of harnesses, chains, and hides hung from the spikes.

As Deets pulled into the yard and weaved Kiowa through the junk and trash, he heard voices inside the sprawling shack. The voices were muffled, so he couldn't make out specifics of the conversation until he'd tied his chestnut to a porch rail and climbed the steps to the porch.

". . . and you just left him out there?" a woman's voice said. It was the voice of Wayne's wife, Mona.

Several men were talking over each other, so Deets couldn't make out what they were saying. He opened the screen door. The inside door stood about six inches open. When he knocked on it, the door creaked open on its leather hinges. The voices died instantly.

"Who the hell is it?" Mona Wayne called.

"Marshal Deets," Deets said as he pushed the door wide and, politely removing his hat, stepped into the large, open room that served as parlor and kitchen.

It was as cluttered with junk as the yard, with crates and old steamer trunks, some of which had rugs draped over them. Animal hides and skulls were tacked to the walls. A large, fieldstone hearth sat against the far wall from the door and it too was loaded down with junk of every shape and size, including a mess of wicker chicken crates, one of which had a sleek golden rooster in it with long, dark-brown saddle feathers.

Mona Wayne raised chickens—had even bred up her own line, which she loudly espoused to be the most productive chickens alive. She sold the eggs as well as the chicks throughout the county. Lupita bought eggs from the woman weekly.

"Well, well, well," Mrs. Wayne said, eyeing Deets. She was a large woman in a shapeless dress, with skin like suet and long, dark-brown hair streaked with gray. She sat in a rocker far to Deets's right, between two piles of crates or something similar, with Indian blankets draped over them to make them more appealing to the eye. "You in on this thing, too, young Marshal Deets?" Mona asked in a faintly mocking tone, rocking slowly in her chair.

Her pale cheeks were mottled red with anger.

"Mona," said one of the three men either standing or sitting around the big woman, like three subjects who've come to pay their respects to some shabby queen.

James Purdy had said the woman's name with gentle admonishment. He added, "This is private business. No need to trouble the young marshal about it."

"Private, huh? Phooey! You left my husband out on the range somewhere, probably dead, and you're tryin' to tell me it's private business?"

"He's dead." Deets moved into the room and stood before the three men—Purdy, Neal Hunter, and Glen Carlsruud. Purdy ran the town's only livery barn. Carlsruud had the Arkansas River Mercantile Company, and Neal Hunter owned the hotel with his pretty wife, Helen, who had once been a saloon singer in mountain mining camps in the first years after the war.

Mrs. Wayne and the three men stared at Deets, incredulous.

The woman's large, round eyes glazed with tears and her upper lip trembled. "How do you know, Marshal? These men said they left him out there last night on their way back from some . . . some errand they felt was so important. Ran off in the middle of the night. I didn't even know Eldon had gone until I got up this morning and found his bed empty."

"A bounty hunter killed him," Deets said, worrying the brim of his hat in his hands. "The bounty hunter who told me eight men from Box Elder Ford ambushed him last night. Shot his partner, Miss Louisa Bonaventure. The bounty hunter is Lou Prophet, a man of some renown."

"Infamy, you mean!" said Neal Hunter, pointing his hat at Deets. He was a darkly handsome, middle-aged man with long sideburns and a thick mustache just now showing some gray.

"Ambushed?" Mona cried. "What in the hell were you boys doin'—ridin' off in the middle of the night to ambush *bounty hunters*?"

"I'd like to know that, as well," said Deets, when all three men merely stood there, defiantly silent, glancing around at each other.

"Mona," Glen Carlsruud said, "we did no such thing." He looked quickly at the other men, as though silently ordering them to fall into step behind him. "No such thing at all. In fact . . . those bounty killers ambushed *us*. Shot Eldon, and his horse ran off, leaving the rest of us long before we knew it."

"That's not how Prophet tells it," Deets said, feeling that chill again, feeling that old weakness in his knees. He was up against the top men in the town, maybe even the entire county, and he was still wet behind the ears as a town marshal, having spent most of his life up to a year ago punching cattle. "He says you ambushed him up by Ramsay Creek. Ambushed him and Miss Bonaventure."

"You'd take a bounty hunter's word over ours?" Hunter asked

Deets threateningly.

Deets didn't know what to say to that, so he said nothing. His heart was grinding nervously away in his chest. His ears were ringing. Nerves. Those blamed nerves of his. He just couldn't tamp them down once they got sputtering around just beneath his skin.

Once, he'd been a man. Now, he was a mere mouse peeping around in the brush, afraid of its own shadow . . .

"What were you doing out there?" Mrs. Wayne wanted to know, pounding her fist on the arms of her rocking chair.

"It was a private matter," said Hunter. "Private business." He looked at Deets again, threateningly. "Our own private business. All you need to know, young Marshal Deets, is that those two bounty hunters ambushed us last night in the dark. If Eldon is dead, it is they who killed him."

Before Deets could respond to that, Purdy said, "Where did you see Prophet?"

Deets hesitated, not sure he should answer the question. The three men stared at him. Mrs. Wayne was staring off into space, letting the information she'd learned here this afternoon sink in, not the least of which was that her husband was dead. The three men's eyes were demanding, threatening. Deets found himself shriveling beneath those hard, commanding gazes.

Turning his hat in his hands, he said, "At the doc's. He brought the girl in. She's wounded bad."

"Yes, well, we had to fire back, of course," Neal Hunter said, glancing conspiratorially at the others.

"I . . . I don't get it," Deets said. "Why would they fire on you?"

"Because they're killers." Purdy turned to Mrs. Wayne. "We sent two men out looking for Eldon. They'll find him and bring him home."

She was staring now at Deets, wide-eyed. Her cheeks were

flushed, lips set in a straight, tormented line. She wanted to say something, but, she, too, felt beaten down by these men—the most powerful men in the town.

"We're sorry for your loss, Mona," Carlsruud said, donning his black bowler. "We'll make sure you're taken care of . . . in Eldon's memory."

As she continued to stare at Deets, her eyes filled with tears. The corners of her mouth wrinkled as she pursed her lips with sorrow and frustration. Obviously, she saw that the town marshal would be of little assistance.

Purdy squeezed the woman's wrist.

"I'll send Helen over, Mona," Hunter said, patting the woman's shoulder and donning his own hat. She kept her accusing eyes on Deets, who lowered his own in chagrin.

The three men strode over to where Deets stood near the door. Hunter glanced over his shoulder at Mrs. Wayne and then turned to the young marshal. He leaned forward until his mouth was only six inches from Deets's left ear.

"I suggest you arrest the bounty hunter, Prophet, for the murder of our friend, Eldon Wayne. That's all you need to concern yourself with, Marshal."

"I think I'd best talk to the county sheriff about this," Deets said and swallowed.

"Sure, sure," Glen Carlsruud said. "We wanna dot all our i's and cross all our t's, of course. You send a telegram off to old Boss Crowley. Keep in mind he's damn near thirty miles from here. He's sixty years old and laid up with the Cupid's itch from those cheap, disgusting whores he frequents . . . and both his deputies are drunks. But you'd best let him know, sure enough." The mercantiler winked, sneering.

Purdy said, "Then you arrest Prophet and wire for the circuit judge. I reckon we're gonna have us a murder trial."

"And keep in mind," Hunter added with a frigid smile, "the

trouble you had a while back. The trouble we helped you get out of . . . young marshal. No one wants to dig up old bones—both literally and figuratively—now, do we?"

He patted Deets on the back, and he and the others walked out of the house.

Deets's heart thudded.

He looked at Mrs. Wayne. She was still staring at him, sneering at him, lips pursed.

Deets cleared the dust from his throat. "Mrs. Wayne, do you have any idea—?"

"Good day, Marshal," she said and turned her head sharply away from him.

Deets pinched his hat brim to her and left.

CHAPTER EIGHT

Sitting on his saddle in Doctor Whitfield's yard, leaning his back against the cool stones of the well coping, Prophet drew deep on his quirley and let the smoke trickle out his nostrils and mouth. He'd been sitting out here, following the shade around the well, for several hours, waiting for word on Louisa.

Each one of those hours had felt like days.

The doctor's screen door slammed. Prophet looked hopefully toward the house. The boy leaped down off the side door's top step and walked toward Prophet, carrying a wooden bucket by its rope handle. His worn, black shoes scuffed dust up around his black socks, which rose nearly to his knees, where the knickers took over.

The boy looked at Prophet tentatively as he moved toward the well, the bucket bouncing against his right thigh.

Prophet took another drag from the quirley, exhaled, and said, "How is she, boy?"

"I'm not supposed to talk to you," the boy said as he hooked the bucket to the winch and began turning the crank, lowering the bucket into the well.

"Oh," Prophet said. "Well, that's understandable." He paused, watching the kid working, the boy chewing his lower lip as he cranked the bucket down into the well. "What's your name?"

"Titus."

"Titus, you're not supposed to talk to me."

Titus glanced at Prophet, sheepish. Prophet grinned. Titus's cheeks flushed. The bucket sank into the water with a gurgling chug, and then the boy began cranking it back up.

"What's the water for, Titus?" Prophet asked.

Titus grunted but didn't say anything as he unhooked the bucket from the winch hook and began hefting it back toward the house, carrying it in both hands in front of him. Halfway between the well and the house, he turned toward Prophet, scrunching up his eyes against the sun and the dust the breeze was lifting.

"Pa says she's got a heartbeat, but that's about all," Titus said.

Those words sent a hard stone tumbling down the well of Prophet's throat and into the cold water of his belly. He nodded to the boy, who turned and continued walking to the house and up the steps and through the screen door, water slopping over the bucket's rim.

A half hour later, when the shadows were growing long across the yard and the birds had that solemn tone now on the heels of the day, Doctor Whitfield stepped out of the house, letting the screen door slap back into place behind him. He stood at the bottom of the steps and looked at Prophet as he rolled down his left shirtsleeve and buttoned the cuff.

Prophet wanted to get up and go to the man. But he wasn't sure he wanted to hear what the doctor had to say. He sat there frozen against the well, another of many quirleys smoldering between his fingers, a dozen or so butts mashed in the dirt near his boots.

Rolling down his right shirtsleeve, Whitfield walked toward Prophet. He looked glum. Downright dark. He wore no hat and his thick, auburn hair blew around in the breeze.

Prophet mashed out the quirley where he'd mashed out the others and heaved himself with a weary grunt to his feet. He cuffed his hat brim back up on his forehead.

"It's not good," the doctor said as he stopped before Prophet. He scowled up at the big bounty hunter, who stood a good four inches taller than he did. "But it could have been worse. The bullet in her torso missed her heart by an inch and lodged against the back of a rib. It tore her up pretty badly. I got the bleeding stopped and I repaired as much of the damage as I was able. The bullet in her leg didn't sever any arteries, but it nicked the bone. Cracked it, in fact. If she makes it through the night, which is doubtful, she's going to be a very sick young lady for a good, long time."

"But she's still alive . . ."

"She's still alive. Now, it's the shock, fever, and infection we have to worry about. Fever could take her by tomorrow morning. Even if and when she's out of that danger, there's the danger of infection."

"Shit."

"Well, what do you expect, Mr. Prophet? That is what guns and bullets are meant to do, aren't they? Rend the flesh?" Whitfield curled his upper lip distastefully. *"Kill?"*

"Skip the sermon, preacher. Can I see her?"

"For five minutes. But don't make any loud noises or disturb her in any way. She must sleep. Sleep is the only thing that can help her now. Sleep and a frequent change of bandages for the first three or four days."

Prophet walked toward the house. The doctor fell back behind him, dragging his bad foot. Prophet stopped and turned back to the man. "You'll keep her here, won't you? With you? I got money—I can pay. What I can't pay for now, I'm good for later. I'll guarantee you that, Doc."

"I don't want your blood money, Mr. Prophet," Whitfield said, stopping beside him now and giving the bounty hunter a look of bald disdain. "I just want you to stay the hell away from here. And if that girl is somehow able to survive the savagery that's been done to her, I want the both of you to ride far, far away from here."

He glanced suddenly toward the door behind Prophet. "Titus, stop eavesdropping and feed the stock!"

Prophet glanced back to see the boy's face disappear behind the rusty screen door. His footsteps dwindled into the bowels of the house.

Prophet said, "Look, I know you don't cotton to my sort, Doc. But I need to stay here. I can't leave her. I need to be close . . ." Prophet's throat grew thick. Tears were trying to ooze into his eyes despite his effort to choke them back. "I need to be close . . . in case she dies."

Whitfield studied him. His voice was less harsh as he asked, "What is she to you?"

"She's everything to me," Prophet said sternly. "And if she's gonna die, I need to be here."

Whitfield continued to study the big man before him with puzzled interest.

He sighed, glancing around in frustration. "Tonight will be her highest hurdle. You can stay here tonight. In the stable with my horse. You can stable your own mounts there. That's as close as you'll be able to come, I'm afraid. You can visit her for five minutes every hour until Titus and I turn in at sundown." He threw up a placating hand at Prophet's dubious frown. "Don't worry. I will rise every two hours to check on her, refresh the cool cloths I'll be using to keep her fever down with. Fortunately, I have a deep well."

The doctor continued limping toward the door. "You can stay with her until I get back. I have another patient to tend in town. If anything happens, send Titus. He knows where I'll be."

Prophet stared at the man's back with interest as he followed him into the house. "Who might this other patient be, Doc?"

Plucking his bowler hat off a peg by the door, Whitfield scowled at Prophet. "That is none of your business." He made a face. "Good Lord, man—you smell like cigarette smoke and horses. Please wash at the well before you come in here again!"

The doctor doffed his hat, grabbed his leather kit off a chair, brushed past Prophet, and limped out into the yard, heading for the stable. The bounty hunter watched him go, curious.

Had one of his or Louisa's bullets pinked another bushwhacker last night? There was a good chance that the doctor's other patient was another man they'd wounded. Prophet would have followed the young pill-roller, but at the moment he was more concerned about remaining close to Louisa's side than hunting her attackers.

He doffed his hat as he pushed through the curtained room that smelled heavily of arnica. Louisa lay under a sheet and blanket, which were pulled up to her neck. Her arms lay straight down along her sides. Her eyes were closed, but the lids were twitching faintly and her brows were furrowed. She appeared to be asleep but feeling miserable even in sleep, which Prophet supposed was natural. It was hard to see her in such a state. She'd taken lead before, but she'd never been hit this severely.

Lying there, unconscious, she looked so young, fragile, pale, and vulnerable.

And miserable . . .

Prophet pulled a slat-back chair up to the side of her bed. He wanted to take her hand in his, but the doctor had told him not to rouse her. She needed to sleep. Screw the doctor. He knew nothing about them. To him, Prophet and Louisa were just a couple of raggedy-tailed bounty hunters. Whitfield didn't know how Prophet's taking her hand might ease Louisa's pain a little.

Prophet took her left hand and held it gently between his. He held it for a long time, staring down at her, feeling helpless and afraid, sort of the way he'd felt before his first skirmish back in eastern Tennessee during the war.

As frightened as a little boy.

Sometimes, Prophet wished he'd never met this girl. They'd been thrown together when the outlaw gang led by Handsome Dave Duvall had stormed into her family's farm, killing the entire family after raping Louisa's mother and her two sisters. Louisa had hidden from the marauders in the brush and afterwards—after she'd seen to her family's burial—she'd headed off on the warpath against Handsome Dave and his tough-nut bunch of renegades.

She and Prophet had met up in eastern Dakota Territory, after the same gang. They'd followed the killers into western Dakota and then south into the Black Hills country, whittling the gang down gradually until they'd snuffed the wick of Handsome Dave himself.

Sometimes Prophet wished he'd never crossed paths with this girl. Before, he'd been free and easy, nary a care in the world except killing his next killer and securing enough money for his next meal and a bottle of whiskey. His next game of stud.

His next doxie.

Now he had Louisa to worry about. Sometimes that worry was an anvil on his shoulders. It was an especially heavy burden now. Louisa was at death's door. If she walked through it, Prophet was tempted to follow her. That's how wretched his life would seem without her in it.

Even though they didn't always ride together, because they were too damned much alike not to be constantly locking horns, he felt the world was a little kinder, softer, with a little more poetry in it, knowing she was out there somewhere, riding hell for leather against bad men of which the frontier had plenty.

Outside, the clattering of a wagon rose.

Prophet turned his head to peer out the window. A chaise buggy was just then rattling into the yard behind a fine, sleek bay horse with three white stockings. A Morgan horse, judging by the clean, firm lines and compactness, the proud arch of its neck. The white socks stood out now in the dusk as the woman who was driving the buggy turned the horse in a broad circle. A striking woman, indeed, from just the brief look Prophet had gotten of her.

Horse and buggy and the woman driver clattered past the window and continued up toward the front of the house.

Prophet rose from his chair and looked out the window. The chaise had stopped near the doctor's front porch. The woman was stepping down.

Prophet glanced at Louisa. Her eyelids were no longer twitching. He walked over to the bed and leaned down. She was breathing. It sounded as faint as a bird's breath, but she was breathing, just the same.

A knock sounded from the front of the house. Prophet pondered it. The woman was here to see the doctor. The doctor wasn't here. Let the boy deal with the woman. Prophet had returned to his chair and was about to pick up Louisa's pale hand again and place it between his own hands, when a knock sounded on the screen door, just outside Louisa's room.

"Hello?" said a woman's voice. "Anyone here?"

"Christ," Prophet muttered. He looked at Louisa, smoothing her sweat-damp hair back from her pale, warm forehead. "I'll be right back, darlin'. You stay right where you are, hear?"

CHAPTER NINE

Prophet ducked through the curtain and turned to the screen door. The woman stood just beyond it.

"Doc's not here," he said.

From the other side of the screen, which turned her into a gauzy brown blur, the woman said, "Oh. Hello. I was told he had an injured young lady here. I came to inquire if he needed assistance."

Prophet toed the screen open with his boot and leaned a shoulder against the doorframe. His heart lurched when he saw the quality of woman standing out there—dressed to the nines in the most lavish gown he'd ever seen and wrapped in a heavy cape made from what appeared the feathers of some exotic, chocolate-brown bird. They ruffled gently in the breeze.

She wore a spruce-green hat with a black veil that lent an exotic, mysterious quality to her face, which was ivory, oval-shaped, and clean-lined, set with smoldering brown eyes and full, ruby lips. Earrings the same green as her hat dangled from her ears down her long, fine neck.

She smelled richly of ripe cherries.

All in all, the entire package was one of lush, ripe, maybe slightly sinful womanhood. She was the kind of woman who made a man feel as though he had ants crawling around in his trousers.

She let her eyes drop and then rise, taking in the man before her.

"And you're . . . ?"

"Prophet. You're . . . ?"

"Verna McQueen. I just now heard that the doctor had a patient. I usually assist with his female patients. It's only proper a woman be near, you know." She tipped her head slightly to look around Prophet. "Clay's not here?"

"If you mean Whitfield, he's off tending another patient. Well, I'll be seein'—" Prophet had started to turn away, letting the door close.

The woman stopped him with, "If the doctor's not here, I should probably look in on his patient—should I not, Mr. Prophet?"

Prophet toed the door open again. "She's resting."

"May I see?" the woman said stubbornly and then smiled to soften it.

Prophet scrutinized her, customarily wary, especially where Louisa was concerned. He shrugged. "I reckon if you work for the doc . . . why not?"

He held the door open with one hand and stepped aside. Verna McQueen carefully climbed the three stone steps, holding her skirts above her ankles, which were delicate and slender, Prophet couldn't help noticing. Her aroma filled his nostrils, made those ants crawl around as though energized by lightning. Under the circumstances, the feeling was annoying.

Verna McQueen pushed through the curtain, and Prophet followed her into the sickroom. The woman removed her cape and her hat, hung both on the chair, and took up the washbasin and cloth that had been residing on a crude wooden stand. She was in her late, well-tended twenties, Prophet judged. Removing the cape had revealed the low-cut, opulently trimmed, and pleated gown and the fullness of her figure. Her skin was translucent cream with undertones of peach.

Without the veil, Prophet could see that she was beautiful

77

enough to have her visage carved in ivory and set into a cameo pin. Her long, almond-shaped eyes were deep brown with copper tints and long lashes, and they had a faintly smoldering, devilish glint in them.

She was a full-figured, exotic beauty—that was for sure. Prophet wondered what she was doing here in Box Elder Ford. The richness of her attire and jewelry—she wore a choker studded with what was obviously a diamond—bespoke immodest wealth.

"Her color is not good." The woman sat on the chair beside the bed and laid her hand against Louisa's forehead. "Very warm. Clammy. She has a fever, all right. That'll need to come down."

"The doc mentioned that."

"Too bad the ice has all melted in Eldon Wayne's icehouse. He usually freezes a tub of water over the winter, to supply the town with ice for as long as it lasts. This year it was gone by the Fourth of July."

Verna McQueen soaked the cloth in the water basin, wrung it out, and gently ran the cloth across Louisa's forehead. "The doctor's well is deep, however. The water nicely cold." She dabbed Louisa's cheeks, rewet the cloth, and caressed Louisa's neck.

Louisa's eyelids fluttered a little, and she moved her lips, but if she made any sounds, they were too low for Prophet to hear.

As Verna continued to bathe Louisa's face in the cool water, she glanced at Prophet. "Who is she, Mr. Prophet?"

"A friend."

"Mmm-hmmm," the woman said, holding the cloth against Louisa's right cheek. It was as though she'd almost anticipated Prophet's response. "And is she your—?"

"No."

She glanced at him, dubious. Drenching the cloth and wringing it out once more, she said, "How did this happen?"

"We were ambushed."

"Was she hit bad?"

"Bad enough. Two bullets. One in her chest. One in her leg."

"And what was Clay's . . . er, Doctor Whitfield's prognosis?"

"I don't know." Prophet sighed. "He said it don't look good. If she gets through tonight, she might have a little better chance."

"This is obviously very hard on you."

"Yeah, well . . . she's a friend, like I said."

Miss McQueen hung the cloth over the side of the washbasin. "Well, I've done what I can. She seems a little cooler." She looked at Prophet. "You look as though you could use a drink."

Prophet looked at her, frowning. He hadn't expected to be invited to a drink by a woman so obviously out of his class. He hadn't bathed since Colorado Springs, a hundred and fifty tough trail miles back. Like the doctor had said, he smelled of horses and cigarettes.

"A drink?"

"Sure. I know Clay has a bottle around here somewhere."

"I need to stay with my friend."

The woman scrutinized him more closely, turning her head and tipping it slightly. She bounced slowly up and down on the heels of her delicate shoes and said, "Maybe some other time."

"Maybe."

"I live right up there," she said, pointing toward the north and raising her finger, squinting one eye beguilingly. "A pretty little house on an ugly old hill." For the first time, Prophet detected a southern accent.

"You live up there all by yourself, Miss McQueen?"

"Yep. Pretty much." Her shimmering eyes were crawling all over Prophet, making him feel a little self-conscious. He didn't think he'd ever been scrutinized so closely. "All . . . by . . . myself." Her gaze dropped to his boots and leaped to his sandy-haired head. "You're tall—you know that, Mr. Prophet?" She smiled, waved, and turned toward the curtained doorway. "Please tell Clay I dropped by . . . to assist . . . won't you?"

"I'll tell him you were here to assist, Miss McQueen."

"Good day, Mr. Prophet. Or good night, as the case may be."

She pushed through the curtain and disappeared. Prophet heard the screen door close. He was back sitting in the chair by Louisa's bed when the chaise rattled out of the yard and back onto the trail. The woman yelled to the horse.

The rattling and the hoof clomps dwindled to silence.

Prophet stared out the window, pondering the lushly gorgeous Verna McQueen, who still had ants crawling around inside his dusty denims, to his dismay.

For some reason known only to some sixth sense he had, a chill touched him.

He scrubbed a big hand across his cheek, deep lines cutting into his forehead, which was floury white where his hat brim had hidden it from the sun. "Now . . . what in hell was she all about . . . ?"

The doctor put his roan mare up to the back of Melvin Bly's barbershop and bathhouse. There was a hitch rack and a stock trough back here. The doctor swung gently down to the ground, tied the mare to the hitch rack, and unhooked his medical kit from the saddle horn.

He looked around to make sure nothing lay between him and the sprawling, adobe-brick and rickety wood-frame structure that he might trip over. Bly was a sloppy fool who didn't tend much to his place. Seeing nothing in his way, Whitfield limped on up the steps to the door, which stood partway open.

It was nearly dark outside and even darker inside. Bly had no lamp burning. The doctor negotiated his way through the barber's boiler room, where he heated water to fill baths, and made his way over to the part of the building where Bly lived.

"Bly?" he called. "Bly, you here?"

He thought the barber might have gone over to one of the saloons, but then a man's gravelly voice called, "Here, Doc!"

Whitfield pushed through a door and into Bly's main living quarters, which was a single, large room outfitted about the way you'd expect a sloppy bachelor with no upbringing to outfit such a place. It was crude and it smelled crude, with the odor of cheap tobacco hanging heavy.

Bly sat in shirt and suspenders at his eating table against the far wall, under a dimly glowing Rochester lamp that hung over the table. The barber's right arm was in a sling.

There was a shuffling sound and the clattering of small nails on the floor. Whitfield turned to see Bly's cat, Jasper, playing with a half-dead mouse behind Bly's cold wood stove. The cat turned its copper eyes to the doctor, meowed in annoyance, and then went back to swatting the mouse back and forth between its paws.

"You could do with cleaning this place up a little," Whitfield told the barber.

"My cleanin' lady ain't worth a damn." Bly laughed ironically.

He didn't look good. His gray eyes, one of which forever wandered to the outside corner of its socket, were heavy-lidded. He was only in his mid-thirties, and he was a relatively large man with a pronounced potbelly, but his lightly freckled cheeks were sallow and gaunt.

Sweat stood out on his forehead. He had thick, unkempt brown hair that was prematurely graying, and long sideburns. He had a Remington revolver on the table beside a whiskey bottle and a speckled blue tin cup.

The doctor had heard that Bly, who was known for his laziness as well as his penchant for alcohol, had been married once, but his wife had left him for another man—a fellow shop-keeper—and they'd left town together amidst the scandal. Bly had never gotten over the shame and humiliation.

Very early that morning, Whitfield had been summoned here to tend the barber's arm. A bullet had shattered his right humerus and cracked the medial epicondyle.

"How are you doing, Melvin?"

"My arm hurts like a son of a bitch."

"It's badly broken, Melvin. You should be in bed."

"Hurts worse when I lie down." Bly lifted his rheumy gaze to Whitfield. That wandering eye made him look both stupid and slightly off his rocker, though Whitfield knew him to mostly be stupid. "He's here, isn't he?"

"Who?"

"Who? Bullshit, Doc. You know who. I seen him ride in with that girl. She took a bullet. You got 'em over to your place, don't you? Come on—everyone knows you do."

Whitfield shrugged. "All right—they are over at my place." He stared down pointedly at the injured, sweating, half-drunk barber. "You keep in mind that my place is off limits to trouble. I won't put up with anyone coming onto my property looking to further their fight with those two bounty hunters. I will not have my boy's life endangered."

"You don't have to worry about me, Doc." Bly lifted his cup to his lips. "I'm done fightin'. I'm prob'ly done with everything else, too, until I can start usin' this arm again. You know how long that's gonna be, Doc? Shit, I got a business to run. I can't shave and cut hair one-handed!"

Whitfield decided it would be best not to tell the man just yet that he'd probably never regain full use of the arm. He set his medical kit on the table and slid a chair up beside the barber. "You just have to be patient, Melvin. Patience and bed rest is what you need. And you really must eat something. I can understand the need for whiskey to dull the pain, but you won't heal without proper fortification. And please go *easy* on the whiskey. All things in moderation."

"I don't have no one to cook for me, Doc."

"I'll see if I can talk Alma Cartwright into coming over and frying you a steak." Whitfield looked at the shelves in the kitchen part of the room, near the wood stove, a sink, and a rusty iron pump. He saw two airtight tins and a wrinkled potato with long, green sprouts. That was all. "Do you have anything edible at all here, Melvin?"

"I usually take my meals at Cartwright's Café. I ain't no cook. Dolly was a cook—a damn good cook, too. But she's somewhere over in Nebraska now, cookin' for Wally Earle and the two brats I heard they got now."

"There is no point in ruminating on the past. We all have our grievances with the Fates, but it's best to suppress them and move forward. Like I said, I'll have a talk with Mrs. Cartwright about getting some food over here. Now, let me check the bandages on that arm. Might need to replace them, though I'm thinking we might be able to wait till morning."

"Oh, shit—that hurts, Doc!" Bly complained childishly as Whitfield eased his wounded arm out of the linen sling.

As Whitfield gently opened the bandage over Bly's upper arm, he glanced tentatively at the man's gaunt, sweating face and asked, "Now that you're a little more coherent than you were this morning, I'd like to ask you how you got into a foofaraw with those two bounty hunters."

"I appreciate what you're doin' for me, an' all, Doc," Bly said, stretching his lips back from his teeth as he stared down at the bandage the doctor was peeling slightly away from his arm, "but that topic's off-limits."

Whitfield glanced at the man again. He waited a few seconds before he said, "It has something to do with . . . her . . . doesn't it?" He pressed the bandage back into place over the wound.

Bly scowled at Whitfield darkly. He licked his cracked lips and hardened his jaws. "Like I done told you, Doc," he said with barely bridled anger, "that ain't a subject I'm allowed to discuss. Now, please, don't you ask me ever again!"

CHAPTER TEN

It was completely dark when young Marshal Roscoe Deets checked the front door of the Arkansas Federated Bank & Trust, which sat on the far east side of Box Elder Ford, on the north side of the main street.

He always started here at the bank on his nightly rounds, checking all the doors of the business buildings in town. After making a full circle of the main street, he ended up here again, where he checked the bank's door one last time.

Usually, unless the bank president, George W. Campbell, had been overly preoccupied with his accounts when he'd left the building around six-thirty, the door was locked. Tonight it was, as well.

Now Deets could go on home and have dessert with Lupita. After a slice of dried apricot pie and a cup of coffee with his pretty wife, he'd make one more round, checking all three saloons to make sure everything was quiet, as it usually was here in the mostly quiet town on weeknights. Then Deets would tramp on home and sleep in his bed snuggled up against the lithe, supple body of Lupita and rise at six to start his marshal's chores all over again.

Deets had to admit that when he'd considered the city council's offer of the town marshal's job, he hadn't taken into account the boredom involved with law dogging. But in stark contrast to his romantic views of what carrying a badge and a six-shooter would entail, it was often mind-numbingly tedious.

Sometimes he found himself kicked back in his chair in his office, sound asleep not because he hadn't slept well the night before but because he was just so damned bored.

Still, it was a good job. A steady paycheck and not nearly as dangerous as cow-punching had been. Few cowpunchers he'd ever known had lived much past thirty-five without getting killed or at least severely injured when thrown by a half-broke bronc, kicked by a calf during branding, bit by a rattlesnake, or struck by lightning. Many caught their death of cold during spring and fall roundups and died from influenza. Many drank themselves to death while numbing themselves from the exhausting grind and the danger, which is what Deets had once done before he'd met Lupita.

All this while earning twenty-five to thirty-five dollars a month.

As marshal, Deets was earning forty a month, and since his position was relatively secure, he'd been able to get a bank loan for building a house for himself and his bride.

Deets knew, however, that his job could be much more dangerous than it was, as the frontier was still largely an untamed place. Many towns across the west were still wide open and at the mercy of coulee-riding owlhoots and out-and-out renegades. In fact, Box Elder Ford had been that way until the city council had hired Bill Wilkinson, a town tamer of some repute, to file down its horns.

And Wilkinson had done just that in spades.

He and a couple of deputies he'd especially hired for their cold-iron savvy had put the owlhoots frequenting this part of the Arkansas River Valley on notice by hanging some, shooting others, and sending several passels off to the penitentiary. After a year of that, Box Elder Ford had become as docile as a newborn lamb. And so far, it remained that way.

Deets didn't like to think about Wilkinson, however. Thinking about the former lawman made Deets's guts turn to jelly. He ran a gloved hand across his face, hitched his gun belt up higher on his waist, and headed on down the boardwalk in the direction of home. He purposefully turned his mind to better thoughts—to a cup of coffee with Lupita out on their porch and to crawling into bed with his wife and enjoying the pleasures of her wonderful body.

She knew how to please a man, Lupita did. She knew how to make Roscoe Deets forget all his worries and all the dark thoughts that snagged in his mind like flies getting tangled in cobwebs. He thought about her smooth body now as he stepped off the boardwalk and angled over toward the side street on which his and Lupita's house sat.

He stopped suddenly.

Shadows moved down the main drag to his right, in the west.

Three horseback riders were moving toward Deets. No, only two riders. One horse didn't have a rider. Oh, yes, it did, Deets saw, his stomach turning sour. Only, the third rider was riding belly down across his horse's saddle. Two other men were walking alongside the horseback riders. The two others were moving along the boardwalk, dropping down off one boardwalk and mounting the other, walking quickly to keep up with the three horseback riders.

As the riders and the walkers approached, Deets said silently, "Ah, shit," and touched a nervous index finger to his cheek, dragging it down into the late-day stubble, digging his fingernail into the skin, making it hurt a little.

The riders were the two men who'd gone out looking for Eldon Wayne—the blacksmith Lars Eriksson and the saloon owner L.J. Tanner, a close associate of the banker, George Campbell. Tanner, a former cavalry soldier and decorated Indian fighter, was Deets's least favorite Box Elder Ford citizen. Tanner sat on the city council, too, so he was in a good position to make Deets's life a living hell, which this matter with the bounty hunters was sizing up to do.

Deets saw now as they approached that the two men on foot were Neal Hunter and Glen Carlsruud. They, too, were city councilmen, as were all the men who'd gone out and gotten themselves entangled in that inexplicable mess-up in the wild-ass Cavalry Creek country. The banker, Campbell, probably hadn't gone though he was likely entangled in the same mess—whatever the mess was. He, too, was a councilman and he was tight with the others.

"The sheriff's wrappin' up for the day, I see," said L.J. Tanner as he reined his buckskin to a halt about ten feet from Deets. "Kinda early—ain't it, Sheriff?"

Deets ground his back teeth but took a deep breath, calming himself. "I always quit around nine-thirty," he said mildly. "A man's gotta sleep, visit with his wife."

Tanner said, "Bill Wilkinson never slept. Leastways, I don't remember him ever not workin'. The way he saw it, wearin' a badge was a full-time job." He gave a goatish smile. "But, then, he didn't have a pretty Mex wife to go home to, neither."

"That's enough, Tanner," Neal Hunter said, walking over from the boardwalk, Carlsruud at his side. "That's enough about Wilkinson. I don't want to hear his name again. Nobody does. Besides, you know he had deputies to back him."

Tanner, who wore a patch over the eye he'd lost in the Indian Wars, opened his mouth to speak. Hunter cut him off with, "They brought in Wayne." He directed the statement to Deets. "Thought you should know, Marshal. He was shot several times—once through the forehead. A killing shot."

"It was murder," Carlsruud clarified. "Probably shot when he was wounded and helpless. I don't think there's any doubt who did it."

Tanner said, "We seen Prophet out there, ridin' along the

88

trail with the girl. We steered wide and holed up out of sight till they was gone. He shot Wayne, all right."

Glen Carlsruud scoffed at Tanner. "Well, why didn't you finish the job, for God's sake?"

Tanner leaned forward, jutting his chin belligerently at Carlsruud. "Why don't you just go find him and finish the job yourself, Glen, if you're so goddamn tough? You know I can't shoot for shit with only this one eye. A few years ago, I'd have ridden out to that post and taken care of them two *alone*!"

Hunter heaved a disgusted sigh and turned to Deets. "Have you arrested him yet? Both of 'em, if the girl's still alive, I mean?"

"I'm working on it, Mr. Hunter."

"Just how are you *working* on it, Marshal Deets?"

"He's over to the doc's place. You know how the doc is about having trouble at his place, with his boy around an' all. I'm gonna wait till Prophet leaves the doc's place and then I'll have a talk with him."

"A talk with him?" Tanner laughed.

"I mean I'll arrest him," Deets said, feeling his nerves popping deep down in his knees. "I'll arrest him just as soon as he leaves the doc's place . . . and I know I got a good reason for arrestin' him," he added, tentative, raking his hand across his bristled jaws.

Carlsruud lurched forward to stand a little ahead of Tanner. "We done told you, Marshal, that you have a very good reason indeed for arresting that no-account bounty killer!"

"That's what you told me—that's true, Mr. Carlsruud. And I know all you fellas hold my job in your hands, that I serve at your pleasure. Shit, you hold our future in your hands—mine an' Lupita's. But what kind of a lawman would I be if I didn't do what the law says and make sure I got a good reason for arrestin' a man before I arrest him? When you hired me, you said you didn't want another Bill Wilkinson runnin' roughshod over

Box Elder Ford."

"Yeah, well, speakin' of Wilkinson," Tanner said. "You didn't much care about none o' that official bullshit with him, did ya? Shit, you just got likkered up an'—"

"That's enough, L.J.!" Hunter scolded the mounted man.

The big, burly, red-haired and red-bearded Lars Eriksson had said nothing so far, which was customary with him. He was a silent, savage, brooding man who lived with his part-Arapaho wife across a dry wash behind his blacksmith shop.

But now the blacksmith scrubbed dried tobacco juice out of his long, tangled, dark-red beard and said, "Why don't you go rustle you up a cat?" He grinned, showing the large gap where he was missing his front teeth. "Let the cat do the dirty work of *arrestin'* the bounty hunter for you." He glanced at his *compadre*, L.J. Tanner, and pantomimed a pistol with his right hand. "Bang! Bang!"

Tanner threw his head back and laughed.

"Lars, goddamnit!" Hunter said in exasperation. "Both of you!" He chuffed another disgusted sigh and then lowered his voice as he said, "You fellas go on ahead to Mona's place. Go on, go on—the lot of you! Helen's over there now, sitting with her. She'll help with Eldon's body. I'll be over soon."

"Oh, hell," Carlsruud said, giving the bottom of his waistcoat a tug. "What a goddamn mess!"

"Yes, and now we've got it in town," Hunter said, keeping his voice quiet but stretched taut with anxiety. "And now we've got to deal with it. Discreetly! So you fellas go on over to Mona's."

Tanner cursed. Then he turned to Deets and offered a seedy sneer. "Say hi to your purty wife for me—will you, Marshal? That woman of yours is some fine female flesh—second finest in town, in fact."

Deets ground his back teeth in fury but said nothing.

Tanner chuckled and touched spurs to his horse's flanks. He

90

and Eriksson moved on along the street, jerking Eldon Wayne's horse along behind them. Carlsruud sighed, gave Deets a dark look, and continued walking along the middle of the street, behind the mounted men and the horse carrying Wayne's body slack across its saddle.

When they were gone, Hunter wrapped an arm around Deets's shoulders and said, "Admittedly, Marshal, this is a messy, somewhat embarrassing situation."

Deets looked at Hunter's right hand draped across Deets's right shoulder. He didn't like it there. He didn't like it there one bit. Tanner's words were still echoing inside his head.

He turned to Hunter standing up close on his left and he said, "Just what is the situation, Mr. Hunter? I gotta know if you want me to do the right thing here. I have to know. Is it . . . does it have somethin' to do with . . . *her*?"

Hunter winced at that. It was as though the young marshal had hauled off and slapped him.

"What you deserve, Roscoe, is neither here nor there. I will tell you exactly what you need to know, and you're just going to have to trust that it is, indeed, all you need to know to fulfill your obligations here in Box Elder Ford . . . and to keep that shiny badge pinned to your vest."

He glanced at the mouth of the cross street lying dark to the south and along which Deets's house sat not far from the corner. "And to keep that house you and Lupita have grown so fond of . . . and are no doubt pondering filling with little Roscoes. Am I right?"

Deets scowled at the man, who was a good three inches shorter than Deets was and who smelled like pomade and shaving oil. Hunter was clean-shaven, arrogant-eyed, and seedily handsome despite pockmarks on his cheeks.

He rolled a shaved matchstick around between his lips, and his breath smelled like tequila. With his wife, Helen, having been sitting over at Mona's most of the afternoon, he'd no doubt dined in one of the saloons, calming his nerves with his favorite busthead.

Deets had never liked Hunter's smug manner, but he'd been grateful to the man for a job, despite what Deets had ended up doing to win it. Now he hated Hunter right down to the man's fancy, store-bought half boots with the little silver buckles gleaming in the starlight, against the floury dirt of the street.

"Am I right, Marshal?" Hunter asked again, smiling without mirth and giving Deets's shoulders a squeeze.

Deets remembered a night over a year ago—a dark night not unlike this one. He remembered the cat's meow and he heard the bark of a pistol. His own pistol. He heard Wilkinson scream and he saw the flash of the marshal's pistol as Wilkinson triggered his Colt Lightning into the dirt near his boots.

Deets shook his head to rid himself of the memory. He pulled away from Hunter, shrugging off the man's arm as though it were a wet, musty horse blanket.

"I'll look into it, Mr. Hunter. That's all I can tell you. Now, if you want my badge because I can't promise you any more than that, then you'll have it. But all I can tell you right now is that I'll look into the situation and get back to you."

Hunter wrinkled his nose and his cheeks flushed in the starlight. "Why, you coward."

"Maybe," Deets said with a shrug, nodding. "Maybe."

"You're just afraid of the bounty hunter. That's what all this is about. You're afraid of him and that girl he rides with." Hunter wrinkled his nose again and twisted his lips into a ghoulish mask. "Just like you were afraid of Wilkinson, so you shot him here in the street when he was distracted. Well, shit, man—why don't you just do what Tanner suggested? Find yourself a cat!"

Hunter laughed cruelly, clapped his hands once, and strode off in the direction of the Wayne house. He kept laughing like a madman. His maniacal laughter echoed over the star-cloaked town until a dog started barking.

CHAPTER ELEVEN

Prophet was sitting in the chair by Louisa's bed when he heard the clomps of a horse entering the yard.

The horse trotted past the house, heading for the small stable flanking the hog pen and chicken coop, where the bounty hunter had stabled Mean and Ugly and Louisa's pinto.

Fifteen minutes later, the doctor shuffled up to the house. He was talking to the boy, who'd been playing around the yard with a slingshot, and now both came inside. While the boy scrambled off to wash for supper, the doctor pushed through the curtain into the sickroom.

Prophet was holding a cool cloth soaked with fresh, cold water he'd fetched from the well to the girl's forehead.

"She's awful warm, Doc," he said.

"That's to be expected. I'll take over."

Prophet rose, leaving the cloth draped across Louisa's forehead.

"How's your other patient?" Prophet asked the young sawbones.

"About as well as can be expected, given . . ." The doctor caught himself, and flushed. He cast Prophet an annoyed look. "Are you still here?"

"A woman came by to see you. A hell of a looker. She said she often helped out with your female patients, makin' it all right an' proper."

Wringing the cloth out in the washbasin, the doctor cast

Prophet another quick, troubled glance. "She did, did she?" He didn't seem all that happy about the information.

"Does the name Verna McQueen ring a bell?"

"Yes, of course. And yes, she does help out from time to time."

"Purty gal," Prophet said, gently probing for information. This town was a puzzle, the lavishly dressed and erotically attractive woman who'd visited him earlier just one more.

"You said that."

The doctor placed the cloth on Louisa's forehead and then hooked his stethoscope around his neck.

"Mr. Prophet, there's little reason for you to be here now. Your partner is still alive and she seems relatively stable. The fever, as I said, is to be expected. Why don't you go into town and get yourself something to eat? I recommend Cartwright's. Mrs. Cartwright stays open till ten and she's a decent cook for these parts. I'd invite you to stay and join me, but I try to keep Titus clear of your sort. And, believe me"—he laughed caustically—"that isn't all that easy out here on the frontier!"

"Yeah, we unwashed types are a dime a dozen out here in the tall and uncut. You ain't from here, I take it?"

"No, I sure ain't," the doctor said, mockingly.

"Well, all right, then," Prophet said when the sawbones didn't bother to elaborate. "Since I've been dismissed, I reckon I'll rustle up some supper." He donned his hat. "But I'll be back to check on her."

"I'm sure you will, Mr. Prophet."

Prophet dropped down the stone steps into the yard. He glanced toward the stable. Like most frontiersmen, he wasn't accustomed to walking more than a few feet at a time, but he saw little reason to saddle Mean and Ugly just to ride into town, which was only about a couple of hundred yards away. The horse had had a big day, just as Prophet had, and Mean needed his rest.

Not that they'd be hitting the trail again anytime soon. Mean and the pinto would get plenty of stable feed for the next several days.

Prophet had no intention of leaving Box Elder Ford until he was sure that Louisa was well on her way to mending.

Still, Prophet could use a walk. The fresh air and exercise might clear his head, maybe relieve the worry gnawing at him the way a dog worries a new bone. He walked out to the main trail and turned toward town, his spurs chinging as he strode. As the outlying cabins of the town pushed up around him and he could see the lights of a saloon ahead, he stopped suddenly and swung around, one hand dropping to the handle of his .45.

He'd heard something. He wasn't sure what. The faint snapping of a twig under a stealthy boot?

He stepped behind the front corner of a low, abandoned-looking cabin on the left side of the trail and stared along his back trail. The trail, pale brown in the starlight, dwindled off toward the south and the doctor's house, revealed by lights glowing in the windows. There were several shanties that also looked derelict—probably the settlement's original dwellings abandoned in favor of roomier, more modern houses.

Prophet waited, squeezing the handle of his holstered .45. He carefully scanned the trail, looking for moving shadows. Spying none and hearing nothing more—the sound he'd heard might have been anything, maybe the breeze nibbling newspaper litter—he moved back onto the trail and continued on into the town.

He found the Cartwright Café on the town's west-central side—a little brick adobe building with a wood-frame second story where the proprietors probably lived. Doc Whitfield had mentioned a woman cook, but Prophet was served pot roast, mashed potatoes and gravy, a generous portion of buttered carrots, and a hot cross bun by a squat man with a large head that could have been carved from granite. He had short, bristly gray hair and one of those faces that appeared incapable of smiling.

His lips appeared eternally pooched out. He breathed loudly and hard. He wore an apron, and both thick arms were covered in tattoos. One had the faded image of a fat, naked lady with a ship's anchor drawn on her belly, marking the man an old sailor whose wife probably preferred he keep the arm and its scandalous marking covered.

It was too hot for shirtsleeves in the eatery, however.

Prophet was the only customer at this late hour. The man, on the far side of middle age, had been cleaning up when Prophet came in, and he didn't look pleased at the interruption. He gave Prophet a couple of owly glances before resuming the chore. As he ate, Prophet caught the man studying him with interest in a window reflection.

Prophet figured the cook was aware of the problem that Prophet had followed into town.

The *seven problems* that were likely on the lurk hereabouts.

Likely, the whole town knew about the conflict by now. With every move he made, he'd have to watch his back. He considered probing the cook about the seven ambushers, but he suspected the gent was customarily taciturn. Now, with Prophet here, he was even more so.

Prophet finished his meal and the cherry pie and whipped cream and a second cup of coffee, all of which were figured into the fifteen-cent price for the meal. His belly was well padded but he felt only modestly better. A rat of sharp, cold dread was still chewing on him. It had nothing to do with the ambushers. They evoked only rage in him.

The dread was for his trail partner.

She'd looked bad. Really bad.

He rose heavily, donned his hat, hitched his holster up on his thigh, and tightened the thong securing it to his leg. He tossed the fifteen cents down beside his well-cleaned plates.

"Thanks partner," he yelled to the cook. Sweeping a pile of dirt and sawdust into a tin dustpan on the other end of the room, the man did not respond.

Prophet gave a wry chuff. Despite his frustration and worry, he yawned as he strode to the propped-open door. Fatigue weighed heavy on him. The Arkansas River Saloon sat down the street a short ways from the eatery, on the other side of the street. There were two horses standing at one of the three hitch racks fronting the place—a two-story mud-brick building with a high, ornately painted false wooden façade.

A drink would file the edges off.

Prophet glanced around cautiously. Seeing no suspicious shadows lurking around alley mouths, the bounty hunter pushed away from Cartwright's and headed across the street. He climbed the steps to the saloon's broad front gallery and peered over the batwings.

The Arkansas River was a large ornate place with a bar and back bar that ran along the right wall all the way to the carpeted stairs at the back. The back bar mirror glittered in the umber light given off by smoky lamps hanging from wagon wheels. Game trophies and oil paintings festooned the walls.

It didn't matter that the pictures were crude. Most men didn't mind a crude painting if it was sporting a naked woman. One even sported three, all dancing in the desert without shoes even though cactus bristled at their feet. All three girls were appropriately well-endowed enough to cause a man filled with whiskey to consider plopping down his hard-earned cash for a tussle upstairs with one of the girls who likely worked the premises.

There was nothing on the saloon that advertised a brothel,

but that didn't mean it didn't sell mattress dances. Most saloons did.

In fact, a pretty brunette in a dark-red corset and bustier with black trim and a small, dark-red hat was standing at the bar. She was talking to the bartender, a tall man with thin hair on top and long hair on the sides and tumbling over his collar in back. He was unshaven and he wore an eye patch. He had a lean, angular face and his lone eye was dark and glib. He immediately flushed when he saw Prophet.

There were three other men in the place. They were dressed in the shabby suits of poor shopkeepers or drummers. They were playing poker at a round table left of the bar. Like the girl's and the barman's eyes, their eyes were on Prophet.

Prophet smelled trouble here. But then, he'd been smelling trouble ever since he and Louisa had ridden into town. Maybe it was time he rooted out what was causing the stench and dealt with it right and proper.

Anger fanned its flames in his cheeks, but Prophet grinned affably, which was his manner, and poked his hat brim back off his forehead. He pushed through the batwings and moseyed up to the bar, about ten feet right of the girl, who gave him the cool up and down.

"Well, there, friend," said the bartender, who didn't sound overly friendly. "What's your poison?"

"I'd like a whi . . ." Prophet let his voice trail off and glanced behind him as two men, one tall and one short, both sporting revolvers on their hips, pushed through the batwings. Prophet hadn't heard the thud of hooves, so they hadn't ridden up to the place. They'd walked, which was damned unusual for ranch hands, which was how these two were dressed.

They swaggered Indian-file to the bar. The tall one strode past Prophet and took a position to his left, on the other side of the girl. The girl tensed, looking straight ahead, nervous. The short gent wore a shabby brown bowler and had a nasty scar running from the right corner of his mouth and down his neck. Probably the stamp of a wild animal of some kind. He bellied up to the mahogany to Prophet's right.

Prophet smiled and pinched his hat brim to both men and then turned back to the bartender. "As I was sayin', I'd like a whiskey. Just one shot. It's late and I'm tired and looking forward to a long night's sleep."

"A long night's sleep, eh?" The bartender grabbed a shot glass from a pyramid and set it down in front of Prophet. Then he popped the cork on a bottle and splashed whiskey into the glass. "Yeah, that sounds kinda good to me, as well." He glanced first at the man on Prophet's left and then at the man on his right. "Don't it to you, boys?"

"A good long night's sleep," said the shorter of the two in a nasal twang. "Yeah, I like the sound of that. A good, long night's sleep."

The man to Prophet's left snorted a laugh.

Prophet sipped his whiskey and frowned with mock puzzlement. "I'm afraid I don't get the joke," he said, cutting his eyes around. "What's so funny about getting a good, long night's sleep?"

He looked at the bartender, who stared at him blandly through his lone, dark, mean eye. Gradually, a slight flush rose in his cheeks. Apparently, he hadn't expected such a direct and frank reaction.

Prophet turned to the man on his right. "You—little man. What's so funny about getting a long night's sleep?"

The little man flushed and his small, round pig eyes darkened. He didn't like being called little. He stared hard at Prophet for a time and then a darker flush rose in his cheeks and he opened his mouth to lick his lips. He cracked a nervous smile and slid his glance from Prophet to the bartender and back again.

"What?" he said haltingly.

"I'm just tryin' to get the joke," Prophet said in frustration, turning to the bartender and then to the man on his left while keeping his shoulders square to the mahogany. "What's so funny about that? Unless it's a secret joke that I wasn't *supposed* to get. In which case I'm gonna have to assume I'm being made sport of!"

The pleasure girl stepped straight back away from the bar. She turned on a heel, strode past the man on Prophet's left, and climbed the stairs at the back of the room. She lost a shoe about halfway up but left it where it fell, kicked out of the other one, and disappeared barefoot into the second story.

The three men playing poker gathered their cards and money and left the premises, the batwings flapping noisily behind them.

Prophet turned to the bartender. "What's your name?"

The bartender slid his eyes to the other two and said tightly, coldly, "L.J. Tanner. I own this place and I don't appreciate your tone. Kind of bold for a stranger."

"Mr. Tanner . . . er, L.J.—do you mind if I call you L.J.?"

Tanner stared at him. Apprehension drifted into his eye. Tightly, he said, "All right—have it your way."

"All right—L.J. it is. L.J., please let me in on the joke, will you . . . so I can finish my drink and go on to bed, secure in the knowledge that I, a stranger in town, ain't just been mocked by three of the plug-ugliest peckerwoods I've seen in a month of Sundays?"

CHAPTER TWELVE

"Easy now, mister," L.J. said, opening his hands. "Just take it easy."

"I ain't gonna take it easy," Prophet said, glowering and leaning forward, one hand on the grips of his .45. "I feel as though I've done been laughed at . . . after I was shot at . . . after my partner, Miss Louisa Bonnyventure, was badly wounded and is now resting uncomfortably on death's doorstep. And that just really piss-burns me bad, see? And I'm going to need someone to apologize . . . so I can leave here and find me a haystack and get that good, long night's sleep I was talkin' about real innocent-like before you three laughed. If I don't get that apology, there's no tellin' what I'm liable to do in the piss-burned condition I'm in . . ."

The bartender opened his hands wide and took one step back from the mahogany. "Just take it easy."

"That ain't what I'm waitin' to hear."

The barman stared at him with his one dark eye.

The man to his right stared at him, too, as did the man to his left. Prophet was watching them both in the back bar mirror, behind L.J. Tanner. They were flushed and sweating and tense as coiled rattlers. The man to Prophet's left glanced quickly, furtively, to the little man to Prophet's right and then he slapped the bar suddenly and said loudly, "All right, all right, I'll give you the apology you're lookin'—"

He stopped abruptly as Prophet wheeled to his right, the

Peacemaker instantly in his hand. The little man had his own Smith & Wesson half raised. His eyes dropped to Prophet's cocked and leveled .45.

He dropped his own gun and screamed, "No!" He stumbled back away from the bar, tripped, and fell over a chair, taking the chair with him as he fell to the floor, cursing under his breath.

Prophet wheeled. The man to his left had crouched and placed a hand on one of his two Schofields, but he froze, leaving the gun in its holster. He grinned sheepishly at Prophet and slid his gaze to the bartender. The barman chuffed with reproof through his nose, lips pressed tightly together.

Prophet backed up to where he could keep all three men in his line of sight. The little man was climbing heavily to his feet. He'd dropped his hat and his sandy hair was hanging in his eyes. His face was flushed with humiliation. He glanced at the revolver on the floor.

Prophet said, "You touch that Smithy, I'll blow your head off, you ugly little pile of shit."

The little man gave a soft yelp and stumbled anxiously back away from the gun. Prophet swung his Colt to the man on his left. That man, too, stepped back and raised his hands high above his shoulders, eyes wide as he regarded Prophet as though he were a wildcat who'd just moseyed in from the countryside looking hungry.

Prophet turned to the barman, who stood a couple feet back from the bar, shuttling glares from the little man to the man on Prophet's left. "You two are useless," the barman told them. "Useless!"

"He's right fast, L.J.," the little man said, indignant. "Just like what they say about him."

Prophet glared at the barman. "So . . . you sicced these two hapless mutts on me?"

Peter Brandvold

The barman glared back at Prophet, nostrils flared. "So what if I did?"

"Why?"

"That's none of your business."

"I'm makin' it my business." Prophet slid his Colt slightly to the barman's right and quirked a wry half-grin. "How 'bout if I blow out that purty mirror you got there?"

"Christ, no!" L.J. shouted, darting forward, holding up his hands, palms out, as though to shield his precious looking-glass from a bullet. "Please! I got a thousand dollars in that mirror, and that's the expensive liquor on the shelves back there." His gaze now was suddenly one of beseeching, but his voice was also edged with subtle warning. "Please."

Prophet glanced at the other two. "Were they . . . or you . . . part of that pack of chicken-livered dogs that ambushed me an' my partner last night? Maybe all three of ya?"

"God, no!" said the tall man to Prophet's left. "We had nothin' to do with that!"

"We didn't even get to town till late this afternoon. Just rode in for a drink after a long, hot ride from Abilene!"

"Shut up about your life story, Donovan, or I'll . . ." L.J. let his voice trail off and returned his gaze to Prophet.

"What about you?" Prophet asked him, pitching his voice with menace. He narrowed one eye. "Your voice sounds mighty familiar. I got me a good ear for voices. Somethin' tells me you were out there last night, at the Ramsay Creek Outpost."

L.J.'s cheeks mottled red. He shook his head slowly, swallowing nervously. "No. Now . . . you got it wrong, see?"

"Do I?"

"Yes, you do."

"You know who was out there, don't you?" Prophet asked.

"No, sir, I sure as hell don't." L.J. glanced fleetingly toward the man on Prophet's left, as if to gauge his reaction.

104

Prophet knew he was lying. About which part of the question, he wasn't sure. Maybe both parts. He doubted he'd get anything out of him, however. Not now. Not yet. He had a mind to blow up the man's precious mirror.

As he turned his pistol once more slightly to the right, the barman said, "That ain't gonna get you any answers, goddamnit! That's destroyin' personal property, and by god if you do that . . . !"

"What?" Prophet said through gritted teeth. "What're you gonna do about it?"

L.J. just glared at him, his lone eye hard, round, and cold.

Prophet glanced at the other two. The man on his left still had his hands raised. Prophet backed up six feet and wagged his revolver at the nearest table.

"I'll take your guns. Set 'em right here. They'll be layin' in the street outside. If I see either one of you go for 'em before I'm well away from here, I'll kill you. And if I ever see you again, I'll kill you. So if you see me first, you better turn around and hightail it in the opposite direction and hope like hell I don't see you before you get gone."

"Fools," L.J. said through a growl.

Donovan picked up his Smithy and, truckling like a whipped dog, staring at Prophet's cocked Colt, set it on the table. His taller partner set both his pistols on the table, as well, and then backed away.

"You fellas got any hideouts?"

"Nope," said Donovan.

"No, sir," said the tall man, raising his hands again.

Prophet narrowed a suspicious eye. "You sure?"

"We're sure," said Donovan.

"What a couple of cowards," L.J. said out the side of his mouth, keeping his nose wrinkled disdainfully.

"Shut up, L.J.," Prophet said. "One more word out of you

and I'm gonna shatter your mirror."

L.J. swallowed. "Please don't do that."

Prophet picked up the revolvers from the table, one by one. Keeping his Colt aimed at L.J., he shoved each pistol down behind his cartridge belt.

"If I find out any of you ambushed my partner out there at Ramsay Creek, you're gonna die. So you'd best start settin' things in order, maybe brush off the suit you wanna be planted in. I ain't goin' anywhere until I know who did that piece of cowardly business under cover of darkness. Outnumbering us eight to two."

Prophet backed to the batwings, stopping to the left of the doorway. He glanced over the louver doors to make sure no one was lurking on the porch with a gun. Glancing over his shoulder, he said, "I'm gonna find out who and why, and then the cowards behind it are gonna pay. And I ain't just talkin' about a blowed-out mirror, neither."

He backed through the doors. As they slapped back into place before him, he stared over their tops at the three men standing frozen around the bar, gazing at him coldly, edgily. "One last thing before I go. If I find anyone lurkin' around the doc's place, there will be no warning. I will shoot first and find out who I shot after the smoke clears."

Prophet turned, walked down the porch steps, and tossed all three revolvers into the street.

He strode west along the dark main thoroughfare, turned south down the cross street, and headed out in the direction of the river he could not see save for a few dull star reflections beyond the trees in the darkness. The town was quiet. Eerily quiet. As Prophet walked, he paused now and then to turn full around and inspect the night around him. Then he continued walking until he entered the doctor's yard. He walked past the side door to the rear of the house and looked into the window of Louisa's room.

Through the thin curtain, he could see the doctor in there, leaning forward in the chair and pressing his stethoscope to Louisa's chest. Prophet couldn't see Whitfield's face from this angle, but the man's jaw looked nervously taut. Prophet tensed, then, as well.

Had she gone?

Prophet strode to the side door, hesitating. He decided not to knock, though he knew he was likely risking the sawbone's wrath. He'd already drawn that, anyway.

"How is she?" he asked as he pushed through the curtain.

Whitefield was stuffing the stethoscope back inside his open medical kit. He scowled at Prophet, waved him out, and then, after a few seconds, he followed the bounty hunter out into the hall near the side door, dragging his bad ankle.

"You were gone longer than I figured you'd be," Whitfield said, adjusting his glasses on his nose.

"Yeah, well, I ran into more trouble than I expected . . . over at Mr. L.J. Tanner's Saloon."

"Sniffing for more trouble, eh?" the doctor said in a reproving tone.

"I didn't sniff the first bit. It came to us. Save the lectures, Doc. How is she?"

"She's still alive. Her pulse is shallow. Her fever is down, however, but it will likely rise again. I will continue to check on her throughout the night." Whitfield filled his lungs as he stared up at the big man before him, like an admonishing schoolmaster. "If I were you, Prophet, I'd leave this town. Your staying here isn't doing either one of you any good. You're just attracting trouble to my place, and I do not allow trouble here."

Anger burning bright behind his eyes, Prophet said, "Doc, I'll be here until Louisa's ready to ride. And just so you know— and you might want to spread this around, though it's probably spreading already, after my visit to Mr. Tanner's saloon—I'm gonna find out who ambushed her. And I'm gonna find out why. And then, because I know the law here won't do a damn thing about it, I'm gonna settle up with those men myself."

"Why are you telling me this, Mr. Prophet?"

"Because you seem to think your problem is with me." Prophet shook his head. "It ain't. It's with the men who ambushed her." He jerked his head to indicate Louisa behind the blanket curtain. "Good night."

He turned and walked out of the house, letting the screen door slap shut behind him.

The doctor opened the door and said, "Mr. Prophet, I've had a change of heart. I don't want you spending the night in my stable."

"Don't blame you a bit, Doc," Prophet said, striding off in the night.

CHAPTER THIRTEEN

Neal Hunter yawned as he pulled his suspenders up over his shoulders and left the room that he and his wife, Helen, shared on the second floor of their Grand View Hotel. Still blinking sleep from his eyes, he ran his hands through his hair and stumbled down the hallway. He descended the stairs and frowned, puzzled, as he passed the front desk in the lobby.

"Where in the hell . . . ?" he muttered as he turned into the doorway opposite the stairs.

Helen was sitting at the table they customarily had breakfast at, in the corner on the far side of the dining room, where they had a view out two large windows—one facing the front porch and the main street, the other facing a side street.

Helen sat in her customary place at the table, her back to the front window. A silver coffee service sat on the table, as well as china cups, saucers, a small china pig creamer that had been handed down in Hunter's family back in Ohio, and a bowl of granulated sugar.

The dining room was still foggy with night shadows though the sun was just then rising. Steam curled from Helen's coffee cup, which she absently stirred cream into while gazing out the side window to her left.

"Oh, there you are," Hunter said, yawning and striding into the room, in his sleep fog, careful to avoid the chairs arranged around the other oilcloth-covered tables.

Helen was the only one in the dining room so far, which

wasn't unusual for a weekday morning. The Hunters did more lucrative breakfast business on the weekends. Soon, however, the two drummers from Denver, likely still asleep in their rented rooms, would be down for their morning meal, and Hunter would have a little cash in his cashbox.

"Helen, where have you been?" Hunter asked as he strode toward the spot where Helen's coffee steamed on the table, in the coppery light angling through the window over her left shoulder. "Didn't you ever come to bed?"

When he'd awakened, he'd been surprised to see that her side of the bed hadn't been slept in.

"I slept on the lobby sofa," Helen said, regarding her husband coolly with her large, round brown eyes. Helen was a pretty blonde, though she'd been prettier a few years ago, when the crow's feet hadn't yet showed up around her eyes, before her face had lost its youthful glow to the ravages of the Colorado sun, and the eyes themselves had started taking on a weary, slightly jaded cast.

The blonde in her hair now came from a bottle, Hunter knew, despite Helen trying to keep it a secret.

She was thirty-three, and the wear and tear of the years and the hard work of running the hotel had taken its toll on the woman, whom Hunter had married back in Ohio, though he'd met her first in the Colorado mountain mining camps. She'd been a saloon singer, and a good one. Only a singer. Not a percentage girl.

"Why on earth would you do that?" Hunter asked her. "It's only Thursday. We won't be getting any late business till the next stage pulls through."

"I wasn't sleepy," Helen said. "After returning from Mona's, I felt restless." She sipped her coffee. Her tone was low, crisp. "I had a million thoughts running through my head, Neal, if you must know." She sipped her coffee again, holding the delicate cup in both her small, work-thickened, lye-reddened hands, her eyes not meeting his.

Hunter sat down in his usual chair. "Oh?"

The *Box Elder Ford Bugle* was on the table—two pages of large print that came out once every two weeks and which Hunter had already read twice all the way through. The Chinese cook always placed it on the table beside Hunter's cup and saucer, whether Hunter had read it or not, so Hunter usually read it again over the cup of coffee that preceded breakfast.

Hunter could hear Huang, pronounced "Wang" by Hunter and all the other locals, banging pans around in the kitchen and opening and closing the rusty stove door.

This morning, Hunter ignored the paper. Tipping the silver pot over his cup, Hunter glanced at Helen. She was staring at him now. It was hard to read her thoughts, though it was easy to see her expression was grave. Maybe a little suspicious, even angry.

"Aren't you going to tell me?" Helen asked.

"Tell you what, dear?"

"How Eldon was killed."

Hunter leaned forward, his arms folded on the table, his right hand wrapped around his cup. "He was shot by a terrible man."

"How did he . . . and you . . . and the other men come to be out there wherever Eldon was shot?"

Hunter smiled as he reached over to place a placating left hand on Helen's right one. "That isn't something you need to worry about."

Helen pulled her hand out from beneath her husband's and said firmly, "That seems to be the answer of choice. It's the answer coming from all you men—Bly, Goose Johnson, Jim Purdy, that fool Carlsruud. Their wives are very upset. I talked to most of them over at Mona's last night. Look, Neal. We want to know why you men snuck out of town so late two nights ago.

111

Snuck out like schoolboys up to no good, mentioning nothing to your wives. We want to know what you were doing that got Eldon Wayne killed."

She added quickly, anticipating her husband's response, "Don't you think we have a right to know?"

Inwardly, Hunter shrank from Helen's uncharacteristically direct assault. It wasn't like her to get this angry and demanding. Usually, she went her way and he went his. While they worked together running the hotel, they didn't spend a whole lot of time together, and their conversations had become almost like the conversations between strangers waiting in a train station.

Hunter sipped his coffee, carefully setting the cup back onto its saucer. "It's not something we want you ladies to trouble yourselves over."

"We already are troubled over it, Neal. Whatever 'it' is."

"Yes, but you shouldn't be. I and the other men have the situation under control."

Laughing with bitter exasperation, Helen said, "Neal, what *situation* got Eldon Wayne killed and left poor Mona a widow?"

"Ready eat?" came Huang's cheerful voice from the kitchen door. The stocky Chinaman wore his white apron and black silk hat embroidered in red and gold. Long mare's-tail mustaches dangled down past his chin. He was wiping his thick hands on a towel.

"Ham and eggs and two pancakes for me, Huang," Hunter called. He glanced at Helen. "You, dear?"

"I'm not hungry this morning, Huang. Coffee is all."

"No hungry?" asked Huang, crestfallen.

"Really, dear?" Hunter asked.

Helen pounded the table, causing coffee to slosh over the top of her cup as well as Hunter's. "I am not hungry, Huang! All I want is some answers!" She hammered the table again and fired a hard, demanding look at her husband.

"Whoa," said one of the two drummers just then moving into the dining room from the lobby, both men doffing their bowler hats. They paused right inside the door, staring warily toward Hunter and Helen.

"Come in, gentlemen," Hunter said, smiling and beckoning. "Everything's fine. My lovely wife didn't sleep well, is all."

"Coffee?" Huang asked them from the kitchen door.

"Coffee, please, Huang," one of the drummers said, the other nodding in agreement.

When the drummers had been seated at a table near the door, Hunter smiled and nodded at them and then lifted his coffee cup to his lips. He looked across the table at Helen, whose face had turned to wax as she scrutinized him angrily.

As Huang came in from the kitchen, his slippers slapping his heels, and headed for the drummers, singing softly under his breath and smiling in his customarily ebullient way, Helen said to Hunter, "It has something to do with . . . *her* . . . doesn't it?" She sort of tossed her head, as though to indicate the north side of town.

Hunter felt his cheeks warm. His lower intestine snaked around in his belly. Trying to compose himself, he frowned as though with genuine bewilderment. "Her?"

"*Her*," Helen said, glancing over to where Huang was chatting with the drummers. "You know who I mean, Neal." That's all she said. She just let it hang there in the air between them like some noxious gas. She stared at her husband with cold, light-brown eyes and pursed lips, as though sealing the words with an invisible hammer.

"Please, Helen. Why don't you go up and lie down? You know we have Eldon's funeral to attend at ten o'clock this morning. In your current . . . confused and overwrought . . . condition, I doubt you'll be able to manage it."

Helen continued to gaze in the same off-putting, waxy way as before, as though she hadn't heard what he'd just said. She glanced at the drummers again. Huang had returned to the kitchen to begin cooking their breakfast, and the men seemed to be absorbed in their own conversation.

Helen ran her tongue along her bottom lip and returned her hard, accusatory stare to her husband. "You know, Neal, I began to suspect something after Vernon Waddell was hauled out of her place feet first."

"What?" Hunter said, chuckling with incredulity.

"Yes, late at night. Three months ago. Maggie Smith told me. She lives near where . . . *she* . . . lives. Maggie was sitting up late with her poor, old, confused father who's gotten his days and nights mixed up, and Maggie saw several men from town, including Gibbons, the undertaker, cart him out of *her* house. Heart attack."

"Yes, I know that Waddell died of a heart attack," Hunter said, keeping his voice down and trying to casually sip his coffee. "Is Maggie sure that he was carried out of . . . *her* . . . house?" He glanced toward the drummers, glad to see that they were still absorbed in their own conversation.

"She's quite sure," Helen said. "Of course, the story as Vernon's wife, Marjorie, told it, was that Vernon got up at night to use the privy and she found him in there later . . . dead. Maggie says that Marjorie's story is hogwash. Maggie is quite certain it was Waddell who was hauled out of that pretty little house on the hill north of town. By that no-account bartender, L.J. Tanner, and a couple of Tanner's hired help."

Hunter chuckled. "How in the world would Maggie know it was Vernon? It was at night and Maggie's father's house is situated a good fifty, sixty yards away!"

"I don't know why she's so certain it was Vernon, but she is. Tanner and the other men drove a wagon right past Maggie's

house. She saw them clearly." Helen shook her head in annoy-
ance. She pitched her voice low and cold as she leaned forward.
"The point is, Neal, someone was hauled out of *that woman's*
house that night and the next morning we all learned of
Vernon's fatal heart attack. No one else in town died that night,
Neal."

Helen sealed the statement with a faintly mocking quirk of a
corner of her mouth and an arch of her brow.

Huang came out of the kitchen and set Hunter's steaming
food in front of him. When Huang had left, the hotelier busily
draped his napkin over his right thigh and picked up his knife
and fork. Helen was watching him, awaiting his response.

He cleared his throat and said, "Well, I'm sorry to hear that,
Helen. I didn't know that about Vernon." He feigned a laugh
but it came out brittle, betraying his nerves. "Who'd have known
old Vernon had it in him to carry on like that!"

"Yes, who'd have known?" Helen finished her coffee and set
her cup in its saucer. "But then, who'd have known one woman
could turn nearly every man in an entire town into a lovelorn
schoolboy. Oh, don't look at me that way. Don't you *dare* laugh
at me!"

She was hissing this out now, leaning low over the table, her
face a waxy mask of fury, no longer caring if the drummers
heard or not. "I've seen how you all treat her whenever she
rides down from her little castle on the hill. Why, every man on
Hazelton Street stares out their shop windows at her, tongues
hanging, or rushes out to help her out of her buggy . . . to open
and close doors for her. To carry her shopping bags for her!"

Hunter could only stare at his enraged wife, stunned. He'd
had no idea that he and the others had been so transparent.

"Anyway," Helen said, straightening in her chair. "That's
when I began to suspect certain things."

"Helen," Hunter said. "She's not married. All alone here in

Box Elder Ford. We're merely being gentlemen."

"Let me just say this, Neal, and then I will say no more about it. I know that this mess you're all involved in with the bounty hunter somehow involves *her*. I don't think I even want to know all the sordid details. But know this, Neal." Helen narrowed her eyes at him as she rose slowly, stiffly from her chair. "I will no longer be taking sedatives to help me sleep, and you will no longer be down here alone at night, manning the front desk. Do I make myself clear?"

Helen didn't wait for an answer. She swung around and, chin in the air, strode across the room, her spruce-green skirt billowing and brushing tables and the backs of chairs. She gave a cordial nod to the two drummers who, having overheard the last, loudest part of the Hunters' conversation, regarded her with flushed, hang-jawed looks.

When Helen had left the room and mounted the lobby stairs, the drummers glanced at Hunter.

The hotelier smiled, nodded, cleared his throat, and started eating although he was no longer hungry.

CHAPTER FOURTEEN

At the cemetery, after a brief funeral service at the Bethany Lutheran Church in town, Minister Calvin Whitehead bowed his head to recite a prayer. The dozen or so mourners who'd gathered around the grave followed suit. The undertaker's two sons had just finished digging the rectangular hole as the mourners had walked or ridden out from the church to the cemetery here on a rise overlooking the river.

Neal Hunter bowed his head, as well, and sighed.

Whitehead's prayers could last as long as it had taken the two Gibbons boys to dig six feet down through rocks and sand. The sun was blazing straight down through the leaves of a cottonwood, searing the back of Hunter's neck.

He was uncomfortable for other reasons, as well. Verna McQueen was one of the mourners, standing not ten feet to Hunter's left. She was fetchingly dressed all in black, almost as though she herself was the widow. Her lush hair tumbled across her shoulders, strands of it dancing in the breeze and fairly sparkling in the sunlight.

Mona Wayne herself wore only a shapeless gray and white frock, and a straw hat with an appropriately black band that she'd probably borrowed for the occasion. She sat near the hole and the closed wooden casket, sweating and weeping into a handkerchief. One of Eldon's battered hats sat on the ground near one of Mona's stout ankles for folks to toss "memorials" into as they left the proceeding.

Peter Brandvold

Hunter didn't know if Helen, standing to his right, had seen Verna or not. He doubted that Helen would make a scene here at Eldon's funeral if she had. Still, his and Helen's argument earlier, and now Verna McQueen showing up to the funeral, was enough to give Hunter a bad case of indigestion.

He jerked with a start when someone poked him from behind. He glanced over his shoulder. Glen Carlsruud stood behind him in a three-piece black suit. Carlsruud canted his head slightly to his right, rolling his eyes in the same direction.

Hunter turned to see what the mercantiler was indicating. He frowned at first, unable to see anything in that direction except patchy green and brown hills spotted with post oaks and juniper. But then Hunter saw the man standing on a slightly higher hill to the northeast of the cemetery, maybe a quarter mile away, and he felt his heart hiccup in his chest.

The man was tall and broad-shouldered. He wore a cream shirt under a brown leather vest, and Hunter could see the gun thonged on the man's right thigh, the funnel-brimmed Stetson on his head. The tips of twin shotgun barrels poked up from behind his right shoulder. The shotgun's bandolier was slanted across his chest. He held a pair of field glasses to his eyes. The glasses were directed at the cemetery.

As Hunter stared back at the man who was undeniably the bounty hunter, Lou Prophet, Prophet lowered the glasses, turned his head to one side and down, as though spitting, and then raised the glasses once more. The skin over Hunter's chest rippled. He felt as though the glasses were directed specifically at him.

Maybe they were.

Hunter felt weak and sick to his stomach. Anger burned in him.

What in the hell was he doing up there, anyway?

Hunter looked around at the other mourners. All of the other

118

men who'd ridden in the pack the night before last were here. Even Melvin Bly, though his arm was in a sling and he looked pasty and jaundiced and in severe need of a drink. No, not all the men from that night, Hunter saw. L.J. Tanner wasn't here, which wasn't all that unexpected. The hard-bitten Tanner did not hold with such formalities as funerals.

But all the rest were here. And the bounty hunter had probably known they would be here at the funeral of one of their fallen. He was probably scrutinizing each of the mourners right now as the preacher droned on, asking forgiveness for Eldon's sins and beseeching Him to welcome Eldon into his open arms. Prophet was probably trying to figure out which of the mourners had been there that night at the Ramsay Creek Outpost.

He was also strategically making his presence known. He was making sure the men who'd ambushed him knew he was hunting them.

Hunter glanced away and caught Verna McQueen staring at him. Verna's chin was dipped slightly, head bowed, but her head was also turned to her right and she was giving Hunter a sly, cunning smile beneath the brim of her black hat. That dubious smile coupled with the bounty hunter's presence there on the nearby hill caused Hunter's guts to churn with more vigor.

What in hell was she smiling about? Had she seen Prophet and was she amused by his presence? Or was her smile more sinister? Was she reprimanding Hunter in her own, subtle, ironic way?

Perhaps she was threatening him?

He'd have to talk to her as soon as possible. He'd have to explain the situation to her. That wouldn't be easy, however, since obviously Helen was suspicious.

He looked away from Verna McQueen. Out the corner of his right eye, he saw Helen move her head. Helen was now gazing toward the preacher, but had she a moment before caught him meeting Verna's oblique, smiling stare? If so, she gave no indication.

The preacher droned on, his head bowed so low that his chin nearly touched his black wool clergy blouse and white collar. His grizzled gray hair blew around the freckled, bald, domelike top of his head.

"For Christ's sake, Reverend," Hunter was on the pointing of shrieking. "That's enough! We're burying only Eldon Wayne here today, not the King of friggin' England!"

Just then a baby started crying, and Whitehead took that as a cue to end his soliloquy. After the mourners had filed past Mona, offering condolences and dropping a coin or two into her husband's old, salt-stained hat, Hunter managed to step far enough away from Helen long enough to grab Carlsruud's arm and whisper, "We all need to meet at Tanner's. Spread the word. One hour. Call it a memorial libation for our dear friend, Eldon, if you like."

Whether or not Helen Hunter had caught the glance her husband and Verna McQueen had exchanged during Reverend Whitehead's belabored prayer, young Marshal Roscoe Deets had. He and Lupita had been standing to the Hunters' far right, at one end of the curve the standing mourners had made around Mrs. Wayne, the Reverend, the coffin, and the open grave.

Deets had gotten a good look at Mr. Hunter and Miss McQueen sharing that furtive glance, Miss McQueen with that funny, almost ominous smile on her pretty, doll-like face.

Right then and there, Deets knew his suspicions had been correct. Miss McQueen had something to do with the powder keg of trouble that was sitting in the middle of Hazelton Street, just waiting for someone to touch a match to the too-short fuse and blow the whole town to kingdom come.

Now Deets fished in his pants pocket for a dollar's worth of change. He could only produce eighty cents, however. With a sheepish smile at the sobbing Mrs. Wayne, he dropped the coins into the hat, hoping that neither she nor anyone else around them was counting. Stepping away from Mrs. Wayne, following the line of mourners out toward the trail leading down Cemetery Hill, he glanced at Lupita.

Deets's pretty, round-faced wife smiled up at him, squeezing his hand.

She said nothing more as she and Deets made their way to the bottom of the hill, where several buggies were parked and two saddle horses were tied to the wrought-iron hitch rack festooned at each end with a winged iron cherub strumming a harp. Deets caught movement in the distance to his right.

He stopped and swung his head in that direction.

His belly soured as he watched the bounty hunter ride his dun horse up to the top of a distant butte, heading away from Deets and the other mourners. The man's broad back bobbed with the lunging of his horse. His faded Stetson was snugged down on his sandy-haired head, and his double-barreled, savage-looking shotgun hung at a slant across his back.

He and the horse crested the butte and then dropped down out of sight on the other side.

Deets had spied the man glassing the cemetery earlier. He was like a ghost, Prophet was. Haunting the town. Making a mockery of Deets's authority. Or whatever authority he had, which wasn't much, the young marshal had recently realized. The badge he was so proud of was a sham, worth about as much as the cheap nickeled copper it was made of.

"Who was that?"

Deets jerked, startled by his wife's voice from just off his right shoulder. She was staring up at him from beneath her straw boater festooned with the black ribbons she'd arranged earlier that morning for the funeral. Under a light tan shawl, she wore a plain, brown and white print dress that wasn't nearly as nice as the red one he'd given her. But the red dress hadn't been suited for a funeral. On her feet were worn, brown, side-button shoes she was unaccustomed to wearing.

Lupita stared up at her husband with concern.

"He was standing on that hill during the funeral," Lupita said. "He was looking through binoculars at us. Why?"

Deets led Lupita along the side of the trail, heading toward Box Elder Ford sweltering in the midday heat, dust lifting as a hot breeze kicked up.

"Don't worry about him," Deets said.

"Now I am worried," Lupita returned, wrinkling the skin above the bridge of her nose as she studied her husband's eyes. "Who is he, Roscoe? Please, tell me. I can tell you are concerned about him."

Deets didn't want to worry her, but she already was worried. Besides, he felt like getting his own worry off his chest, although merely speaking about it certainly wasn't going to get rid of the cause. No, only action would get rid of the cause. Deets severely doubted he was up to that kind of action . . . again.

"That's the bounty hunter who killed Eldon," Deets told his wife as they continued walking down the hill, to the right side of the trail. He could hear the other mourners speaking behind him as they, too, headed back toward town.

"*Dios mio*," Lupita said, staring dully forward in shock. She looked up at Deets. "What was he doing up there?"

"Sending a message, I guess."

"How unholy of him . . . to spy on the funeral of a man he killed. How disrespectful!"

Deets chuckled morosely.

"You are concerned," Lupita said, looking up at her husband again.

"Yeah, I'm a little concerned. But that don't mean you need

to be, honey." Deets patted Lupita's hand. "I've . . . I've got it all under control."

"Are you going to arrest him?"

Deets chuckled again.

"What is so funny?"

"I was just thinkin' how you sound like Hunter, Carlsruud, and the others. They all want me to arrest him, too. Only thing is, I don't know if I got any cause to arrest him." Well, it wasn't the *only* thing. There was a little problem with his nerve, as well, though of course Deets wasn't going to admit that to his wife. "They and several others shot his partner, a young lady. She's over at Doc Whitfield's place, gettin' tended. Might live, might die. Meanwhile, Prophet's on the lurk and makin' everybody nervous as rabbits at a rattlesnake convention."

Lupita studied on that for a time, frowning down at the ground as they turned onto their street and headed for their little house. "Why did they shoot this young lady, Roscoe?"

"That there I don't know," Deets said. "They won't tell me nothin'. All I know is a passel of 'em rode out of town together a couple nights ago and not all of 'em came back upright. Wayne and Melvin Bly took bullets—Wayne, of course, fatally." The young marshal kicked a rock in frustration. "What I *should* do is get everybody, including the bounty hunter, Prophet, in one room and have 'em all lay their cards on the table for me."

"So . . . why don't you do that?"

Deets and Lupita stopped walking as a buggy came rattling up behind them. Deets turned to see the polished leather chaise of Verna McQueen rolling up from the direction of the cemetery, her smart Morgan trotting handsomely in the traces. Miss McQueen dipped her chin cordially and smiled winningly with her rich, red lips and said, "Good morning, Marshal. Good morning, Mrs. Deets."

She passed on by, dust lifting from her high, thin, red wheels.

"Miss McQueen," Deets said, pinching his hat brim to the woman.

"She is so beautiful," Lupita said, gazing admiringly after the buggy, which was crossing Hazelton Street now, heading north. "Why do you suppose she lives alone? A woman so beautiful must have had many suitors."

Deets glanced at his young wife. Since she was half-Mexican, Lupita lived on a veritable island here in Box Elder Ford, subtly shunned by the white women. Aside from a couple of full-blood Mexican women, the half-Arapaho woman the blacksmith had married, and the occasional saloon girl, Lupita was the only woman in Box Elder Ford without pure white blood running through her veins.

She didn't seem to mind the lack of social interaction. After all, she'd grown up on a small, remote ranch with only her father and brother and a few wild horses and some chickens, until Deets had taken her away from there only a little over a year ago. Growing up, her closest companion outside her family was a coyote she'd raised from an orphaned pup.

The lack of socializing, however, had kept her in the dark about such things as the rumors going around town about Miss McQueen.

"Yeah, you'd think she would marry, wouldn't you?" Deets said, staring at the sleek, black buggy curving up the trail between buttes on the north side of town. "Maybe she's just got so many choices she can't make up her mind."

"Hmmm," Lupita said, also staring at the chaise, speculatively.

"Well, I'd best get back to the office," Deets said, thinking that he might soon pay a visit to the woman they'd just been talking about. Maybe from Miss McQueen he could get some answers, but he wasn't sure he really wanted any.

Deets doffed his hat and leaned down to kiss Lupita's cheek.

"Wait, Roscoe," Lupita said, clutching his arm. "You still

haven't told me all that concerns you. I am your wife. You should share such things with me."

"All in good time, honey," Deets said, giving her slender shoulders a reassuring squeeze. He himself wasn't at all sure about anything. "All in good time."

CHAPTER FIFTEEN

One hour after the funeral, Neal Hunter met Glen Carlsruud out front of the Arkansas River Saloon. They exchanged matching frowns and turned to the batwings over which L.J. Tanner could be heard shouting, ". . . and then he threatened to blow out my friggin' mirror!"

"Shit!" said big Lars Eriksson as Hunter and Carlsruud pushed through the batwings and let them clatter into place behind them.

The two stopped just inside the saloon. Hunter scowled when he saw L.J. Tanner, Eriksson, Goose Johnson, Jim Purdy, and the sick-looking Melvin Bly gathered around a table in the middle of the room. There were three other men there, as well— two shopkeepers and the round-faced and portly banker, George Campbell, who had not taken part in the fracas up at the Ramsay Creek Cavalry Outpost, but who was listening in scowling consternation at Tanner. The saloon owner was the only one standing. He had a boot propped atop a chair and he was leaning forward on that knee, holding court, as Tanner tended to do.

Tanner's beefy half-breed bartender and business partner, Arnell Three-Bears, stood behind the bar, toweling out a beer mug with a typically bland expression on his wide, flat, crudely chiseled features framed in long, coal-black hair hanging to his shoulders, the ends haphazardly hacked off with a knife.

Like Tanner, Arnell wore a patch over one eye, which he'd

apparently lost in some grisly childhood accident when he and his brother had been practicing with their slingshots down by the river. Behind their backs, Tanner and Arnell were often wryly, mockingly referred to as the "Blinky Boys," though Hunter failed to see either the reason for or the irony in the moniker.

It had most likely arisen because Hunter and Arnell, both bullies, were roundly feared. The popularity of Tanner's saloon was owed to the fact it was roomy, handily located in the center of town, served the best liquor at the best prices, and provided the best whores, though Tanner, who mistreated the girls, had trouble keeping them.

Hunter thought he only had one, possibly two, at the moment, both girls probably asleep upstairs.

"Gentlemen," Hunter said, scowling and casting a cautious glance over his shoulder, "don't you think it might not only be wise but prudent to take this meeting to the privacy of the billiard room? For chrissakes!"

"Yeah," said the liveryman, Jim Purdy, who dressed more like a well-to-do rancher than your typical, shit-shoveling livery stall swamper. "He was on that bluff overlooking Cemetery Hill. Watching the funeral through a pair of binoculars. No tellin' where he is now!"

"Can you believe that?" exclaimed Melvin Bly. He'd just taken a deep sip from his beer mug and wiped his mouth with the palm of his good hand. "Skulkin' around up there in plain sight, watchin' us like he was darin' us to ride up there and tell him not to!"

"Gentlemen!" Hunter wheezed out, trying to keep his voice down.

"All right, all right," said Tanner, removing his boot from the chair and straightening. "Let's head for the billiard room, boys."

As the others rose from their chairs and started tramping

toward a door at the back of the main drinking hall, Hunter turned to Arnell Three-Bears. "A pitcher of beer and a bottle of whiskey, Arnell. The good stuff."

"It's all good stuff," Tanner said, scowling his typical belligerence.

"Ah, stow it, L.J.," Hunter said, having no time for the saloon owner's schoolyard bravado.

He brushed past the man, heading for the billiard room, but he stopped abruptly and swung around toward the two men who had not been part of the eight who'd ridden out two nights ago.

"Henry? Jack? I'm sorry, but this is a private meeting."

The men glanced at each other, crestfallen.

"And keep everything you've heard here today under your hats, for chrissakes," Hunter said, glaring at the impertinent L.J. Tanner, who merely returned a flat stare. Turning to the rotund banker, Campbell, he said, "You're welcome, of course, George."

Campbell might not have ridden out that night, but he'd been part of the group who'd decided to go. Since Tanner worked closely with him, using his belligerence and, if necessary, his brawn to force repayment on mortgage loans, it was roundly assumed that Tanner had ridden in the fat man's stead. Hunter doubted that Campbell had ever straddled a horse in his life.

When the two extraneous men had left, grumbling, Hunter and the others gathered in the billiard room. They sat around one of the only two tables in the long, narrow room, against the far wall, between two tall windows. There were two billiard tables running nearly the length of the room, and Tanner sat on the edge of the one nearest the table the other men sat around, doffing their hats, clearing their throats, and exhaling cigarette or cigar smoke. Tanner held a half-filled beer mug in his right hand.

When they'd all gotten comfortable, Arnell Three-Bears brought in a pitcher of beer, a whiskey bottle, and a stack of shot glasses. He also brought beer schooners for Hunter and Carlsruud.

As he turned to leave the room, Hunter said, "Arnell, make sure we're not interrupted, will you?"

The half-breed merely grunted, went out, and closed the door behind him.

Hunter filled his and Carlsruud's beer mugs and then splashed whiskey into each of the shot glasses.

"How's the wing?" he asked Bly.

"Aches somethin' fierce," Bly said, sulking.

He lifted his whiskey to his lips and threw back half. "I still can't believe that son of a bitch was bold enough to stand atop that butte yonder, watchin' the funeral."

He chased the whiskey with a deep swallow from his beer schooner. "And Deets just stood there as though he didn't even see him!"

Tanner said, "Wilkinson would have dealt with this little problem when it first rode into town. Soon as we asked him to. Gibbons's boys would have dug another hole up on Potter's Field and they'd already have them friggin' two bounty hunters dumped into it an' snugglin' with rattlesnakes!"

Hunter said, "You wanted Wilkinson retired as badly as the rest of us did, L.J."

"Yeah, well, maybe I did. And maybe it was a mistake. What were we thinkin' when we hired that kid?"

"We hired the kid," Campbell said in a resonate voice that bespoke the refinement of his moneyed class as well as the sonorous lilts of his Virginia upbringing, "because we knew we could control him. We ceased being able to control Bill Wilkinson. The power went to his head—you all remember that. It wasn't all that long ago."

Tanner hung his head like an admonished schoolyard brat. Campbell was the only man in town who could cow Tanner, but only because Campbell held the note on the Arkansas River Saloon and paid Tanner handsomely to flex his muscles for him. Most of said flexing consisted of Tanner merely paying "courtesy" visits to the homes in Box Elder Ford of slow loan repayers or even just glaring at same from across his saloon floor. That was usually all it took.

Hunter said, "I suggest we forget Deets for now. We'll think about what to do about him once this little problem has been cleared up."

"And how do you propose to do that?" the bleary-eyed Bly asked, wincing against the pain in his arm, which he was cradling across his chest.

"Look—there's seven of us, for chrissakes," Tanner said. "I say we gang up on the son of a bitch."

"What?" Campbell said. "Shoot him on the street? In front of the women and children and the men not part of this nasty little problem?"

"After dark," Jim Purdy suggested, taking a deep drag off his loosely rolled quirley and blowing the smoke toward the ceiling.

Campbell shook his head. "Not in town, boys. Not in town. We cannot look like savages. Besides, we do have a town marshal."

"He's not gonna do shit!" Tanner said, laughing.

Campbell said, "Yes, but if we did that—shot a man down in the street—we'd be making a mockery of the young marshal. He'd be useless to us forever more . . . whatever we decided to do with him, and I don't think I'm going to be for cutting him loose." The fat banker gave a sly, heavy-lidded smile and puffed the fat stogie in his soft fingers. "He just bought a house. How would he pay for it without a job?"

The others chuckled—some with genuine humor, some ironically, casting each other furtive glances.

"Well, he's already a mockery," Tanner said and sipped his beer.

Turning to Tanner, Hunter said, "Why should we have to gang up on him? Why don't you take care of him, L.J.? You had quite the gun reputation in your day."

"Stow it, Hunter." L.J. glared through his one eye at the hotel owner. He did not add what the others already knew but did not discuss: Tanner could talk a good game, but his shooting skills had gone with his eye.

He still carried a pistol, but mostly for show, to keep the peace in his saloon after the sun went down and all breeds of man came to town to drink, gamble, carouse, and generally turn his wolf loose.

Tanner had gone out to Ramsay Creek that night, but only because he had the others to back him. Who'd have thought eight guns could not bring down both bounty hunters? The problem lay in the fact that the bounty hunters had split up, and the gang had only gotten the girl.

"Well, something needs to be done," said Glen Carlsruud, slamming a hand down on the table. "Good Christ—didn't you see him out there?" He hooked a thumb in the general direction of the cemetery.

"He came in here last night and threatened to blow out my back bar mirror!" Tanner exclaimed.

"Why?" Campbell asked Tanner. "Does he know you were out at Ramsay Creek?"

"No," Tanner said. "I don't think so."

Hunter said with a knowing smile, "L.J. turned a couple of dogs loose, I heard. A couple of incompetent dogs."

Campbell turned a fatherly frown on the saloon owner. "Is that true?"

Tanner scowled into his beer glass, took another sip, and

swallowed, gritting his teeth. "Well, shit—it would have looked like a saloon fight. It was a slow night and—oh, what the hell? So I chose the wrong dogs! It didn't work!"

A silence descended over the table. In consternated thought, the men smoked and drank. Tanner belched and was cast a reprimanding look by the banker.

Purdy splashed more whiskey into his shot glass. "Has anyone told . . . you know . . . about what happened?"

"You mean," Hunter said, "about our incompetence?"

Campbell said, "I saw her ride over to the doctor's place yesterday. I'm sure Whitfield told her what transpired. But it would probably be . . . prudent . . . wise . . . if I rode up and had a talk with her." The banker arched a brow over his beer mug, which he held to his mouth in the same hand holding the cigar. "What shall I tell her?"

The others looked around at each other.

Hunter wore a stricken look. He shook his head. "What nonsense we let ourselves get talked into. What nonsense!"

"Sounded like a good idea at the time," Tanner said, chuckling.

Lars Eriksson, the blacksmith, hadn't said a word since Hunter had walked into the saloon. Now he said, leaning far back in his chair against the wall and staring blankly off toward the billiard room's close door, "The consequences—they would have been bad. Real bad." Now he quirked the corners of his thick-lipped mouth, causing his heavy beard to rise on his big, freckled, sunburned face.

"Men will do anything for something like that," Purdy said, raking a sheepish hand across his face. He shook his head and stared at the floor so intently you'd have thought he'd dropped a coin. "Pretty much anything . . ."

Another silence. Tanner was staring at the floor as well, but he was grinning. He seemed to be the only one in the room who saw any humor in the situation, however.

Carlsruud poured half his whiskey into his beer and watched it foam. "Gentlemen, we are right where we were when we all came in here. Right now we have a madman on the loose. He's hunting us. What are we going to do about it? I understand, George, that you don't want him shot down in the street like a rabid coyote. But you weren't out there that night. He's not hunting you, though of course he probably would be if he knew you were in on the planning."

Campbell choked on cigar smoke. "What are you implying, Glen? Are you going to *tell* on me?" He coughed again, leaning forward over his enormous, bulging belly.

Hunter said, "I think what Glen means, George, is that we all have more to lose than you do."

"How is he ever going to find out who was out there?" Campbell asked, spreading his hands. "Let him stomp around here with his tail up all he wants. If we all keep our damn mouths shut and do nothing to expose ourselves, we'll be fine. Eventually, he'll have to leave."

"And we'll have failed," Hunter said, rolling his eyes to indicate the north end of town.

"I'll explain it," Campbell said. "I'll explain how it happened. All will be well."

"How can you be so sure?" Purdy asked. "You don't hold a note on that little house up there, George. Do you? I heard it was paid for."

"*Pssst!*"

Hunter and the others turned to Eriksson, who'd gotten up out of his chair and strolled over to the window nearest the table. The big blacksmith beckoned and pointed to indicate that the window was open a good six inches.

Hunter was the first one to the window. He stood beside Eriksson, following the big man's gaze outside. His heart skipped a beat when he saw the butt of the half-smoked cigarette still smoldering in the dirt nearly directly below the window.

Chapter Sixteen

Prophet moved around the saloon's front corner and mounted the gallery. He pushed through the batwings and strode toward the door at the back of the room.

"Hey, where you goin'?" demanded the big half-breed standing behind the bar.

Prophet kept walking.

"Hey!" The half-breed pounded both fists atop the bar, scowling, red-faced.

"Stay there and you won't get hurt," Prophet said.

The door ahead of him opened. Prophet slid the Richards around from behind his back and took it in both hands, the lanyard still around his neck and shoulder. He aimed the barn blaster straight out in front of him and drew both rabbit-eared hammers back to full cock.

The square-jawed, handsome gent who ran the hotel stood in the doorway, staring at him. The others stood behind him, looking over his shoulders at the bounty hunter. The square-jawed man, whose name Prophet believed was Hunter, looked at the shotgun in the bounty hunter's hands, and then he took one step back, opening his hands before him.

The others, to a man, looked as though they were filling their drawers.

"I'll put an end to this right now!" came the half-breed's voice behind Prophet.

Hunter slammed the door in Prophet's face. Hearing heavy

135

footsteps behind him and seeing the big half-breed's shadow slide across the floor to his left, Prophet dodged right.

As he did, there was a thundering blast.

Prophet whipped around. The half-breed was crouched over the double-barreled shotgun smoking in his hands, and he was staring in wide-eyed shock at what he'd done to the billiard room door.

The shotgun blast had taken a fist-sized chunk out of the door's top panel and peppered the rest of it with pellets. That was just one barrel. As the big man slid the gun toward Prophet, Prophet squeezed the left trigger of his barn blaster.

The blast from the ten-gauge rocked the room.

The buckshot ripped through the half-breed's chest and belly, lifted him two feet off the floor, and hurled him five feet straight back.

He hit the floor on his ass, rolled backward then sideways, and piled up near the batwings where he lay shivering and dying on the floor.

Shouting erupted behind the closed door. A man's horrified face—the hotel man's face—appeared in the fist-sized hole in the top panel. The face disappeared as Prophet turned to the door and brought his right leg back. He thrust it forward, hammering his right boot against the door, just beneath the knob. The door exploded inward. Prophet stepped into the room and caught the door's bounce off the wall with his left foot.

He aimed the Richards straight out from his right hip.

"That's too bad," he said. "Somethin' tells me him and me coulda been pals under different circumstances." His tone belied the friendly words. Anger was a hot iron laid against the back of his neck. "How 'bout you stupid bastards? You wanna be my pals?"

Five of the small group stood in a ragged semicircle about ten feet in front of him. The bartender, L.J. Tanner, was one of them, standing to Prophet's far right. He held his open hand over the butt of his holstered Schofield revolver. When Prophet's gaze dropped to that hand, Tanner slowly raised it, palm out, in supplication.

"Easy, now, big man," he said. "Easy, now . . ."

Three of the eight-man group stood behind the five. Two were standing, that was. A third man—the fat, impeccably dressed man with an egg-shaped head whom Prophet had seen going to and from the bank—was just now rising from where he'd been hunkered beneath the table they'd all been sitting at when Prophet had overheard their meeting from outside the window a few minutes earlier.

The fat man was red-faced. Sweat streamed down his cheeks. He was wheezing like a landed fish, his thin-lipped mouth forming a small O on his clean-shaven face.

One of the others, the man who ran the mercantile, hurried over to him, took one of his arms, and helped him to his feet.

"Good Lord," the fat banker wheezed, staring in horror at Prophet's coach gun aimed at the group.

"Oh, I don't think the Good Lord'd have much to do with you boys. Ole Scratch is more your style. Mine, too, but for other reasons than lurin' folks into a bushwhackin'."

"What the hell are you talking about?" Hunter said.

"It was you boys that was talkin' about it . . . only you forgot to close the window yonder. Now, I didn't hear all of it, but I heard enough to know seven of the eight of you was the ones who threw that lead into my partner and likely would have killed both of us if you weren't such a bunch of cork-headed fools, not to mention lousy shots."

"That's ridiculous," Hunter said, giving a short chuckle severely lacking in sincerity. He had his hands raised to his shoulders, fingers curled toward the palms.

"Shut up, Neal," Tanner said out the side of his mouth, flaring a nostril at the hotel man. To Prophet, he said, "So . . . what're you gonna do about it? You gonna gun us all down right here . . . in cold blood? Now, you mighta had cause to shoot ole Arnell there . . . the damn fool . . . but none of us here is armed."

Very slowly, Tanner lowered his right hand to the butt of his Schofield. "Easy, now," he said as with two fingers he unsnapped the thong from over the hammer and lifted the gun from its holster. He held the revolver up high and gave a mocking half-smile as he opened his fingers.

The gun dropped to the floor with a dull thud.

Several of the others jumped at the noise.

"Good Lord!" wheezed the fat man, standing with the mercantile owner behind the others, before the table they'd all been sitting at.

"Fat man," Prophet said, "since you're here with them, I'm assumin' you're *in* with them. Please inform me if that's a mistaken assumption on my part."

The fat man also had his pudgy hands raised. He looked dubiously around at the others. The others looked back at him. He cleared his throat and moved his lips, as though trying to say something. Unable to come up with the right words, he slid his eyes around again, self-consciously, then lowered his gaze to the floor and pressed his thin, pink lips together.

From outside rose the sound of running footsteps. They grew louder until boots pounded on the saloon's front gallery.

"Jesus Christ!" exclaimed the young marshal, Roscoe Deets. "What in God's name . . . ?"

Prophet turned his head to one side and said over his shoulder, "Like I told these others, Marshal, I don't think God or Christ would have much to do with this bunch."

"Prophet?"

"Party's back here, in the billiard room." Prophet smiled over his shoulder at the marshal standing in the open batwings and staring down in horror at the lumpy figure of the dead bartender.

Deets looked at Prophet. The young marshal held his pistol down low over his empty holster.

"Come on back," Prophet urged. "I do apologize for the mess I made in there, but I shot the barman in self-defense. I was just walkin' through the saloon all innocent-like, wantin' only to have a chat with these seven bushwhackers. The devil's seven, I call 'em. And the banker who, it seems, was also in on the bloody deal."

"Arrest him, Deets!" barked Hunter. "Arrest him now! He shot Three-Bears and he's threatening us with a shotgun."

"Now, that ain't gonna happen," Prophet said, turning his head back toward the sheepish crowd gathered before him. "But you can come on back and join the party, just the same, Marshal. I'd appreciate it if you'd holster that six-shooter, though. If it were to accidentally go off it might cause me to jerk one of my two hair-triggers here and the blast from the ten-gauge would likely blow at least two of these fellas' heads clean off their shoulders."

"Oh, Jesus," wheezed the fat man under his breath, sweating profusely.

Deets stepped over the dead bartender and strode slowly, apprehensively through the saloon's main drinking hall. As he approached the billiard room, he said, "What's going on?"

"These here are the remaining seven that bushwhacked me and my partner," Prophet said, his voice pitched menacingly soft. "I eavesdropped on their little meeting from outside that open window. Oh, I didn't hear it all due to wagon traffic and the wind and whatnot, but I heard enough to know it was them. Minus the fat banker back there. He's likely too fat to straddle a horse. But he was in on it, too. Otherwise, he wouldn't have been part of the meeting."

Prophet glanced over his shoulder at Deets standing four feet behind him, staring into the room. He was still holding his revolver straight down over his right hip.

"Holster it," Prophet said mildly. "And come on in. You might as well hear what I have to say to these boys. You're part of it. You got a big part in it, you bein' the local law an' all."

Prophet stepped to his right, giving the marshal some room.

Deets studied Prophet. Then he looked at the men standing like cowed children in the room before him. He holstered his Remington and moved into the billiard room, stepping toward Prophet's left and turning to face him. "What's all this about?"

"Some lawman you are, Deets," said Tanner. "Worthless piece of—"

"Shut up, Tanner!" Hunter said.

"My sentiments exactly," Prophet said to Tanner. "Besides, if he'd tried to take me down, your shoulders would look awful damn funny, seein' as how they'd be minus your head."

Tanner narrowed his eyes at the big bounty hunter.

Hunter's gaze flicked toward the double bores of Prophet's coach gun, and he swallowed. "What're you gonna do, Prophet?"

"Me? Nah, I ain't gonna do nothin'. It's you boys that's gonna do all the doin'. First thing you're gonna need to do is pray real hard that that young lady over there at Doc Whitfield's place don't die. If she does die, all bets are off. You fellas are wolf bait. In the meantime, what you're gonna do is go home and think over the mistake you made out there at Ramsay Creek. Then what I *hope* you'll do next is go on over to Marshal Deets's office and confess what you done. And why you done it."

Prophet looked at Deets, who was frowning at him, puzzled, wary.

A low muttering rose from the crowd. They were speaking out the sides of their mouths to each other.

Prophet grinned.

"That's right," he said to Deets. "I'm gonna turn it over to you, young marshal. I got faith that you'll do the right thing. You'll lock 'em up for attempted murder and assault, and you'll call a judge in and have a trial. It'll be all legal-like. If that happens, I'll wash my hands of the whole affair, comforted by the fact that the wheels of justice are turnin' smoothly in the right direction."

Tanner said, "You're full o' shit, Prophet!"

"It's been said before," the bounty hunter allowed.

He moved forward, stopped in front of Tanner, and looked down at the man, who was about three inches shorter. Tanner glared up at him but his eyes flickered faintly with apprehension. Prophet whipped the Richards around and slammed the butt into Tanner's belly.

Tanner grunted loudly and jackknifed, dropping to his knees and clutching his belly. He fell over on his left shoulder and drew his knees toward his gut, groaning and writhing and wheezing raucously as he tried to draw a breath.

"Like I said—it's been said before. But until now I never run into anyone stupid enough to say it when I've been holdin' a gun on 'im." Prophet chuckled. "Consider that a lesson, free of charge."

CHAPTER SEVENTEEN

"That's all you fellas have to do," Prophet said as Tanner continued to writhe and groan on the floor. "Go on home and have a little heart-to-heart with yourselves, possibly your wives"—he chuckled wryly—"if you got the *cojones* for it, and then saunter on over to the jail and confess your sins to Marshal Deets."

"And if we don't?" asked the big blacksmith standing near the window, his nostrils flaring.

"Then the marshal's gonna have to arrest you."

Deets said, "It's their words against yours, Prophet. There's seven of them. How do I know who's telling the truth?"

"Oh, come on—look at 'em," Prophet intoned, raking his scowling gaze across the room. "Do those look like the faces of men that don't have blood on their hands?"

Deets looked around. Slowly, he turned his head back to Prophet. He looked as though he'd taken a bite out of an extra tart lemon.

"What if the girl dies?" he asked.

Prophet turned to the others, narrowed one eye, and said gravely, "If she dies and they're not behind bars and charged with murder, then I take it out of your hands, Marshal."

He backed toward the door, keeping the Richards aimed straight out from his right hip. "If she dies, there won't be a one of them left alive to see the next sun come up."

He backed on out the door, then turned and strode to the

batwings. He stepped over the dead bartender and went out.

As he slung the Richards over his shoulder and behind his back, a wagon moved toward him from his left. Not a wagon but a buggy. A chaise with its top down. The lovely Miss McQueen was driving, looking like the distillation of all things sweet and summery in a fetching yellow frock with matching picture hat with lime-green feathers. The dress was form-fitting, low-cut, the well-filled bodice edged in lace.

Smiling brightly, twirling a parasol above her head in her white-gloved left hand, she turned the Morgan toward the saloon and said, "Whoa, boy," halting before Prophet. Her smile faded somewhat, and shallow lines cut across her forehead as she glanced behind him, at the barman lying just inside the batwings.

"Good heavens," she said. "Is that Arnell Three-Bears?"

"Beats me," Prophet said. "I never had the pleasure." He glanced over his shoulder. "Now I guess I never will."

She returned her eyes to Prophet, and the smile returned. Her lips slid back from white, perfect teeth. "You look like a man who could use a ride, Mr. Prophet."

Prophet studied her, sizing her up. His eyes kept returning to her cleavage, which was what the bodice was intended to do. She didn't seem to mind. Prophet gave a wry chuff and, spurred by curiosity as well as his natural male attraction to an irresistible female form, he dropped down off the saloon's gallery and stepped up into the buggy. Miss McQueen slid over for him, tucking her frock beneath her bottom as she did, favoring him with her beguiling smile and flickering eyes.

"Where to?"

Prophet set the Richards on the floor behind his boots and dug his makings sack out of his shirt pocket. "Oh, I don't know. The doc said my partner made it through the night and her fever was down. I reckon I don't need to pester Whitfield about her again for a few hours." Opening the tobacco pouch and digging out his wheat papers, he said, "Surprise me."

She smiled again, turned her head forward, and shook the reins over the Morgan's back. "I know a beautiful place."

Prophet looked at her breasts jiggling around inside the corset, the lace edging ruffling in the wind blowing over the Morgan. "I bet you do," Prophet said, chuckling and dribbling tobacco smoke onto a wheat paper troughed between his fingers. "I bet you do . . ."

Miss McQueen laughed as she put the Morgan on down the street, heading east. As Prophet rolled his smoke, he saw several men slowing on the boardwalks on both sides of the street and casting him and the woman incredulous stares. Prophet pinched his hat brim to one man and then raked a thumbnail across a match. He leaned forward to cup the flame to the quirley.

Miss McQueen didn't say anything as she drove the chaise on out of Box Elder Ford. The trail soon narrowed and became a shaggy two-track as it curved through the trees paralleling the river on Prophet's right. Cottonwoods and box elders stood tall on both sides of the trail, the leaves flashing in the sunlight as the breeze rattled them.

They drove for fifteen, maybe twenty minutes, bouncing along the trail, which was badly rutted in places. Occasionally they jounced over exposed tree roots. The trail curved south with the river, and soon the town was out of sight behind them and the buttes that formed a wall along the river's far shore.

Miss McQueen turned her sparkling smile on Prophet once more as she abruptly steered the Morgan off the trail. There was no trail here—only tall, green grass waving in the breeze and shaded by the deciduous forest. Cottonwood seeds danced in the winey air and fell in the grass like a light snow dusting. She pulled up to within twenty feet of the river, which was wide and flat and the color of coffee with a good dollop of cream in it. Prophet saw that there was a deep, horseshoe-shaped gouge in the near bank, and here the water gently swirled. It looked darker than the rest, deeper, and it was well shaded by the trees leaning out over the bank.

"Here we are," Miss McQueen said.

Prophet climbed down off the chaise. He took a last drag off his quirley, dropped the butt onto a patch of bare ground, and mashed it out with his boot heel. He walked over to where Miss McQueen still sat on the buggy's front seat as though waiting, and raised a hand to her. She placed her hand in his with a cordial nod and rose from her seat.

Placing his hands on her slender waist, he lifted her down to the ground and she stood before him, her breasts brushing his belly. Staring up at him, she said, "You're tall."

Still staring up at him, she reached behind her head, removed a few pins, and doffed her picture hat. She set the hat on the buggy seat and shook out her rich, dark-brown hair. It spilled beautifully down across her shoulders, glistening in the sunlight.

She took his hand and began to lead him away from the buggy but then stopped abruptly, reached into a canvas satchel under the seat, and pulled out a small, tin, hide-covered flask.

"You come prepared," Prophet said.

"We should have a wicker basket filled with cold chicken and pickled eggs, not to mention a bottle of French wine, but I guess this will do . . . for now."

Miss McQueen removed the cap and took a sip. She closed her eyes as she swallowed, then stretched her lips back from her teeth as the firewater hit her belly. She extended the flask to Prophet, who took a drink.

"Brandy," he said, running the back of his hand across his mouth. "Good stuff."

"Good," she said, saucily turning away and striding into the grass, heading toward the river. "But I can do better."

145

The rich, wavy tresses of her hair slid across her slender back as she moved off through the brush. Tufts of downy cottonwood seed clung to it.

Prophet glanced at the coach gun, which he'd left under the chaise's front seat. He brushed his hand across the walnut grips of his Peacemaker and started following Miss McQueen into the tall grass, deciding he wouldn't need the barn blaster out here. He'd made a good many enemies in town—at least, he'd enflamed those who were already his enemies—but they'd likely stew on their troubles for a good, long time before they decided to do anything about them.

He wondered with amusement how many, if any, would spill their guts to the young marshal. Probably none. They were arrogant bastards, to a man. To their way of thinking, the fact that they had money and were considered "important" townsmen put them above the law. They'd try to find another way out of their situation.

Prophet's musings ended abruptly when he saw Miss McQueen sitting near the water on a tree stump. She lifted one knee, hiked up her skirts, and began rolling a stocking down her leg. She tossed her garter belt, and Prophet snagged it out of the air. He twirled the lacy garment on his finger and then draped it over his gun butt. He removed the cap from the flask and took another drink, keeping his eyes on the woman, who'd removed both her stockings now.

She was barefoot in the grass, the cotton dancing in the air around her.

She rose from the stump and began unbuttoning her dress as she regarded Prophet demurely. He sat back against another stump and felt a warm wave of passion roll through his loins on the crest of the brandy flush. Sitting there, sipping the brandy, he watched her skin out of the dress and a thin, lacy chemise.

Wearing only a pink, whalebone corset, she turned around to

146

face the river and glanced coyly over her right shoulder at him.

"A little help, Mr. Prophet?"

Prophet walked over to her, gave her the flask, and began unlacing the corset. When he was half done, she chuckled, "You've done this before."

"Oh, a time or two."

"I like a man who knows his way around a corset."

"I like a woman who knows when to get shed of such contraptions."

He peeled the shell-like garment from around her waist and tossed it into the grass. She turned to him, splendidly naked, her full, proud breasts thrusting toward him. She lifted her hands to them, massaging them gently as she backed away through the grass.

She had her chin down and she was giving him that phony, bashful smile again, the sun glinting in her brown eyes.

At the edge of the river she stopped, lowered her hands from her breasts, winked at him, then twisted around, sprang off her well-turned calves, and dove off the bank and into the pool.

She knifed the water cleanly, hardly lifting a wave.

The pool wasn't more than ten feet wide. She came up only a few feet from where she'd gone in, brushing water from her eyes and sliding her wet hair back behind her ears. She glanced over at him. Blowing water out her pooched lips she swam across and out of the hole and into the river.

Gradually, the water grew shallow, and she was crawling. She turned over on her back and raised her arms behind her, stretching them over a sun-bleached log suspended between stones. The water was not deep enough to cover her.

Her breasts rose above it, floating, cherry nipples tipped to the sky. The water gleamed over the lower points of her body and around her, like a massive sequined gown.

She kicked a foot, splashing. "You coming in?"

"Why not?" Prophet looked around carefully, scrutinizing the trees on both sides of the river.

"What are you looking for?" Miss McQueen asked. "I don't think anyone else knows about this hole. I've been riding out here from time to time all summer and I've never seen any sign of anyone else. It's my secret place." She smiled coquettishly. "Or . . . I guess it *was* my secret place."

Prophet scanned the area once more. He didn't trust anyone around Box Elder Ford. Not seeing anyone creeping up on him through the trees, he doffed his hat and unbuckled his gun belt. He coiled the belt around the holster and set it on the stump.

He kicked out of his boots, shucked out of his pants, shirt, and summer drawers, and stood on the bank overlooking the pool—a big, naked man, lumpy with muscles, lightly haired, his manhood awakening. He was sunburned where his clothes didn't cover him—mainly his neck and head. The rest of him was floury white.

The woman kicked her foot again and laughed. "I'm glad to see at least a part of you isn't shy." She pronounced "shy" like "shaw." The same way he'd pronounce it. He'd noticed that, unlike his own, her southern accent came and went. It usually came when she was feeling frisky.

Prophet looked down, chuckled, shrugged, and dove into the pool.

The water was tepid but refreshing. He felt the sweat and dirt of the trail melt away. Lifting his head out of the water, he swam over to her. The sandy bottom rose and he walked up the sloping shelf until he was on all fours, crawling to her.

Watching him, arms hooked over the log, she opened her legs and began mewling before he'd even mounted her.

Chapter Eighteen

Verna McQueen groaned and clamped her teeth down on Prophet's shoulder.

She writhed beneath him, shuddering.

A few minutes later, spent, Prophet rolled off of her. He lay with his head angled back against the log, half floating in the shallow water, the sand making a smooth, comfortable bed beneath him. She rolled toward him, lifted her right leg over his, and kissed his chest, pulling his right arm around her shoulders.

"You're a man, Mr. Prophet. It's nice to have a man around here."

"There's plenty of men around here, Miss McQueen."

"There's plenty of men around here, sure enough," she said, her accent still slow and soft and lilting as she continued to press her lips against his chest, her right hand trailing down past his belly. "But no *men*."

"Why do you stay here, then?" Prophet asked her, probing her gently while staring at the sky over the river and enjoying the delicious sensation of her warm, wet, supple body folded against his. "A woman who looks like you, with your . . . *talents* . . . could pretty much go anywhere, have any man she wants."

She looked up at him, frowning. "Settle down, you mean?"

Prophet chuckled and pressed his lips to her forehead. Her breasts felt good, her nipples like delicate rosebuds pressed against his belly. "I reckon you do have a certain freedom. And

149

the money can't be bad. But—hey, girl—we all get old."

"Don't I know it?" she said, turning her mouth corners down. "But I intend to enjoy myself while I can. Make a good livin' . . . doin' what I do"—she smiled and lowered her head to press her lips against his private parts—"while I can. Besides," she added, resting a cheek against his stomach and still fiddling with him down there, "I've been a lot of places—a girl on her own. I like bein' settled in one place. Bein' well liked."

"Forgive my indiscretion, but how long have you been . . . uh . . . doin' what you do?"

"Few years. I was married once, for a little while. He died when a freight wagon ran him over on a trail one night—drunk as a lord. A wealthy Texas rancher, he was. He plucked me out of an Abilene saloon. His sons didn't like me, so after he died so tragically they ran me off the place. Ungrateful bastards. I think they themselves yearned for me. They were ashamed of themselves." She giggled. "And they, of course, thought I was out for their old man's poke. Which, I guess I was in a way, but rest assured, Mr. Prophet—"

"Might as well call me Lou, Verna, since we've become such pals, an' all, and we're both former graybacks."

"Rest assured, Lou, I made that old man very, very happy." She reached up and pinched his nose, crossing her eyes delightfully as she laughed.

"I don't doubt it a bit, Verna," Prophet said. "I surely don't. I also reckon there's no place you could go you wouldn't be well liked," he added, groaning against her ministrations. "By the men, that is. The womenfolks—now, they could be a problem."

"Not so far they aren't," Verna said. "I think for the most part they like to get their men out of their beds a night or two every week." She chuckled. She lowered her mouth over him and after a while she lifted it and turned to him. "You're an old Reb, Mr. Prophet. It is an honor. I just want you to know that. I

150

come from the Rebel country myself and how well I remember the men. They are . . . and you are . . . like no other."

She lowered her head again. After a few minutes, Prophet ground his heels into the sand, shuddering.

"Where'd you grow up down south?" she asked him when she'd rested her head against his belly, dreamily lolling against him in the water.

"North Georgia."

"Came west after the war, eh?"

"Nowhere else to go."

"So you came out here to hunt bad men for a livin'. No . . . not for a livin' . . . for that fork-tailed, yellow-toothed demon, Ole Scratch!" Verna laughed and rubbed her cheek against his belly, staring up at him dreamily.

Prophet smiled curiously at her.

"Oh, I know all about you, Lou Prophet. I've read about you in the newspapers. You and your comely young partner, Miss Bonaventure, or 'The Vengeance Queen,' as the scribblers call her."

Prophet rested his head back against the log. "No kiddin'. Well, I'll be damned."

"You're right famous—don't you know that?"

"I don't read the newspapers much. Few are handy where I go. When I'm in a town I got better things to do than read newspapers."

"I bet you do," Verna said, chuckling as she snuggled against him.

"Verna?"

"Yes, Lou?"

"Since you probably know most of the men in Box Elder Ford, maybe you can help me solve my not so little puzzle."

"What puzzle is that, Lou?"

"Why did those sumbitches, Hunter and Tanner and the others, bushwhack me an' Louisa out at the Ramsay Creek Outpost?"

Verna didn't say anything. She stared down at Prophet's chest for a time, her eyes long, slanted, and thoughtful. Then she stuck out her tongue and touched it to the skin just below his left nipple. "Mmm. You taste like an old Rebel. Like well-aged bourbon."

Prophet glanced down at her, frowning again. "Answer me."

"Oh, I don't know, Lou." She sat up and stared down at him, her eyes suddenly grave. "You must've wronged 'em somehow."

"How?"

She hiked a bare shoulder and looked off toward the buggy parked up on the bank, shadows and sunlight flickering over it and the grazing Morgan. "Oh . . . how would I know, Lou? You're a bounty hunter. Maybe you crossed paths with one of 'em . . . sometime in the past. And they got the others to throw in against you." She ran her right hand down her arm, looking away dreamily, the water rippling around her bare thighs. "Yeah . . . that must be how it is."

She turned to him, concern pinching the bridge of her nose. "Could be any one of 'em. Who knows? Lou, you're in grave danger here. I feel it in my bones." She placed her hand on his belly. "Are you frightened?"

"Frightened?" Prophet sat up and looked around, making sure he and Verna were still alone out here. "Nah, I ain't frightened." It was a lie and he knew it, but he didn't want to think that those cowards could have that effect on him. "I'm piss-burned about what they did to my partner. Piss-burned at their cowardly act."

"How did they ever know you were going to be out at the Ramsey Creek Outpost, Lou?"

Prophet looked at Verna staring curiously at him. He'd almost forgotten about the scrap of paper someone had slipped under his door in Colorado Springs. "Someone sent me a formal invitation. Louisa, too. The notes were worded the same but in different hands."

Verna shook her head. "Quite the mystery, isn't it, Lou?" She leaned down and kissed his nose. "But don't worry. I'm sure you'll figure it out. And whoever's responsible for such a nasty deed will get their just desserts!"

She climbed to her feet and cupped her breasts in her hands, smiling down at him beguilingly. "I don't know about you, but I could use a drink. Did you leave any brandy in the flask?"

"Oh, there might be another shot," Prophet said, staring at her thoughtfully as she turned, dropped into the pool, and swam to the bank. She pulled herself up onto the grass, rose, and scooped the brandy flask off the tree stump. She raised it. "Cheers!"

She took a sip and then set it back down on the stump. Prophet watched her stare down at his holstered .45. A slight tremor of apprehension passed through him as she reached down and slipped the Peacemaker from its holster.

"My, what a big gun," Verna said above the river's quiet gurgling and rippling.

Prophet rose and walked down into the pool. She smiled at him from the bank, hefting the revolver in both her hands. "A big gun for a big man, eh, Lou?"

Prophet swam across the pool, glancing up at the woman smiling down at him, trying but failing to twirl the heavy Peacemaker on her finger. He gained the bank and hoisted his dripping body up out of the water and onto the grass.

"How many men do you suppose you've killed with this gun, Lou?"

She pointed the gun in his direction, frowning at him

Prophet hesitated. For a second, the barrel was aimed at his heart. Her finger was curled across the trigger. The barrel

153

wavered, as though the gun was too heavy for her to control.

Prophet walked over to her, closing his hand over the gun. He smiled as he gently pulled it out of her hand.

"Don't you know it ain't nice to aim guns at folks? Unless you're aimin' to shoot 'em?"

"If that gun could talk—eh, Lou?"

Prophet shoved the piece back into its holster. "Well, it can't, and that's probably just as well." He glanced at her. "You like guns, do you, Verna?"

She moved over to where her clothes lay in the grass. "A girl in my line of work best know how to shoot one if she wants to survive. That's all I know about 'em."

Sullenly, pensively, she began dressing. Prophet did, as well.

When he'd stomped into his boots and strapped his gun around his waist, cinching the buckle, she asked for help with the corset. He laced it for her and kissed her neck, resting his hands on her shoulders. She was a moody girl. As though to acknowledge the fact, she placed her right hand on top of his, on her shoulder, and glanced up at him with genuine demureness for a change.

"Thank you for a wonderful afternoon, Lou," she said quietly as she continued dressing.

Something was bothering her. Prophet wondered what it could be. A general tendency toward darkness? Some of the most beautiful, bubbly women were so stricken. He'd known enough such women to know that it was often best not to press them about their moods. He himself was that way, after all, and when he felt the shadows moving in on him, he didn't like to talk about it.

"Thank you, Miss Verna." He ran his fingers through his damp hair, which the breeze was quickly drying, and snugged his hat down on his head. "I reckon I'd best get back to town and look in on my partner."

As they walked together slowly back through the grass to where she'd parked the buggy, Prophet said, "I . . . uh . . . don't know how to ask this discreetly, Miss Verna, but . . . how much do I owe . . . ?"

"Oh, you don't owe me a thing, Lou Prophet." As they approached the Morgan, she stopped and turned to him, her bright smile in place once again. "Let's just call this afternoon my attempt to prime the pump, so to speak. Perhaps you'll stop by my little house on the hill sometime while you're still in town? If you come before five, I serve cookies and tea." She gave a husky chuckle at that.

"I'd like nothing better," Prophet said. "I'll be here a few more days for sure, and—"

A bullet hammered a box elder two feet to his right. Close on the heels of the crunching thud came the flat crack of the rifle.

Prophet jerked with a start, crouching and bolting forward, covering Verna's body with his own. He hadn't meant to run her over but she gave a little scream as she fell backward.

Prophet grabbed her arms to break her fall, letting her settle onto her knees.

As another bullet screeched through the air over his head and snapped a branch off a juniper to his right, the Morgan gave a whinny and leaned into its collar, pulling the chaise along behind it. The buggy's brake was engaged, its front left wheel holding taut, so the horse jerked it along haltingly, unable to pick up any speed.

As Prophet heard the metallic rasp of another cartridge being levered into a rifle breech, he threw himself onto Verna, and, holding the girl taut in his arms, rolled twice until he and the woman were lying behind a stout cottonwood.

The rifle shrieked two more times, the second bullet chewing into the side of the cottonwood, bark raining down on Prophet and Verna, who said nothing but lay shuddering beneath him.

155

"Stay down!" Prophet yelled, sliding his Peacemaker out of its holster.

He shot a look around the right side of the cottonwood. He saw the silhouette of a man aiming a rifle from around the side of another tree about forty yards away.

Prophet snapped his Peacemaker up and fired.

He continued firing—one shot after another, the gun thundering and bucking in his hand, flames lapping from the barrel—until the hammer pinged on an empty chamber.

CHAPTER NINETEEN

When the echoing roars of his own gun had subsided, Prophet heard a hoarse, rippling sob. Through his wafting powder smoke, he saw the shooter running away from him, stumbling through the brush and trees.

"Stay down, Verna," Prophet said, glancing around as he quickly opened the Peacemaker's loading gate and shook out the spent shells. He filled the cylinder with fresh brass from his shell belt, spun the wheel, clicked the loading gate home, and began walking out away from the cottonwood, following the shooter.

He looked around for other possible ambushers, but saw and heard only the one running away from him. The man was sobbing and grunting, occasionally cursing. The brush crackled beneath his boots.

Prophet stopped.

Suddenly, he'd lost sight of the shooter. He couldn't hear him, either.

Just as suddenly, the man slid his head out from behind a tree about fifteen feet ahead of Prophet. The man gritted his teeth and widened his dark-blue eyes as he raised his rifle once more.

Prophet jerked up the Peacemaker and fired without aiming.

The shooter's head snapped straight back on his shoulders. The man staggered, tripped over his heels, and fell like a toppled pine.

Prophet looked around. Spying no signs of more shooters, he strode forward and stopped near the dead man's boots. The dead man stared up at him wide-eyed, as though he were surprised by his fate. He had a long, gaunt, pale face and thin, gray-brown hair, more brown than gray along the sides and in his sideburns, which dropped to his earlobes.

He was one of the seven. Purdy, Prophet thought he'd heard him called. He wore a brown vest over a blue wool shirt and a blue stone bolo tie with silver tips. He had shit on his boots. Prophet thought he'd seen him around one of the town's livery barns, giving orders to two young hostlers.

Footsteps sounded behind Prophet. He glanced behind him to see Verna walking toward him, tentatively, holding her hands together in front of her belly. Her rich lips were slightly parted.

She stopped near Prophet, looked down, and shook her head. "Jim Purdy."

"One of the devil's seven," Prophet said gruffly. "Good riddance, *amigo.*" He glanced around, finding it odd that none of the others had shown up yet. He grabbed Verna's left forearm and squeezed. "You stay here with Purdy. I'm gonna have a look around."

"Damn fool," was all she said, staring reprovingly down at the dead liveryman.

Prophet went back to the chaise. The Morgan had stopped only a couple of dozen yards from where the buggy had originally been parked. Prophet grabbed his Richards out from beneath the seat and held the stout popper in both hands as he tramped through the trees, moving first upstream along the river and then down. He moved out away from the Arkansas and circled back to where Verna stood near Purdy. She was leaning almost casually against a tree.

"Looks like he came alone," Prophet said, peering curiously down at the dead man, whose eyelids had partly closed, though the eyes behind them still looked shocked. "Why in hell would he do that?"

"Silly man," Verna said, staring down at Purdy and slowly shaking her head. "Whatever possessed you to try such a fool stunt?" She sighed, looked at Prophet, and shrugged. "One down, eh, Lou?"

"I reckon."

A horse whinnied. Prophet looked through the trees to see a saddled horse standing by the river. He walked over, still looking carefully around him, incredulous, and untied the horse's reins from a branch of a young cottonwood. He led the sorrel gelding back to where Purdy lay in the grass near Verna and lifted the man up and over the horse's saddle. The horse shook its head as though not happy about having to carry a dead man on its back. It whickered, blew, and whickered again.

"Easy, boy," Prophet said, wishing he had some rope. Purdy wasn't carrying a riata, and the horse wasn't outfitted with saddlebags in which the bounty hunter might hope to find something to tie the dead man to his saddle with.

"Taking him back?" Verna asked.

"Yep."

She didn't say anything but only pooched her lips out slightly, giving a queer, oblique smile.

"Where the hell is it? Where the hell is it?"

Roscoe Deets rummaged around in the bottom drawer of his roll-top desk in the town marshal's office. He looked under and between old ledger books, tax documents, judiciary dockets, old court summonses, and a crudely put together folder of local statutes. They were all the documents that had come with the job.

Deets had gotten rid of everything that had personally belonged to Bill Wilkinson and his deputies—couldn't get rid of

159

it fast enough after Wilkinson was dead—but the desk was still packed with wanted dodgers, manila folders, and other paperwork that Deets had been told to leave alone, as the sheriff would need to consult certain documents on his monthly run through Box Elder Ford.

"Monthly run?" Deets had silently scoffed to himself a time or two.

He hadn't seen old Boss Crowley a single time since he'd been made town marshal. As far as Deets knew, the county outside of the jurisdiction of individual town marshals was left to its own devices. In other words, the ranchers settled disputes between themselves with guns, knives, and hang ropes. Deets had seen that for himself the five years he'd worked for old Jasper McRae up near the Jasper Buttes, not far from the Kansas border. McRae had been as quick as most old-time ranchers to play cat's cradle with a man's head if he suspected that that man had been stalking his range with a running iron, doctoring brands.

"Goddamnit!" Deets said now, slamming the bottom drawer and mopping sweat from his cheek with a sleeve of his pin-striped shirt. "Where in the hell is it?"

He knew he'd left a bottle in here. He'd rid himself of most of the whiskey he'd stored here after he and Lupita were married and she'd made him promise to give it up. When he'd met her, he'd been a soak. A common affliction of the range rider. He and some fellow cowpunchers had distilled the stuff themselves. He hadn't really given it up, however, until he'd shot Bill Wilkinson. He'd had to get half-drunk to confront the tyrannical gunfighter and lawman, and then he'd probably been so quick to shoot him because of the busthead.

And because of the cat.

That damned cat that had given a screech and surprised Wilkinson, distracting him, which Deets, scared out of his wits, had instinctively used to his full advantage. He wouldn't have done that sober. At least, he didn't think he would have. He'd intended to confront Wilkinson fair and square and inform the man he was taking his job and let the cards fall where they may.

He'd given up whiskey after that—for good and true.

At least, he'd gotten rid of all the quart bottles he'd kept here and hidden behind the buggy shed at his and Lupita's place. But this morning, just after he'd watched the undertaker's boys haul the bulky body of Arnell Three-Bears away in their wagon, he'd remembered a small, flat bottle he'd half-consciously held onto.

In the event of an emergency.

But where in the hell had he put it?

There were two other desks in the office. Rather, one desk—a small roll-top sitting in the middle of the room and abutting a square-hewn roof support post—and a small, wobbly square table of warped, hammered-together planks and with an apple crate beneath it that served as storage. The roll-top and the table had served Wilkinson's two deputies.

Thinking he might have stowed the bottle in the small roll-top, Deets headed that way.

He'd just opened a drawer when a shadow crawled along the rough wooden floor behind him. He whipped around and looked out the window over his desk to see Miss McQueen's leather chaise pull up in front of the office from the left. As Deets scowled through the dirty window, he saw that Prophet was riding with Miss McQueen on the chaise's front seat. The wagon pulled a little to Deets's left.

It was then that he saw the sorrel trailing the chaise. A man was sprawled belly down over the saddle.

"Oh, no," Deets groaned, throwing out an arm like a distraught child, letting his fist slap down against his thigh. "Oh, Christ—what now? *Who* now?"

Deets walked wearily over to the door and stepped outside. Several men were coming along the street, heading toward the marshal's office, glowering after the sorrel and its grisly cargo. Prophet climbed down out of the chaise. He was smoking a cigarette. He removed the cigarette from between his lips, tapped ashes into the street, and freed the sorrel's slip-knotted reins from the back of the buggy, letting them drop in the street.

"There you go, Marshal," Prophet said. "More business for your undertaker."

Deets stared hang-jawed at the big man. Prophet turned and pinched his hat brim to Miss McQueen, who was still sitting in the buggy, the reins in her gloved hands. She wasn't wearing the big picture hat she'd been wearing before. Her hair looked disheveled, maybe a little damp, Deets thought.

"Ma'am, I did enjoy the day," Prophet said, giving a mock-courtly bow.

"And I did, as well, Mr. Prophet," she said, dipping her chin. "Give my regards to your partner and please relay my wishes for a speedy recovery."

"Will do." Prophet turned and walked off down the street.

Deets stared, mouth open, wanting to call out to the man, but something held him back. The man had so much gall; it was off-putting.

"You just gonna stand there, Deets?" This from Neal Hunter, who was holding up the head of Jim Purdy by its hair. Purdy's lower jaw was slack, his eyes half-open. Hunter let the liveryman's head slap down against the side of his horse. "You're not going to arrest him for this?" He canted his head toward the dead man. "He killed Purdy, for chrissakes."

"Oh, it was all in self-defense, Mr. Hunter—I assure you," said Miss McQueen. She gave a superior smile and batted her lashes mockingly. She turned to Deets. "Mr. Purdy ambushed him. Or tried to. Might have hit me, the fool. If you ask me, he got what he deserved."

She turned her head forward, shook her reins over the Morgan's back, and rattled off down the street. At the next cross street, she swung north and disappeared behind Bly's barbershop. Bly himself stood outside, his arm in its sling, staring toward Deets and Hunter and the dead man sprawled across his saddle.

Soon, they were all here, gathered around Purdy and the sorrel.

All seven of the eight who'd been in the saloon earlier in the day, being cowed by Prophet. The banker was even ambling up now, huffing and puffing against the walk over from the bank. He was mopping sweat from his forehead with a red silk handkerchief.

"Good Lord, who is it now?" he said, moving up to the horse.

"Jim," Hunter said. He looked past Deets. Deets followed his gaze to Hunter's wife, Helen, standing on the boardwalk fronting their hotel to Deets's right, staring back at her husband.

Leaning against an awning support post, she held a towel. The sleeves of her gingham dress were shoved up her arms. She stared back at Hunter without expression. Slowly she turned and walked back into the hotel.

What the hell was that all about? Deets wanted to know.

Or, no. Maybe he didn't. Christ, what kind of a bailiwick did he find himself in here, anyway? He'd thought this would be an easy job. Of course, his having to kill Wilkinson to get it should have been a sign . . .

Damned fool, he told himself.

"What happened?" the banker asked Hunter. He, Tanner, Carlsruud, and big Eriksson were all standing together near Purdy. Bly remained in front of his barbershop.

"What happened?" Hunter said to the banker. "Prophet just killed our mayor. That's all."

They all swung their gazes toward Deets.

Deets said, "Miss McQueen said it was self-defense."

"She did," Hunter said to the others fatefully. "She did at that."

Tanner scowled. "What the hell kind of a game is she playin' here, anyways?"

"Shut up," Hunter said under his breath, his cheeks coloring. "Just keep your trap shut, L.J."

Tanner swung around and headed back across the street to his saloon, adjusting his eye patch as he went. He lifted his revolver halfway out of the holster he wore on his right thigh, and let it drop back down again. Lifted it, let it drop, as though he were semi-consciously practicing his draw.

He pushed through the batwings and disappeared.

Deets swung around and went back into his office.

"Where is it?" he asked himself aloud, looking around frantically. "Where in God's name did I hide it?"

CHAPTER TWENTY

Louisa could see one of her pistols beneath her carefully folded clothes piled on an old, sun-faded brocade armchair parked in a corner of the narrow room she was in. Weakly, she stretched her left arm out, but there was no way she could reach the Colt from the bed. She'd thought there might be a chance, but she'd been unconscious so long that she'd lost her depth perception.

She didn't know where she was, but she felt like hell. She ached as though she'd been run over by a fully loaded lumber dray. Worse, she was unarmed, and that, coupled with her physical condition, left her vulnerable, indeed.

She had a very vivid recollection of the ambush at the Ramsay Creek Outpost.

She had to get to that Colt.

She threw back the bedcovers. She was naked save for a bandage wrapped tightly around the lower half of her upper torso, leaving her breasts bare. She also wore a plaster of Paris cast on her left leg, from the thigh to her shin. That leg weighed as much as the lumber dray she'd been run over with.

Still . . .

She sat up, wincing against the raw pain pulling in her chest. Just sitting up made her feel weak and out of breath. Her head swam. Dark spots shifted around before her eyes like tiny, black hands opening and closing. She held still, drew a deep breath, and then lowered her left foot to the floor. Carefully, gritting her teeth, hearing the bed squawk precariously beneath her, she slid her left leg to the edge of the bed, as well.

Suddenly, the narrow bed seemed to pitch like a rowboat. She gave a scream as she felt herself falling, and then the floor with a flowered rug came up to smack her left cheek and hip.

Fiery pain exploded in her chest and leg. The flames leaped all through her body. She heard herself groan as she lay slumped on the floor.

Shuffling footsteps sounded outside the curtained doorway of the room. Louisa's heart pounded fearfully. She heaved herself up and dragged herself several feet across the floor, taking the rug with her, and shoved her hand under her clothes stacked on the chair. The floor shuddered as someone loudly approached her room making a stomping, dragging sound.

Louisa shoved her right hand under the clothes, flicked the keeper thong free of the Colt, and pulled the silver-chased piece from its holster. As the curtain parted, Louisa swung the revolver toward the man just then entering, and clicked the hammer back.

Her throat was raspy from nonuse as she said tautly, "Who the hell are you?"

The man's face blanched behind his spectacles. "Good Lord!"

He stumbled back against the wall by the curtain, raising his hands to his shoulders. He wore a rumpled white shirt, suspenders, and broadcloth trousers. He had thick, dark-brown hair parted in the middle, and an open, intelligent face, which was lightly freckled.

More footsteps sounded in the hall behind him—a lighter, faster tread than the man's. The man turned his head quickly, throwing an open hand out toward the hall. "Titus, stay there!"

He looked warily at Louisa and then turned again to the hall from which the footsteps had died. "Go back to the kitchen and stay there."

Seeing no threat in the man, Louisa began to lower the pistol slightly but she kept some steel in her voice as she said, "I asked you a question."

The man's handsome face flushed with anger as he stared down at her. "I am the doctor who dug those bullets out of your hide, Miss Bonaventure. And if your way of thanking someone for saving your life is making them stare down the maw of one of your fancy revolvers, then you'd better mend your ways or get thrown out of here."

Louisa depressed the Colt's hammer and lowered the gun to the floor. She was happy to. It weighed nearly as much as her plaster-encased right leg. "Sorry, Doc." She dropped her chin, groaning against the pain she was keenly aware of now that the danger had passed.

"For chrissakes!" The doctor hobbled toward her, dragging one foot, and dropped to a knee. "What in the hell were you thinking of?"

"I was shot, Doc," Louisa said. "And I take that rather personal. When I woke up and . . . oh, Jesus, that hurts! . . . and saw that I had no gun near, I guess I panicked."

The doctor grunted as he picked her up in his arms and eased her back onto the cot, which groaned and barked against the floor, banging the wall. He moved awkwardly because of his own bum leg. He straightened, reaching behind to clutch the small of his back, breathing hard. He glared down at his patient as Louisa drew the bedcovers up to cover her nakedness.

"You've no need of a pistol in here." The doctor crouched to scoop the revolver off the floor. "In fact, I had intended to get rid of this and the other one. I won't have weapons in my house. Not my own, not my patients'. I have a young son and I do not want his life endangered, and neither do I want him becoming familiar with firearms. Only bad can come of a gun. If you're not the perfect example of that, I don't know who is."

He was rummaging around under Louisa's clothes. He pulled

her shell belt and two holsters off the chair. He shoved the Colt into the one empty holster and coiled the belt around both holstered guns.

"Look, Doc," Louisa said. "I'm as naked as a jaybird under here. If you take my guns away—"

"Oh, I'm quite sure you'll feel even more naked, Miss Bonaventure. I know who you are and what you and Mr. Prophet do for a living. But those are my rules, and until you're fit to leave here, you'll have to obey them or make other arrangements. In your condition, I have no idea what those arrangements would be."

"Sorry, Doc."

That seemed to appease him a bit. He stood staring down at her with a little less heat than before. "Damned fool move. You could have opened up those wounds." He set the guns on a bureau and pulled a straight-backed chair up beside the cot. "Lie back and I'll have a look."

Louisa rested her head back against the pillow. She sucked a breath as the man pulled the covers down to her waist, exposing her breasts above the thick, tightly wrapped bandage.

"I do apologize," he said, a sheepish note in his voice. She saw that he avoided looking at her bosom. "I do like to have a woman here to do such things in my stead, but I haven't been able to find reliable help since my wife . . ." He paused as though he'd found himself saying more than he'd intended. As he peeled up part of the bandage, he said, "Well, since my wife died. She was a good assistant and cared for the bandaging of my female patients."

"I'm confident in your professionalism, Doctor."

"Whitfield. Clayton Whitfield . . . reluctantly at your service, Miss Bonaventure."

"You don't much care for bounty hunters, that it?"

"That's it," he said as he lowered his head to examine the

wound beneath the bandage.

"That's all right. I don't much care for them, either."

Whitfield gently pressed the bandage back into place against her chest. "Looks all right from the outside. If you've opened up anything *inside,* you're in trouble."

He drew the covers up to her neck. "And if you're so against the profession yourself, why do you practice it?"

"There's a lot of bad men out there who need killing, Doctor Whitfield. So, tell me, am I going to heal?"

"So far so good . . . as long as you don't keep falling out of bed and crawling around on the floor in here. When you're in my house, Miss Bonaventure, you're safe. No need for guns. The people in this town know that I do not put up with violence. I have a young boy to raise alone, and I'm very protective of him. The town respects my wishes."

"What happened to your leg, Doc?"

Whitfield scowled at her, incredulous.

Louisa hiked a shoulder. "Sorry if the question was impertinent. I'm the curious sort, and when I'm curious about something, I just come right out and ask about it. Besides, I figure that any man who's seen me in my birthday suit can put up with an impertinent question or two."

The doctor continued to scowl down at her. Gradually, the indignation left his eyes behind his glasses and he thumbed the spectacles up his nose and chuckled. "Yes, well—I suppose you're right. I"—he glanced down at the limb in question—"I broke it rather severely two years ago, just after I moved my family out here. My wife and I, Diana and I, had ridden into the country to deliver a baby. Diana was a midwife, a good one. On the way home, we rode into a thunderstorm. The buggy horse spooked and broke into a dead run. Ran us straight into a ravine."

He stared at the wall on the far side of the bed. "Diana was killed. I was left . . . with something much less severe, but . . . it's a constant reminder of that wretched night."

Louisa gazed up at the man as he continued to stare at the wall. She felt as though a strong fist had grabbed her heart, squeezing.

"I'm so sorry, Doctor. I . . . me and my big mouth. I shouldn't have asked."

"No, it's all right," Whitfield said. "For a long time I didn't care to talk about it. And there's really no one around here I feel comfortable enough discussing it with." He snorted softly, glancing at her, vaguely puzzled. "Except, I guess, you, Miss Bonaventure—a bounty huntress, of all people."

He frowned down at her in shock.

"Good Lord," he said. "A sentimental man hunter!"

"Huh?" Then she realized what he was talking about. A tear was rolling down her right cheek. Quickly, she brushed it away. "Oh, that. Well . . . yeah, things have always gotten to me. Injustices like that, especially. When there isn't even anyone to see about it. Except God, I reckon, and he's a little too big for my pistols."

Whitfield sighed, nodded, and rose slowly from his chair. "Yes, there's no one to see about this. Your pistols are worthless here, Miss Bonaventure. The Fates have turned their tricks, as they so often do."

He slid the chair back against the wall. "You'd best rest. You'll be here for a few more days. I need to keep a close eye on those wounds, make sure your fever is staying down. In a week or so, you should be able to move into the hotel in town, and finish recovering there."

"Don't worry, Doctor," Louisa said. "I can pay for your services. Lou's probably got my. . . ." She let her voice trail off. "Where is Lou, anyway? He must have brought me here."

"Oh, he did, indeed." Whitfield drew his mouth corners down

distastefully. "He's around somewhere. The first several hours after he brought you here, I practically had to lock my doors to keep him out so I could tend your wounds. No doubt he'll be paying you a visit soon. He stops by every few hours or so. I'm sure he'd camp out here in your room if I let him. Partners, are you?"

"Sometimes, when I can stand the smell," Louisa said, wryly, fatigue pressing down on her, making her eyelids heavy. "And I can endure his pranks and what he calls jokes."

"Indeed," Whitfield said. "I'm sure he's quite the burden. Well, I'll let you sleep."

"Thanks, Doctor," Louisa said, closing her eyes, already half-asleep. "I'll . . . I'll be out of your hair soon, I'm sure . . ."

"Indeed." Whitfield drew the door partway closed, pausing to stare through the crack at his comely patient.

A bounty hunter with the vocabulary of a literate person. One who cries at sad stories.

Rather easy on the eyes, as well . . .

He latched the door and shuffled off down the hall.

CHAPTER TWENTY-ONE

Prophet cantered Mean and Ugly up to the doctor's side door and swung down from the saddle. He'd just dropped Mean's reins when the door opened and Whitfield dropped down a step and stopped suddenly, frowning in surprise at his visitor. He had a gun belt and two holsters in his hands.

Prophet recognized Louisa's fancy rig.

"Ah, there you are," Whitfield said, quietly closing the door and dropping down one more step.

Prophet's heart thudded. He didn't like the expression on the doctor's face. He seemed pensive, troubled. "What's wrong?"

"Oh, nothing, nothing." Whitfield held up Louisa's gun rig. "I was about to store this out in my stable for your partner. Don't like guns in the house where Titus can get at them."

"Oh." Prophet felt relief wash through him. "She's alive, then."

"Yes. In fact, she was conscious just a few minutes ago. She fell out of bed, crawled across the floor, and got her hands on one of these. I thought she was going to shoot me." Whitfield gave a wry snort.

"That's Louisa."

"I assured her she had no need for these on my premises."

"Are you sure about that, Doc?"

"People in this town respect the wishes of their only doctor, Mr. Prophet. Call it an unfair advantage or whatever you like, but my withholding services can prove costly."

He held the guns out, and Prophet took them and stowed them in his saddlebags. He turned to Whitfield. "Can I see her?"

"No." Whitfield shook his head. "She just fell back asleep, and sleep is the best thing for her now."

Prophet sighed and looked away. "Well, I'm glad to hear she's still kickin'. Did she hurt herself fallin' out of bed?"

"It doesn't look like it. She's a tough girl. A spirited girl."

"That she is. Well . . ." Prophet gathered up Mean's reins.

"Why don't you come in for a drink, Mr. Prophet?"

Prophet had turned a stirrup out. Now he glanced in surprise at the doctor. "What's that?"

Whitfield jerked his chin at the house. "Come in and have a drink. I have a bottle of Spanish brandy in my liquor cabinet. I don't drink much, so it's just been gathering dust. I mean"—he shrugged, offering a rare, sheepish half-smile—"if you've a mind. If you've nowhere else you need to be."

"No, no," Prophet said. "It's just that—well, I'm a little surprised by the invitation, Doc."

"I'm afraid I've been a trifle impolite," the doctor said. "A little quick to judge, perhaps."

"Well, hell," Prophet said. "It's bad luck to turn down a free drink."

Prophet started forward. Whitfield cleared his throat meaningfully, glancing at the double bores of the shotgun hanging up above Prophet's right shoulder.

"Oh, right," Prophet said, and slung the Richards's lanyard over his saddle horn.

He followed Whitfield through a kitchen and parlor and into the doctor's office separated by French doors from the rest of the house. It was a small room, book-lined, and with a neat desk outfitted with a green-shaded Tiffany lamp. The room that flanked it, through a half-open door, appeared to be an examination room. In the main office, the smell of medicines mingled with the aroma of pipe tobacco.

Whitfield produced a cut-glass decanter from a plain walnut cabinet with glass doors. He filled two goblets and handed one to Prophet. "Have a seat."

Prophet sank into a short, horsehair sofa flanking one wall while Whitfield sat in a wingback armchair beneath an oval-framed daguerreotype of himself when younger and a beautiful woman with her hair neatly lifted, rolled, and secured with an ornate tortoiseshell comb. She wore a ruffled white dress and held a bouquet of wildflowers.

Whitfield glanced up at the picture. "My wife." He sipped his brandy and studied the image for a time, then turned back to Prophet. "She's dead. Buggy accident. Same accident that gave me this bit of additional grief."

Prophet set his hat down beside him on the sofa. "I'm sorry to hear that, Doc."

"Your partner asked about Diana. She seemed quite moved by the story."

Prophet sipped the brandy. He could tell it was good stuff, but he'd have preferred a couple belts of Tennessee Mountain. Brandy tasted bitter to his unrefined palate. Like wine. Give him a beer and a bourbon any day of the week. "Does that surprise you?"

"I guess it did, yes."

"Louisa's not your typical bounty hunter. She comes packing a whole steamer trunk of heartbreak."

"Oh?"

"Her family was killed a few years back by an outlaw gang led by the bull demon of all demons, Handsome Dave Duvall."

"Duvall?" Whitfield looked surprised.

"Yeah. Know the name?"

Whitfield shook his head. "No. I mean . . . I knew some Du-

174

valls back where I came from, in Ohio, but I'm sure it's not the same family."

"Doubtful. I think Duvall hailed from Alabama, but as a fellow Confederate, I recognize no kinship with that rabid coyote. Dead now, anyways, thank god."

Whitfield looked down at the drink he held in both hands. "I see."

"Duvall was a child killer. A rapist and a murderer of women. That, you see, Doc, is sort of Louisa's specialty. Hunting down men who do harm to women and children. It's her calling and she practices it with a religious fervor I ain't seen since I left the healin' preachers and snake charmers in the north Georgia mountains."

Whitfield remained pensive. Something did indeed seem to be pestering the man, even more so now than when Prophet had just ridden up to the house.

"You all right, Doc?" Prophet asked.

Whitfield glanced up at him and quirked a phony smile. "Yes, I'm fine. Just a little tired, I guess."

"I'm sure Louisa's been a burden, having to check on her every hour."

"She'll be less so now. She still has a slight fever but it will gradually diminish. Now we just have to make sure there's no infection. I'd like to keep her here for at least the next week. Then she should be able to move over to the hotel. She should fully recover before she returns to the saddle."

"What're the charges, Doc?" Prophet reached into a front jeans pocket. "Between us we got . . ."

Whitfield waved his hand. "No need for that yet. We'll settle up when she leaves here. I sense that despite the lowliness of your occupation, you are an honorable man, Mr. Prophet. She certainly seems like an honorable woman, anyway."

"Oh, I'm honorable. Don't bathe much and tell stupid jokes,

but you can trust me farther than you could throw me uphill."

Whitfield chuckled. "Yes, she told me about your jokes."

"She asked about me, did she?"

"Of course. I sense that you're close."

"Sometimes more than other times. I reckon we're cut too much alike to not get along like gators of the same swamp."

"You sound like brother and sister."

"That's pretty much what we are, Doc."

Whitfield took another sip of his brandy. He didn't seem to be enjoying it all that much. "Tell me what's going on in town, Mr. Prophet. Between you and the men you think ambushed you."

"Oh, I know they ambushed me, Doc. I heard it from their own lips, though I'll admit I was a might deceptive. I listened to 'em talkin' in the billiard room after Wayne's funeral. Now I got the *who* of it answered. So's I just need to know the why. If they confess their sins to your local lawdog, and if he'll lock 'em up and call for the circuit judge, all will be well between me and Box Elder Ford."

"That's a tall order, I'd imagine."

"I would, too, but when they ambushed me an' Louisa that night, they were fillin' a tall one themselves. And they fucked it up. Pardon my French, but I'm mad as an old wet hen."

"So you have poor Roscoe Deets in the middle."

"There's no need for him to be in the middle. He wears a badge. This is his town. He should act like it."

"We had a man like that before Deets showed up. That's why Deets is in there now."

Prophet laughed without mirth and shook his head. "Well, I reckon you get what you pay for. But if there's gonna be any justice . . . and peace . . . in Box Elder Ford, Deets is gonna have to live up to that badge on his coat."

"And what if neither your ambushers nor Deets complies

with your demands, Prophet?"

"Then I reckon I'll be taking matters into my own hands."

"And the town be damned."

"Doesn't have to be that way."

Whitfield took another, larger swallow of his brandy, set the glass on his right thigh, and stared at Prophet dubiously through his glasses. "To use a stockman's expression, don't you think you're stomping a little high, Mr. Prophet?"

Prophet felt his cheeks warm with anger. He leaned forward on his knees. "They ambushed that girl in there. Could have killed her. Could have killed me. And I don't even know why."

"I'm not saying you don't have the right to be angry. I'm just wondering if you're not stomping a little high, placing this entire town in a whipsaw."

"It doesn't have to be that way," Prophet said, "if Roscoe Deets would grow up and be the lawman he calls himself."

Prophet drained his glass.

"Mr. Prophet?"

He looked at Whitfield. "I know how you feel about her, but don't take it out on the whole town. It's just eight men who ambushed you. There are two hundred innocent bystanders here in Box Elder Ford."

Prophet sank back against the couch, holding his empty glass on his leg. "What would you like me to do?"

"Sometimes things happen and there's really no one to see about them. Sometimes you just have to cut your losses." Whitfield stared pensively down at his own glass, then drained it. "Those men . . . they might have been desperate. You don't know what compelled them. I'd imagine it was something very . . . powerful, maybe beyond their ability to control. They felt that they had no option. I know those men, and none of them is a cold-blooded killer. Desperation compels men to do the oddest, most foolish things. Things that they might not otherwise do."

"What was it?"

"Huh?"

"What compelled them?" Deep lines cut across the bounty hunter's leathery forehead as he narrowed his eyes at the doctor. "Come on, Whitfield. You know, don't you? What was it?"

Whitfield rose from his chair. "I was speaking in general terms, Mr. Prophet. Now, if you'll forgive me, I need to call my son and start preparing supper." He held his hand out for Prophet's glass.

The bounty hunter stood, glowering in frustration. "All right. Thanks for the drink, Doc." He donned his hat. "But if you decide to tell me, I'm all ears." He strode out of the room. "I'll see myself out."

Prophet had stabled Mean and Ugly in the Federated Livery and Feed Barn and was heading down Hazelton to look for a room and a meal, when he stopped suddenly. He poked his hat brim back off his forehead.

Doc Whitfield was just then crossing the street a half a block ahead. The doctor was riding his horse, and he didn't have his medical kit hanging from his saddle horn. He wore a corduroy jacket and a bowler hat. He crossed Hazelton and continued westward one block before swinging down a cross street and heading north.

Prophet poked his hat up from behind and scratched the back of his head.

He continued tramping forward and on into the lobby of the Grand View Hotel. A pretty but weary-looking blond woman in her early thirties was manning the front desk, doing bookwork. She glanced up as Prophet strode to the desk and her cheeks colored a little.

She looked Prophet up and down, critically.

"Can . . . I . . . help you?"

"I'd like a room."

She gazed at him, nodded once, an odd, amused light entering her brown-eyed gaze. "You're the one who has all the men of Box Elder Ford looking as though the bogeyman were after them—my husband included."

"Oh, he is," Prophet said, smiling grimly. "Indeed, he is. But that's just between them and me, Mrs. Hunter. I see no reason why you and me can't be friendly."

"Well, then." The woman chuckled and turned the register book toward Prophet. "How long will you be staying?"

"As long as it takes, Mrs. Hunter," Prophet said, scribbling his name. "As long as it takes."

He pinched his hat brim to her, hefted his saddlebags on his shoulder, scooped his Winchester off the desk, and climbed the stairs.

In his room, he dropped his gear on the bed and glanced out the west-facing window, trying to cast a look up the hill to the north, the direction in which Whitfield had headed.

Why was it that everything in Box Elder Ford seemed to begin and end on the north end of town?

CHAPTER TWENTY-TWO

Doctor Whitfield swung down from his saddle and made his way to Miss McQueen's front porch. She didn't have the red lamp burning in the front window yet, which was the signal to the men in the town that she was open for business, but she likely would soon. It wasn't like Verna to take a night off. She liked money too much for that.

She also liked the power she wielded in her supple body.

The burning red light meant she was ready and waiting. The burning blue lamp meant she was with a customer. Why the women of the town hadn't caught on to that, Whitfield had no idea. Or perhaps they had, but they merely ignored this neat, mini-Victorian house up here on the north end of town. Maybe they saw Verna as performing a handy function for them, as well.

He'd often wished Diana had seen it that way . . .

The doctor shambled up onto the porch, neatly painted powder blue with white trim and furnished with two wicker chairs with a small, wicker table set between them. The table had a white satin cloth draped over it. It was outfitted with a decanter of fine Spanish brandy and two overturned glasses. The setup was for waiting customers. They could sit out here and sip Verna's complimentary brandy while they waited for her current client to leave.

Whitfield had never seen anyone taking advantage of the chairs or the brandy. Most of Verna's clients were far too discreet to risk being seen up here on her porch, even in the dark of night. She did not cater to saddle tramps, drummers, or range riders. By keeping her prices high, she'd successfully culled her clientele so that only the wealthiest and best behaved rode up the hill from town.

Whitfield rapped on Verna's front door. When he'd rapped two more times and received no response, he tried the door. It was open, as Verna felt secure enough here in Box Elder Ford to often forget to lock.

Whitfield stepped into the lavishly and tastefully appointed parlor with its delicate cherry wood tables and shelves and several plush velvet chairs and fainting couches arranged around a small, brick fireplace in which no fire danced this summer night. Verna's canary, Birdy, cheeped in his large, gilt-washed cage that hung down over her baby grand piano, which Verna played beautifully.

Verna must have heard Whitfield enter, for she called down from somewhere upstairs, "I'm not taking customers this evening, I'm sorry. Please come back tomorrow night—will you, hon?"

Whitfield liked her smooth, subtle, gently lilting southern accent, but he kept his mind on the business at hand.

"It's Clay," he called up the stairs at the far end of the parlor. The steps were carpeted in the same burgundy as the fainting couches. The mahogany newel post was carved in the shape of a naked angel in flight.

"Clay?" There were the faint tinkling sounds of water. She was bathing. "My goodness—to what do I owe the pleasure?" She sounded genuinely surprised. "I'll be right down."

Whitfield had no intention of waiting. With one hand on the banister, he climbed the stairs to the second story, which was one large bedroom and dressing room broken up with ornate room dividers and decorated with candles and Chinese lanterns.

The spicy aroma of opium hung in the air. No lanterns or candles had yet been lit, and the room was made even more sensuous by the sharp-edged shadows and prisms of early evening sunlight through which gold dust motes sifted.

"I said I'd be down," Verna gently remonstrated the doctor.

She was lounging back in her long, porcelain, zinc-lined bathtub that sat before another cold fireplace, to the right of Verna's high, canopied bed. She was partly in honey-gold sunlight, partly in shadow. She had a long, finely turned leg up, the foot resting on the opposite knee. She was slowly running a sponge along the calf, the water sounding like glass chimes in a light wind.

Outside, birds chirped in the branches of a cottonwood near one of the room's three, large windows.

"Didn't feel like waiting."

"My goodness!" Verna chuckled. "Been a long time, Clay. I guess you got tired of your priestly existence down there, eh?"

Whitfield walked over to a teak table and poured himself a glass of brandy. "I'm not here for that, so take your time."

"Oh?" Verna lowered her leg into the water and rested her arms along the sides of the tub. A table stood by the tub, and a small silver and stone-crusted opium pipe rested in an ashtray. It was hard to tell through the sunlight-striped shadows, but her eyes appeared touched with a dreamy, glistening opium cast. "What are you here for, then, Clay?"

Whitfield sat down in a lion-clawed, blue velvet chair far enough away from the tub that he couldn't see the woman's body in the shadows, which was good. He never wanted to see her body again.

"Why no visitors tonight, Verna? It's not like you, taking a night off."

"I took a ride in the country this afternoon." She smiled dreamily past Whitfield, and her eyes were lit by a far window.

"Plumb wore myself out, I guess."

Whitfield was vaguely curious, but he let it go.

"I had a visitor this afternoon, as well. Prophet."

She turned to him, the dreamy smile still quirking her lips. "That makes two of us, then. He joined me in the country. Sweet man."

Whitfield studied her, puzzled, but then he chuckled sardonically and massaged the back of his neck. "Oh, I see."

"What do you see?"

"Sleeping with the enemy?"

"Oh, we didn't sleep." Verna laughed a little too loudly at that and slapped her right hand down against the edge of the tub. "I think I made him quite happy, in fact."

"I bet you did."

"He's a big man, full of vinegar. But I think I can get my second wind for you, Clay." She patted the side of the tub. "Would you like to join me?" She glanced at the opium pipe. "A little spice might loosen you up a little."

"No. That will never happen again."

"No, I suppose not," Verna said with a fateful sigh. She looked at him with a half-beseeching, half-mocking smile. "Would you be a dear and pour me a brandy?"

Whitfield contemplated that. Then, rising with a sigh, he set his own drink down and poured one for her. He took it over to the tub and gave it to her without looking at her. As he turned away, she wrapped her left hand around his wrist.

"It wasn't my fault," she said quietly. "It wasn't your fault, either. You must remember that. Terrible things happen."

He pulled his wrist free of her hand and sat down again in the chair. He sipped the brandy and turned to Verna, who was sitting back in the tub now, raising her own glass to her lips. "Prophet mentioned a name that I think you'll recognize, Verna."

She arched an anticipatory brow.

"Whitfield said, 'Duvall.' "

She stared at him, brow leveling.

"You recognize that name—don't you, Verna?"

She blinked slowly, and in a low, even voice said, "Indeed."

"So that's what all this is about. He . . . or they . . . killed your brother."

She blinked again slowly and spoke with a lightness that belied her eyes and her words. "Don't say it like it's such a small thing, Doctor. Whoever Dave was . . . whatever he became after he left home . . . he was my brother. We Duvalls stick together, avenge our own. That's the way it's always been." Her voice had acquired a deep southern lilt, more pronounced than usual. "Ever since I read about his death in a newspaper, and the names of the two bounty hunters who killed him, I swore on my mother's and father's memory that I would seek restitution in blood."

Whitfield stared at her, aghast. "The Old South lives."

"Oh, it does." Verna sipped her drink and swallowed.

Whitfield said, "How in hell did you know Prophet and Miss Bonaventure were even going to be out at the old Ramsey Creek Outpost?"

"I called them there." Verna smiled in delight at her scheming. "Last week, a friend in Colorado Springs sent me a telegram informing me that she'd entertained Mr. Prophet in her brothel. Just a couple of weeks before, another dear friend and business associate informed me that she'd read in a newspaper 'society' column that the infamous Vengeance Queen herself, Miss Louisa Bonaventure, was spending a couple of months in Denver, enjoying the opera. I made it worth both my friends' time to get messages to both bounty hunters"—she smiled, white teeth glistening in the fading, golden light from the window—"telling each that they could learn about the fate of the other by riding out to Ramsay Creek."

Whitfield's expression was still one of disbelief. "My god, you're cunning."

"Aren't I, though?"

"Since you had such a network of people keeping eyes out, why didn't you just have them each killed where they'd been discovered? Surely you must have a gun-for-hire amongst your acquaintances."

"That would have been too easy. This way, leading them into an ambush, was more fun."

"But you sent amateurs." Whitfield shook his head quickly, smiling with the realization. "But that was part of the fun, too, wasn't it? Sending amateurs. Sending men from Box Elder Ford . . . your clients whom you knew you could control. Would have fun controlling, in fact. It was probably a little test—only not so little—to see how much power you had over them. To show *them* how much power you had over them. Threatening that if they didn't feel up to the task you'd—what? Inform their wives?"

Verna threw her head back, laughing. It was more like a witch's cackle. "Don't be silly, Clayton! I don't give a damn about their wives. Most of them don't, either."

Whitfield scowled, bewildered. "What was it, then?"

She lowered her brows at him, as though she'd just realized she was speaking to an idiot. "Why, that I'd strike my tent and take my business elsewhere, of course." She smiled again, slitting her long lids with their long, brown lashes and taking another sip from her glass. "There are some men in this town, Clayton, who can't live without me."

Whitfield drained his brandy, setting the empty glass down on the floor by his right shoe. He leaned forward on his knees, entwining his hands together. "I frankly had no idea what kind of a monster you are, Verna."

"Monster?" She seemed surprised by the insult but not offended. "They killed my brother. An eye for an eye. It's the

185

southern way."

"I'm not talking about that. I'm talking about involving the townsmen. So brashly wielding your power under threat of closing those beautiful legs."

She gave a heavy-lidded smile, lifting one of the appendages in question, water dripping into the tub. "They are pretty, aren't they?"

"You know, I came here because I thought I could talk some sense into you. I thought maybe I could get you to let the townsmen off the hook, though that's probably too late now, anyway."

"Oh, yes—I heard that Prophet gave them an ultimatum. Either they turn themselves in to our boy marshal and confess their sins, or he'll be on the prowl like a hungry mountain lion. I bet they're all trickling down their legs even as we speak."

She giggled devilishly.

"Yeah, that's what I figured," Whitfield said. "This is all sport to you." He rose and shuffled toward the stairs. Halfway there, he stopped and turned back to her as she lifted the pipe from the table. "You know, I always blamed myself for what happened to Diana. The storm, our fight over you, so that I was too distracted by the argument to take cover sooner. But now I realize that I'm not the only one to blame. Because you're a devil, Verna. A devil in a very pretty package. But a devil, just the same."

"Oh, come now, Clayton." She was lighting the pipe, blowing opium smoke and speaking between puffs. "Don't you think you're being just a tad overly dramatic?"

"We'll see, Verna. I think I know who to see about you."

He was almost to the stairs when the woman called to him casually, "I wouldn't do that, Clayton. I wouldn't go to Prophet." She set the pipe on the table, tipped her head back, and blew smoke at the ceiling. "I know how much the boy means to you, Clayton."

She turned to him, and she was indeed a devil—a fiend with red-glowing eyes in the sunset light streaming through the window. "If you go to Prophet, Titus is likely to end up at the bottom of your cold well."

CHAPTER TWENTY-THREE

Prophet spent most of the next three days kicked back in a rocking chair of the Grand View Hotel's front stoop, facing the street. From here, he had a pretty good view of the entire main street, Hazelton Street, and the comings and goings of the shopkeepers and businessmen.

It was a quiet three days. Business appeared to be churning as usual, townsfolk strolling in and out of the shops and saloons, the occasional ranch or farm or mine supply wagon clattering into town to pull up to the loading dock of the mercantile. Cowboys from nearby ranches cut the trail dust in the town's saloons.

It was late summer, and hot. A slow, heavy, desultory air lay over Box Elder Ford like a cloud of dreamy ease. The dust kicked up by the wagons took a long time to settle. Occasionally a brief windstorm blew dirt and horseshit around, rattling the shingle chains, banging loose shutters, and shepherding tumbleweeds and trash to and fro.

The local stagecoach came through only once in those three days, carrying only mail and two sullen-looking old women wearing bedraggled mob caps. One stared blankly out the coach's window as the coach rattled on past Prophet after it had switched teams, continuing west toward the mountains. Two mongrels barked at the coach, giving chase before suddenly stopping to nip playfully at each other and running off down an alley.

There was no rain. In fact, Prophet could have counted the clouds he'd spied in the near-faultless, broad-arching sky on one hand.

When the bounty hunter wasn't on the hotel porch, he was taking a meal, wetting his whistle, strolling about here and there with the Richards hanging down his back, attracting incredulous stares or downright glares from most quarters.

By now, what he was here for, his beef with the six remaining businessmen, had likely made its way through town and probably across a good chunk of the county, as well. Ladies of the town walked past him, whispering. Occasionally a couple of boys would skulk sheepishly, a little fearfully around the hotel, wanting to get a look at the bounty hunter who had the drawers of so many of the town's most prominent men tied in knots.

None of his six quarry made any move to fulfill his demands. It didn't appear that the town's young marshal was even on duty to write down their confessions if they chose to confess, which Prophet thought unlikely, anyway. The bounty hunter had seen neither hide nor hair of Deets since the day Prophet had killed Arnell Three-Bears and laid down his own brand of law across the street in the Arkansas River Saloon.

Several times a day, he checked on Louisa, whose condition was improving to the point that she was starting to talk about getting up and moving around. She wanted to back Prophet's play when the cyclone hit, which surely it would sooner or later here in Box Elder Ford.

Likely sooner rather than later. Prophet could tell by the quick, angry glares fired his way that his presence was rattling his six quarry. Soon, they'd feel pressed to the point of doing something about it.

Prophet assured Louisa that he could handle the matter himself, that what she needed to do was stay in bed and listen to Doc Whitfield.

189

Prophet blew a long plume of cigarette smoke over the porch rail. He stared out over the toes of his boots crossed atop the rail and saw L.J. Tanner staring out at him from over the Arkansas River Saloon's batwing doors, beneath the shake-shingled roof of the saloon's front gallery.

Tanner had his arms resting atop the doors, and he was glaring with his one eye across the street toward Prophet. Prophet stared back at him. Tanner held the stare for almost a full minute. Then he curled his nose in disgust, lowered his arms, adjusted his eye patch, and turned back inside.

Prophet smiled.

Footsteps sounded inside the hotel lobby, growing louder. The screen door squawked open and Helen Hunter stepped out.

"Mr. Prophet?"

Prophet dropped his boots to the floor, doffed his hat, and stood. "Yes, ma'am?"

"Oh, you don't need to get up. What a southern gentlemen you are!" Mrs. Hunter smiled, blushing and pressing her pink dress against her left thigh. She held a glass of something sugary in her other hand. She came out and extended the glass to Prophet. "So hot out here, even in the shade—I thought you might like a glass of lemonade."

"Oh, Lord o' mercy!" Prophet intoned, salivating at the sugary concoction. He saw a wedge of lemon floating around inside it. "Thank you, ma'am. Thank you."

"I always make up a batch early in the morning and then store it in our springhouse, so when I bring it up in the afternoon, it's nice and cool. I do so love a glass of lemonade on a hot summer after—"

Her husband's voice barked from the bowels of the lobby behind her: "Helen!" Angry footsteps stomped toward the porch.

Mrs. Hunter whipped her head around. "What is it, Neal!"

she barked back at the man. "Can't you see I'm having a conversation?"

Hunter pushed through the door and stepped out onto the gallery. When he saw Prophet, he hardened his jaws. "What in the hell are you talking to him for? He's a goddamned killer, for chrissakes!"

Hunter grabbed his wife's wrist and jerked her back into the lobby.

"Neal, unhand me!" Mrs. Hunter demanded, though apparently without favorable result, for the screen door slapped shut. Then Prophet heard the two stomping off into the hotel, Hunter barking angrily and Helen complaining against his grip on her wrist.

Prophet donned his hat, slacked down into his chair, sipped the lemonade, and smacked his lips. "Damn—that's good."

Later that night, lying in his bed on the hotel's second floor, Prophet opened his eyes. He'd heard something.

The soft squawk of the floor outside his room.

He'd heard it before—last night, in fact. It had sounded as though someone had been out there, skulking around. But when Prophet had grabbed his Richards and gone to the door, there'd been no more sounds. When he'd opened the door and investigated the hall, the hall had been empty. Now he waited, ears pricked, listening.

There it was again, the faint squawk of a floorboard.

Prophet grabbed the Richards hanging by its lanyard from a front bedpost. He threw the single sheet back and stepped out of bed and out of the line of any possible fire that might come bursting through the door. He pressed his left shoulder against the wall and crept toward the door.

There was a soft, single tap on the panel.

Prophet froze, scowling.

191

He had the Richards aimed at the door. His thumb was hooked over both hammers but he did not peel them back.

Two taps sounded on the door.

Then a woman's raspy voice, "Mr. Prophet . . . ?"

Prophet stepped up to the door, still wary. He wasn't about to be lured into another trap. For all he knew, there were six would-be shooters waiting outside his door with Winchesters cocked and ready.

The woman's voice came again, louder this time: "Mr. Prophet?" It was Helen Hunter.

Prophet stepped a little closer to the door but did not step in front of it. "What is it?" he said.

"Could you open the door, please?"

"What for?"

Slight pause. "Please open the door, Mr. Prophet. I assure you that my husband is asleep. It's only me out here . . . Lou."

Prophet turned the key in the lock. The bolt made a metallic grinding sound as it retreated into the door. Prophet stepped back and took the Richards in both hands. "It's open."

The door clicked, opened, hinges whining. Wan yellow light emanated from the candle she held in one hand, on a little tray. It lit her face but the rest of her was in shadow. She had a lacy wrap of some kind around her shoulders.

She looked down at the shotgun in Prophet's hands. "No need for that, Lou."

As she stepped into the room, Prophet looked into the hall behind her, which was lit with the milky glow of the moon. He could see no other shadows out there. Mrs. Hunter quietly closed the door behind her and turned to Prophet, who lowered the shotgun to his side.

She looked up at him. Her head came only to his bare chest. He wore only summer-weight longhandles, the legs of which dropped midway down his bulging thighs.

"Can I help you, Mrs. Hunter?"

She slid the wrap off one shoulder and then off of the other shoulder, and it fell to the floor, leaving her standing naked before him save a gold necklace with a fob of some kind hanging down into the valley between her heavy breasts.

"Indeed you can, Mr. Prophet."

She moved toward him, raising a hand.

"Hold on, Mrs. Hunter."

"Oh, really?" she tittered, placing her hand on his bare chest, over his bulging left pectoral.

"You're a married woman." It sounded like a foolish thing to say, but it was true, and Prophet did not make a habit of sleeping with married women. Not only was it dangerous, it wasn't the way he'd been raised by Ma and Pa Prophet back in the Blue Ridge Mountains of northern Georgia.

"Oh, but he's such a little man, Lou." She lowered her hand, sliding it ever so slowly down his belly, tickling his lightly haired skin with her fingertips, until she'd found what she'd been looking for.

She hefted, gently squeezed.

The blood in Prophet's loins instantly quickened.

"A very tiny, little man." She stepped closer, gently nibbling Prophet's chin. The tips of her breasts pressed against his belly. "Besides, does it really matter . . . given our circumstances?"

Her hand felt good down there.

"Nah," Prophet said. "I reckon not."

He leaned the Richards against the wall, peeled his underwear off, and then took the candle out of her hand and set it on the bureau. He stepped to her. Her lips parted as she gazed up at him, her eyes raking his large, tall, rugged body. Her hair was down. He could hear her breathing. He took her in his arms and kissed her before picking her up, laying her down on his bed, and mounting her.

She laughed and then groaned as the bedsprings began to sigh.

Down at the other end of the hall, Neal Hunter stood staring through his half-open door at the room into which Helen had disappeared. His heart thudded slowly, the burn of anger rising and spreading from his buttocks into his back. The back of his neck chafed.

Slowly, he closed the door and turned the key, locking it.

Helen returned to their room around ninety minutes later. When she rattled the doorknob, finding the door locked, she gave a laugh and walked away.

Hunter didn't sleep all night. His heart hammered like a war hatchet against his breastbone. First thing the next morning he walked across the street to the Arkansas River Saloon. L.J. Tanner was drawing a beer from one of his kegs while his friend, Lars Eriksson, was hauling another one in from the back room.

He carried the big keg over his right shoulder, leaning forward and grunting, his broad face as red as raw beef, veins forking in his freckled forehead.

"How you doin', Neal?" Tanner said as he cracked an egg into his beer.

"Give me one of those," Hunter said.

Tanner looked at him. "Never knew you to imbibe before noon before, Neal." He grinned and cast a glance at Eriksson coming up behind the bar from the far end.

Turning his faintly mocking gaze to Hunter, he said, "What's the matter—that guest of yours over there starting to smell like rotten fish? I've noticed that Helen's been sportin' a rosy glow lately. She doesn't seem to mind."

Hunter threw the punch before he even knew he was going to throw it. Tanner caught his fist atop the bar and held it, scowling at its thrower. "Holy shit, Neal," he laughed. "I never knew you to throw a punch before noon, either. In fact, I never knew you to throw a punch at all!"

He laughed again and shared another snide glance with the big Norwegian, who'd just placed the beer keg onto its rack. Eriksson regarded the hotel owner with wide-eyed surprise.

Hunter withdrew his fist. He felt even more deflated than he had before he'd walked in here. "Just give me the beer and the egg. And we gotta talk about . . ." He turned to thrust his arm and angry finger at his hotel. *"Him!"*

Tanner filled a mug. "It's done."

"What?"

Tanner swept the head off the beer with a stick, set the mug onto the counter, and cracked an egg into it. "Two days ago, Danny-Boy Price from Kansas came in here. He was lookin' for work, wondering if I knew if any of the ranchers had anything."

"Wait a minute, wait a minute," Hunter said, holding his beer on the bar's zinc top. "Who's Danny-Boy Price? You must remember, L.J., I don't run in your circles."

"Oh, that's right," Tanner said with a sardonic snort. "I forgot. Forgive me all to hell, Neal. Danny-Boy's a gun-for-hire. Him an' me once scouted for the army together, before I lost my eye. Anyway, I told him about the situation, and when he heard the names Prophet and Bonaventure, he said it's going to cost us, and he wants to bring in two more men. I agreed to his price . . . on yours and everybody else's behalf since I don't see as we have any choice . . . and he sent out a couple of telegrams. He's upstairs, waiting for the other two to show up. Laurie's showin' him a time . . . free of charge, of course."

"Who're the other two?"

"Joe Bastion and Asa Wade, commonly known as 'Slash.' In fact, don't call him Asa. I once did that, and . . . well, anyway, they're gonna cost us five hundred apiece."

Hunter raised his mug and downed half of his beer in a single draught. He lowered the glass and licked the foam and egg off his upper lip. "Is that for both of 'em?"

"Yep. They're gonna burn Prophet down first. Then the Vengeance Queen." Tanner sipped his own beer.

"How? You know Whitfield's rules."

Tanner chuckled. "Price, Bastion, and Wade don't follow *anyone's* rules, much less the rules of a crippled sawbones." He smiled at Eriksson and took another sip of his beer. "Now, we just gotta wait for Bastion and Slash to get here."

He looked up as the sound of straining bedsprings carried through the ceiling. A girl moaned.

Tanner frowned. "Sure hope ole Danny-Boy don't wear Laurie plumb out before his friends get here!"

CHAPTER TWENTY-FOUR

The next day, L.J. Tanner was sweeping the floor of his saloon and grumbling under his breath about no longer having his swamper, Arnell Three-Bears, around to perform such lowly chores. Instead, Arnell was pushing up rocks and snuggling with diamondbacks on the little bluff across the river known as Potter's Field.

Good help was hard to find, but Tanner wasn't about to pay for the half-breed's funeral.

All that was left of Arnell were the bloodstains on Tanner's floor. Though L.J. had scrubbed and scrubbed at the stains, he couldn't seem to get them out of the wood. Maybe in time they'd fade, but at the moment they were a grisly reminder of Lou Prophet's barn blaster.

Hearing his only whore groaning again upstairs to the accompaniment of her worn-out bedsprings, Tanner lifted his head to yell, "Goddamnit, Danny-Boy—how many free pokes are you . . . ?"

Tanner let his voice trail off when sharp slapping sounds rose from out in the street. He turned to see Roscoe Deets's pretty little Mexican wife shuffling by in rope-soled sandals, carrying a small crate of grocery goods up high against her comely, brown bosoms. She wore a straw sombrero and the low-cut red dress she nearly always wore, as though it were maybe one of only two or three dresses she owned. The skirt of the dress danced against her long, slender legs, and her straight, dark-brown hair

197

fluttered out behind her shoulders as she strode on past the Arkansas River Saloon, heading east, the sandals slapping her heels.

Tanner moved to the door and called, "Hey, there, *Senorita*. I mean, *Senora* Deets!" He chuckled at his purposeful mistake.

Lupita Deets stopped and glanced back at him. She looked sad, crestfallen. Without much heart, she said, "Hello, *Senor* Tanner."

She turned and continued shuffling away but stopped again when Tanner said, "Hey, where's your husband, the marshal? Ain't seen him around much lately."

"He is sick," said the girl.

"Sick, huh?"

"*Si.*"

"That's too bad."

Her head and shoulders bowed, she said unconvincingly, "He will be all right in time. I will tell him you asked, *Senor* Tanner."

She started walking away again.

Tanner called, "Anything I can do to help?"

Without stopping or even glancing back at the saloon owner, Lupita merely shook her head. Tanner watched as she shuffled away, dust rising from around her sandals and brown feet, admiring the way the dress clung to her legs. A pretty girl, Lupita. But then, Tanner had always been fond of young Mexican women. There was something undeniably alluring about those dark eyes and that dark hair and smooth, nut-brown skin.

He'd once had a Mexican whore working for him, but she hadn't liked the way he'd treated her. She'd slipped out on him only two weeks after she'd started.

Tanner grimaced at the ceiling through which he could hear his current whore groaning. Knowing what Danny-Boy was doing up there, and having seen Lupita Deets out in the street, looking so sad, caused a burn of desire to rise up into Tanner's belly.

He leaned his broom against the wall, removed his apron, tossed it onto a table, and then stepped out through the batwings and onto the gallery. Lifting his black slouch hat trimmed with a conch band, he smoothed his thin hair back from his temples.

He dropped down the gallery steps and walked out into the street, swinging right and following the girl's scuffed sandal tracks. He could see her a half a block ahead. Pulling his hat down snug on his forehead, Tanner jogged forward as two horseback riders passed on his left. They were the only two others on the street, as it was hot and bright and most folks were sticking to the shade.

"Mrs. Deets? I say there—*Senora* Deets?"

She stopped and turned to him, frowning, straining slightly against the weight of the groceries in her arms.

Tanner jogged up to her. "Don't know what got into me. Where are my manners? I should have offered to help you with your burden."

"That is all right, *Senor* Tanner," Lupita said. "You are a busy man. Besides, it is not so—"

"Nonsense, nonsense. You let me help you with that."

"Really, it is not neces . . ."

She let her voice trail off as Tanner took the small, tightly packed crate from her. "Of course it's necessary. Your husband's sick and you're obviously feeling a mite off your feed about it. The least a good citizen . . . and gentleman . . . can do is carry your groceries home for you."

"Thank you, *Senor* Tanner," Lupita said as she drew her chin down and started walking alongside the saloon owner.

She said nothing as they walked along the partly shaded right side of the street, heading toward the cross street on which her and Deets's house was located. Tanner glanced at her. Her brown cheek was screened by her coarse, dark-brown hair, which brushed her shoulders and arms.

"So ole Roscoe is sick, eh?" Tanner said, feigning concern.

"*Si.*"

"Tell me, Lupita. I mean, it ain't none of my business, and I assure you I'll keep it just between you an' me, but . . . is Roscoe drinkin' again?"

Lupita looked at him quickly, fearfully. But then tears shone in her eyes and she lowered her head again as she said, "*Si.* He is drinking again."

"Ah, that's a damn shame. See, I knew Roscoe had a problem. Back when he was working for old Chester McCrae, he and a couple of his *compadres* would ride into town on Friday nights already lit up like Chinese lanterns. But he promised me and the rest of the town council he'd given it up."

"He promised me that, too, *Senor* Tanner." Lupita turned quickly to Tanner again. "Please do not fire him, *Senor* Tanner. Please do not tell the others. It is just a small setback. It is a bender. My papa was the same way. When he is sober again, I will talk to him and he will listen to reason. He does not want to lose me, and I know he does not want to lose his job."

"It's this bounty hunter mess, ain't it?"

"What?"

Tanner kicked at a horse apple in mock frustration. "It's this bounty hunter mess that got him all antsy and pulled him back into the bottle. Damn, that man . . . and that girl. They sure have complicated things in Box Elder Ford, I don't mind tellin' you, Miss Lupita. But it's a passing thing. Roscoe has to understand that. And he's tough enough to face up to Lou Prophet."

"I know that and you know that, *Senor* Tanner," Lupita said as they turned the corner and headed for her and Deets's house, "but Roscoe does not know that."

"As soon as he comes out of it, *chiquita*, I'll talk to him."

Lupita glanced at him skeptically, hopefully. "You will?"

"Of course, I will. Hey, listen—we all got problems. Sometimes just knowin' we got friends who care helps a whole damn lot, pardon my French."

As they entered her and Deets's yard, Lupita said quietly, "The back door, please, *Senor* Tanner. Roscoe is sleeping upstairs, and I don't want to wake him."

"Sure, sure."

As they walked along the side of the house, Lupita glanced at Tanner skeptically. "You will not tell the other town council members?"

Tanner gave her a winning smile. "I said I wouldn't, didn't I?"

Lupita smiled, flushing. As they turned the rear corner of the house and headed for the back door, Lupita said, "I don't know how to thank you, Mr. Tanner." She stopped and turned to take the box of groceries from him.

Tanner held onto the box and, smiling lasciviously, said, "I think you do."

She frowned, staring at him with befuddlement in her chocolate-brown eyes. Then her dark cheeks turned darker and she pulled a little harder at the box in Tanner's hands. "I will take this now, *Senor* Tanner."

Tanner pitched his voice low with both lust and menace as he said, "You know what I think, *chiquita*? I think you need a man. I think you need a real man. Not some young drunk who turns tail and runs at the first sign of trouble."

Lupita's voice quavered as she tugged at the box. "Please, *Senor* Tanner, give me the box. I must go inside now. I have work—" She gave a startled cry as Tanner suddenly released the box and grabbed her. She dropped the box, and as the groceries

201

spilled out on the ground around her sandals, she opened her mouth to scream.

Tanner clamped his hand over her mouth, and the scream sounded like a moan. He wrapped his free arm around her shoulders and shoved his face up to within six inches of hers, tipping her head back.

"Let's go on over to the stable yonder, *chiquita*, and I'll show you what it's like with a real man."

She moaned against his palm clamped down hard on her mouth, and tried to wrestle out of his grip, but he was far larger and stronger than she.

"If you don't," Tanner said. "If you keep makin' a big fuss over it, I'll see that Roscoe's fired. Understand? Now, you like your little house here, don't ya? Prob'ly wanna fill it with little half-breeds? Well, that ain't gonna happen if you don't come nice and quiet with me over to the stable and act like a woman's supposed to act." The saloon owner grinned. "Understand, *chi-quita?*"

She stared at him through those terrified brown eyes. Her lips were moist and warm against his hand, fueling the fires of his goatish desire.

"Understand?" Tanner asked her again and gave her head a quick, savage shake.

She blinked once, twice. Tears shone in her eyes. They dribbled down her cheeks to roll up against Tanner's hand.

She nodded once.

Slowly, Tanner lowered his hand to his side. Lupita did not scream.

Tanner took her hand and led her back to the small stable and buggy shed Roscoe had built at the rear edge of his and Lupita's property. Deets's chestnut gelding stood in the small corral abutting the stable, eyeing the pair curiously as it chewed hay and switched its tail at flies. The hot, dry breeze stirred the leaves of the cottonwood partly shading the stable.

A squirrel chittered angrily in the branches.

Tanner opened the stable's side door. He stepped aside, and Lupita stared up at him for a second before she moved on through the door and into the stable's heavy shadows, brushing tears from her cheeks.

"Why are you doing this, *Senor* Tanner?" she asked quietly.

Tanner closed the door and walked over to her. The empty stable was neatly kept, with gear hanging from spikes in the walls. There were three stalls standing side-by-side though Deets had only one horse. More of the young marshal's optimism, Tanner thought.

He walked up to Deets's pretty little wife and slid her hair back from her cheeks with the backs of his hands, staring hungrily down at her. "Because you're the prettiest little thing in the whole damn county, *chiquita*. Don't you know that?" He stepped back and hardened his voice, keeping it low. "Now, take that pretty little dress off."

Lupita sniffed, lowered her head, and began unbuttoning the dress. When she had it open, she slid it off her shoulders, stepped out of it, and set it on a saddle rack.

"The rest of it," Tanner ordered.

Sobbing quietly, she reached down and pulled her camisole up and over her head. Her hair tumbled down around her shoulders and small, pert, brown-nippled breasts.

"Jesus," Tanner said throatily, swallowing. He placed a hand on her right breast and fondled it roughly. "Niiice."

When Lupita had removed her lacy drawers and set them, too, on the saddle rack, Tanner brusquely picked her up and set her down on the clothes piled on the racked saddle. She gave a small cry and then she just sat there on the saddle, naked and sobbing, as Tanner unbuckled his cartridge belt. He let his gun and holster fall to the hay-strewn floor. He unbuttoned his pants and lowered them and his underwear to his knees.

He stepped forward and, holding his jutting dong in one hand, spread her left knee wide with the other.

"Nice and quiet now, *chiquita*," he warned, sliding himself forward against her. "Nice . . . and . . . quiet. Ohh, *yeah!*"

Suddenly bright sunlight swept over him as the stable door opened behind him.

"Huh?" Tanner said, awkwardly turning, stumbling over his trousers.

"Roscoe!" Lupita cried.

CHAPTER TWENTY-FIVE

Deets stumbled through the stable door, the golden sunlight showing copper on the naked, brown body of his young wife sitting on the saddle rack, knees spread wide. It shone, too, on L.J. Tanner, whose denims had been shoved down to his knees although, as he swung around toward Deets, they dropped down to his boots.

Deets saw the man's erect dong jutting up from between the hanging coattails of his shirt.

Deets was so badly hung over that it took his drink-fogged brain nearly five seconds to fully realize what had been happening in here. As he did, he saw the corner of the one-eyed Tanner's mouth begin to quirk a mocking grin.

That smile was like a keg of black powder detonated in Deets's head. The young marshal bounded forward, cocking his right fist.

"Hey, now!" Tanner screamed.

"Roscoe!" Lupita cried.

Deets slammed his fist so hard against Tanner's jaw that he heard cracking sounds issuing from both his fist and the saloon owner's face. He felt the pain of the blow jolt up his arm and into his shoulder. Tanner grunted, twisted around, tripping over his pants and underwear, and hit the stable floor on his belly. Then Deets was kneeling on him, hammering his head with one savage blow after another.

Tanner gave a gurgling cry and raised his arms to shield

himself from the blows. He turned his head to stare up at Deets between his arms.

The bald terror in the man's lone eye only fueled Deets's fury. Only half-hearing Lupita's screams and the whinnies of his frightened horse in the corral, the young marshal continued to punch the saloon owner wildly, working so furiously that only about half of his blows landed square on the man's head, the rest glancing off his head or smacking his hands and arms.

Unsatisfied with his and Tanner's position, Deets grabbed Tanner's arms and began to pull him toward the door.

"Roscoe, stop!" Lupita cried. *"Stop!"*

She grabbed at Deets, but in his insane state, not realizing what he was doing—she was a mere obstacle to the beating he intended to give Tanner—he threw his arm out, smacking her shoulder and sending her reeling against a stall partition. He dragged the groaning and grunting Tanner out into the yard, into the sunlight, and then he kicked him hard in the belly with the toe of his boot.

"Ohh!" Tanner cried, jackknifing.

Deets drew the man's head up by his hair, and holding it thus with one hand, he landed two solid blows on the man's jaws and a third one smack against his nose, which exploded like a ripe tomato, splattering both Tanner and Deets with blood. Then he drove the toe of his boot once more into Tanner's belly.

When Tanner folded again, Deets kicked him in his left side, hearing a rib snap.

Deets kicked him again, rolling him over. He kicked him again and again until Tanner, yowling and mewling, had rolled nearly all the way to the back wall of Deets's house, dust sifting around him. He intended to continue kicking him until he'd turned every bone in the man's body to powder, but then Lupita threw herself on his back and wrapped her arms around his neck.

"Roscoe, that's enough!" she screamed. "That's enough! That's enough!"

She pulled Deets back onto the ground, where he sat on his butt, leaning back against Lupita, who kept her arms wrapped around his neck, pressing her face against his back.

"That's enough, my love," she said softly now, sobbing. "You saved me. That is enough."

Deets continued to glare at Tanner who lay writhing, beaten and bloody, the man's trousers still twisted around his boots. The man's shirt was torn and filthy. He'd lost his eye patch and the scarred, empty socket was puckered and caked with dirt and bits of the sage Deets had kicked him through.

The man's lone eye was swollen and nearly closed.

"You're crazy," Tanner whimpered into his arms, moaning. "You're goddamn *crazy!*"

Deets turned around to face Lupita. She'd donned her dress, but she hadn't buttoned it. Her hair was disheveled, and tears were rolling down her cheeks from her anguished, brown eyes.

"Oh, Roscoe!" she cried, hugging him tightly.

"It's all right, Lupita," Deets said, wrapping his arms around her, squeezing. "Don't you worry. He'll never hurt you again. I'll see to that myself. In fact, that son of a bitch is never gonna hurt no one ever again."

He glanced over his shoulder at Tanner, and hardened his jaws once more. He raised his voice, making sure that Tanner would hear him.

"In fact, if the son of a bitch ain't out of town by midnight, I'm gonna kill him. I'm gonna kill him and burn his fuckin' saloon to the ground!"

★ ★ ★ ★ ★

An hour or so later, Lou Prophet was rolling a quirley on the hotel's front porch. A glass of lemonade, his second of the afternoon, sat on the porch rail before him, the sunlight turning the tiny sugar crystals to gold dust. The slice of lemon in the glass glowed like a miniature sun.

He leaned forward, elbows on his knees, rolling the smoke and looking around.

He wasn't sure what, but something told him that hell was about to pop. There was no single, identifiable reason for him to think so. It was just the feeling he had. He'd learned in his many years of hunting men, and the trouble involved, to trust that feeling. It had kept him out of a grave . . . so far.

The street was nearly empty, but he saw a single portly man moving toward the hotel. He could tell from even a block away that it was the banker, George Campbell, easily the fattest man Prophet had so far seen in Box Elder Ford.

The man was shaped like a rain barrel with legs, wearing a three-piece, spruce-green suit and black string tie. He wore an opera hat on his egg-shaped, bald head. Little pince-nez glasses were perched on his pudgy nose.

As he made his way, taking little, mincing steps in his black shoes, he glanced at Prophet, stopped, removed the glasses from his nose, and stuck them into a breast pocket of his suit coat. He scowled at the bounty hunter sitting at his usual place on the porch, and swerved toward the Arkansas River Saloon.

He glanced at Prophet several more times as he crossed the street. Prophet pinched his hat brim to the man, who turned sharply away, the back of his bald head beneath his hat turning red, and disappeared into the saloon.

Prophet scratched a match to life on his gun holster and touched the flame to the quirley. As he lit the cigarette, he spied another man moving toward Prophet's end of the street.

This man came slowly, haltingly along the street's other side, sticking to the shadows widening out from the building fronts. As the man moved closer, Prophet saw that it was L.J. Tanner.

Tanner was walking as though he had a full load in his drawers, and he was holding his right arm across his belly, as though he'd injured the limb. He brushed his left hand against the walls of the buildings he passed, clomping slowly, heavily, uncertainly across the boardwalks.

Prophet frowned as he puffed the quirley, staring at the saloon owner.

Drunk?

Or injured?

Injured, he concluded a few seconds later when he saw that Tanner's clothes were badly disheveled. His shirttails were hanging out of his pants and his face was a smeared mess of half-dried blood. His lone eye appeared to be swollen. He wasn't wearing the patch over the other eye socket.

"Why," Prophet said, feeling his mouth corners quirk in a grin, "he's had the shit kicked out of both ends. Now, who in the hell would have done that . . . ?"

Tanner staggered over to his saloon and clomped up the steps, his boots sliding off every other riser so that he had to grab the rail to keep from falling. When he finally gained the porch, he dragged his boot toes over to the batwings and on inside.

"Good Lord, Tanner!" Prophet heard Campbell's voice echo from inside the saloon, "what in the hell happened to you?"

If there was a response, Prophet didn't hear it.

The bounty hunter sat in his chair, smoking and sipping his lemonade, pondering the saloon owner's condition. A half hour later, two horseback riders came into town from the east. They were hard-faced men wearing battered, broad-brimmed hats and at least two pistols apiece.

One was small and wiry, and he wore a thick, blond mus-

tache with upswept ends. He wore a blue calico shirt and suspenders, and he rode a cream gelding.

The other man was bigger, heavier, and slope-shouldered. He
had a thick, gray-brown beard and he wore his long, gray-brown
hair in a braid down his back. A cream felt sombrero with a
brown leather band shaded his broad, mean-looking face with
close-set eyes and a nose like the prow of a clipper ship.

They both looked around cautiously as they rode, lightly
bouncing in their saddles, holding their reins up close to their
chests. When their eyes found Prophet on the hotel porch, they
scrutinized him carefully, warily, and then swung their horses
toward the Arkansas River Saloon.

They dismounted and continued to cast frequent, wary
glances toward Prophet. The bigger man spat a stream of chaw
into the street, ran a gloved hand across his mouth, and said
something under his breath to the smaller man. The smaller
man chuckled, and, adjusting his double shell belts and two
Colt Peacemakers on his lean hips, glanced again at Prophet.

Batting their hats against their denim-clad thighs, causing
dust to billow, they mounted the saloon's porch and pushed
through the batwings.

"Now," Prophet said, sitting slowly back in his chair, staring
toward the saloon with a speculative glint in his eyes, "what
have we here?"

The Arkansas River Saloon's sole whore, Laurie, dabbed at
Tanner's split bottom lip with a cloth she'd dampened with water from a tin pot. Tanner was sitting gingerly at a table near the
bar, and the whore stood beside him wearing a gauzy black
wrap over her corset and bustier.

She was a pretty brunette with freckles all over her body, but
she was looking tired and worn out.

"Ow—goddamnit, Laurie, that hurts!" Tanner roared when

she'd pressed too hard on his lip, causing blood to bubble up from the gash and sending what felt like a hot, razor-edged stiletto of pain into his jaw. "Go easy, damnit!"

"I'm tryin' Mr. Tanner! I'm tryin'!" she cried.

The gunslinger, Danny-Boy Price, sat across from Tanner, beside the stout banker, George Campbell. Both men were nursing whiskeys and staring at Tanner incredulously. Price grinned, lowered his chin, and chuckled, shaking his head.

"What's so goddamn funny, Price?" Tanner spat out with a tooth that went rolling across the table to pile up against the banker's shot glass.

Laurie gasped. "Oh, *ooooo!*"

Campbell lifted his drink high, staring down in revulsion at the bloody tooth before him.

Price laughed and shook his head. Tanner was about to give the gunslinger an earful when he heard boots clomping up the porch steps. Two figures appeared on the porch—one taller and broader than the other. The big man, Joe Bastion, stepped through the batwings first, followed by the smaller man, Asa "Slash" Wade.

Danny-Boy Price turned around in his chair to intone, "Well, look what the cat dragged in! Come on in, boys, and you can watch Miss Laurie try to put our Mr. High and Mighty employer back together again. He fell down and hurt himself!" He clapped his hands together once and laughed.

The big Bastion scowled down at Tanner. "What in the hell happened to you, L.J.? I didn't know there was still any Injuns to fight out thisaway!"

The three gunmen laughed.

Campbell sat in his chair, turning sideways to inspect the two menacing-looking, hard-eyed, trail-dusty newcomers with the wide-eyed fascination of a boy. Both killers wore two pistols apiece. Wade also wore a horn-gripped bowie knife riding beside the Peacemaker positioned for a quick cross-draw over his belly.

Bastion had a long, folding barlow knife hanging from a leather thong around his neck. A silver, jewel-crusted medallion hung from the same thong. It clacked against the knife when he moved.

Tanner grabbed Laurie's wrist and shoved her hand away from his face. Gritting what was left of his teeth with pain and fury, he leaned forward in his chair. At least as far forward as he could without grinding his broken ribs to the point of causing him to pass out. He thrust his hard jaws and spade-shaped chin at the killers sitting or standing before him.

"You got three now," he said, flaring his nostrils.

"Three what?" asked Wade.

"Three people to kill. The sumbitch across the street. His partner, Bonaventure. And the town marshal of Box Elder Ford—Roscoe Deets!"

Tanner sat back in his chair, which creaked against his shifting weight, and said, "I'll pay for Deets out of my own pocket."

CHAPTER TWENTY-SIX

Late the next night, Prophet opened his eyes and stared at the dark hotel room ceiling.

He'd heard something out in the hall. He wasn't sure what it was, for he'd heard it in his customarily light sleep. But he was relatively sure what it had been.

He sighed, smacked his lips, groaned, and ran a hand down his face. He wasn't sure he was in the mood tonight for Mrs. Hunter's ministrations. He was fairly certain his quarry was close to making its move, and he needed to keep his edge. He also needed his sleep, however shallow.

He tossed his covers aside and rolled out of bed. He'd just gained his feet when what sounded like the detonation of a dynamite keg in close quarters filled the room. The door of his room burst open, spitting wood from the pumpkin-sized hole in its upper panel. A silhouetted figure stepped forward and there was a bright flash as flames leaped from the barrel of a sawed-off shotgun, the lead pellets causing the bed to leap as they tore into the mattress where Prophet had been lying only two seconds before.

Prophet stumbled back against the wall, ears ringing. As the gunman stepped farther into the room, Prophet grabbed his Richards off the near bedpost and raked back both heavy hammers.

"Shit—look out!" the gunman shouted, his shadow wheeling.

Prophet tripped both triggers at nearly the same time, the

second blast sounding like the echo of the first. The flash of the flames lapping from the Richards's maw briefly lit up the room and the back of a man bounding out of Prophet's open doorway and down the hall.

Several sets of boots hammered the carpeted floor, fast fading as the gunmen—there must have been two or three—headed for the stairs, shouting.

Prophet tossed the Richards aside, grabbed his Peacemaker from the holster also hanging from the bedpost, and ran to the door that had bounced off the wall to stand partway open. He could feel the reverberations of the ambushers' pounding boots through the floor beneath his bare feet.

The hall was empty. The gunmen were gone.

Down the hall to Prophet's right, a door latch clicked. A door opened slightly and Neal Hunter's voice said, "Good god— what the hell's going on?"

Prophet said through a snarl, "You keep your head inside that room unless you want it blown off, Hunter. Your three hired guns just came to finish the job you started, and when I'm done with them I'm gonna come for you. So you just stay there less'n you want me to deal with you right here and now!"

The door slammed. The key turned with a ratcheting click in the lock.

Prophet gave a wry snort and started pulling his clothes on. There was a good bit of light in his window, which meant it was later than he'd thought. Dawn pushing close to sunrise, most likely.

Prophet was betting the three hired guns had been over at the Arkansas River Saloon all night, diddling Tanner's whore and drinking themselves up into a cold-blooded killing fury.

An ambusher's drunken, chicken-livered fury.

Prophet stomped into his boots, buckled his cartridge belt around his waist, grabbed his hat, and refilled both barrels of the Richards with fresh ten-gauge wads. He clicked the gun closed, strapped it over his head and shoulder, and picked up his Winchester. When he was sure it was fully loaded, he racked a shell into the magazine, off-cocked the hammer, and strode out of his room.

"Here we go," he muttered.

He turned carefully at the top of the stairs, peering cautiously into the lobby below. Spying no movement around the bottom of the stairs, he moved down slowly, holding the Winchester down at an angle from his right hip. He had his index finger drawn snug against the trigger, thumb on the hammer.

The lobby was empty. It was filled with smoky blue shadows, for the sun was climbing higher.

A shadow moved in the doorway to the dining room. Prophet swung the Winchester toward it. Helen Hunter gasped and placed a hand to her breast. She was fully dressed and wearing an apron, probably already at work in the kitchen, helping the Chinese cook.

Prophet turned the rifle back toward the door.

"Get back in the kitchen," he said quietly.

She stepped back and strode quickly across the dining room.

Prophet moved to the front door, which was open, and peered through the screen. The street was filled with brown-purple shadows touched with pearl. The air was soft and cool. Birds were raising their usual early morning ruckus, darting about the false façades on both sides of the street, flapping wings glinting silver.

Prophet stepped slowly out through the screen door. He eased it closed and stood on the porch, scrutinizing the street, the alley mouths opening onto it, looking for his would-be killers. They'd tried to kill him the easy way, because that was the kind of spineless killers they were. They probably figured the worst thing that could happen was that they'd lead him out here onto

215

the street, where they could try again.

Well, here he was . . .

When he spied no one scuttling around behind rain barrels or stock troughs, he began moving down the porch steps. Movement to his left.

He turned to gaze eastward, where two men were just then striding out into the street from an alley by the bank. Another man walked out from an alley mouth directly across from them, on the south side of the street. They took positions about six feet apart, spread out in a line, casually holding rifles on their shoulders or, in the case of the man on the far right, resting in his crossed arms.

They stared toward Prophet, who chuckled as he strode out into the street.

"There you are," he said. "I thought maybe you'd lost your nerve!"

The men, just shadows in the dim but quickly intensifying light, glanced at each other. The one on the far left said, "Shut up, you old warhorse. You're gonna die here this mornin'."

"Talk's cheap, peckerwood." Prophet grinned.

He stood waiting, rifle resting on his shoulder.

The others seemed a tad reluctant to get the ball rolling. Prophet wasn't reluctant. He was eager to do away with this batch of hired killers so he could get started on the men who'd hired them to do their blood work.

He brought the rifle down quickly, aimed, and clicked the hammer back. His sudden movement seemed to startle the other three, who sort of jerked with starts as they began bringing their own weapons to bear.

Prophet aimed quickly, fired, and saw through his powder smoke the middle shooter, a big man who he thought might be Joe Bastion out of Kansas City, twist around and stumble back as he fired his own weapon through a window to Prophet's left.

Bastion grunted.

The other two cut loose with their carbines, the bullets screeching over and around Prophet and blowing up dirt at his feet. He returned fire, but both men were jostling around now, moving toward Prophet and cocking and firing their Winchesters, making poor targets.

Prophet fired and pumped, fired and pumped.

The smallest of the three shooters yowled and then hobbled quickly off to his left, throwing himself down behind a stock trough.

Bastion was down and crawling off toward the right side of the street. As he passed the third man, who Prophet recognized as Danny-Boy Price, also out of Kansas—his family had been Jayhawkers—Prophet drilled Price through his left shoulder.

Price jerked back with a shrill curse and triggered his carbine into the street as he dropped to one knee, his back now facing the bounty hunter. Screaming shrilly, Price reached for his two pistols, heaved himself to his feet with another shrill scream, and extended both revolvers straight out from his shoulders.

Prophet triggered his rifle three more times, sending all three shots into Price's chest, causing dust to billow from his dirty clothes.

Each shot sent Price stumbling backward and nodding his head sharply as though in drunken agreement with something, firing each pistol wildly around the street. As he fell, Prophet's own Winchester pinged on an empty chamber. As the other two shooters sent lead hurling toward the bounty hunter, Prophet ran crouching toward the Arkansas River Saloon.

Bullets hammered the street round him. They hammered stock troughs and the saloon's awning support posts. One carved a hot, shallow line across the back of Prophet's right leg, and another carved a similar line across the side of his neck. He ran up onto the porch and fell flat, facing the direction from which the two shooters had now, suddenly, stopped shooting.

He aimed his Peacemaker straight out in front of him, hammer cocked.

He was having trouble picking out a target. The sun was on the rise, spreading light and shadows.

He could see one man crouched behind the far end of a stock trough a half a block away from him and on the same side of the street. That would be Bastion. The other, shorter man had disappeared, probably hunkered down in the alley mouth by the bank.

Silence had fallen over the street. Dogs barked in the distance, and somewhere a baby cried.

Bastion was keeping his head down. Prophet could see the crown of his Stetson moving. He was probably reloading his pistols, preparing for another onslaught. Prophet glanced toward that alley mouth by the bank.

The street in front of it was touched with salmon light from the east.

Prophet crabbed back along the saloon's front porch. He slipped through the rail at the far end and leaped to the ground. Quickly, he stole around behind the saloon and made his way down the alley that paralleled the main street. He holstered the Peacemaker and swung the Richards around in front of him, thumb on the hammers.

When he'd gained the far end of what he thought was a millinery, he stole up alongside it, heading back toward the main street.

He stopped when the tall gunman, Bastion, appeared ahead of him, hunkered down behind the stock trough. Bastion had doffed his hat, and he was edging looks up over the trough toward the saloon, looking for his quarry. He had one pistol in his left hand. He had clamped his other hand over his thigh, and he was grunting and groaning softly, obviously in pain.

Bastion glanced toward the other side of the street, turning his head right and left and back again, looking for the other shooter. Beyond him, near the other side of the street, Danny-Boy Price lay spread-eagle on his back.

Prophet wanted to get a little closer for the coach gun.

He'd taken two more steps when his left spur dragged on some scrap lumber. Bastion turned quickly toward Prophet. Prophet squeezed the Richards's left trigger. He watched Bastion blow back away from him as though on a stiff wind to pile up in the middle of the street, quivering.

Holding the smoking Richards down low by his belly in one hand, closing his other hand around the grips of his holstered Peacemaker, Prophet stepped up to the mouth of the alley. He poked his head out of it, looking around.

No sign of the third shooter.

He crept out into the street where Bastion was gurgling and shivering, the sunlight now glistening in the large, gaping hole in his chest. The sun was half up, and there was now more light than shadows. There was no one on the street. At least, no one that Prophet could see.

Looking around, he moved slowly down the middle of the street toward the west, occasionally stopping to turn full around and make sure the third shooter wasn't sneaking up behind him.

As he approached the hotel on his right and the saloon on his left, there was a quiet, wooden scraping sound. He looked around. He spied the rifle aimed at him from a second-story hotel window and had just started to pull his Peacemaker, knowing he was too late, when a rifle cracked hollowly to his left.

Roscoe Deets stood on the saloon's front porch, aiming a Sharps carbine toward the hotel, slanted upward. Smoke curled from the rifle's barrel. There was a groaning sound, and Prophet

219

followed it to the second-floor window, out of which a man and a rifle fell.

Man and rifle hit the hotel roof simultaneously. The man rolled down the slanting roof and over the side to land with a heavy thud in the street ten feet in front of Prophet.

Prophet looked around cautiously and then walked forward to stand over Neal Hunter, who lay on his back with a puckered blue hole in the middle of his forehead. Blood trickled up out of the hole to run down into his wide-open right eye.

Movement ahead.

Prophet looked up to see the big blacksmith, Lars Eriksson, striding toward him, a rifle in his hands, the mule ears of his boots dancing in the morning breeze. As Eriksson stopped and jerked his rifle to his shoulder, Prophet started to raise his Peacemaker.

He hadn't gotten the revolver even half up before something hammered the back of his left leg, just above the knee. The knee buckled as the bark of the gun behind him reached his ears, and he dropped, twisting around and yelling, "Ah, *shit!*"

They were all going to swarm on him now like buzzards.

CHAPTER TWENTY-SEVEN

Prophet saw the short, mustached killer poke his head out from around the hotel's far front corner. He grinned and stepped out, leveling his carbine for a killing shot.

The thunder of a rifle on the saloon porch distracted him for the half-second Prophet needed to raise his sawed-off and trip both triggers.

The short, mustached killer's head turned bright red in the morning sun as it flew back off his shoulders to roll up against the saddle shop behind him. The killer's headless body, spewing blood, dropped to its knees and fell belly down in the street.

Prophet swung back around to face west, where Lars Eriksson lay on his side in the middle of the street, stretching his right hand out toward his old Spencer repeater.

Marshal Roscoe Deets was moving down off the saloon's front porch, aiming his Sharps rifle at Eriksson.

"I said hold it," the kid warned, loudly racking another shell into his rifle's chamber.

Eriksson turned his flushed, sweating face toward the town marshal, flaring his nostrils and curling his upper lip. "You go to hell!"

He lunged for the rifle.

Deets raised his carbine, aimed down the barrel, and drilled a slug through the side of the blacksmith's head, just above his right ear. Eriksson gave a sigh and rolled over, blood pooling in the street beneath him.

Boots thundered on the saloon's front porch. L.J. Tanner burst through the batwings, raising a Winchester and bellowing, "Oh, no! Oh, no you don't!"

Deets spun around toward the saloon owner, racking another cartridge into his carbine's chamber. Prophet whipped up his Peacemaker and before Tanner could get a single shot off, the bounty hunter and town marshal ripped several rounds each into Tanner's chest, causing him to fire his rifle into the porch ceiling and dance a bizarre two-step, turning two complete circles before tumbling backward over the porch's front rail, bouncing off a hitch rack with a snapping crack and piling up on his back in the street.

Prophet glanced at Deets. Lowering his smoking rifle, Deets glance back at him. Then Deets frowned and stared past Prophet toward the east. A clattering rose from that direction. A woman was loudly hurrrahing a galloping horse.

Prophet turned to see Verna McQueen's Morgan pull the chaise onto the main street from the north, moving so fast that the chaise's two right wheels left the ground and nearly dumped Verna McQueen herself into the street. The chaise dropped back onto all four wheels, jostling the woman violently. She recovered quickly and whipped her reins against the Morgan's back.

"He-*yahh*!" Verna wailed. "He-*yahhh*, you cayuse!"

She scowled over the horse at Prophet.

Prophet said, "Oh, shit," as the horse, buggy, and raging woman bore down on him. She was a half a block away and coming hard and fast, her hair blowing out behind her shoulders, dust billowing thickly up behind the fast-spinning wheels.

Prophet's wounded leg felt as heavy as stone. He couldn't move.

"Lou!" someone cried.

Pistols crackled.

Verna dropped the reins and sagged in the chaise's front seat.

The horse screamed and careened sharply to Prophet's right. The buggy fishtailed, Verna bouncing around on the seat like a rag doll in a cyclone.

The buggy's right side bounced off the saloon's front porch, breaking apart, wheels flying in all directions. As the buggy, now in two pieces, bounced over L.J. Tanner's inert form and rolled past Prophet, narrowly missing the bounty hunter, the Morgan galloped off to the west, whinnying shrilly and pulling only the double tree.

"Holy shit!" Prophet said, blinking against the dust and grit in his eyes.

As the dust cleared, he saw Verna McQueen lying only four feet behind him, all blood and dust and two staring eyes. She wasn't moving.

"Lou!" came the voice again.

Louisa came from around the far side of the millinery store, hobbling on a pair of wooden crutches and her stiff right leg. She wore her brown skirt, calico blouse, and shell belt with two holsters. She was holding one of her .45s, but now, squinting her eyes to see through the billowing dust, she holstered the Colt and continued shambling toward Prophet.

She stopped and looked around at Tanner, Verna McQueen, Neal Hunter, and Lars Eriksson. She glanced at Deets, who'd leaped onto the saloon steps to avoid being pummeled by the chaise. Now the young marshal took his carbine in one hand, ran the sleeve of his other arm across his mouth, and shook his head once.

"Roscoe!" came another female voice.

A pretty young Mexican woman came running along the street's right side.

"Roscoe!" she shouted again, holding the skirt of her red dress above her sandals.

"I'm all right, Lupita," Deets said, striding toward her. "It's okay. I'm all right. You shouldn't be out here, honey. You don't want to see this."

As Deets hurried over to his young wife, Louisa turned her gaze back to Prophet.

Prophet gazed up at her. "Don't you look fit as a fiddle."

Louisa looked at his bloody leg and pursed her lips.

"Now look at what you've done to yourself."

Prophet gave a snort. Then he looked at Verna's twisted body, and he frowned, puzzled.

"Her name was Duvall," Louisa said. "Doc Whitfield told me."

"Duvall?"

"It doesn't ring any bells?"

Prophet's eyes widened in shock. "*Handsome* Dave Duvall?"

"She was his sister. Tight bunch, you southern folk."

Prophet sighed, shaking his head. "So that's what all this was all about. Holy shit . . ."

There was a muffled crack from the east.

Prophet grabbed his Peacemaker and stared down the street. The sound seemed to have come from the bank.

Deets, who was holding his young wife in his arms, glanced over his shoulder at Prophet.

"Campbell," Deets said. "I reckon he didn't want to face that judge I had in mind for him. Don't worry—Bly and Carlsruud will." He glanced toward the barbershop, which doubled as a bathhouse. A CLOSED sign hung in its window.

Deets smiled shrewdly.

Louisa turned from Deets to frown down at Prophet. "Huh?"

"Long story," Prophet said.

Louisa dropped down beside him, unknotted his neckerchief from around his neck, and tied it firmly around his bloody leg. "Well, I have a feeling we're both going to have plenty of time to discuss it . . . over at Whitfield's. Come on—let's get you over there before you bleed out."

"Ah, shit," Prophet said, heaving himself to his feet. "That uppity sawbones ain't gonna like this a bit."

He limped down the street, angling toward the cross street and the doctor's house. Louisa shuffled along beside him on her crutches. Whitfield came around the corner ahead of them, driving a buckboard wagon, his medical kit on the seat beside him. He scowled as he looked around, spectacles glinting in the morning sun, and wagged his head in disgust.

"There's our ride now," Prophet said.

"Lou?"

"Hmmm?"

"I don't want to get shot again," Louisa said. "It hurts like hell."

Prophet laughed and kissed her cheek. "You're in the wrong line o' work, darlin'."

★ ★ ★ ★ ★

Bring Me the Head of
Chaz Savidge!
OR THE BOUNTY POACHERS

★ ★ ★ ★ ★

CHAPTER ONE

Louisa Bonaventure pulled one of her pretty pistols and said, "All right, Lou—how would you like to do this?"

"What's that?"

"I said—how would you like to do this?" The comely, hazel-eyed blond bounty hunter flicked open the Colt's loading gate and spun the cylinder, making sure all six chambers showed brass.

"I'm sorry," Prophet said, placing a hand behind his left ear. "I thought you said, 'Lou, how would you like to do this?' But my hearing has obviously been compromised by all your rants over the years. Probably sawed both eardrums down to nubs. Say it one more time, but speak a little slower and louder, will you, Miss Bonnyventure?"

Louisa arched a brow at him. "Excuse me for not finding the same humor in you that I'm sure the parlor girls do."

Prophet broke open his ten-gauge Richards coach gun, and looked down the barrels. Both tubes were loaded with fresh paper wads.

The big, ex-Rebel bounty hunter, born and bred in the north Georgia mountains, said, "You'll have to excuse *me* for being more than a little surprised that you asked my advice on how to do this job—one I've been practicing for a good three times longer than you have, I might add. It's just that on those too-few occasions that you've asked for my advice, you've failed to follow it."

"You're just sore that I doubted your tracking skills back there. All right—let me apologize." Louisa had holstered her first pretty Colt and was checking the second one.

"All right, go ahead." Prophet looped the sawed-off ten-gauge's leather lanyard around his neck and shoulder, so that the barrel of the wicked-looking gut-shredder peeked up from just behind his right shoulder.

He shucked his Winchester '73 from the saddle boot strapped to the saddle of his hammer-headed lineback dun, appropriately named Mean and Ugly. As he checked the loads in the long gun, he bestowed upon his curvy, peach-skinned, hazel-eyed partner an expectant look.

Instead of apologizing, however, Louisa turned her head sharply away and then shucked her own Winchester carbine strapped to the saddle of her brown and white pinto.

"I'm waiting," Prophet said.

Louisa racked a round into the carbine's breech, patted her horse's rump, and turned toward the thick copse of autumn-naked box elders and cottonwoods that the gray morning light was just now delineating. She and Prophet were in western Dakota Territory, and it was appropriately cold for mid-November.

"I said I'm waiting," Prophet repeated, setting his rifle on his shoulder and brushing past Louisa as he walked into the woods.

As Louisa followed, cradling her carbine in her arms, she said, "Forget it. I no longer feel apologetic."

"That's more like it."

"Huh?" she said behind him.

Keeping his voice low, Prophet glanced over his shoulder at her, grinning. "You had me worried there, girl. I've always held that when Louisa Bonaventure started to feel contrite about *anything,* hell would freeze over and the devil would get icicles in his beard." He glanced at the gray sky. "Hope it don't get that cold!"

Louisa turned her mouth corners down at him, and flared a nostril.

Prophet stepped carefully through the woods, trying to make as little noise as possible. He managed to snap a few twigs beneath his boots and cause dead leaves to crackle. He glanced behind him.

Louisa followed him off his right flank, about twelve feet away. She wore a cream Stetson, a brown knit poncho, and faded blue denim trousers with the cuffs stuffed into her riding boots. Her light-blond hair jostled over her shoulders. She didn't seem to be taking any more care with her steps than Prophet was, but he'd be damned if she didn't move as quietly as an Indian.

She wasn't the tracker he was, however. She'd lost the sign of the gang they'd followed out from Colton, where the outlaws plundered a saloon for fifty-two dollars three days ago, in a marshy area where several creeks forked in grassy country. She hadn't believed the killers had come south, because she hadn't seen the sign where they'd left the bog in rocky country. Prophet had seen it and he'd followed it.

He supposed they complemented each other that way—him and Louisa. She was pretty and lithe, quiet and stealthy, while he was ugly as sin, big and lumbering, but he could track a June bug across a roiling millpond.

Louisa was also ornery and impetuous, not always given to caution, whereas Prophet had learned during and after the war he'd fought in, and lost most of his family in, to be mild and cautious. He'd learned that life would end, so he'd learned to take his time. To live *lightly*, to enjoy the little things like a falling leaf or a pretty woman's fleeting smile on a bustling street.

That's likely why he and Louisa stayed together—or at least kept moving back toward each other after getting sick to death of each other and forking paths.

They complemented each other.

That and the fact that he loved the girl.

That and the fact that *she* loved *him,* though it would have taken long, slow Apache torture to get her to admit it.

That was the hell of it, he thought. They loved each other. That gave their lives a problem. Before they'd met up with each other, they'd had no such problems. They'd joined forces when they'd both been trailing . . . and killing . . . the Handsome Dave Duvall gang that had murdered Louisa's family down in Nebraska Territory.

Back then, before Prophet had met up with the pretty, stalwart blonde who had a killing fury burning through her, she'd looked as though she'd been born merely to wear pink ribbons and frilly dresses and to play gentle tunes on a parlor piano. For his part, he'd lived only to whore and play cards and hunt men for the bounties that funded such a devil-may-care lifestyle.

But now he lived for her, as well. And in this business, living for someone else could get you killed quicker than it takes a hammer to fall on a chambered round.

Prophet held up at the edge of the woods and stared into the clearing beyond. Louisa came silently up beside him, and dropped to a knee.

A small log cabin hunched at the far side of the clearing, maybe a hundred yards away. A thin, gray skein of smoke unfurled from the stone chimney climbing the cabin's left wall. A two-track trail jogged into the clearing from Prophet's left and ended in the barren, hard-packed yard that included a log barn just ahead and to the right, about fifty yards from Prophet's and Louisa's position.

Several joined corrals angled off the barn's far side. Prophet could see six or seven horses milling around the corrals, likely waiting to be fed and watered. It was still early but the sun would be up in a half hour.

A windmill and stock tank stood in the middle of the yard, between the barn and the cabin. The wooden blades clattered lightly in the morning breeze. That was good. The clattering would likely cover his clumsy approach. He just had to hope the horses didn't alert the men in the cabin to his and Louisa's presence.

And he had to hope there were no dogs. Dogs were not a man hunter's friend. Dogs could get you killed quicker than love.

He didn't see any dogs, though. He just hoped none returned from a night of hunting out in the fields to spy the interlopers and lift a ruckus.

Oh, well, you couldn't dot all your I's and cross all your T's. Life didn't come all wrapped up in certainty. We were all wolf bait, when you got right down to it. Some of us sooner than others . . .

A vision of a smoky battlefield covered in bleeding, howling, dying men swept in front of the bounty hunter's eyes. He quickly brushed it away with his gloved fist and said, "All right—let's check out the barn first. They might be holed up in there. We'll slip around to the right, stay close to the trees, and then you take the front and I'll take the back."

Louisa gave him a skeptical, faintly suspicious look. "Why am I taking the front?"

"You asked me how we're going to do this, right? Well, that's how we're gonna do it." Prophet started moving through the trees at the edge of the woods but stopped and turned back to her. "But if you're scared to take the front, just say—"

"Shut up, Lou."

"Right."

Prophet continued moving through the trees, stepping over branches, deadfalls, and dry leaves. In truth, he wanted Louisa to take the front because she was stealthier than he was. You

233

needed more stealth to enter the front of a place than the back.

He wasn't worried about her handling any incurred fire. There were few better than the Vengeance Queen, as she was called throughout the frontier, with a pair of six-shooters. She was no slouch with a carbine, either.

Prophet stopped when they were near the rear of the barn, with the barn between him and Louisa and the cabin.

"All right," he said, knowing that's all he needed to say.

Louisa stepped out of the woods ahead of him and, holding her Winchester in both hands, strode to the rear of the barn. Prophet stayed in the trees, watching her. She canted her head toward the barn wall, listening, then turned toward him and hiked a shoulder.

She slipped around the corner of the barn and walked toward the front. Prophet couldn't help taking a moment to admire how the young woman moved—straight-backed, long-legged, and cool. Utterly fearless.

Louisa moved as quietly as an Apache warrior, as though grass or gravel didn't dare crackle when she stepped on it. Prophet gave a wry snort at the thought.

When she'd slipped around the front of the barn, Prophet moved out of the trees. He looked around carefully as he moved to the barn's rear wall. There was a single, small door back here. It might be locked. He hoped it wasn't. Especially if the front doors were not locked. That meant Louisa would be on her own until he could run around to the front.

Quietly, gritting his teeth, he tripped the metal latch. It was rusty and loose, and it clattered a little when he tripped it. The door groaned on old, dry leather hinges. So far, so good. He stepped inside, blinking against the dense night shadows. The usual barn smells of hay and ammonia billowed against him.

He drew the door closed, so he wouldn't be outlined against the relative light beyond it, and moved ahead along the hard-packed earthen floor of the barn's main alley. He walked between two rows of stables that appeared empty. There was the smell of dry rot and horse piss, of straw, moldy tack, and mouse droppings.

He couldn't see very far ahead. It was too dark, and the ceiling support posts from which tack hung impeded his view. He heard no sounds except the muffled clattering of the windmill and the soft wheezing of the breeze under the barn's eaves.

There was a clipped grunt. It was a muttered, "Oh!" And then there was the thud of a body hitting the floor.

Prophet quickened his pace and raised his voice, "Louisa?"

He stopped, levered a round into the Winchester's breech, and aimed the rifle straight out from his shoulder, blinking against the barn's dense shadows.

He took another two steps forward, stopped again, and frowned.

A large, dark figure hung before him. Some farming or ranching implement, most likely. Maybe a hay harness.

Beneath and beyond the object, he saw another figure sitting on the barn floor. He could see blond hair falling down from beneath Louisa's hat. She was leaning back against the barn's large door, one knee up, the other leg stretched out before her. She reached out and picked up her rifle, and brushed it off with a gloved hand.

"Louisa?" Prophet said again, his voice sounding inordinately loud in the close, silent quarters.

His eyes were adjusting, and the light angling through the seams in the barn's walls and through two sashed windows at the front were intensifying.

"I'm all right," Louisa said in a strange, wooden voice as she slowly gained her feet.

Her attention was on the object hanging from the ceiling before her. Between her and Prophet.

He moved forward, swung carefully around the object, and slowly realized that it wasn't what he'd thought it was.

What he'd thought *they* were.

As he moved closer, he saw that they were not one object but several. Four, in fact. He stepped around the right side of the four people hanging from a rafter, and scowled, bile churning in his gut. There were four of them, and they were all facing Louisa and the front of the barn.

Prophet stopped a fair distance away from Louisa, who also stared up at what was apparently a family hanging there, ropes looped around their necks, strung over the beam and then tied off at the bases of the ceiling support posts behind them.

A balding man of middle age in worn coveralls.

A woman of roughly the same age, flecks of gray in her hair, which had spilled out of its once-neat bun. She wore a plain gray dress. She'd been wearing low-heeled black leather shoes but she must have kicked out of them when they'd hanged her. The shoes lay on the floor nearly directly beneath her stocking-clad feet.

A tow-headed young man of around sixteen or so hung beside the woman, tongue out, eyes tipped up toward the ceiling as though to get a look at his Maker.

A girl close to the same age as the boy, maybe a year or two younger, hung beside him. She was the only one who was naked save for a badly torn and soiled chemise, one strap hanging down her arm to reveal one tender, pale nubbin breast that appeared raw and chafed from manhandling.

The girl had a wide-eyed, startled expression. Her lower jaw hung slack. She had thick, curly, light-brown hair that was so badly mussed and spiked with straw and dirt that it didn't even look like hair anymore. She had many cuts and abrasions on her face. Her fingernails were bloody—likely from the blood of her savage attackers, whom she'd tried to fend off to little avail.

Feeling sick, Prophet turned to Louisa. It was startling, how she gazed up at the hanged family without expression. It was almost as though she wasn't really seeing them but was just standing there, gazing off into the distance, waiting for a train.

Prophet glanced to his left. The tack from four horses lay against the wall over there—four saddles, four saddle blankets, and four bridles. There were some coiled *riatas,* as well. The saddlebags and bedrolls were likely inside with the men to whom the tack belonged.

The men whom Prophet and Louisa were hunting.

Prophet turned back to Louisa. She turned to him, then, as well. Now her eyes were hard and cold, her lips set in a firm, straight line. Her chest rose and fell heavily as she breathed. Her cheeks were mottled red.

Her eyes bored holes through Prophet.

He almost thought he could hear the screaming in her ears, the loud thundering of the Vengeance Queen's heart.

A family had been murdered here. A girl raped. Not so different from what had happened to her own parents, to her own sisters and brother . . .

Prophet held up a placating hand. "Okay, now," he said. "Okay, now . . . just hold on, girl. We're gonna have to take this nice and . . ." He let his voice trail off as Louisa loudly pumped a cartridge into her carbine's action and wheeled toward the door behind her.

"Louisa, goddamnit, pull your horns in!"

But then she slid the door open with a loud grunt, and bolted outside.

CHAPTER TWO

"Louisa!" Prophet rasped, lunging for her and missing. He gaped at her from the barn's open doorway. "Get back here!"

She didn't stop. She didn't even hesitate. She strode straight away from the barn toward the cabin crouched about two hundred feet beyond, thin gray smoke unspooling from its chimney.

The sun wasn't up yet. The cabin looked stark and gray against the barren woods flanking it. Many yellow and brown leaves clung to the cracks between the shakes of the cabin's roof. Some slid around in the breeze, making dull scratching sounds.

Prophet's heart hammered as he watched the headstrong Vengeance Queen walk toward the shack as though she were going to join the killers for breakfast, and she was famished. Her blond hair jostled down her slender back. She carried the carbine down low in her right hand but now, halfway between the cabin and the barn, she raised it.

As she kept walking, she aimed at the cabin and fired.

Prophet started at the rifle's hiccupping crash. The bullet blew through the window just left of the door, making the flour sack curtain dance.

Magpies lighted from the trees behind the cabin, shrieking raucously.

"Shit!" the big bounty hunter groaned, moving out away from the barn and raising his Winchester '73.

Louisa jacked another round and fired.

That shot plunked through the window right of the door.

As Louisa kept walking, within twenty yards of the cabin now and closing quickly, men inside the shack began cursing incredulously. One voice rose louder than the others: "Wha—what the hell was *that?*"

Thumps rose and furniture barked as the killers scrambled out of their cots, likely reaching for weapons. Louisa stopped, pumped two more rounds through the second window right of the door, and then strode to the door itself.

As she tripped the latch and rammed the butt of her rifle against the door, throwing it wide, a man appeared in the shack's far left front window. He was shaggy-headed and he was wearing balbriggans. He looked around wildly, turning his head to his left as Louisa bolted through the door.

Prophet snapped his own rifle to his shoulder, and shot the man in the window before he could get his own rifle aimed at Louisa. The man yelped and stumbled back out of sight.

Prophet couldn't see the Vengeance Queen now, but he could hear the thundering blasts of her Winchester. She fired quickly, methodically. He could almost see her in his mind's eye, cooling picking out her targets.

He ran forward, pumping another round into his own rifle, resisting the urge to fire another round into the cabin. He might hit Louisa. Inside, beneath the steady thunder of her Winchester, men screamed and shouted and jumped around, causing chairs or cots to screech against the floor. Glass shattered; there was the wicked whine of a ricochet off an iron stove.

Prophet ran around the side of the cabin, heading for a rear door, if there was one. He ran hard, holding his Winchester up high across his chest, pumping his arms and legs. His hat blew off.

"That fool-crazy polecat!" he kept muttering. "That fool-crazy polecat . . . gonna get herself plucked and greased for the pan!"

Inside, the steady, rhythmic shooting continued. But now there were others shooting besides Louisa. One or two others were flinging lead as well. Prophet recognized the slightly more hollow pops of pistol fire. The rifle fire continued steadily until Prophet reached the cabin's rear corner.

Then Louisa's Winchester must have run out of lead.

Prophet dashed around the cabin's corner and then halted, throwing himself back against the cabin's rear wall. The back door flew open and a man lunged out, bellowing and staggering before he broke into a shambling run. He was short and stocky and tufts of ginger-colored hair stood up around the bald, freckled crown of his head.

He wore only balbriggans and wool socks. He had a shell belt and rifle in his right hand. He held a bundle of clothes under his right arm. He ran off into the trees, casting a desperate look back over his right shoulder at the cabin, where Prophet could hear only pistol fire now.

The shouting inside had died.

"Hold it!" Prophet shouted, leveling his Winchester on the man's spine.

The man snapped a wide-eyed look over his left shoulder, then turned his head back forward and lunged into a faster run. Prophet was about to pop a pill through the man's back, but then another figure lunged out the cabin's rear door.

Prophet wheeled as the second man dropped to his hands and knees.

He was tall, thin, and hawk-nosed. He, too, was only half-dressed. Blood shone on his longhandles and in a deep, nasty gash that ran from the nub of his cheek to his left ear, the lobe of which was gone, leaving only a ragged fringe.

The man turned his head toward Prophet.

"No, by god!" he bellowed, flaring his nostrils furiously and raising a smoking revolver in his right hand.

Prophet lined up his Winchester's sites on the man's forehead, and squeezed the trigger. The Winchester leaped and roared. The man's pistol popped. The bullet slammed into the wall of the cabin to Prophet's right. The man's head snapped wildly back, a quarter-sized hole puckering the skin in the middle of his forehead.

As the man flopped over on his back, a pistol barked once, twice from inside the cabin. The bullets hammered into the man's chest, causing his body to quiver.

"Save your lead, you crazy wildcat!" Prophet yelled. "He's dead!"

Racking a fresh round into his Winchester's breech, he took off running after the man who was getting away through the trees. He had to admit he was glad that Louisa was uninjured—or that at least she was still well enough to shoot a dead man twice. She'd dodged another bullet—or two dozen of them, rather. Her luck wouldn't hold, though. The luck of someone as crazy as Louisa was never did.

He swept his partner from his mind and concentrated on the killer bolting through the woods ahead of him.

Prophet was big and lumbering, but the man ahead of him was in his stocking feet, which slowed him down considerably. The bounty hunter gained on his quarry, who leaped deadfalls as he fled through the woods. Prophet leaped the same deadfalls, grunting, throwing out his arms and rifle for balance.

As the man left the woods and started running along the crest of a low rise, Prophet stopped and aimed the Winchester straight out from his right shoulder.

"Hold it, Savidge, or you're crowbait!"

The man whipped another fearful look over his shoulder but kept running. Prophet drilled two rounds into the ground around the man's feet. He jumped wildly, as though trying to avoid the slugs. He stopped, dropped his bundle of clothes, and raised his hands. He still had the rifle and cartridge belt in the right one.

"Turn around," Prophet ordered.

Chaz Savidge turned around. Prophet had recognized the bank robber, stagecoach robber, train robber, and cold-blooded killer from several wanted dodgers he'd carried around in his saddlebags for the past several years. Savidge was wanted in several states and territories. He had a two-thousand-dollar bounty on his head.

A bounty that size made even a seasoned man hunter like Lou Prophet's mouth water.

Savidge was an odd-looking bastard. He had a thin, ginger beard that clung to his face in patches. His forehead was high. It bulged at the top, like the crest of a granite crag. His eyes were dark and set improbably close together. His nose was long and hooked, his pale lips thin and chapped.

He was missing a front tooth, which Prophet could see when Savidge stretched his lips back and said, "You can go to hell!"

"We all can, Chaz. Drop the guns or I'll pump one through your belly, watch you die slow."

"You the law?"

"No."

"That's good, because what you did back there . . . comin' in when we was asleep, blastin' away . . . that was . . ."

Savidge let his voice trail as he focused his little, dark eyes on something behind Prophet. Prophet heard footsteps. They grew louder, and then he could hear Louisa breathing as she strode up behind him. The bounty hunter could smell his partner's distinct female aroma on the breeze. It was laced with the peppery odor of powder smoke.

Savidge gave a wry chuff and said, "Why . . . that's a *girl!*"

242

"Good eye, Savidge. Now, drop the guns or I'm gonna send you on to St. Pete and let him decide what to do with you. I doubt he'll have much trouble . . . once he riffles through all the paper you got on your head."

Savidge wrinkled his nostrils in frustrated defeat. He opened his right hand. The rifle and cartridge belt with its holster and Colt .44 dropped to the ground.

Savidge kept his eyes on Louisa, who stopped beside Prophet. She was thumbing fresh cartridges through her Winchester's loading gate. She didn't say anything as she regarded the killer coldly.

"Why, that's nothin' but a girl who . . . came in there . . . done all that."

Savidge was deeply confounded.

"Nothin' but a girl," Prophet said.

"Nothin' but," Louisa said, pumping a round into her Winchester's breech and taking one step toward Savidge.

"Louisa, take it easy," Prophet said.

"I'm gonna kill him," Louisa said coolly, staring at Savidge.

"Hey, now, wait a minute!" Savidge said, backing away, holding his hands up higher. "I done tossed my guns down. That was the deal!"

"What about the folks in the barn?" Louisa asked him.

Savidge stared at her, his little, too-close-together eyes darting around in their sockets like frightened mice scurrying around in a hole.

"Louisa, settle down," Prophet said. "We're taking him in alive."

"Why should he get to live?" Louisa said. "The folks in the barn didn't get to live."

"There's a two-thousand-dollar bounty on his head," Prophet told her. "Seems Uncle Sam wants this bastard alive so they can play cat's cradle with his head their ownselves. Don't know why

243

Sam should get all the fun, but that's the way it is. They won't pay if he's dead. I've dealt with Sam before."

Louisa just stared solemnly up at Chaz Savidge. Her blond hair blew around her shoulders in the wind. She had her Winchester aimed at Savidge from her right hip. "I don't care about the money."

"Maybe you don't, but I do. I, for one, have about three dollars and some jingle in my pockets, and my stomach's been growlin' for nigh on three weeks. Stand down, Louisa!"

"I'll buy you a meal in the next town, Lou," Louisa said in her dull, even voice, which she kept so low that Prophet could barely hear her above the breeze scratching around in the barren branches behind him. "I'll buy you some whiskey and even a whore. I know that's all you're worried about. Whiskey and whores and having enough money to gamble away. So I'll even slip you a few extra dollars to buy into a stud game. How would that be?"

Her voice fairly dripped with sarcasm.

Rage was beginning to boil inside of Prophet. "Louisa, you got little more jingle than I do. We do this for a living, not the religion of it. Now, stand down, partner!"

"I do it for the religion of it, Lou."

Prophet stomped up beside her. "Stand down!"

Chaz Savidge was flushed and flustered. He kept his hands up even with his head, palms out. He was breathing hard.

"What is she—*loco*? She can't just out an' out kill me. It ain't right. Especially a girl doin' it. That ain't *right*!"

"What's not right is you killing innocent folks. Raping innocent girls."

"I had nothin' to do with that! That was the others."

Louisa smiled grimly.

"It's true. I had none of that. That . . . that's just not how I am. I don't operate that way."

"Oh, I think you do."

Prophet reached over and jerked the rifle out of Louisa's hands. Inadvertently, she tripped the trigger. The bullet sailed off behind Savidge but not before drawing a red line across the outlaw's bulging left temple.

"Hey!" the outlaw screamed, brushing his hand across his forehead and looking at the blood on his fingers. "She's god-damn crazy!"

Prophet tossed her rifle away.

Louisa glared up at him for a full thirty seconds. Her jaws were so hard they made her cheeks dimple. "I got two more," she said, lifting the bottom of her poncho above the pearl handles of her pretty matched Colts.

Prophet leveled his Winchester at her belly. "If you use 'em on him, I'll shoot you."

She stared up at him, her right eyelid dropping slightly down over that eye. "You wouldn't. What's more, you couldn't."

"On principle," Prophet said, "I would. And I could. I don't do that. I don't kill in cold blood. And I'm not gonna let you do it, either."

"Mighty high principle for a man who has so few."

"I got that one."

"What about whiskey and whores?"

"Those I don't got." Prophet felt his nostrils flare as he held the Vengeance Queen's icy stare. "This one I got. I'm a bounty hunter. I stop when the hunt stops. I'm not judge and jury. I leave that up for them more qualified. If I don't stop there, where do I?"

"I don't think there's anyone more qualified, Lou." Louisa glanced at Chaz Savidge. "We saw his work. You saw that girl they raped. Probably ravaged her in front of her folks. Why wait for a man who never saw *her* slam a gavel down on this sick bastard? Besides, a lawyer might get him off. You know it happens."

"Then it'll happen, but we won't have no part in it." Prophet adjusted his gloved hand around the neck of the Winchester still aimed at his partner's belly. "We get Savidge to the train station and we haul his worthless ass back to Denver. We turn him in to the U.S. Marshal in the federal building there. We collect the two thousand dollars and be on our way."

Louisa glanced at Savidge.

She turned her opaque gaze back to Prophet. She walked up to him, stopped where the barrel of his Winchester was pressed taut against her belly, and then hauled off and slapped him. She slapped him so hard that the blow sounded like a pistol shot.

"Ouch!" Savidge said.

Prophet stared down at the girl. He grabbed the neck of her poncho, drew her to him violently, and kissed her. She didn't resist. She mashed her own lips against his, turned her head, placed her gloved hands on his face, and groaned like a wildcat in heat.

Prophet pulled his mouth back from hers and released her. Spittle stringed between their lips and broke. Louisa's cheeks were flushed, her chest rising and falling heavily as she breathed. She quirked her mouth corners slightly, then turned away sharply, retrieved her rifle, and strode back in the direction of the cabin.

Savidge shuttled his disbelieving gaze between the two bounty hunters. "Christ almighty!" the outlaw intoned, his heavy brows ridging above his eyes. "You're both fuckin' *loco*!"

CHAPTER THREE

Prophet and Louisa buried the dead family in four separate graves in a clearing behind the cabin. The hard work of digging four holes in the cold, hard, late-autumn ground took several hours, but burying the innocent dead was as much Louisa's way of doing things as *not* playing judge, jury, and executioner was Prophet's way of doing things.

He put his back into it.

Afterwards, he held his hat down low while Louisa said a few words over the mounded dark soil and the rocks they'd gathered to keep the predators out of the family's eternal resting place. Prophet had fashioned crosses out of dead branches and strips of rawhide, and sunk them into the ground at the head of each grave.

As for Savidge's three dead partners—Louisa insisted that nothing more be done to them than that they be dragged into the yard where the magpies, coyotes, and wildcats could feed. And that was just fine with Prophet. His back was sore from digging, anyway, and all of Louisa's prattle about whiskey had made him yearn for a drink.

After the dead killers were lying belly up in the yard and several crows were already waiting in a line along the peak of the cabin's roof, Prophet and Louisa fetched and mounted their horses. They'd already ordered Savidge into his own saddle, on his dappled gray with one black sock, and cuffed his hands behind his back. His ankles were shackled, the shackle's chain arcing beneath the dapple's belly.

Prophet had built the shackles himself, with the help of a savvy blacksmith, and the chain's length was easily adjusted. A large key opened each jaw-shaped, iron shackle.

The ugly outlaw stared down at his bloody brethren from beneath the edge of his flat-brimmed Stetson. He wore a sheepskin coat, knit scarf, and gloves. "Damn peculiar, the way you two are just gonna leave the boys out here. They were friends of mine, goddamnit. They were human, too, just like that family you took so damn long to bury."

In her characteristically soft, menacing tone, Louisa said, "Tell me, Mr. Savidge, did that family beg you and these three other dogs for their lives?"

Savidge looked at her dubiously. "What do you mean?"

"I'm asking you if they begged you not to kill them. And the girl—I bet she begged you not to rape her. I bet she begged you all the while it was happening, didn't she? Just as I bet her parents and her brother begged you to stop."

Louisa raised her voice slightly. "Didn't they, Chaz?"

Savidge chuffed and looked at Prophet. "What the hell's her problem, anyway? What kind of a question is that?"

"You killed 'em," Prophet said. "You should know."

Savidge looked at Louisa as though he were watching a hungry-eyed wildcat moving slowly toward him. Then he glanced at Prophet again, laughed mirthlessly, and said, "Just take me to the goddamn marshal in Denver. Hell, I'll feel a whole lot safer in the federal lockup. That girl there—she's just plain *loco*!"

"I think you just answered her question, Chaz," Prophet said, reining Mean and Ugly around and touching spurs to the horse's flanks. "And I think she just answered yours."

"You're both pure-dee, bonded *loco*!" the outlaw intoned as Prophet jerked the man's horse along by its bridle reins.

As Prophet, Louisa, and their prisoner loped out of the yard, heading southwest for the nearest train depot at the little settlement of Cody, in western Dakota Territory, a fine snow had begun to fall. Clouds had moved in while the two bounty hunters had dug the graves, and the breeze had turned cold.

Prophet thought they should have stayed at the cabin, but he hadn't bothered suggesting it. He knew enough about Louisa's haunted past to know that if they'd spent the night at the murdered family's home, she'd have been hearing the remembered screams of her own mother and sisters as the Handsome Dave Duvall gang had raped them, as well as the screams of her brother and father as they'd been murdered.

She wouldn't have gotten a wink of sleep. Prophet wouldn't have, either. He'd likely have been up all night, rocking the sobbing young woman in his arms.

Earlier he'd been ready to kill her. Or he thought he'd had. Now, he really didn't know. But that one rule of his meant a lot to him, maybe even more than Louisa did.

Nah, he wouldn't have killed her. He reckoned he'd never know for sure, though. Maybe he loved her enough to kill her at such a time, to save her from ruining them both. She didn't really value her life all that much, anyway, and he was convinced that deep down she knew why he'd have to kill her, and that she'd even want him to.

Because she valued his life more than her own.

Leastways, Prophet hoped he never had to weigh such a dilemma again. He'd been faced before with her killing unarmed men, but most of them had been at death's doorstep or Prophet hadn't been in a position to intervene.

No, he hoped he never had to weigh it again . . .

The snow continued to fall throughout the late afternoon, gradually growing from bran-like flakes dancing on the wind to cottony snowflakes. As the sun sank behind the clouds, and the light leeched slowly out of the gray sky, turning it a darker and darker blue, they made night camp in a creek bottom sheathed in box elders and cottonwoods.

As Chaz Savidge sat tied by the fire, Prophet gathered firewood while Louisa got a pot of coffee ready to boil and skinned the rabbit she'd shot late in the afternoon, knowing they'd need supper that night. Prophet was handy with a six-shooter. At least, he'd thought he was, before he'd met Louisa. But he wouldn't have attempted the shot Louisa had made from horseback with anything but his Winchester.

The Vengeance Queen, however, had calmly unsheathed one of her fancy Colts, clicked the hammer back, aimed straight out from her right shoulder, and nearly shot the jackrabbit's head clean off its shoulders from a good forty-five yards away, leaving the meat pristine.

The rabbit had lay kicking its headless body in a circle.

"Holy shit," Chaz Savidge had said with quiet, cautionary admiration.

"Do you like that, Chaz?" Louisa had said.

"I like it just fine . . . as long it's a rabbit's head you're blowin' off . . . and not mine."

"Give it time," Louisa had said, swinging down from her saddle. "Lou's gotta sleep sometime, doesn't he?"

She winked across her saddle at the prisoner, then strode off to retrieve the rabbit.

Savidge looked at Prophet. "That girl's plumb—"

"I know," Prophet growled, watching her weave among the trees. "Believe me, I know."

That night after they'd all eaten—including Savidge, though Louisa had seen little point in allowing a rapist and killer anything but week-old biscuits and water—they sat around the fire as the snow continued to fall, the large, cottony flakes sizzling in the flames and onto the rocks forming a ring around them.

Prophet cleaned his guns to keep his mind off not having any whiskey. Savidge's gang had apparently drained all their own bottles the night before, and the bounty hunter had found none anywhere in the cabin.

The settlers must have been teetotalers, God bless them . . . much to the bounty hunter's keen disappointment.

Louisa cleaned her own guns because it was a habit with her, in the same way that good Catholics went to mass every morning and sometimes every evening, and said their Hail Mary's.

She performed the task with sober, almost spiritual contemplation, her hazel eyes reflecting the fire's dancing flames. She even wiped down each of the bullets adorning her cartridge belt, slipping each back neatly into its little leather loop when she was finished.

Savidge sat against the tree he was tied to, a single blanket covering him from neck to stocking feet. He watched Louisa with fear and fascination until his eyes grew so heavy he couldn't watch her anymore, though Prophet knew he felt as though he had to keep an eye on her, to make sure she didn't swing one of those pistols at him, in much the same way she'd done to the rabbit, and blow his head off.

Savidge's head fell back against the tree. Then his chin dipped toward his chest, and low, ragged snores began crawling up out of his throat to flutter his lips.

When Prophet finished cleaning his Richards coach gun, he loaded the sawed-off gut-shredder and propped it against his saddle. He poured himself a last cup of coffee, lifting the pot from its hot stone perch with a leather swatch, and then offered the pot to Louisa.

"Mud?"

She looked at him obliquely, pressing the tip of her tongue to her lower lip, and then shook her head slowly, as though she'd had trouble understanding the question. As though she were

251

distracted by the heavy, solid weight of the pearl-gripped Colt in her hands.

Prophet set the coffee pot back onto its hot rock, then sagged back against his saddle. He drew his blankets up against the steely breeze and gently falling snow, blew ripples on the piping hot brew, and sipped.

He set the cup on his belly and looked across the fire at Louisa once more.

She was still running an oiled cloth over her six-shooter. But she was staring back across the fire at her partner, keeping her tongue pressed to her bottom lip in that funny, distracted way she'd been doing when he'd last looked at her. She was cleaning the pistol in her hands slowly, but she was thinking about something else.

She was thinking about something else and sort of smiling. At least, it might have been a smile. Whatever she was thinking about was lifting a flush in the nubs of her peach-colored cheeks.

Prophet frowned. "Girl, what do you have on your . . . ?"

He let his voice trail off as she shoved her pistol into its holster beside her, and rose. She had a faintly troubled, consternated look on her pretty face. She kept her eyes on Prophet as she stood on the far side of the fire, and shrugged out of her coat.

"Whoa, now," Prophet said, glancing at Chaz Savidge snoring against the tree to his right.

He turned to Louisa, who was now unbuttoning her shirt, her eyes fairly burning holes through her trail partner.

"Whoa, now," he said again, quietly, unable to take his eyes off the girl undressing before him.

He'd seen her naked before. But it always seemed a rare treat.

He'd made love to her before. But that always seemed an even rarer treat. Especially after an experience like the one

252

they'd had today—an experience that had opened Louisa's own, soul-deep, forever-agonizing wounds.

An experience that had opened up a gaping vacuum inside her—a vacuum save for the hammering misery that lived there like some prehistoric monster in a deep, dark cavern in remote mountains.

When Louisa had tossed away her shirt, she lifted her cotton chemise up over her head, and threw it away, as well, knocking her hat off her head as she did. Her thick hair rustled around her head in the breeze, dancing across her pale, naked shoulders.

"Christ," Prophet said as she leaned forward, her pink-tipped breasts sloping out away from her chest as she kicked out of her boots and began peeling her denims down her long, fine legs.

Either the fire had grown hotter or a fire inside Prophet himself had been kindled. He found himself flushed, heart beating insistently against his breastbone.

He glanced at Savidge once more. The outlaw was still asleep.

He turned back to Louisa. She stood naked before him, her denims and men's longhandles and pink drawers twisted around her bare feet. The flames licked up around her legs, caressing her perfect body with umber light and shadows.

The shadows rippled across her breasts. The nipples jutted with need.

Louisa stared at him hungrily, cupping her breasts in her hands, gently massaging them, squeezing them.

Prophet cleared his throat as he glanced at Savidge once more, and said, "Louisa, not now. Not *here!*"

She didn't say anything. She just folded her long, slender, buxom body into her blanket roll, breasts jostling, and rested her jaw on the heel of her hand, gazing at Prophet from across the fire. Her eyes were painted umber now by the flickering flames. Her jutting nipples brushed the blanket beneath her, the fire dancing across the outside curve of the one nearest the flames.

She was like some wild animal in heat, lying over there, lust pulsating in her eyes. Prophet could smell the lust on her, the uncontrollable compulsion to fornicate. She moved her legs beneath the blankets, writhing with desire.

Her bosom swelled as her chest rose and fell heavily.

Prophet glanced at Savidge. He turned back to Louisa. Sweat trickled down the side of his right cheek.

"Shit on a pole!" He'd never been able to deny her before, so he wasn't sure why he thought he could have done so now, Savidge or no Savidge snoring nearby.

The outlaw had had a long day. He'd likely sleep through it.

Prophet set his coffee aside, rose quickly, breathing hard now as he stared at the girl's long body lumping her bedroll comprised of sewn-together, striped trade blankets. She writhed slowly, hungrily, staring at him like a she-wolf in the keenest, most agonizing heat imaginable, a look of grim seriousness making a stone mask of her face.

Prophet grabbed his Winchester and leaned it against a tree near Louisa. He tossed another log on the fire.

After glancing at the snoring prisoner once more, he kicked out of his boots, shrugged out of his coat, and skinned out of his shirt, jeans, and longhandles. The air only a few feet away from the fire was cold, but it was so hot inside his skin that the air near the fire—near Louisa—was hot enough to give him the fantods.

Naked, he moved to her.

She rose to her knees, letting the blankets slide off her shoulders, down her back. Staring up at him from beneath her brows, she cupped him with one hand, gently massaged him with the other hand. As she did, a light grew in her eyes and her lips very gradually began to slide back from her teeth. Prophet wasn't sure if it was a smile or a snarl. It caused chicken flesh to rise across his shoulders.

Louisa bowed her head and closed her mouth over him.

"Shit . . . on . . . a . . . pole!" he wheezed through gritted teeth, grinding his heels into the ground.

She toyed with him, bringing his blood to a near boil, for close to a minute. Then, unable to restrain her own needs any longer, she slid her mouth back off of him, and slumped down into the bedroll, extending a hand to him. Her cheeks and breasts were mottled red.

Prophet dropped down into her blanket roll, and took her in his arms as she rolled onto her back, turning to face him.

She wrapped her arms around his waist and flattened her hands on his buttocks, scuttling down beneath him and raising and spreading her knees, giving him plenty of room. She groaned. She gasped softly as he mounted her, and when he slid himself inside her hot, waiting portal, she gave a mewl that rose from deep in her belly.

She arched her back, threw her head back against the ground, and bucked up against him, meeting his downward thrusts, which quickly grew savage as his own desires grew to a vehemence that matched the woman's own.

"Those bastards," she cried, digging her fingertips into his ass, bucking up against him and turning her head from left to right and back again. "Oh, those bastards!"

"I know, Louisa," Prophet said, toiling away on top of her, placing his hands on both sides of her face and using his thumbs to slide her sweat-damp hair back away from her feverish cheeks. "Let it go. Let it all go."

"Bastards!" she sobbed, groaning.

"I know."

"Bastards!"

"Let it go."

"Devils!"

"Let 'em go, honey!"

She opened her eyes suddenly. She lifted her head up off the ground and pressed her mouth hard against his, kissing him as they continued to hammer away at each other like two lovers who'd been apart for a long, long time. She stuck her tongue in his mouth, nibbled his lips until he thought they would bleed, and then she squeezed her eyes shut and gave his right shoulder a violent shove with the ends of her fists.

Prophet rolled onto his back.

Louisa climbed on top of him, breathing hard, the sweat dripping down her body showing golden in the firelight. She held his staff, impaled herself on it, began grinding up and down.

Up and down.

Up and down.

She was mewling like a trapped wolf now but Prophet had lost all concern, so enraptured was he, as always, by the girl's insane, pain-induced desire that always reminded him of a volcano that had been waiting for eons to blow its top.

At one point in their violent thrashing, Prophet saw sparks rise over Louisa's left shoulder. A corner of their blanket had leaped into the fire. Flames were chewing away at it, gray smoke rising.

Prophet rose to a sitting position, knocking Louisa onto her back between his legs, where she lay writhing, a faraway look in her eyes—a golden-skinned beauty bathed in firelit sweat. Her breasts and belly rose and fell and expanded and contracted as she breathed, clawing at Prophet's broad chest and groaning.

Quickly, Lou slapped the blanket's flames out against the ground, and then rolled Louisa onto her back, and finished her.

He knew she'd finished by the eerie echoing of her scream that always reminded him of the vaulting, catlike cry of some mysterious forest beast he'd once encountered in the Oregon mountains, years ago.

Prophet held her till she slept.

Then he rose, dressed, built up the fire once more, and crawled into his own blanket roll.

The frenzy of the dustup had allowed Savidge to slip his mind.

He whipped a look at the outlaw now, whom the fire's built-up flames now revealed more clearly, sitting against the tree he was tied to, eyes open and staring in wary befuddlement.

The ugly killer shook his head slowly, his lower jaw sagging. "Yessir," he said tonelessly, "when I see that U.S. Marshal in Denver, I'm gonna give him a big, fat ole kiss on the mouth. You two are *loco*!"

CHAPTER FOUR

It snowed just enough during the night to make the ground white the next morning. While the squall had pulled out and the sun was rising in a cloudless sky at seven a.m., a deeper chill than yesterday's now laced the breeze.

Prophet crunched through the half-inch of fresh powder and dumped his armload of wood beside the fire he'd built when he'd first risen from his blankets. His black enamel coffee pot gurgled where it hung on its iron tripod over the snapping, crackling flames.

The bounty hunter lifted the collar of his buckskin mackinaw against the chill and turned to where Louisa was draping a feed sack over her pinto's snout.

"Coffee's almost rea—"

Prophet stopped and turned his head toward the north. He'd heard something. Mean and Ugly must have heard it, too, because the hammerheaded dun, tied to a picket line near Louisa's and Savidge's mounts, whinnied inside his feed sack, and shook his head in warning.

Prophet rose and retrieved his Winchester from where it had been leaning against a box elder.

"What is it?" Louisa said.

Just then Savidge gave a startled gasp as he lifted his head from a dream. "Oh, Jesus!" He looked around, blinking. "I dreamt a big ole silvertip had just wandered into camp, and here I was, all trussed up like a hog for the slaughter!"

"Shut up," Prophet said, racking a round into his Winchester's breech and moving slowly into the trees north of the camp.

"What is it?"

"I said shut up."

"You're actin' awful owly for someone who got as much as you did last night," Savidge drawled.

"Shut up," Louisa told him, retrieving her own carbine.

"Heard somethin'," Prophet told her. "Not sure what . . . but somethin'."

Beyond the narrow swatch of woods, a grassy hill rose to a low ridgeline. The snow-dusted, autumn-cured bromegrass carpeting the slope whipped and danced in the breeze. Prophet was halfway through the woods when he stopped and quietly racked a cartridge into the Winchester's breech.

A rider had appeared, following the line of the ridge from the east, moving from Prophet's right to his left.

Another rider appeared behind the first one, riding out from behind a chokecherry thicket. There was another and another until there were four men riding along the ridge before the first rider swung his horse off the ridge and angled down the slope toward Prophet.

The others swung their own mounts around to follow the first man down the incline.

"Halloo, the camp!" the first rider hailed, waving an arm.

He was a big man in a buffalo coat wearing a peaked buffalo cap with earflaps tied beneath his chin. Tatters of snow-white hair poked out from under the cap. The man's face was bright red from the cold. His nose was especially red. Shaped like an ax handle, it glowed as red as a ripe apple hanging from a tree in late September.

"Friend or foe?" Prophet called.

The lead rider grinned at that, showing brown-encrusted

teeth beneath his sweeping white mustaches. "Lou Prophet, if that's you down there, you wild Rebel cayuse, I'm foe!" He leaned back in his saddle and bellowed a laugh that sent a pair of crows cawing out of the higher branches.

"Foe all the way, yessir!" he said through his laughter.

Prophet studied the man, able to more clearly make out his features now as he approached the bottom of the hill. "Ben Ryder, is that you, you hog-walloping, blue-tongued bastard?"

Ryder laughed and slapped his thigh.

Ryder reined his strawberry roan to a stop at the edge of the trees, and swung heavily down from his saddle. He was roughly Prophet's height—six-foot-four—but he was far heavier in the gut, which shelved out his buffalo coat. "How you been, Proph?" he said, chewing off a glove and throwing out his bare hand toward the bounty hunter.

Prophet shook it. "I can't complain overmuch, Ben, and even if I could, who wouldn't shoot me for it?" Grinning, he glanced at the three other men riding up behind Ryder. "Well—say, you got the same group together. Hidy, Kinch," he said, smiling at the shortest man of the group, just now reining his steeldust to a halt and leaning forward against his saddle horn.

Kinch, a rangy fellow with drooping, Mexican-style mustaches, returned neither the greeting nor the smile.

"Hidy, Coyote—you're lookin' no worse for the wear," Prophet said before sliding his gaze to the third man of the group, also easily the tallest. "Ghost, how you been?" Ghost Callaghan was two inches over seven feet tall. Still, he was known to move with uncanny stealth, like a ghost in the night, thus the moniker.

Ghost merely shrugged his shoulders and raised his hands as though in surrender to the question. His sharp-featured face was easily as large around as a full-sized dinner plate. His eyes were weirdly spaced a good three inches apart.

"Still a chatty lot—I'll give them that," Prophet said.

Ryder chuckled. "You know I'm partial to a quiet trail, Proph. I reckon that's why we never rode together. I couldn't think straight with all your palaver!" He sniffed the breeze blowing through the trees. "Say, is that Arbuckles I'm windin'?"

"Sure is," Prophet said, swinging around and beckoning as he tramped back to the fire. "Oughta be done right about now. Follow me in, boys, and I'll fill your cups." He raised his voice. "Louisa, hold your fire. We're among friends!"

"Friends, huh?" Louisa scoffed as Prophet and the others, all four leading their horses, moved through the trees.

Prophet glanced around the group as they tied their mounts to branches at the edge of the camp.

"Ben Ryder, Kinch Duggan, Coyote Perry, and Ghost Callaghan—you all remember my lovely partner, Miss Louisa Bonaventure."

"These men are no friends of mine," Louisa pronounced. "And I resent your bringing them into camp, Lou. They're animals."

Ben Ryder canted his head to one side in sadness. "Let's not be that way, Vengeance Queen! It's been a long time—goin' on two years now, I s'pect, since my eyes were last allowed to feast on your lovely and enchanting countenance." He opened his arms. "Come on over and give ole Ben a hug!"

"Go to hell."

Prophet said, "Now, Louisa, that's no way to act toward trail brothers. Ben and me and Coyote and Ghost go back a long ways. We all turned bounty hunter around the same time, just after the unchecked War of Northern Aggression, and been swappin' lies ever since."

Prophet laughed, though Louisa didn't crack a smile.

Prophet broke the laugh off abruptly, incredulously, and said, "Boys, grab your cups and go over and help yourself to the java.

261

Don't mind my partner. She woke up on the wrong side of the old mattress sack, but she's not so trigger happy before noon."

"Damn near *burned* her mattress sack right *up* last night!" snorted Chaz Savidge. "Shoulda seen the way these two was goin' at it. Like two rabid dogs in heat. I never seen the like! Say, I could use a cup of that belly wash my ownself. You boys have your fill but leave me a swallow or two, will ya?"

"Say, who do we have here?" Ryder asked, on one knee by the fire and using the leather swatch to remove the coffee pot from the tripod hook.

He was staring at Savidge.

"Nobody," Louisa said, crossing her arms on her chest.

"No, no. That ain't nobody."

Ryder filled his cup, then turned the pot over to Kinch, waiting in line with the other two men. The fat, older bounty hunter sipped his coffee as he stared across the fire at Prophet's and Louisa's prisoner. He sipped again, thoughtfully, then lowered the cup, wrinkling his snow-white brows in recognition, and pointed across the flames.

"Say, that . . . that there is . . . that there is *Chaz Savidge!*"

"Chaz Savidge?" said Kinch Duggan as he filled Coyote Perry's coffee cup. "Who's Chaz Savidge?"

"Chaz Savidge is one of the slipperiest *hombres* known to run roughshod over the western frontier. Why, if I remember, he's wanted in a good half-dozen states and territories!"

"You don't say," said Coyote Perry, his steaming cup in hand.

"One and the same," Prophet said.

"Don't he have somethin' like two thousand dollars on his head?" Ryder was studying Savidge, who was blushing like a schoolgirl from all the attention.

"Two thousand, give or take," Prophet said, standing a little back from the fire, holding his Winchester atop his right shoulder. "Somethin' like that."

Holding his cup of hot coffee in one hand, the hulking Ghost Callaghan had slipped back away from the fire to walk up in his stealthy way behind Louisa. He crouched now, nearly touching his wedge-sized hawk's nose to the woman's hair. Drawing in a deep breath, he closed his eyes and quirked his mouth corners in a mesmerized smile, savoring the Vengeance Queen's aroma.

Louisa wheeled and buried the toe of her riding boot in the big man's crotch. She hadn't pulled the kick a bit but gave the giant all she had.

Ghost jackknifed violently, expelling a loud, ragged groan of displaced air. He dropped his coffee cup.

Red-faced, he crossed his hands over his battered groin. He groaned and staggered backward, bunching his lips and glaring up in fury at Louisa from beneath the single, shaggy brow trailing across the ridge above his wide-set eyes.

"Ghost, what in the hell were you thinkin', pard?" Ryder regaled the giant. "Where are your manners? Were you born in a barn? Don't you know it ain't polite to go stealin' up on a girl like that? And, in the Vengeance Queen's case, don't you know it's just plain *dangerous?*"

Kinch Duggan said, "Ghost, goddamnit, you embarrass us all!"

Coyote Perry sipped his coffee, chuckling.

Ghost remained bent forward, groaning and grunting and holding his battered balls in his hands.

"Well, that'll learn him," Prophet said, opening and closing his hand around the neck of his shoulder-propped repeater.

"I want to be the first to congratulate you, Proph," Ryder said with a sincere dip of his chin. He turned to Louisa and did the same again. "And you, too, Miss Louisa. That's quite a payday you got there. A pair of bounty hunters could live a good, long time on three thousand dollars."

"Not the way Lou goes through it," Louisa said.

"Three?" Prophet turned to Ryder. "I thought the reward was two thousand." He slitted one eye. "Say, Ben, do you know somethin' I don't know? And . . . you weren't after ole Savidge your ownselves, now, were you, boys?"

"Of course they were," Louisa answered for the others. "What else do you think they're doing way out here in the middle of nowhere? Do you think it's just a coincidence they rode into our camp this morning? They've likely been on Savidge's trail for months."

Silence.

The newcomers glanced sheepishly around at each other. Even Ghost did as he slowly straightened from his crouch, his broad, craggy face deep-lined and flushed from misery.

Finally, Ben Ryder laughed and shook his head. "Okay. All right. You got us, Miss Bonaventure. Should have known you'd figure it out. I was gonna mention it sooner or later, but I gotta admit I was a little dumbfounded to see the outlaw here in your camp. I mean, there's just the two of you and there's five of us in my group, and we couldn't snag him, so, hell—I reckon we got us each a slice of humble pie to eat. Big ones. There you have it."

He sighed, shrugged, and sipped his coffee. "You two brought down one of the slipperiest *hombres* on the frontier, and there's nothin' we can do about it but congratulate the victors and drink your coffee. I reckon that'll have to do, eh, boys?"

Ryder laughed incredulously, and took another sip.

"I reckon that's all we can do," groused Kinch sadly, crouching to refill his cup.

Ghost, who rarely spoke, spat in his guttural, simple-minded way through gritted teeth while glaring at Louisa, "She kicked my oysters so far up my belly they won't shake down till spring!"

"Ghost, you had it comin'!" Ryder said.

"It hurts like hell!"

"How 'bout if I kick 'em into your throat?" Louisa asked the savage giant. "Then you won't have to think about 'em till next Christmas. Neither will the syphilitic doxies down in Deadwood."

Ghost flared his large, pitted nostrils at her.

"Louisa," Prophet scolded. "That's enough. Can't you see the poor man's in agony?" He turned to Ryder. "Allow me to apologize for my partner's poor behavior."

"Only if you'll accept my apology for that of the big man, Lou."

"Deal. Say, what's this about a three-thousand-dollar bounty on ole Savidge's ugly head, Ben?"

Ryder backed up to a log, pinched his buckskin trousers up his broad thighs, and sat down with a grunt. "They changed the reward, Lou. It ain't two thousand no more. Uncle Sam upped it a thousand to three."

"I'll be damned," Prophet said, raking a gloved hand down his cheek and studying his prisoner sitting back against the tree.

Savidge wore a self-satisfied grin. "Shit, whoever gets a three-thousand-dollar reward on his head? Has Black Bart ever had three thousand dollars on *his* head?"

Louisa said, "As far as I know, Black Bart never raped and murdered the governor of Utah's granddaughter."

"That'll do it," said Kinch. "I bet that right there's the reason."

It was true. Chaz Savidge and the now-dead rest of his gang had run down a stagecoach on which the granddaughter of Utah's territorial governor had been traveling with her aunt. She'd been a saucy twelve year-old, and apparently Savidge's boys hadn't been able to resist her.

Nor had they been able to resist killing the girl with a rock once they'd finished with her.

They'd killed nearly everyone on the coach, including the

girl's aunt. A former Indian agent had survived his wounds long enough to tell the grisly tale to a sheriff's posse.

"Three thousand dollars," Prophet said, rubbing his cheek in awe. "Me an' Louisa gonna be shittin' in high cotton!"

"That's only four nights in Dodge City for you, Lou."

Ryder walked over to the fire to refill his coffee cup, draining the pot as he did and setting it on the ground. "That ain't all that's changed about the bounty on Savidge's head, Lou."

"Oh? Pray tell!"

Kinch was sitting on a rock near Ghost. Grinning devilishly, he said, "You don't need to take in nothin' but his head."

Louisa hiked a brow. "What's that?"

Ryder said, "The reward has been changed to 'Dead or Alive.' You can take him in either way. It says in smaller print at the bottom that if ya kill him, you can just bring his head in for positive identification."

Coyote said, "Apparently, the governor was gettin' frustrated that nobody was able to run down the beast, so he upped the offer and made the job a whole lot easier."

He and the others turned to the prisoner.

Sitting against his tree, Savidge looked around at the others staring at him with renewed interest, and blinked in horror. "Don't none of you get any ideas." His gaze landed on Louisa. "My head'll stay right where it is, thank you. You got no cause to go sawin' it off!"

"Louisa, stand down!" Prophet said, when he saw how his partner was looking at Savidge.

CHAPTER FIVE

Ryder chuckled. "Temptin', ain't it, Miss Bonaventure? Wouldn't have to feed him or listen to his bullshit. Wouldn't have to tie him up every night, tie him to his saddle every morning. I assume you're takin' him back to Denver. That's a fair piece!"

"We'll manage it," Prophet said.

Ryder looked at him. The fat man blinked slowly. He was moving to his right, sort of toeing the ground, trying to look casual as he traced a semicircle around Prophet, moving up on the bounty hunter's left side, exposing him to the creek side of the camp.

Prophet also "casually" kicked a stone and moved to stay on the east side of Ryder. As he did, he saw the others spreading out around him and Louisa, their hands hanging down over the handles of their guns. Louisa had noticed the movement. She turned her head slowly back and forth, rolling her gaze around, keeping the men in the periphery of her vision.

As she did, she backed up, not wanting them to get directly behind her where she couldn't see them.

Prophet moved up to stand in front of Ryder, keeping the fat bounty hunter between himself and the creek.

"Say, Ben, I been wonderin'," Prophet said, scratching the back of his head and scowling with feigned pensiveness, "where's your old pal, Spider Dotson?"

Ben stopped his slow stroll, and smiled, crossing his arms on his broad chest. "Spider? Oh, well . . ." He scowled suddenly, sadly. "Spider's dead, Lou. Took a bullet down in Wichita. We was takin' in an owlhoot named Harley Mason, and Mason got the drop on us, I'm afraid. He was sittin' in a privy and fired through the half-moon in the door!"

"What a way to go," said Coyote Perry, shaking his head sadly, though he had a tense look on his pale face as he slowly moved his hands down toward the grips of the two pistols on his hips. "Shot by a drunk owlhoot through a privy door!"

"That's funny," Prophet said.

"Nothin' funny about it, Lou," Ryder said, offended.

"I could swear I just seen ole Spider moving in them trees back there along the creek."

He'd just gotten "creek" out when he whipped his Winchester down off his shoulder, aimed, and fired not six inches to the left of Ben Ryder's left ear.

The blast evoked a shrill yelp from the woods along the creek. At the same time, Ryder himself screamed and, stumbling back away from Prophet, clamped a hand over his ringing left ear while fumbling a long-barreled Smith & Wesson from the holster on his right thigh.

Prophet pumped another round into the Winchester's breech and popped a pill into the fat's man's belly. As he cocked the long gun again, he saw and heard Louisa go to work with her two fancy Colts, sending Kinch Duggan and Coyote Perry dancing off into the trees, triggering their own pistols into the air or the ground, bellowing.

Ghost had just unholstered his own six-shooter and was aiming at Louisa, when Prophet raked out a sharp curse and flung a round into the side of the giant's head, just above his left ear.

Ghost's own shot sailed wild as he staggered sideways.

Louisa wheeled and triggered both her Colts into the big man's chest.

Ghost pinwheeled and stumbled off into the woods before falling with a loud, crackling thump and lay kicking.

Kinch lay unmoving on his side, but Coyote was trying to heave himself up onto his hands and knees. As he reached for his dropped revolver, Louisa calmly walked up to him and finished him with one round to the crown of his skull.

Prophet walked over to where Ben Ryder lay on his back, clamping both hands to his bulging belly, which was oozing blood through the ragged hole in his buffalo coat. His red face was pain-wracked. He threw his head back and howled.

"Why, you wily Rebel sonofabitch!" he yelled, sobbing, casting his pain-bright gaze to Prophet.

"Tryin' to poach a bounty, eh, Ben?" Prophet said. "We took Savidge down fair an' square. He's ours."

"Ah, shit," Ryder said, grunting, "We been trackin' that bastard for weeks. We couldn't believe it when we seen you two ahead of us. We . . . we just couldn't let him go. Goddamn you, Lou, you deafened me." He brushed a hand toward his left ear. "I can only hear church bells tolling in that ear! Otherwise, nothin'!"

"They ain't tollin' for you, Ben."

Ryder glared up at the big bounty hunter standing over him. "Look what you done—you went and killed your old pal, Ben Ryder, you ornery sonofabitch!"

"About one pull of a whore's bell before you would have killed me, Ben." Prophet glanced at Chaz Savidge looking on in grave distress. "And sawed ole Savidge's ugly head off."

Savidge made a sour expression. "Savage!" the outlaw wailed at Ryder. "Damn savages—fixin' to hack a man's head off for profit!"

"Ah, hell," Ryder said, breathing heavily now, his face turning pale and sweat-bathed as he looked over at Savidge, "you're just a child rapist and murderer."

He gave a ragged sigh, and his body fell slack. His chest and belly stopped rising and falling. His hands fell to the ground. He turned his head to one side and half-closed his eyes.

Louisa had walked over to stand beside Prophet, staring down at Ryder.

She glanced at her partner. "You knew?"

"As soon as I saw them," Prophet said. "None of those tinhorns has taken down their own bounty in years. When he made the mistake of sayin' there were five in his group, I started looking around for Spider. He's the best shot of the bunch, which ain't sayin' much."

"Good on ya, Proph!" Savidge said, delighted, an enervated shine lingering in his gaze. "I knew you could do it. Two against five, and you took 'em all down quicker than a whore can blow a—"

Prophet cut him off with, "Don't get any ideas."

He'd spoken to Louisa, who was staring dubiously down at their prisoner.

"Yeah, don't get any ideas!" Savidge echoed the bounty hunter.

"I'm not gonna cart a bloody ole head back to Denver. I've had to do that before, and it wasn't purty *or* sweet-smellin'!"

Louisa narrowed a speculative eye at the sky. "It's cool enough." She looked at Savidge again. "He wouldn't get to smelling too awful bad. Leastways, not any worse than he smells now."

Savidge made a face, and shuddered.

Late that afternoon, Josephina Hawkins adjusted the powder-blue print dress she'd donned after her hot bath, and walked to her kitchen window.

Since she'd bathed in the kitchen, whose windows faced the bunkhouse on the other side of the yard, she'd pulled the flour sack curtains closed. When she and George Hawkins had first been married ten months ago, and Josephina had moved off her parents' small farm and into Hawkins's log cabin, she'd sewn little felt roses into the curtains, to lend them color.

Now, the little blood-red roses danced against the window fringed with frost and dusted with the snow that had been falling all day, foretelling another long—no, endless—Great Plains winter.

As Josephina stared out the window at the bunkhouse, which was a boxlike, one-room log cabin with a brush roof and a single ladder-back chair sitting against the wall just left of its plank-board door, the door itself opened. Josephina felt a flush rise in her cheeks as the hired man, Henry Otherday, stepped outside, smoothing his thick, coal-black hair back with one hand and then donning his Stetson hat with the other.

Josephina took two steps back away from the window, which was finely scraped waxed paper stretched between brittle sashes. The paper made annoying popping and wheezing sounds when the breeze blew it, which it was doing now.

Mr. Otherday stood looking around for a time, as though judging the weather. He wore blue denims and a corduroy jacket over a cream wool shirt and black neckerchief. His dark hair hung down over his ears. He held out one of his large, brown hands, as though to catch the downy flakes that were falling, and then brought his palm to his mouth, and licked it.

"Oh," Josephina laughed. "Oh, my gosh. He's eating snow!"

She wasn't sure why that thrilled her, but it did. She couldn't imagine her husband, Mr. Hawkins, ever doing such a thing. But then, Hawkins was eighteen years Josephina's senior, and Mr. Otherday was probably right around Josephina's age of nineteen.

He'd been working for Mr. Hawkins since just before the roundup. Mr. Hawkins wanted to carry the young half-breed

271

over the winter, because his rheumatism was making it hard to keep up with even his less taxing winter chores, and then he'd have ready help in the spring for calving and branding.

At least, that's what Mr. Hawkins had told Josephina. Josephina secretly opined that the real reason her husband wanted to keep a hired man on the place was so that he could spend more time at the woodcutters' camp down on Mulberry Creek. There was a small saloon there, which employed three girls of various ages.

Josephina wasn't sure why, but her ears did not burn at the notion of her husband as a whoremonger. Rumors about his infidelities to his first wife had circulated throughout the county, so Josephina had known what she'd been getting into when she'd accepted the man's marriage proposal.

She hadn't married him out of love, anyway. She'd married him because her parents couldn't afford to support five daughters and two sons on their little dirt farm five miles from here, and she'd needed a place to live. Otherwise, she herself might have ended up working for room and board down at the woodcutters' camp and enduring all manner of indignity just to feed herself.

Now she gave a little gasp of excitement as Henry Otherday began walking toward the cabin. Her heart lurched in her chest. At the same time, shame caused her ears to burn. She was a married woman. She had no right to feel so light in the head at the prospect of enjoying a meal and maybe part of an evening with her husband's hired man.

The two of them—Josephina and Henry Otherday—alone in her husband's cabin!

Mr. Hawkins's own transgressions gave her no right to transgress in a similar way. But then, she was only cooking supper for the hired man, she reminded herself. She had no intention of letting things go any further than that. In fact, the thought increased the burning in her ears, and added a shrill, admonishing hum.

It caused her heart to flutter and her breath to grow short.

She'd been raised a good Christian girl. In fact, her mother had read to Josephina and her sisters and two brothers from the Good Book right up until the very night before Josephina married George Hawkins. If Josephina's family knew that she was entertaining a man alone in her husband's cabin tonight, they'd likely disown her.

Outside, the sound of footsteps grew. There was a thump as the hired man stepped up onto the small boardwalk fronting the Hawkins's shanty.

A light knock sounded against the door.

Josephina gave another gasp, stepping back.

Oh, dear Lord—what had she done!

CHAPTER SIX

"Please, come in, Mr. Otherday," Josephina said, turning quickly toward the range, pretending that she'd been tending the two chicken leg quarters frying in a small, cast-iron skillet and not staring at the door and having second thoughts about inviting the hired man into Mr. Hawkins's cabin for supper.

The door squawked open, giving a little shudder on its leather hinges. Josephina felt a breath of cool air blow in to caress the backs of her legs and her bottom. On that breath of cool air, she smelled the sagey, manly musk of Mr. Otherday coupled with the infernal stench of horse and cow manure that lingered forever over the ranch yard.

The young man's smell, a familiar one now, caused a nerve to jerk to life in Josephina's belly.

Turning the chicken in the pan, Josephina glanced over her shoulder. "Good evening, Mr. Otherday. Supper's almost ready. You can peg your hat and coat there by the door. There's water on the stand, if you need to wash."

Mr. Otherday offered a cordial smile touched with a shyness that Josephina had detected in the young man the very first time he'd smiled at her, when Mr. Hawkins had finally introduced the two a full three days after Otherday had been hired and living in the little bunkhouse.

It hadn't been much of an introduction. Mr. Hawkins had just said, "This is Henry Otherday, Jo. He'll be stayin' in the bunkhouse."

That was all he'd said, and then the two had gone to work. But not before Mr. Otherday had cast Josephina that boyishly shy smile of his while his brown-eyed gaze had flickered with quick, furtive male interest across her body.

Henry Otherday didn't say anything. He glanced at Josephina and then looked away, doffing his hat and hanging it on a peg by the door. Facing the front wall, he shrugged out of his jacket and pegged it, as well.

Then he walked over to the zinc-topped washstand on the other side of the door, and washed.

As he did, Josephina took their plates off the table, which she'd already set, and filled them with the chicken, mashed po- tatoes, milk gravy, and corn she'd harvested from her irrigated garden patch. As she set a basket of hot cross buns and a dish of butter onto the table, she glanced at Mr. Otherday and caught him studying her in the small mirror hanging from a nail over the washstand.

When his eyes met Josephina's, he ran the towel over his face with a start.

Josephina jerked her gaze away, as well, and said, "Well, then . . . supper is served." She heaved a sigh. "I hope it's ed- ible. While mother is a wonderful cook, and most of my sisters are, as well, I'm afraid it's a gift the Good Lord didn't see fit to bestow upon me."

Mr. Otherday hung the towel on the nail beside the mirror, and turned to the table. His brown eyes took in the two steam- ing plates on the oilcloth-covered table, and he smiled at Jose- phina, shrugging. "Looks mighty good to me, ma'am. I mean . . . Miss . . ."

"Please call me Jo. All my friends do, and I don't see why I can't count you among my friends, Mr. Otherday. Lord knows I have few enough!"

She laughed nervously, almost having to choke back a sob of loneliness.

For she *was* lonely.

So, so lonely.

Sometimes her heart felt as thin and brittle as an old newspaper left out in the weather for weeks.

Mr. Otherday placed his hand on the back of his chair and stared down with a suddenly troubled expression at the steaming food on his plate. Finally, he looked up at her from beneath his black brows, and he smiled oddly as he said, "Are you sure . . . you know . . . it's all right?"

He had a very deep, almost guttural voice, and he flattened his vowels. He had the voice of a much older man. It was an odd, almost toneless rhythm, and a particularly Indian one, Josephina had come to know, having been raised here in the Dakota Territory, home to many bands of Sioux, some of whom were still allowed to roam freely with travois and wagons as long as they also lived in peace with the whites.

Josephina frowned, feigning befuddlement. "Why wouldn't it be all right? You're Mr. Hawkins's hired man. It's only right that I feed you from time to time."

Mr. Otherday glanced skeptically at the door. "I know . . . but . . ." He let his voice trail off. Josephina knew that he'd been going to say that Mr. Hawkins had warned him to stay away from her. That George had likely forbidden him to go anywhere near his wife or the cabin. Of course, Josephina didn't know this for sure, but she'd lived with Mr. Hawkins long enough to know the kind of man he was.

Mr. Otherday had worked alongside him long enough to know, too. Thus the look of wariness and sheepishness in the young half-breed's eyes.

"When Mr. Hawkins sells stock in town, he's usually gone for three days at least," Josephina said quietly, recognizing the sheepishness in her own voice. Tension drew tight in her, as though Mr. Hawkins were standing right outside the door, listening. "Sometime an entire week," she added with a phony laugh, as though her husband's behavior merely amused her.

She removed her apron and hung it on the back of her chair. "Please, Mr. Otherday. Do sit down. The food is getting cold!"

The hired man shrugged as he pulled his chair out and sat down. He immediately picked up the chicken leg quarter in his hands.

Josephina said, "Would you like to say grace, or should I?"

Otherday gave that bashful, cockeyed smile of his again, and returned the chicken to his plate. He wiped his hands on his trousers and bowed his head.

Josephina said a quick table prayer, and unfolded her napkin on her lap. She noticed that Mr. Otherday ignored the napkin beside his plate as he eagerly went to work on his food. Josephina marveled at the abandon with which the young man ate, busily stirring the gravy into his potatoes, mixing the corn into the potatoes and gravy, and then lifting the chicken to his mouth, tearing and chewing.

Normally, she would have been repelled by such a poor display of manners, but it wasn't all that different from how Mr. Hawkins himself ate. About the only difference was that Josephina's husband used a napkin from time to time, instead of his trousers.

She was overjoyed at the young man's delight in the food she'd cooked for him. Once, out of an undeniable rush of curiosity, she'd slipped into the bunkhouse when Mr. Hawkins and the hired man were off tending cattle on the range. About all that Mr. Otherday ever ate, it appeared, were canned goods—especially canned beans and peaches—that he purchased from the grocery shop in town. He had only one cook pot, a scorched and dented tin coffee pot, one tin plate, one wooden-handled fork, a spoon, and a skinning knife, which he apparently used as a table knife.

Josephina had run her hands over these utensils, and felt a shudder of intrigue along her spine. She'd liked how the bunkhouse smelled, as well. It smelled of Mr. Otherday, which she'd found somewhat heady.

The half-breed ate with such concentration that Josephina decided not to distract him with idle conversation. So they ate in silence, the young man finishing a good ten minutes before Josephina herself did. He merely stared down at her plate, waiting for her to finish. This made her self-conscious, and she left some chicken on the bone before she declared herself done.

"Let me clear and scrape the plates," she said, rising from her chair.

She took her plate and Mr. Otherday's plate to the dry sink and began scraping what few leavings there were into a wooden bucket. As she rinsed the plates from a kettle of soapy water, she became aware of him standing behind her.

She hadn't heard him move, but he was standing behind her, all right. His manly, wild tang was heavy in her nostrils. She could feel the heat radiating off of him, pushing against her from behind. He was like a fully stoked stove.

"I'll be through here in just a minute, and then I'll cut us each a slice of—*oh!*" she said when he placed his hands on her shoulders.

She dropped a plate into the kettle of soapy water. She felt as though she'd been struck by lightning. A jangling, burning, searing, tearing heat rippled all through her. What felt like hot tar puddled low in her belly, making her knees quake.

As he wrapped his arms around her, and closed his hands over her breasts, he pressed his face against the side of her neck, nuzzling her. She felt his slightly chapped lips open. She felt the hot, wet, aggressive caress of his tongue along her neck.

He groaned as he licked her and massaged her breasts through her dress.

"Oh," Josephina said, wanting him to go away so badly . . . to keep doing what he was doing so badly. . . .

She just stood there, stricken, as the hired man licked her neck and nibbled her ears. Gradually, he opened her dress and slid it down off her shoulders. She watched the garment open and pull away from her bosom.

"Oh . . . no," she said, moaning, lolling her head back against him. "Oh . . . god . . . no. . . ."

But then he'd run his hands up inside her chemise, and her bare breasts were in his work-callused hands. Her nipples came alive beneath his manipulations. Her bosom was like a bared nerve, sending shudders of pure horror and pure ecstasy through every nerve in her lust-wracked body.

Her ears registered the clomps of a horse's approach long before her brain did. She turned toward the hired man pressing up against her, and glanced at the scraped-paper window to see Mr. Hawkins's face glaring in at her.

Glaring in at *them*! Mr. Otherday still had his hands on her breasts, his lips on her neck.

Josephina slapped hands to her mouth and screamed.

The hired man whipped around to the window, but George was no longer there. A boot thumped on the boardwalk. The door flew open, and George Hawkins bolted in to stand just in front of the dark opening, glaring at the two mashed up against the dry sink together.

"Figured!" George Hawkins said. "I just *figured*!"

"No!" Josephina cried, tearing at her hair in misery.

Her husband bolted inside the cabin and reached down to grab a stick of split firewood from the pile near the potbelly stove. Otherday shoved Josephina away from him, and strode around the table. As he did, he pulled a knife out of his right boot, and thrust it out offensively, crouching, facing the man coming toward him.

"You damn half-breed savage!" Hawkins bellowed, and swung the log.

Otherday ducked. The log whistled through the air over his head. The momentum of the blow turned Hawkins sideways. Otherday thrust the knife at Hawkins, slicing the right side of the rancher's shirt, just beneath his arm.

Blood oozed through the tear.

Hawkins looked under his arm at the slice. Josephina could see that he was glassy-eyed, drunk. He brushed his hand against the tear in his shirt, and looked at the blood on his palm.

He cursed savagely and whipped the log at the half-breed's head once more. Mr. Otherday hadn't ducked fast enough, and the log clomped him on the side of his head, just above his ear. His head wobbled drunkenly as he fell onto the end of the table, scattering glasses and cups.

He pushed himself off the table, blinking as though to clear his vision, and came at Hawkins once more, slashing the air with the knife, his long hair flying out around his head.

Hawkins was grinning devilishly now as he faced the half-breed. Both men shuffled their feet, shifting their weight from foot to foot and nearly turning a complete circle there at the end of the table, in front of the open door, facing each other like wild dogs determined to tear each other's throats out.

"No!" Josephina heard herself scream through the numbness of shock, shuffling around on the far side of the table from the men. *"No! No! No! Stop! Please, stop!"*

Otherday jabbed the knife toward Hawkins once more. The rancher stumbled back, getting a funny look on his face. Blood welled from the hole on his left side, between his belly and his chest. He glared with even more fury at Otherday now. He gave a drum-rattling bellow as he swung the log at the younger man.

Otherday took the blow on his left shoulder and bounced off a ceiling support post.

"Stop fighting—you're going to kill each other!" Josephina screamed, wildly shaking her head.

Hawkins thrust the log backhanded.

There was a crunching thud as the log smashed into the half-breed's mouth and nose, splitting his lip and causing two rivers of blood to stream from his nostrils. Otherday plopped down on his rear, eyes rolling back in his head, his hair hanging in black strands down his face and across his cheeks.

Hawkins bolted forward and, crouching low at the waist, swung the log with a bellowing grunt from right to left. Josephina screamed again when she heard the horrible, crunching thud as the log connected with the hired man's head.

She heard the half-breed's knife clatter to the floor.

She dashed around the table toward the fighting men. She didn't know she'd picked up the cast-iron potato pot until she'd swung it with all her might against the back of her husband's head. It clanged against the crown of Hawkins's skull.

Hawkins dropped the log and staggered forward, almost tripping over Otherday, who lay writhing on the floor. Shocked by what she'd done, Josephina dropped the pot.

Hawkins groaned and closed his arms over his head. He cursed loudly, then straightened and turned to where Josephina stood, staring in horror at her husband. Hawkins's eyes were even glassier than before as he staggered toward her.

He didn't say anything.

He just glared at her glassily, stupidly. His expression was as flat as an attacking grizzly's. Blood trickled down from his right nostril. His face was ghostly pale.

"I'm sorry," Josephina said, shaking her head and sobbing as she stumbled backward, between the table and the cabin's front wall. "I only . . . I only wanted you to . . . *stop!*"

Hawkins pursed his lips and mewled as he lunged for her, spreading his arms wide.

Josephina screamed and continued to stagger backward.

Hawkins pushed his arms out at her, as though they'd turned to lead and he could hardly lift them. His hands raked her shoulders, then fell to his sides. Josephina tripped over one of Hawkins's feet, and fell backward. As she fell, he fell.

They hit the floor together, her husband on top of her. She'd slammed the back of her head so hard against the puncheons that the room dimmed as it spun.

Josephina looked down at her husband. His head lay against her half-exposed bosom, resting on his left cheek. His mouth was slack. His tongue hung out a corner of it. He was drooling. His eyes were like two opaque marbles, staring up at her, unblinking.

Josephina's head sagged back against the floor, and she was out.

CHAPTER SEVEN

Tied to his saddle, Chaz Savidge said, "I'm so hungry my stomach thinks my throat's been cut. You think they'll give us somethin' to eat?"

"We're only here to buy feed for the horses," Prophet told his prisoner as he, Savidge, and Louisa rode into the humble ranch yard. "If they have any to spare. Out this far, they probably don't."

The horses clomped through a three-inch dusting of powdery snow that glistened like diamonds in the midmorning sunlight, which was of a weak, watery hue that made the scattered buildings and corrals look bleached out and sallow. Wind gusts shifted the snow around, clearing tan patches of the hard-packed yard.

A beefy, saddled zebra dun stood at the edge of the yard, cropping brittle cornstalks from a garden patch.

"Halloo the ranch!" Prophet called, halting Mean and Ugly and Savidge's horse, which he was leading, a good distance catty-corner from the cabin.

Louisa stopped her horse beside Prophet.

Prophet studied the horse cropping the cornstalks.

Louisa leaned out from her pinto to get a better look at the front of the brush-roofed cabin. "Looks like the door's partway open. I don't see any smoke rising from the chimney pipe."

"That saddled horse is odd, too."

Prophet cupped his gloved hands to his mouth and hallooed the cabin once more, louder. Strangers didn't just ride up to a

283

cabin this far out on the frontier. Not if they didn't want to risk getting shot out of their saddles.

Still, no response. The horse stopped foraging to turn a puzzled look at the newcomers, absently chewing a brown cornhusk.

"Strange," Prophet said, swinging down from Mean and Ugly's back.

He removed the lanyard of his sawed-off Richards coach gun from around his neck and shoulder, and hung the barn blaster from his saddle horn. The sawed-off ten-gauge tended to put people off. He adjusted the wool muffler he'd tied over his hat and ears, and tramped toward the cabin, looking around cautiously.

Some folks this far out got skittish from solitary living, and they tended to shoot at strangers before finding out what they wanted.

Prophet walked up to the cabin, keeping his hand away from the Peacemaker thonged on his right thigh, beneath his buckskin mackinaw. The door was indeed open. It teetered back and forth in the breeze, its hinges creaking softly.

Snow and dead leaves had blown through the door to litter the crude puncheon floor within.

"Hello?" Prophet said again as he stepped up onto the boardwalk and nudged the door open with the back of his hand.

He stepped over the threshold, and stopped, scowling.

A dark-skinned, dark-haired man lay on the floor about ten feet away from the door. His eyes were open, but the man was dead. Prophet knew what dead eyes looked like, and this halfbreed was dead, all right. Blood had dribbled out his nose and ears and from a nasty gash on the side of his head to congeal on the floor beneath him.

Prophet turned to his left, and his scowl grew more severe.

Another man lay dead on the floor. A bigger, older man with

a horseshoe of gray-brown hair around the top of his otherwise bald head. He lay half atop the young woman beneath him, who was sitting up and looking around bewilderedly, her eyes fogged from a recent sleep.

The young woman's dark-brown hair had come loose from its bun and hung in tufts around both sides of her heart-shaped, brown-eyed face.

The girl looked around the cabin and then lifted her dull gaze to Prophet. She frowned slightly, uncomprehendingly.

"What happened here, miss?" Prophet said.

She looked at him as though she hadn't heard him, as though she were trying to puzzle out who he was, as though she thought she might know him but was having trouble recollecting his name.

Prophet turned to poke his head out the door. He beckoned to Louisa and then walked over to the brown-haired girl. Her print dress was partway open, exposing a cambric chemise and the high plains of her breasts.

Prophet pulled the dead, older man off of her and then offered her his hand. She placed her hand in his, and then he wrapped his arm around her waist and pulled her to her feet. She didn't seem able to keep her balance, so he picked her up and sat her on a sofa that lay against the far wall, on the other side of a potbelly stove.

The dead younger man lay nearby, still staring. The girl's eyes found him, and a deeply concerned look passed over her face. Tears glistened in her brown eyes.

Prophet looked at her. He looked at her partly open dress and then he looked at the dead young man and the dead older man. Vaguely, he heard Louisa pull the horses up in front of the cabin. She stepped inside and looked around.

She glanced at the girl and then she walked over and looked down at the older man. She glanced dubiously at Prophet and then peered down at the younger man. She turned to the girl sitting on the couch, who was sobbing into her hands now. Louisa sat down beside the girl, glanced again at Prophet, and then wrapped her arm around the girl's shoulders.

The girl bawled louder, tears oozing from between the fingers clamped over her face. Her head and shoulders bobbed as she cried.

Suddenly, she pulled her hands away from her face and looked wide-eyed at Louisa and then at Prophet. "You won't tell my folks, will you?"

Prophet and Louisa shared another incredulous glance.

Louisa said, "No, we won't tell your folks, dear."

The girl placed her hands on her face again and continued sobbing uncontrollably.

Chaz Savidge called from outside, "Hey, what the hell's goin' on in there? Gettin' a little cold out here, and I'm hungry!"

Louisa said, "Best put the horses up, Lou. I think we'll be spending the day."

Prophet sighed. They didn't have a day to spare. They'd likely miss the train to Denver. But Louisa was probably right. There didn't seem anyone else around, and the girl was in no condition to be left alone. What had happened seemed pretty simple and clear to him—deadly simple and clear—and now there likely wasn't a man on the place.

He'd ride out later and see if the girl had any close neighbors who could take her in.

He left the cabin and pulled the door closed and latched it.

"Did you hear me, Prophet?" Savidge said from atop his horse. "I'm hungry!"

"Shut up."

Prophet dropped down off the boardwalk, fished keys out of his pocket, and went to work uncuffing and unshackling the prisoner. He stepped back, drew his Colt, and cocked it.

286

"Get inside."

"That's more like it."

Massaging the blood back into his hands, Savidge swung his right boot over his saddle horn and dropped to the ground. He grinned mockingly at Prophet, climbed the boardwalk, and stepped into the cabin. Prophet moved in behind him, carrying the cuffs and leg irons.

Savidge stopped just inside the door and looked around. He turned to the girl still sobbing on the sofa, in Louisa's arms, and he laughed, shuttling his amused gaze between dead men.

"Good Lord, girl—what you been doin' in here?"

Prophet shoved him forward. "Shut up, Chaz. One more word out of you, and you're gonna look funny with your head turned backwards."

"Ouch!" Savidge chuckled.

Prophet cuffed the prisoner to a ceiling support post in the middle of the cabin, and shackled his ankles together, leaving only a few chain links between them. The bounty hunter would have preferred to keep the seedy killer away from the girl, but he and Louisa needed to keep a close eye on him. Lou had a feeling the girl was too preoccupied with her grief to pay the killer much attention, anyway.

"If he gives you any trouble," Prophet said, rising and shoving the keys back into his pocket, "shoot him."

"My pleasure," Louisa said as Prophet began dragging the dead younger man out of the cabin.

"But only if he gives you trouble," he wryly admonished his partner.

When he had both dead men lying out in the yard fronting the shack, Prophet led his party's three horses to the barn standing just north of the small shack that, judging by the flour sack curtains in the window and the chair sitting beside the door, was the bunkhouse.

287

Which of the two dead men had been the hired man? Most likely the young one. The saddled horse had likely belonged to the older gent, the girl's husband. That's how it worked on the frontier. Girls married older men more capable of supporting them than your average younger gent. Girls rarely married for love on the frontier.

It was an old story. As old as folks had been walking the earth.

What would become of the girl?

Prophet gave a slow sigh as he went out and retrieved the saddle horse still foraging in the garden patch. When he had all four horses stalled and tended and munching parched corn from wooden buckets, he headed back to the shack with his rifle and the Richards hanging butt-up behind his back.

Halfway across the yard, he stopped and jerked a look to his right. A man was running at a crouch near a small fringe of trees just beyond the edge of the yard. As Prophet watched, the man, carrying a rifle, dove down behind a low hummock of ground.

Now, what?

Footsteps sounded behind Prophet. He wheeled, unslinging the Richards. A bearded man was running down the side of the bunkhouse, heading for Prophet and raising a carbine. He wore a red plaid mackinaw and a flat-brimmed black hat. A yellow muffler encircled his neck.

As he stopped and slammed the butt of his rifle to his shoulder, Prophet rocked the Richards's left hammer back, and squeezed the eyelash trigger.

The explosive thunder shattered the wintery morning quiet of the yard.

The man in the red plaid mackinaw was blown up off his feet and straight back with a shrill scream, triggering his rifle into the side of the bunkhouse. Another man poked his head out from behind the rear corner of the bunkhouse, glanced down in shock at the quivering form of the man in the red mackinaw, and then snaked his own rifle around the bunkhouse corner.

Prophet cut loose with the Richards's second barrel, blasting several large chunks of wood out of the side of the bunkhouse, only inches from where the head of the other rifleman had been before he'd pulled it back behind the rear wall to prevent it from being blasted off his shoulders.

Behind Prophet, the cabin door opened. Louisa strode out wielding both her Colts, and dropped to a knee on the board-walk.

"Come on, Lou!" she said tightly and began flinging lead to cover Prophet's retreat to the cabin.

The bounty hunter slung the empty gut-shredder over his shoulder and ran across the boardwalk and into the cabin, turning sharply, palming his Peacemaker and throwing lead back through the door, toward where he'd just seen powder smoke wafting above that hummock near the trees.

"Come on, girl!" he called to his partner, spying another man running on the far side of the pole corral off the barn's right wall.

He triggered another shot and saw his bullet plume dust two feet in front of the man who'd just dived behind a hay crib. Louisa ran into the cabin, and Prophet kicked the door closed.

"What's happening?" Savidge said, owl-eyed, "What the hell's happening? Who *is* that?"

As a bullet crackled through a waxed paper window and clanked off a cast-iron pot sitting on the dry sink, Savidge yowled and ducked.

"Somethin' tells me it ain't Santy Claus," Prophet grumbled.

He crabbed toward the window right of the door.

"I got me a feelin' we've been shadowed by more bounty poachers," Prophet said.

"Oh, come on!" Savidge said, ducking as another couple of bullets plunked through the paper windows to zing like angry hornets around the cabin. "I'm *your* prisoner! Don't you bounty hunters have no *honor*? Shit, I may be a killer, but I got honor, goddamnit!"

"I guess these fellas didn't get the telegram," Louisa said, poking her Winchester out the window to Prophet's right. She triggered three quick shots, angling her rifle from left to right, the long gun blasting and leaping in her gloved hands.

Prophet swung a look back at the girl still sitting on the sofa. She was looking around as though she knew something bad was happening but she wasn't sure what. A ragged bullet hole shone in the wall over her right shoulder.

As Louisa continued returning fire, Prophet ran crouching toward the girl in the print dress, and pulled her off the sofa. He shoved her belly down to the floor.

"You stay down there—all right, honey?"

"What's happening?" she said thinly, closing her arms over her head.

"I do apologize, sweetheart," Prophet said, running back to the window right of the door. "But I reckon we've led some wild dogs to your ranch. Or . . . our prisoner has, anyways."

He glanced at Louisa, who'd just emptied her Winchester, the hammer pinging onto an empty chamber. "Did you see anyone on our trail? I didn't!"

"They must be savvy." Louisa turned away from the window, pressed her back to the cabin wall, and began punching fresh cartridges into her Winchester's breech.

"You two are careless!" Savidge reproved them, dropping as low to the floor as he could, trussed up as he was. "I mean, really careless! No one ever told you about watchin' your *back trail*? Someone really oughta teach you your jobs!"

"Shut up, Savidge," Louisa said, gritting her teeth as she continued to reload, rifles crackling out in the yard like Mexican firecrackers, "or I'm gonna remember that all we need to bring back to Denver is your head!"

CHAPTER EIGHT

Prophet poked his own Winchester out the window before him, and fired four quick shots, targeting mostly puffs of wafting powder smoke. He couldn't get a good look at any of the dogs who'd stalked them here. After he'd killed the man in the red mackinaw, they'd become less careless.

"How many out there, do you think, Lou?"

Prophet aimed carefully at a man who'd just dropped behind a stock trough at the front of the corral, and fired. He grinned devilishly as he heard a yelp, and ejected the spent, smoking shell casing onto the floor behind him. "Judging by the rifle fire and the smoke I've seen, we've got a good six or seven out there."

The rifle fire tapered off.

After nearly a minute of tense silence, from somewhere across the yard a man yelled, "Hello, the cabin! Prophet? Lou Prophet?"

Prophet glanced incredulously at Louisa, who arched a dubious brow at him. "Right famous you are, Lou. Or is it *infamous*?"

Prophet shouted through the shredded bits of waxed paper hanging from the window's sashes before him, "You have me at a disadvantage, friend!"

"Name's Burrow. Earl T. Burrow. We met in Omaha once. You spilled a beer on me, sucker-punched me, and ran out with the doxie I'd already paid for!"

Louisa gave Prophet another blank look. "*In*famous it is."

"I don't think I ever sucker-punched anyone in my life, friend. Without good cause, leastways. Can't say as I remember the night in question, but then there's quite a few nights I don't remember!"

"Glassed you a ways back, Prophet! There's six of us out here. We're bounty hunters hired by Milford J. Osborne, Governor of Utah Territory. He's payin' us each three thousand dollars to bring him the head of Chaz Savidge, the man who raped and murdered his granddaughter!"

"Oh, Lordy!" Savidge whimpered behind Prophet, scuttling even lower to the floor. "Oh, Lordy, Lordy, Lordy!" He sounded as though he were actually crying.

"Not even he can help you," Louisa told him.

"Oh, Lordy, Lordy, Lordy, Lordy, Lordy!" Savidge gritted his teeth at Prophet. "You can't let 'em take my head, Lou! You can't let 'em! You can't let 'em, you hear? You gotta be man enough . . . and woman enough," he added, glancing at Louisa, "to stand up to those stinking headhunters!"

"Shut up, or I'll start hacking right now just for the peace and quiet," Prophet drawled.

He looked over the top of the window frame. A man lay in the brush atop the bunkhouse directly across the yard from Prophet. All the bounty hunter could see of him was a rifle and a black bowler hat. He thought he could see glasses glinting in the washed-out sunlight, as well, but he couldn't be sure from this distance, and through the bending brush atop the bunkhouse.

"Sorry, gents," Prophet yelled. "But you're a little late to the dance. Me an' my partner are the ones who took ole Savidge down, and we're the ones who'll bring him in. I don't cotton to bounty poaching, and that's what you fellers are tryin' to do. It does seem to be common practice of late, but it piss-burns me right down to my toenails. What's the world coming to, for god-sakes? I'm gonna kill every last one of you cowardly sonso'bitches unless you pull out *pronto!*"

"There you go, Lou!" Savidge cheered. "There you go! You give it right back to 'em in spades!"

Louisa looked coolly at the killer, the nubs of her cheeks coloring in anger. "One more word out of you, Savidge, and I'm gonna hack your foul head off myself and toss it out there like a rotten cantaloupe, the reward money be damned."

"You must not be as hungry as I am," Prophet said.

The girl turned a frightened, puzzled look over her shoulder at Prophet and Louisa. "Why . . . why do they want his head so bad?"

"Never you mind, hon," Louisa told the girl. "Suffice it to say he's bad."

"He's not the only one," the girl said, pressing her cheek despondently against the floor once more.

Prophet and Louisa shared a glance.

From atop the bunkhouse, Earl Burrow yelled, "That's how it's gonna be, Prophet? I mean, it's up to you. You can live or you can die. If you choose to live and throw us Savidge, we'll give you a note for a thousand dollars. We'll pay both you and your partner five hundred apiece—once we get paid, of course."

"How generous!" Louisa shouted through her own shredded window. "How about if you kiss my ass?"

"There you go—that's tellin' 'em," Savidge said, miserably. "Oh, Lordy—I'm gonna get my head hacked off and shipped to Utah!" He started sobbing again. "Fuckin' Mormons are gonna do some weird-ass dance around it!"

The man on the bunkhouse yelled, "Miss Bonaventure, there's nothing I'd love to do more than kiss your pretty, pink ass. Too bad you're gonna be dead, so you won't be able to enjoy it!"

With that, laughter erupted among the bounty poachers. Then all seven shooters began hammering lead at the shack again, drowning their own guffaws beneath the thundering fusillade.

The bullets plunked into the log walls and screeched through the windows. Some ground into the indoor walls; every now and then one ricocheted off a pot or pan or off the potbelly stove, screeching wickedly as it bounded around the cabin like a horsefly seeking flesh.

They were shooting so steadily that neither Prophet nor Louisa could return fire without risking getting their heads blown off. They were merely hunkered low against the wall, gritting their teeth.

Savidge mewled and writhed on the floor as the bullets zinged around him.

The girl lay belly down on the floor, covering her head with her arms.

"That cuts it!" Prophet said.

He crawled on hands and knees through the kitchen, between Savidge and the girl, and pushed through a curtained doorway. He crawled down a dark hall between two more curtained doorways, one on each side of the hall. At the rear of the shack was a small pantry area stocked with airtight tins and dry goods. He thought there'd be a back door around here somewhere.

He looked around, keeping low as an occasional bullet curled the air above his head and plopped into a wall or tore a picture off a nail and dropped it on him.

There was no door.

Prophet cursed and crawled back into the main room.

"There's an escape tunnel."

Lying on the floor near the sofa, the brown-haired girl was looking at him, wide-eyed.

Peter Brandvold

"What's that?"

"Mr. Hawkins built this place when the Sioux were still on the warpath. He dug an escape tunnel, in case they burned him out. They were always burning folks out back then. My pa built one beneath our cabin, too."

"Where is it?"

The girl pointed to a throw rug on the puncheons before the kitchen range. Prophet crawled over to it, throwing the rug aside. Sure enough, there was a trapdoor with a pull ring.

He looked through the chairs beneath the table. Louisa was scowling curiously at him from her position in the cabin's right front corner.

"You stay here, partner," he called beneath the crackling rifle fire. "I'm gonna see if I can work around behind 'em and show 'em the error of their ways!"

Louisa started crawling toward him. "I'd best go with you, or you'll get yourself shot!"

Prophet shook his head adamantly. "I do appreciate your concern for this big, old, ugly hide, sweetheart. But you gotta stay here and hold 'em off in case they try to burn the place."

Louisa stopped crawling. Staring at him through the chairs beneath the table, she drew her mouth corners down.

Prophet grinned at her. Then he swung his gut-shredder behind his back and lifted the trapdoor up and out of the floor. He let it slam back against the floor, on the other side of the hole, which pushed cool, loamy-smelling air up at him rife with the smell of meal and root vegetables.

He looked at the girl, who was gazing back at him from where she lay before the sofa.

"Thanks!" he called.

"I hope it's not caved in," she said. "Our tunnel at home caved in after a time, and there was no point digging it out, since we never used it after the Sioux quit, except for a root cel-

296

lar. That's we used this one for—Mr. Hawkins and me—so watch your step at the bottom of the ladder."

"Got it."

Prophet grabbed his Winchester and dropped his legs into the hole. He climbed down the wooden rungs, feeling the air growing cooler around him. The light from above showed him the gunnysacks gathered at the bottom. Garden potatoes and carrots spilled out the necks of two open sacks, the potatoes sending out long, waxy, curling ears.

Prophet stepped off the ladder, negotiated his way around the foodstuffs, and moved down the tunnel. He had to crawl, as the ceiling was only about four feet high. He didn't like dark, cramped places. He could feel his muscles tightening up, his heart quickening.

No, he didn't like dark, cramped places one bit.

He had to fight off the imagined images of a cave-in—of the ceiling collapsing and dirt tumbling down on top of him, suffocating him. During the war, he'd spent plenty of time in mountain tunnels, and he'd never gotten used to it.

Soon he got beyond where the light from above penetrated, so he stopped, dug a lucifer out of his shirt pocket, and scraped it to life on his thumbnail. Down here, the rifle fire sounded like muffled belches. The shooting was tapering off, as the shooters were likely growing concerned about popping off all their caps.

Soon, one or two might make a play on the cabin. They had to be wondering if they'd killed anyone inside and if the odds were now enough in their favor to make a full-out assault.

Prophet held the match out before him. The flickering, watery light didn't illuminate much ground, but it showed him the way. Holding the match in one hand, his rifle in the other, he continued crawling awkwardly, slowly, the crown of his hat raking the tunnel's low ceiling. The tunnel wasn't shored up with wood, and clumps of dirt and rock had fallen from occasional spots in the ceiling to litter the tunnel floor.

The cavern didn't seem to curve but led straight east from the cabin.

Prophet felt the walls and ceiling closing in on him. A few times, he thought they actually were, but it was just his nerves. It was cool down here, but sweat trickled down the backs of his ears and between his shoulder blades.

His own raking breaths echoed. They seemed to belong to another desperate man following him.

He nearly went through his entire store of lucifers before he came to an earthen wall. The match burned his fingers. He cursed, dropped it, and lit another one. He held it up and saw the rotting wood rungs of a ladder built into the tunnel's right side, leading up into darkness.

Prophet let his last match burn out and then grabbed the ladder's first rung. He climbed blindly, hearing his breaths echo off the walls around him. The crown of his hat nudged something solid. Prophet reached up, placed the heel of his hand on what he assumed was the cover over the tunnel—it felt wooden—and pushed.

The damn thing wouldn't give!

Prophet grunted again as he pushed.

Nothing. No give whatever. The cover, which might have gotten buried under sod or brush, held fast to the ground.

Shit!

Had he come all this way to find that the exit cover wouldn't open?

The bounty hunter placed his hand against the underside of the cover once more. He gave a deep, groaning grunt as he heaved. The cover gave way so suddenly that Prophet's momentum jerked him upward with another, shriller grunt.

He settled back against the rungs of the ladder and stared out of the hole into hazy daylight—where three men in animal skins or fur coats and wielding rifles stood in a semicircle around the hole, staring down at him.

One was grinning and aiming an old Springfield repeater at his head.

CHAPTER NINE

"Hidy, fellas," Prophet said, returning the man's grin. "Anyone got a light? I'm plumb out of matches."

The three bounty poachers leveled their rifles on him. The man who'd been grinning said, "Climb on out of there, you son of a bitch!" He extended his left hand. "Your rifle first, Prophet."

Prophet sighed. He tossed the Winchester up out of the hole. The man who'd been grinning but who now merely looked smug caught it one handed and tossed it into the brush behind him. He was tall, and he wore a wolfskin coat and a heavy blond beard. He had a deep scar across the bridge of his nose. Prophet thought he'd seen him before and was vaguely trying to place him.

"Get up out of there."

Climbing wearily out of the hole, Prophet glanced around. He was about a hundred yards straight east of the cabin, in some wild brush and sickly looking oaks at the edge of the yard. The shooting around the cabin had died. The chill breeze jostled the brush and whipped the ends of the bounty poachers' scarves around their necks, nipping at their hat brims.

Prophet said, "How'd you fellas know about the . . . ?"

"There was a red flag on the cover," the blond-bearded poacher said, glancing at where the cover lay in the grass, near a wooden stick to which had been attached a red bandanna. "I seen it when I was circlin' the cabin. I grew up in these parts, and I figured it marked an escape tunnel from the wild Sioux days. My own pappy had one like it. When the shootin' stopped from inside the shack, I had me a feelin' you was gonna use the tunnel here to work around us."

He grinned again, working a wad of chaw around inside his cheek.

The man's name gained a foothold on Prophet's brain.

"Homer Johnson?" he asked. "Rotten Homer Johnson from Bismarck?"

"I never cared for the 'Rotten' part," Johnson said.

"I heard it was fittin'," Prophet said. "Since you been back-shootin' your quarry for years now, afraid to look an owlhoot in the eye. Now you've turned to poachin' bounties." Prophet shook his head and clucked in disgust. "Look how low you've become, Homer."

Johnson's cheeks flushed above his tobacco-stained beard. He snapped his rifle around and buried the butt in Prophet's belly. Prophet jackknifed as the air was hammered from his lungs. He dropped to his knees in misery, fighting to rake a breath into his chest.

Johnson chuckled as he pulled the bounty hunter's Peacemaker out of its holster and tossed it away. "There you go, big man. How do you like that?" He pulled the Richards off Prophet, tossed it away, and glanced at the other two men flanking him. "This here's Lou Prophet, fellas. In case none of you have ever had the pleasure. Look at the big bounty man now—down on his hands and knees, squirmin' around like a landed fish!"

"Shoot the son of a bitch," one of the others said, "and be done with him."

"In good time," Johnson said. "I wanna have some fun with him first. I want him to watch me with his purty partner, the Vengeance Queen herself, when we drag her out of the shack along with Savidge." He grabbed his crotch and glared down at

301

Prophet. "I got somethin' special for her. She's gonna like it just fine, too!"

Prophet burned with fury, but at the moment all he was able to do was continue trying to work air into his lungs so he didn't pass out. Johnson pulled the bowie knife out of the sheath on Prophet's right hip, held it up, and whistled his appreciation at the finely tempered, razor-edged Damascus steel blade.

"I know just how I'm gonna kill him, too." Johnson grinned. "After I use his big bowie here to separate Savidge's head from his shoulders."

He glanced at the others. "Teddy, you and J.W. take the tunnel. When you reach the cabin, you shouldn't have too much trouble. You won't be expected. Just remember to take Miss Bonaventure alive. I don't care if you don't take anyone else alive, but make sure you take her alive—understand?"

The shortest poacher of the three said, "Why do we have to take the tunnel? Why don't you take the fuckin' tunnel!"

" 'Cause I said so, and me an' Burrow's in charge. That clear enough for you, or do you boys wanna fork trails?"

"Christ almighty—let's get on with it," said the third man, whose hairless face was badly pitted with smallpox scars.

He climbed down into the black circle of the tunnel entrance, the rungs squawking against his weight. Cursing a blue steak and glaring at Johnson, the little man followed him down into the ground.

Prophet cursed under his breath. That told him he was getting some air into his lungs, anyway. His belly ached all the way to his spine, but he had to do something fast, before those two poachers made it through the tunnel to the cabin.

Johnson had been right. Louisa wouldn't be expecting anyone from that direction.

Bad luck. Just pure, one-hundred-proof bad luck that Johnson had happened to spy the exit to the tunnel!

Prophet drew another, deeper breath and looked up at Johnson. The poacher had Prophet's bowie in his hands. He was flicking his thumb across the razor-edged blade, frowning down at the weapon devilishly.

"Sharp," Johnson said as he stepped slowly toward where Prophet was still down on all fours, raking raspy breaths through gritted teeth, his anxiety over the poachers reaching the cabin now making him as miserable as had the butt of Johnson's rifle. "I bet you could scalp a man right quick with a knife this sharp."

He looked down the blade at Prophet, and smiled. Tobacco juice dribbled out the corner of his mouth and into his beard. Prophet thought of this man taking Louisa, and another volley of fury hammered through him like rounds fired by mountain howitzers.

"Sure would like to have the scalp of Lou Prophet dangling from my belt," Johnson said. "Now, that there would be a conversation piece if there ever was one!"

Johnson crouched over Prophet. The poacher jerked Prophet's head up by his hair and swept the bowie toward Prophet's forehead. Prophet gave a bellowing cry and, gritting his teeth and narrowing his eyes, hammered his right fist up against the underside of Johnson's chin with a killing fury and the resonating crack of shattering bone.

The bowie fell from Johnson's hand.

Johnson grunted and flew straight back off his feet to plop down on his rump with a stupid look in his dung-brown eyes, which were rolling around in their sockets like two coins spun on a table.

"Oh," he said as though around a mouthful of beans. "Ohh!"

Blood spilled out his mouth. The blood was flecked with the small shards of the man's tobacco-stained teeth.

As Johnson comprehended what had just happened, his eyes widened in shock as more blood and more bits of his teeth oozed out from between his lips. *"Ohh-ohhhh!"*

Prophet grabbed the bowie. He rose and stood over the horrified Johnson.

"There you go, you rotten son of a bitch," Prophet said, drawing yet another, deeper breath into his lungs, the fury having returned more of his strength to his brawny frame. "How do you like that?"

Johnson looked up at him in terror.

As Prophet took another step toward him, crouching and drawing the bowie back behind his left shoulder, Johnson opened his mouth to scream. He got out nothing more than a clipped yowl before the edge of the bowie sliced across his neck, drawing a red line from ear to ear.

Johnson flopped back against the ground, jerking as he bled out and died.

Prophet retrieved his weapons, then hurried down into the tunnel mouth, using only two rungs and then leaping to the bottom. He wheeled, raised the Winchester, and fired six quick shots into the darkness, in the direction of the cabin. The screams of the two bounty poachers reached his ears like the distance-muffled yelps of dying wolves.

"There you go," Prophet said, ejecting the last spent casing and climbing up out of the smoky hole.

He looked through the screen of shrubs and brush toward the cabin and beyond. There were three other poachers around here somewhere, waiting for Johnson's signal, most likely. Someone moved out away from the side of the barn. The hatted figure carrying a rifle was looking toward Prophet.

The bounty hunter raised his rifle in what he hoped was a sufficient signal, and then pushed through the brush and began moving along the southern edge of the yard, swinging wide around the cabin. He hoped to be mistaken for Johnson, who'd been roughly Prophet's size.

He was far enough away from the barn that the man standing there probably couldn't see much more than his vague outline. If any of the others could see more than that, he'd be wolf bait.

There were worse things than wolf bait . . .

Burrow had been lying in the brush atop the bunkhouse, but Prophet couldn't see him up there now. He'd probably stepped down to prepare for a run at the cabin.

As Prophet walked, the only bushwhacker he could see remained by the barn, facing him, resting his rifle on his shoulder. The bushwhacker stood behind the front corner of the barn, which shielded him from the cabin . . . and Louisa's Winchester.

Prophet hoped Louisa didn't see him walking out here and mistake him for one of the bushwhackers. She usually identified her targets before dropping the hammer on them, but sometimes you didn't know what the Vengeance Queen would do.

Prophet walked with his own rifle hanging casually low at his side. He wondered when the man by the barn—or the other two squirreled away out of sight, including Burrow—would see that Prophet was not Johnson and commence firing.

He got his answer two strides later, when the man by the barn said, *"Hey—that ain't Johnson!"* and jerked his rifle down.

Prophet stopped, aimed his rifle straight out from his waist, crouched, and threw a .44-caliber chunk of whistling led toward the man by the barn, who jerked back, firing his own rifle wide, and then twisted around to bounce his right shoulder off the barn's wall.

"Pull out!" the wounded poacher cried, running away along the barn, clutching his left shoulder. "Pull out! Pull out!" He yelled something else but by then he'd swung around behind the barn, and his words were muffled and drowned by the breeze.

From the far side of the yard, another man shouted, "God-*damnit!*"

A rifle blasted from the front of the cabin. Louisa fired three, four, then five shots. Prophet heard the metallic rasp as she pumped another round into her Winchester's chamber, but no more reports followed.

Prophet broke into a run, dashing across the open yard between the cabin and the barn. He ran down along the side of the barn, noting blood droplets in the blond weeds growing up along the barn's stone foundation.

Prophet ran around the barn's rear corner. He raised his rifle to his shoulder but held fire. Three horseback riders were galloping away through the brush, climbing a low rise and then disappearing down the other side.

Their hoof thuds were quickly drowned by the moaning breeze.

"Shit!" Prophet said, angrily slapping his hat against his thigh.

He'd wanted to lay them all out with Johnson and the two in the tunnel.

The bounty hunter cursed again, donned his hat, and walked back up alongside the barn. He moved out away from the barn, heading for the shot-up shack. The shack's front door opened, and Louisa stepped out, holding her Winchester.

"How'd it go?" she called.

Her breath vapor was shredded by the wind.

Prophet felt his ears warm with chagrin.

He shrugged, scratching the back of his head with his Winchester's barrel. "Pretty much how I figured it," he lied.

CHAPTER TEN

Earl Burrow galloped his steeldust gelding into a shallow, wind-blown valley a half a mile beyond the ranch where Burrow's group had just gotten the shit shot out of them by two bounty hunters.

Two bounty hunters—one of them a *girl*!

At the bottom of the valley, near a partly frozen slough that was fringed with cattails and smelled like a privy, Burrow checked the steeldust down.

"Goddamnit!" he cried, batting his weather-stained bowler against his thigh.

Hooves thudded behind him. He turned to see "Whiskey" Charlie Meyers galloping his black mare down the hill, holding his Winchester in one hand and flapping the rifle like a wing as his horse plunged toward Burrow. Meyers's long, black hair blew back behind him in the wind. He wore buffalo fur ear-muffs under his hat, and a big, billowy red neckerchief flopped down the front of his buffalo coat.

"What the hell was *that*?" he shouted, red-faced with fury, his nose running, as he jerked the black to a stop beside Burrow. "What the hell was *that*?"

"You saw what I saw," Burrow said, glancing behind him once more as another horse shambled over the crest of the ridge and started down into the hollow.

The horse's rider—Kenny Sanchez, a bounty hunter from the Arizona Territory who'd once served with Burrow in the frontier Indian-fighting army—leaned far back in his saddle, making a face. He had his left hand clamped over his bloody right shoulder. His unshaven face was pale and pain-wracked. He stretched his lips back from small, square, tobacco-stained teeth, cursing in Spanish.

Sanchez's horse trotted past Burrow and Meyers and probably would have kept trotting clear to Canada if Meyers hadn't ridden up and grabbed the bit, stopping the mount at the edge of the gamey slough.

"Whoa, whoa!" Meyers said, the bit clattering against the horse's teeth. "Kenny, how bad you hit?"

"Shit!" Kenny yelled, and, as though in response, rolled sideways out of the saddle. He screamed again as he hit the ground with a solid thud and the crackle of brittle weeds.

"Oh, for Christ's sake!" Burrow swung down from his saddle. He thumbed his glasses up his nose, snugged the bowler down tighter on his red-haired head, and knelt beside the writhing Sanchez. "Kenny, how bad?"

Sanchez stopped writhing, though not shivering, and looked up at Burrow, his brown eyes cast skeptically. "I don't think it's too bad, *amigo.*"

Burrow knew that his former fellow trooper was remembering the dictum of their platoon back in Apacheria: "Leave no wounded man behind to die at the hands of the enemy." Of course, there were no Apaches up here on the plains, and damned few Sioux.

But the wolves and the cold wind could be almost as merciless. Doctors didn't exactly grow on trees in these parts, any more than they did in Arizona.

Burrow opened Sanchez's coat, lifted the left side to peer under the flap toward the shoulder, and made a face.

"You're losin' blood fast, Kenny."

"I got plenty of blood, *amigo.*" Sanchez chuckled, turning it into a joke, but then he coughed raggedly and rested his head back against the ground, again stretching his lips back from his teeth in misery. "Ah, shit."

Meyers swung down from his horse and stood beside Burrow, staring down at Sanchez.

Sanchez looked up and slid his beleaguered, fearful gaze between them. "*Por favor, amigos,* don't kill me. I am not ready. We were so close . . . so close to the money. I wanted to ride west . . . spend the winter in Frisco. I heard the girls there have slanted eyes . . . they're from the Orient . . . and there's a tobacco called"—he convulsed, coughing, before rasping out: "*opium!*"

He smiled again, dreamily, and closed his eyes. "It makes you feel . . . real . . . good!"

When he opened his eyes again, his smile disappeared.

He stared up in horror at the pistol aimed down at him. Raising his hands in front of his face, he screamed, "*Noooo!*"

Burrow's Schofield .44 roared, punching a quarter-sized hole through the palm of Sanchez's right hand before drilling a similar-sized hole through Sanchez's forehead.

Sanchez's hands dropped to his sides. He turned his head away and gave what sounded like a disgusted sigh as his last breath left him.

"Great," Meyers said. "That's just great. There were seven of us not a half hour ago. Now there's two!"

He gave a savage kick to one of Sanchez's boots, then stomped several yards away and stared out at the partly frozen slough, his fists on his hips. "What the hell happened?"

"Don't lose your nerve." Burrow sat on a rock, removed a glove, and began unbuttoning his coat to dig his makings sack out of his shirt pocket. "We're still gonna get Savidge. Leastways, we're gonna get his head. One way or another."

He cursed as he pulled the small, canvas sack out of his shirt pocket.

"Who the hell's that?"

"Who the hell's who?"

Meyers glanced over his shoulder at Burrow and then pointed to the northeast. Burrow rose from his rock and stared off toward where a horseback rider was cantering his horse along the edge of the slough, following an old buffalo trail pocked with deep wallows.

"Hard to say," Burrow said, nervously fingering the pouch in his hand. "But he's headed this way."

The redheaded, bespectacled bounty hunter walked over to his horse and slid his Winchester out of the saddle scabbard. He pumped a round into the Winchester's action, off-cocked the hammer, and rested the barrel on his shoulder. Meyers used the thong drooping from the hem of his buffalo coat to tie the flap up above his walnut-gripped Colt holstered low on his right hip.

Both men watched the rider canter around the curve of the slough and continue toward them—a lanky man in a long, black wolf coat with the head of the wolf still attached and serving as a hat of sorts, with fur flaps sewn on to drop down over his ears. The flaps were tied beneath his chin.

As he continued to approach, Burrow saw that the lean man had extremely long, dark-blond hair liberally bleached an off-yellow by the elements. His long, thick beard was of the same color. His ruddy cheeks were deep-lined and of the texture of old saddle leather. His blue eyes were set beneath brows thick and shaggy enough to resemble oversized caterpillars well on their way to becoming butterflies.

He was grinning as he reined up before the two bounty hunters regarding him incredulously. He looked at the dead man on the ground beyond Burrow, then regarded the two bounty hunters once more, pursing his lips and shaking his head in disdain.

"What a couple of sorry sacks of shit I'm lookin' at now!" he scolded in a thick English accent. "Rarely, on the Queen's honor, have I seen the like!"

Scowling, Burrow lifted his rifle off his shoulder and let the barrel sag in the general direction of the newcomer without aiming the rifle directly at him. "Who in the hell are you—besides bein' a wise-assed foreigner, I mean?"

"Yeah," Meyers said, scowling his disdain, as well, "who in the hell are you—ridin' in here like you own the whole damn territory . . . ?"

The lanky man—tall and thin, with no extra tallow that Burrow could see, though he was wearing a lot of clothes, including fringed buckskin trousers—swung down from his saddle. He removed his mittened hand and extended the large, red paw to Burrow.

"Rutherford H.L Chivington the Fifth, at your service, gents. Call me Squire. Most folks do."

He had that big, toothy grin on his face again. Burrow found him more than slightly patronizing, even mocking. The man had a good opinion of himself—that was for sure. And he didn't have a very good opinion of anyone else. At least he didn't make much of Burrow and Meyers. That was gallingly obvious.

When Burrow didn't shake the man's hand, Chivington didn't seem offended in the least. He held it out to Meyers for another rebuff and then shoved his hand back into the fur-lined, elkskin mitten, under which he wore a thin, doeskin shooting glove.

"You're English, ain't ya?" Burrow said, as though he were asking the man if he'd been birthed by a cow.

Chivington chuckled. "How did you know, my good man?" He laughed again. "Yes, of course I'm English. Born and raised in London, don't ya know. My mum and pop served the King and Queen, they did."

"What're you doin' over here, if you're from such a tribe that served the King and Queen?" Meyers asked, skeptically. "You a remittance man?"

Chivington pursed his lips to consider the question, lowering those shaggy blond brows and nodding slowly. "I guess you could call me a remittance man. Yes, I could be called that." He looked up devilishly at the two before him, his lustrous blue eyes twinkling in the washed-out sunshine. "I wouldn't mind being called that at all, though, truth be known, my family was of the servant class. Dear old Mum and Pa sent me here to this wild new land going on thirty years ago now, when I was only fifteen years old. You see . . ."

He looked around as though making sure no one else was within earshot, then, keeping his voice as well as his chin dipped low, stepped closer to his two-man audience to confess, "You see, even at that young age, I was hung like a mule and owned the passion of a rogue griz too long in hibernation."

He gestured lewdly with his entire body. "I put a bun in the oven of the visiting Princess of Denmark, don't ya know, one wild night after too much rum punch and the lighting of the palace Christmas tree. Slipped her underfrillies down those porcelain legs in Prince Albert's study, and went after the lusty little Dane like she was little more than stable trash."

He winked as he thrust his hips. "And that's exactly how young Ingrid took the studding, too, I might add. She yowled like common stable trash and damn near laid my poor pink ass wide open with her fingernails. But she made up for the injury in spades"—Chivington winked, grinning—"if'n you get my drift, buckos."

The Englishman roared loudly, then quieted quickly.

He brushed a sheepish fist across his nose. "Ingrid's guilt rode her as hard as I had that pie-eyed night, especially when it was discovered the poor girl was with child. She confessed the tryst to her mum, who complained to Victoria, her cousin. After that I was considered a pariah at Buckingham Palace. Fearing for my life, not to mention certain gelding by the palace guards, my folks bestowed their life's savings upon me and sent me here to the New World to avoid dear Victoria, who, understandably, I reckon, was more than a little miffed at having her beloved Danish niece impregnated by an unshod steed from the cobbled, coal-begrimed slums of east London!"

The Englishman fell back against his beefy cream stallion, laughing raucously.

Burrow and Meyers shared a puzzled scowl.

Burrow turned to the still-laughing Brit, and aimed his rifle at the man's flat belly. "Thanks for your life story, you four-flushin', limey bastard. Now, suppose you tell us what you're doin' here. You been followin' us? You a bounty hunter, maybe?"

He canted his head toward the man's horse. He'd spied a large, brass-framed rifle jutting from the man's fur-clad scabbard to which was attached a smaller scabbard housing a brass tripod.

Chivington looked at the gun. Then he turned back to Burrow and Meyers. "Eighteen-Seventy-Four Sharps sporting rifle," he said, proudly. "Fashioned and re-fashioned to suit my own particular needs. Outfitted with a Malcolm telescopic scope that makes a man four hundred yards away appear to be dancing a jig within ten feet of the end of the barrel . . . give or take," the Englishman added with a smile.

His pale features flushing with exasperation, Burrow said, "You been followin' us!"

"Yes, my good man—I have been following you," the Englishman said with a patient air, as though he were dealing with a couple of cork-headed fools. "You've been following Prophet, and I've been following you."

"You've been followin' us followin' Prophet!" accused Meyers.

"Yes, my good man." The Englishman smiled indulgently at Meyers. "I've been following you following Prophet. However, let me point out, that I was on Prophet's trail before you were. Before you and several others, I might add. Rarely have I seen Dakota so crowded this time of the year. As soon as I saw Prophet and the Vengeance Queen in Dakota Territory, I figured they were after the same man—or men—I was after. Who else but Chaz Savidge would they be after out here, at this outlandish time of the year?"

He shrugged, bunching his lips inside his shaggy beard, which was as sleek as the fur of his wolf coat. "When I was hunting buffalo a few years back," he added, patting the sheathed Sharps, "I'd always follow the Sioux or Cheyenne braves, because they knew where the largest herds were. I'd wait till they were finished taking two or three from a herd of hundreds, and then I'd set up the Sharps here and drop twenty inside of an hour!"

"You're a poacher," Burrow snarled. "A bounty poacher."

Chivington glowered. "I don't like that term. I'm a man of opportunity. I'm a businessman. A good one. You see, I'm not as young as I used to be. I'm neither the tracker nor the hunter I once was. When I see a younger, more capable man or men on the same trail—why not let him do the dirty work?"

"And then you blast the poor bastard with the long-range cannon there," Burrow said, "and take his quarry."

"Exactly!" Chivington exclaimed like a schoolmaster congratulating the class fool for finally answering a question correctly. "Far easier to bushwhack a man who doesn't know it's coming than an outlaw constantly peeking over his shoulder for shadowers. Now, gents, let's get off our bloody high horses, shall we? Right here, you've been doing—or *trying* to do—the same thing I've been doing—*successfully*—for the past several years."

"We don't make a habit of it," Burrow objected. "It just so happened Chaz Savidge stomped a boot down in Prophet's and that crazy blonde's bear trap before we had a chance to ensnare him ourselves. We got a whole lot more money riding on Savidge than Prophet does."

Meyers gave Burrow a castigating look.

"Oh?" Chivington said with interest, arching a brow the size of a small sparrow. He tugged at his chin whiskers with a mittened hand. "I had me a feeling. How much will you be getting for Savidge—if you don't mind my askin', of course?"

"None of your business," Meyers said. "Now, why don't you pull foot before we grease you right here!" He closed his hand over his gun handles.

"Gents," Chivington said. "I saw what happened here. You started out with seven men, and you're down to only two. What makes you think you two are going to be able to take Lou Prophet and Louisa Bonaventure down *alone?*"

Burrow and Meyers glared at him, ears burning. They looked at each other. Then they glanced at the long rifle hanging down the side of the Englishman's stud horse.

They looked at Chivington, who grinned at them, showing a mouthful of large, horsey, grime-encrusted teeth.

CHAPTER ELEVEN

Prophet saved his own horse to saddle last, after he'd saddled Louisa's pinto and Savidge's dapple. He took the heavy wool saddle blanket down off a stall partition, shook it out, and tossed it up and onto Mean and Ugly's back.

As Prophet reached for his saddle, Mean gave a shake.

The blanket billowed off the horse's back to the floor.

Prophet turned to the horse, his cheeks warming in fury. "Why you cussed beast," he said. "What in the hell did you do that for? You don't think I been through enough trouble so far today?"

Mean and Ugly kept his head facing forward, ears back slightly. He gave his tail a single, ornery switch.

Prophet walked around to the other side of the horse to retrieve the blanket. Again, he shook it out and tossed it up onto the dun's back.

"I don't got no time for your high jinks today, Mean," the bounty hunter warned. "You wanna hit the trail as bad as I do. You're just bored and the shootin' made you cankerous, and you wanna play games. Well . . ."

Again, the horse shook the blanket off his back.

This time Prophet grabbed it before it hit the floor.

"Goddamn, you wretched, ugly cuss!" he bit out. "You know what I'm gonna do as soon as I strike Denver? Even before I turn Savidge's head in for the reward money? I'm gonna find me a glue factory, and I'm gonna—"

Prophet stopped and whipped toward the barn's double doors, his Peacemaker already in his fist and his thumb raking the hammer back. He held fire when he saw the silhouette of the girl from the cabin standing between the partly open doors, against the wintery, washed-out daylight behind her.

"Mr. Prophet?"

Prophet depressed the Colt's hammer. He strode quickly forward, glanced around the yard, and then ushered the girl inside the barn, drawing the doors closed. "You shouldn't be out here, miss. I left three of them shooters alive, and they could be back at any time."

"I'm sorry," the girl said. "I didn't mean to be any trouble."

At first, Prophet thought she was being sarcastic. He and Louisa and Chaz Savidge had led a whole pack of trouble to her front door. Her place was so shot up that if it hadn't been constructed of stout logs, it likely would have disintegrated into a pile of oversized matchsticks by now.

She stared up at him sincerely, the light streaming through the cracks between the logs of the wall glistening in her wide, brown eyes.

Prophet chuckled. "You're no trouble, miss. We . . . my partner an' me an' our prisoner . . . we've been trouble."

"Yes, well, there was plenty of trouble here before you arrived." She looked down. "But you already know that."

Prophet drew a deep, slow breath, frowning down at her. "Miss, what's your name?"

She looked up at him again. "Josephina Hawkins."

"Which was your husband?"

"The older one. The younger one was . . . he was my husband's hired man."

"Enough said."

She placed a hand on his forearm. "Mr. Prophet, will you please take me with you? To wherever you're going? I don't care

317

where it is. But I can't live here anymore."

Prophet considered this, nodding. "Why, sure. Why, sure. You can't live in that house now. I should have figured on that. Tell you what—we'll take you to the nearest neighbors, and—"

"No!" Josephina dug her fingers into his forearm.

"I can't stay anywhere around here anymore, after what happened. My folks . . . my family . . . they live only five miles away. When it gets around that Mr. Hawkins and Mr. Otherday . . . fought over me . . ."

She let her voice trail off. Tears shone in her eyes and began to dribble down her cheeks. "No, no. I can't stay here. I can't live around here ever again. I'd never be able to look anyone in the eye again. Certainly, no one would marry me. Please, Mr. Prophet, take me to wherever you're going."

"Well, hell, Miss Josephina, Louisa an' me—we're riding clear down to Denver with—"

"That's perfect! Denver's a long ways away from here, isn't it? Denver's perfect. If you get me there, I'll figure out my next step. But I can't remain here. Please, you must take me with you!"

"Miss Josephina, I'm sure your family would come around. It might take some time, but, they *are* your family and this *is* your home."

"If I remained here, Mr. Prophet, for the rest of my life the shadow of what happened here yesterday would follow me around. My family would disown me. No man would ever have me. Why, just to survive, I'd probably end up working down at the woodcutters' camp!"

The thought seemed to chill her. She crossed her arms over her breasts and shivered.

Prophet caught the drift of what the woodcutters' camp was. Judging by the girl's expression, fellows probably did more than just cut wood there.

Prophet silently opined that there was really no reason that anyone need know exactly what had happened here before he and Louisa had showed up. There were enough dead men around and enough bullets in the cabin for several interpretations.

But, of course, Josephina would always know. And folks would still wonder and come to their own conclusions.

"Earlier," the girl said, staring desperately up into Prophet's eyes once more, "when those men were shooting and the bullets were flying around inside the cabin, I wanted to lift my head up off the floor so that one of those bullets would find me and put me out of my misery. For some reason, I couldn't do that. I didn't have the courage."

Her lips quivered. She tucked the bottom one under her front teeth, dropped her chin, and sobbed.

"All right," Prophet said, placing his hands on her shoulders and drawing her against him, holding her. "All right. I'll saddle whatever horse you want, and we'll take you just as far as you want to go."

She stopped sobbing, stepped back, and brushed the tears from her cheeks. "Thank you, Mr. Prophet."

"You might not be thanking me for long, Miss Josephina. It's a long ride to Denver, and there's no telling how many other bounty poachers are going to be doggin' our heels."

"I'll take my chances, Mr. Prophet. I'd like the coyote dun. His name is Herman. My pa gave him to me for a wedding present."

"All right, then." Prophet led her over to the doors, which he opened, glancing cautiously around the yard. "You best go on back to the cabin. I'll lead the horses over when I'm done saddling them."

The girl slouched out of the barn and angled across the yard toward the shack. Louisa was standing on the boardwalk fronting the place. She looked at the girl walking toward her, and then she looked at Prophet. She frowned curiously.

Prophet shrugged, then moved back into the barn to finish his chores.

When he had all four horses saddled and ready to go, Prophet threw the barn doors open and stepped out into the yard.

He left the horses in the barn as he walked around, holding his Winchester up high across his chest. He scanned the yard and the terrain surrounding it, making sure that the three surviving poachers hadn't returned. He'd wounded one of the three fairly severely, judging by the amount of blood the man had left in the grass by the barn.

That made two healthy men left of the seven who'd originally ambushed the ranch. The third likely wouldn't be a threat.

But those two . . .

Burrow had seemed determined.

Determined enough to make another play on Prophet and Louisa, when he had only himself and one other man? Prophet had to assume he'd make the attempt. Three thousand dollars was an alluring bounty. Prophet wouldn't mind getting his hands on that much money himself, but the three thousand he and Louisa would have to split between them would have to suffice.

However, he'd like to discuss with the territorial governor of Utah the vermin he'd hired to fetch the head of the man who'd murdered his granddaughter. The governor had essentially, albeit unknowingly, put a bounty on the heads of both Prophet and the Vengeance Queen.

As satisfied as he could be that the yard was clear of bushwhackers, Prophet led the horses out of the barn and across the yard to the cabin. It was midafternoon. The air was cold but the snow had stopped falling. Prophet thought they could reach the rail line by noon of the next day if today they got at least three more hours of travel behind them.

He stopped the horses and took another look around. Apprehension caused the short hairs under his collar to bristle. Still, he spied no movement anywhere around the yard.

Behind him, the cabin door clicked open. He glanced over his shoulder to see Louisa step out, clad in her coat, hat, and scarf, and holding her rifle in her gloved hands.

"What is it?" she asked.

"Not sure."

"What are you feeling?"

"I feel like someone's drawing a bead on me."

"I've been keeping pretty close watch, and I haven't seen any riders—or walkers, for that matter—approach the yard since you went out to the barn."

"Yeah."

"But you have that feeling . . ." Louisa sounded uneasy, herself. She'd come to begrudgingly respect the short hairs under her partner's collar.

"Yeah, I got that feelin'. Let's hope it's just a feelin." Prophet walked up onto the boardwalk. "We have to pull out or we're gonna miss that train for sure. I think it only runs once every couple days. You keep watch while I get our prisoner out here and mounted."

Prophet went inside. Josephina stood near the door. She had a bag of grub and a carpetbag packed. She wore a heavy buffalo coat and knit cap and heavy mittens. She looked worried. Obviously, she'd seen Prophet and Louisa through the window.

"What's wrong?"

"Maybe something, probably nothing."

Prophet dropped to a knee beside Savidge, who looked up at him skeptically. "You sure them headhunters ain't still out there? You look spooky as the devil on the Sabbath, Proph."

"Shut up."

"Hey, listen, *amigo*," Savidge said as Prophet unlocked the shackles from around the man's ankles. "I ain't really worth all this. I mean, your life's in danger here, Lou. Why don't you just turn me loose? Shit—I got me a grand idea? How about if—?"

"Shut up."

"How 'bout if you and me and the purty Vengeance Queen ride on down to Arizona Territory? Hell, Miss Josephina's welcome, too, if she so desires!" He cast the frightened-looking girl a lusty wink. "I got me a little cache of gold hid down there. I been addin' to it every year. You know—a little nest egg of sorts for my later years."

"You been sockin' nuts away for retirement, Chaz?"

Prophet slung both sets of cuffs over his shoulder, then swept the Richards off his arm and aimed both stout barrels at his prisoner.

Savidge said, "I got pret' near fifty thousand dollars saved up. Now, don't *fifty* thousand split *four* ways sound a hell of a lot better than *three* thousand split *two* ways? Especially when you prob'ly won't live to buy a spoonful of whiskey with that measly fifteen hundred!"

"Hmmm," Prophet said, stepping aside and wagging the Richards at Savidge. "Hmmm. Food for thought."

Savidge walked out onto the boardwalk.

Behind him, Prophet said, "Louisa, we're headin' for Arizona Territory!"

Savidge swung around, eyes snapping wide in shock. "Really, Lou?"

"No, not really," Prophet snarled. "Get up there on that horse before I beef your ugly hide!"

"Ah, hell, Proph! You ain't thinkin' sensible. What chance you think you have—any of us has—of reachin' Denver in one piece?" He swung up onto the dappled gray and looked around warily. "I could get my head blown off just any old time!"

"Don't get your shorts in a twist," Prophet said. "Your head is worth too much to get it blown off. Chopped off, maybe . . ." He glanced back at Josephina, who'd followed them out. "Ready to ride, miss?"

"I reckon I am, Mr. Prophet. Thank you."

"Ain't she polite?" Savidge said. " 'I reckon I am, Mr. Prophet. Thank you.' "

"Shut up, Chaz," Louisa scolded the man as she crouched to close a shackle around his left ankle. "Do you have to talk every second of every damn minute?"

"See there?" Prophet said, handcuffing the outlaw's wrists behind his back. "Now you got her cussin' like a brakeman. Miss Bonaventure ain't normally one to sport a blue tongue. She'll fill you full of lead and send you dancing off to hell screaming, but she's as reluctant as a parson's wife to curse."

"Some of us were raised properly," Louisa said.

Prophet chuckled ironically at that.

When he and Louisa had their outlaw secure, Prophet helped Josephina onto the saddle of her coyote dun to which she'd strapped a blanket roll. She'd also hung her carpetbag and grub sack from the horn. Prophet handed the girl her bridle reins.

"You can ride, I take it, Miss Josephina?"

"Oh, yes, I can ride," the girl said. "My husband preferred I stayed home and tend chores around the cabin, so I haven't ridden for a while, but I'm sure it'll come back to me."

"What's gonna come back to you, miss—if you'll forgive me for sayin' so—is a whole mess of ugly, nasty saddle sores!" Savidge laughed.

Louisa swung her carbine up and buried the stock in the outlaw's belly.

"*Ohhh!*" Savidge groaned as his breath was hammered from his lungs, jerking forward in the saddle. "*Ohhh*—Lordy—that

323

. . . just . . . wasn't . . . *nice!*"

Prophet chuckled as he swung up onto Mean's back. He didn't laugh long, however. As he turned his horse out away from the cabin, the reins of Savidge's mount in his left hand, he cast a cautious look around the yard.

Those short hairs spiking the back of his neck were twitching like a watch witch over an underground ocean.

CHAPTER TWELVE

From a distance of a quarter or a half a mile away across the gently rolling prairie, the fire was little more than a pinprick of orange, faintly guttering light.

Prophet studied the light from a rise to the north of where he, Louisa, Savidge, and Josephina Hawkins had bivouacked just after sundown and built a small cook fire of their own. Prophet had spotted the distant flames an hour ago, when he'd scouted around the camp for more possible poachers.

Well, he'd found said poachers.

Of course, the fire could belong to range riders or hunters or even to woodcutters or sheepherders. But Prophet was no juniper. He was new neither to the west nor to the business of bounty hunting. He had to assume the fire belonged to men shadowing him and Louisa, out for the improbably valuable head of Chaz Savidge.

Grass crackled behind Prophet.

He turned to see Louisa's vague shadow moving up the slope. Their own cook fire guttered behind her, a coffee pot hanging from the iron tripod over the flames.

Savidge sat against a birch tree beside the fire, the man's knees raised to his chest. He was staring up the slope toward Prophet. The girl, Josephina, sat on a log on the opposite side of the fire from Savidge. She had a blanket over her shoulders. She leaned forward, hunched against the cold, the coffee cup in her hands sending steam up to bathe her face, which the fire's umber flames caressed with dim light and deep shadows.

Josephina, too, was staring up the slope toward Prophet.

Louisa dropped down beside the bounty hunter. She held a steaming plate in one hand, a steaming cup in her other hand. On the plate was a charred venison steak resting on a mound of pinto beans, and a baking powder biscuit. Josephina had contributed the grub, and she'd cooked it, too, insisting on doing her part.

"What has you so preoccupied up here?" Louisa asked, setting the plate down beside Prophet. "Eat. Just don't expect such service every night."

"Holy shit—that smells good! I didn't realize how hungry I was."

Prophet picked up the chunk of venison, and dug into it, chewing ravenously.

Keeping her head beneath the brow of the rise, Louisa stared toward the north. "Campfire?"

Prophet groaned in the affirmative as he chewed.

"How long's it been there?"

"Good hour now," Prophet said, setting the venison down on the plate and starting to shovel the beans into his mouth. They'd been cooked in the venison drippings, and they were mouth-watering good.

"You think it's him—Burrow? You think he's that much of a fool—to keep coming after us when he's only three-men strong, with one of those men likely toting a bullet if he's even still alive?"

"You know, girl, I stopped trying to gauge the intelligence of other men a long time ago. Doing so'll get you planted under a low mound of rocks with no other marker to speak of. I just try to play the trail as smart as I can, and assume everyone else on the frontier is up to no damn good."

"You're a wise one, Lou Prophet." Her words were touched with irony.

Prophet shrugged as he ripped another chunk of meat off the venison steak.

Louisa studied the distant, faintly flickering fire ensconced in a dark hollow. "How you wanna play this?"

Prophet stopped chewing and looked at her. She arched a brow at him. Prophet gave a snort, then swallowed his last mouthful of the food and wiped his gloves in the grass.

"I'm gonna give it another hour, then I'm gonna go over and have a look. You stay here with Savidge and the girl, in case they sneak around me. That fire could very well be a diversion, and Burrow could be sneaking around us right now."

"I'd best douse the fire, then."

Prophet nodded.

Louisa reached for his plate, then left it where it was. She moved closer to Prophet, and wrapped her arms around his neck. She kissed him. The warm, wet knife of her tongue stabbed between his greasy lips. Then she pulled her head away from his, and gave him a commanding look.

"Be careful."

"What—you don't think you can spend that whole three thousand by yourself?"

"Sure, but you'd have such a much better time than I would, you whore-mongering fool."

With that, she rose, picked up his plate and fork, and strode back down the hill toward the fire. Prophet watched her go. He enjoyed watching Louisa coming and going. It never failed to give him a boyish thrill, and he never knew when another look at the Vengeance Queen would be his last.

So he took the time to appreciate this one.

He remembered their recent night together. His back still ached sweetly from the clawing she'd given him. He remembered her pale hips thrusting hungrily up against his.

Chuckling and cursing, he shook the remembered pleasure from his mind, and turned back to the fire.

Behind him, he could hear Louisa talking to Savidge and Josephina. Savidge said something in an objecting tone. Prophet heard the scuffing sounds as Louisa kicked out their fire.

"Gonna be a cold night," Savidge groused, his voice low but clear in the chill air.

"Could be colder," Louisa told him.

After that, there was nothing but silence in the hollow in the hills below Prophet. He held his position there on the crest of the rise, watching the fire flickering half a mile away, under a sky awash with twinkling stars. The fire diminished, then burned brighter again.

Someone was tending it.

When the stars' slow glide across the heavens told him an hour had passed since Louisa had left him, Prophet picked up his rifle, rose, adjusted the Richards coach gun's position behind his back, touched the Peacemaker to make sure it was still thonged on his thigh, and started down the hill's north slope.

He hurried down from the brow of the hill, so the stars wouldn't outline him. Halfway down, he slowed his pace. He took his time as he tramped well south of the fire, following a meandering, dry creek bed generally west.

Stones and bleached cow skulls glowed pale along the narrow watercourse. In the far distance to the west, coyotes yammered insanely before quieting suddenly, like scolded children.

A wolf kicked up its long, mournful howls in the opposite direction. Nearer, an owl hooted. There was the constant scratching of mice and other burrowing creatures in the grass and occasional woods around Prophet.

The night was alive.

The creek dropped between steep cutbanks lined with

brambles and willows. Prophet couldn't see the fire until the creek bed rose once more, and then the pinprick of wavering light shone again, a half-hearted beacon in the darkness.

Prophet followed the creek's northward curve and then left the stream and followed a shallow crease between barren hills. Several times, he again lost track of the fire. Disoriented for some time, he climbed to higher ground and loosed a relieved sigh when he saw its flickering glow again, farther to his right than he would have thought and slightly obscured by trees or bumps of higher ground, maybe picketed horses.

Fifteen or twenty minutes later, he was crabbing on all fours through a sprinkling of woods tufting this bowl between low, pale hills. The fire lay directly ahead of him. Someone had built it up again recently, for it glowed vibrantly beyond the tangled, black webbing of brush and branches.

Prophet wondered how long he'd been out here. At least an hour. Maybe closer to ninety minutes. In that case, it was likely around nine o'clock. Most travelers would be settling in by now.

Wary of an ambush, Prophet slowed his pace as he drew nearer the fire. He could smell the smoke from time to time as the breeze jostled it toward him. Slower and slower he crawled, setting the Winchester softly down beside him with each crawling stride.

He breathed though his mouth, wincing at every soft crackle of grass beneath his big, lumbering frame.

Louisa should have come, he thought. She was quieter. But she was also less dependable and predictable, because she was more emotional. She'd never admit it, of course, but she'd made mistakes because emotion had clouded her judgment.

Eventually, her hot-headedness would get her killed. But not tonight.

Prophet hoped not tonight . . .

He crawled up to a deadfall log at the very edge of the firelight. The light spread a dull, umber glow across the top of the log. The fire was lower now, the sphere of light it spread, weaker. But Prophet could see two men lying around it—one on the left side, one on the other side of the flickering flames.

He couldn't see the men themselves, but he could see the man-shaped lumps they made in their coats and blankets.

He looked around. He'd passed two picketed horses about twenty yards back. He couldn't see them now. They'd made soft whickering sounds as he'd passed, and one had stomped but not loudly enough for anyone around the fire to hear, thank God.

So there were two men now.

Where was the third? Dead?

Prophet studied the camp before him. Neither man moved. He thought he could see the chest of the man on the left rising and falling as he breathed, but that could have been a trick of the firelight. He was wary of the old trick to arrange blankets to look as though men were slumbering under them.

These blankets looked genuinely filled with men, however.

Prophet looked behind him and then to each side and beyond the flames, which were dancing lower and lower. He saw no sign of a third man. Just these two.

Prophet's heart quickened as, gripping the Winchester, he rose slowly and stepped over the log. Still looking around and pricking his ears almost painfully, listening to the woods surrounding the fire, he moved over to the man on the fire's left side.

He pressed his boot toe to the man's side. "Hey."

The man didn't move. Prophet looked around. Nothing moved in the darkness surrounding him. The only sounds were the occasional scratching of small critters and branches.

"Hey, wake up," Prophet said, poking his boot toe deeper into the man's side.

Still, nothing.

Cold sweat trickled down Prophet's back. The short hairs under his collar were dancing a nervous jig.

"Wake up, there," Prophet said, louder, and opened the man's blankets.

A red-haired man, Burrow, lay staring up at him. His mouth was twisted in horror. A long, wide gash shown across his throat. The man's chest was covered with a thick blood pudding.

"Holy Christ," Prophet raked out, stepping over the dead man to the other man on the other side of the fire.

That man lay on his side. Prophet kicked him over, and he lay staring up at Prophet with much the same expression as Burrow. His throat, too, had been cut from ear to ear and he was still trying to scream a scream that, even when new, likely hadn't made it past his vocal chords.

Cold sweat bathed Prophet as he stared down in wonder.

Who . . . ?

Then the word snapped like a small-caliber pistol in his brain: *Trap!*

Before he even realized what he was doing, he was launching himself off the heels of his boots and into the darkness beyond the fire. At the same time, he heard a low screech, like the beginning of a scream issued by a very old woman.

The screech grew until it merged with the thumping roar of a high-powered rifle, and slammed loudly into a tree inches from where Prophet had been standing, spraying bark and large wood chunks in all directions.

Prophet hit the ground and rolled, wincing as the Richards dug into his back and then hammered the back of his head as he rolled farther away from the firelight. As he rolled, he realized with a sickening feeling that he'd lost his rifle.

There was another loud thud as a second large-caliber slug plowed up dirt and dead leaves just off his right hip. The furrow the slug made was like that gouged by a man's fist.

The rifle's hiccupping roar rolled like thunder.

Prophet scrambled wildly behind a broad tree bole, slamming his back up against it, as he heard the clink of a shell being pulled out of the rifle's breech and another one being slid into the chamber.

The shooter was close. Maybe only fifty, sixty yards away. He had to be up high, too. Maybe in a tree. And he must've had a scope on that cannon . . .

Prophet edged a look around the side of the tree.

There was the tooth-gnashing screech of another bullet shredding the cool night air. Before Prophet could pull his head back, the bullet carved a scalding line across his right cheek before hammering the ground with a heavy thud like that of a stamping horse's hoof.

Prophet groaned against the pain in his cheek and threw himself forward, away from the tree. He rolled once, twice, three more times, trying desperately to get out of the shooter's range. But he knew that a Big Fifty Sharps had a wickedly long range—especially when an expert shooter, probably an ex-sharpshooter or buffalo hunter, was wielding it.

Yeah, a Big Fifty. He knew what they sounded like. He'd heard a few during the war, many more when he'd tried his hand at buffalo hunting before the waste of that massacre had disgusted him and he turned to hunting men instead.

As the big gun thundered twice more, the shots spaced about five seconds apart—the shooter was a seasoned son of a bitch, all right—Prophet found himself rolling down a slight hill. That was good. He needed to get lower. And he needed to get into heavier cover.

As he crabbed to his left, his left leg barked at him, burning. He looked at it. Blood shone across the outside of his thigh, through a gash in his denims and balbriggans. It glistened in the starlight.

Another bullet whooshed over his head, trailing the hammering blast by half a second.

Ka-funk! went the bullet blasting into the side of another tree. Bark rained. The tree quivered from the concussion of the blow, barren branches scraping against each other.

Prophet wanted to return fire, but he only had the shotgun and his Peacemaker. Besides, the shooter wasn't giving him time. And every time he moved, the shooter seemed to see it. Or he saw the brush moving around him, and that's what he was keying on.

Another bullet came hurling toward Prophet to plume dust and leaves a foot to his left. Prophet sucked back the pain in his cheek and leg, and hurled himself farther down the slope and into heavier brush. Yet another bullet came snapping through the brush just over his head. It caromed shrilly off a large rock just beyond him.

He crawled forward quickly. The shooter must have seen the brush move.

Another bullet screamed and split a sapling in half just ahead of him, throwing the upper part of the tree on top of him.

Christ almighty, the bounty hunter silently told himself, lying flat against the ground, deciding he might be better off holding still for a time. *You're out-positioned and overpowered. You might have just come to the end of your trail, old son.*

CHAPTER THIRTEEN

Louisa threw back the last of her cold coffee, and huddled down inside the blanket she'd drawn over her shoulders. She wore her wool blanket coat over a heavy serape, but it was a cold night. The chill penetrated her every fiber.

She set her cup down and glanced to her right.

Savidge was curled on his side, inside his blanket roll, head on his saddle. He snored softly, occasionally stopping to smack his lips. How comfortable he looked down there, under his blankets. Louisa felt the burn of deep rage, remembering that nearly naked, bloody girl hanging in the barn with her murdered family.

All hanged.

Louisa's right hand trembled faintly with the nearly irresistible urge to pull her pistols and shoot the rapist and killer through the head that everyone seemed to want so badly. She heeled the impulse. She'd feel good for a time, knowing that Savidge was dead, the girl and her family avenged, but then Lou would be angry with her, and she would no longer have the anticipation of watching the man stretch hemp at a public hanging.

That would be a joy, indeed.

As long as she and Lou were able to get the man to Denver. So far, the trip hadn't been a picnic, and it wasn't anywhere near finished. They still had to get to the rail line and hope they hadn't missed the twice-weekly train, though they likely had. If so, they'd have to wait for the next one. When they did get Savidge on the train, it would be a three- or four-day pull down to Denver.

Josephina murmured to Louisa's left, where she lay curled in her own blankets on that side of the fire. The girl was shivering in her sleep, moaning softly, turning her head from side to side. She was cold and she was having a nightmare. There was only one part of that that Louisa could help.

The Vengeance Queen rose from her log, retrieved her own bedroll, and arranged it over the slumbering girl. Josephina lifted her head with a startled gasp.

"Shhh," Louisa said, placing two fingers to her lips. "I covered you with my bedroll, that's all."

"What are you going to use?"

"I don't think I'll be going to sleep anytime soon. Lou's not back yet."

The girl sat up, and looked around. "What time is it?"

"Around nine."

"Cold," Josephina said, shivering inside her mound of blankets.

"Do you wish you would have stayed home?"

The girl shook her head and glanced into the cold darkness beyond the camp. "I'd rather freeze to death out here."

A distant, rumbling blast caused the girl to gasp again with a start.

Louisa jerked her head up, frowning toward the north.

Savidge stopped snoring and lifted his head from his saddle. "What was that?" he said thickly.

There was another thunder-like, rolling blast.

"Lou," Louisa said, tonelessly.

Wheeling, she grabbed her rifle and turned to Josephina. "Stay here," she ordered, and canted her head toward Savidge. "And stay away from him."

She racked a round into her Winchester's breech and ran up the northern rise.

Josephina stared after Louisa, a slender shadow that moved up and over the crest of the rise. She quickly dropped down the other side, fading from view.

Josephina suddenly felt very alone. Cold and alone.

"They ain't gonna make it," Savidge said. He was a man-shaped shadow leaning back against the birch.

"Please, be quiet," Josephina said.

"I'm just sayin' they ain't gonna make it."

"And I asked you to be quiet, Mr. Savidge."

"It's somethin' we gotta think about." Savidge stared at her darkly through the darkness. "If they don't come back, what're you gonna do? What am I gonna do?"

Josephina clutched her arms and shivered as, knees drawn to her chest, she stared off in the direction in which Louisa Bonaventure had disappeared.

There was another echoing blast. It sounded like a cannon, though Josephina didn't remember ever hearing a cannon before. Maybe once, during a Fourth of July celebration in town . . .

"You hear that heavy report?" Savidge said, his voice pitched low with menace. "That's a Big Fifty. Buffalo Rifle. Fires a bullet bigger'n your nose. And as fast as it's being fired out there, I'd say the shooter knows his way around it pretty damn good. That's about one shot every five seconds. Yeah, he was likely a hide hunter, all right. You see, the Big Fifty is a single-action weapon. You gotta remove the spent shell and replace it with a fresh one after every shot."

Savidge shook his head darkly. "Nah, Prophet walked into a trap. And that hot-headed girl is gonna follow him into it. Prophet's likely pinned, soon dead, and—"

"Please, shut up, Mr. Savidge!"

"—and Miss Bonaventure's gonna be dead here in a few minutes, when she—"

"Please!" Josephina fairly screamed, clamping her hands over her ears.

"—walks into the same trap. I'm sorry, but we gotta face facts, Miss Josephina."

The heavy reports kept echoing in the north. Josephina jerked with each report, as though the bullets were being hurled at her heart. She turned to Savidge and slowly lowered her hands from her ears, her blood racing in her veins, her stomach aching with fear.

"I ain't all that bad," Savidge said, stretching his lips back in an oily grin. "Not half as bad as they want you to believe. They've exaggerated my transgressions to make themselves feel better about turnin' me in to hang. My gang—now, they were a bad bunch, I'll confess that much." He shook his head. "But I never went in for what they did—to women an' such. And I never killed a man who didn't have a gun aimed my way."

"Really?" Josephina said.

"My word's bond."

"No, it's not."

Savidge frowned. "What's that?"

Josephina shook her head. "You're a rapist and a killer, Mr. Savidge. That's why you're here. That's why so many bounty hunters are after you."

"No, you see, that's what I'm tryin' to tell you. I ain't half as bad as they all would have you believe. I'm *good* to women. Hell, I was raised with three sisters, and I still write to my ma twice a year."

"Why are you telling me this?" Josephina said, jerking again with another echoing blast of that savage weapon.

"Because I want you to know you can trust me. I'm the only

337

one who can get you out of here. Hell, I can get you safely down to Denver and beyond, if you want. A purty young gal like yourself wouldn't have a chance, goin' it alone."

Josephina jerked as another echoing report rolled over the northern ridge. It sounded like the hammer of God. She couldn't help but imagine the flesh those large bullets were tearing out of Mr. Prophet . . . maybe out of Miss Bonaventure soon, as well.

Savidge said, "We don't have much time. Whoever's firing that gun likely has two or three more men sidin' him. They know where we're camped, and they'll come for us soon. *Us.* You don't think they're gonna be very nice to you when they come strollin' in here, do you? Killers like that? *Bounty poachers?* Hell, no—they'll take what they want from you, kill you, take your horse, take my *head,* and—"

"Were you lying about the money?"

Savidge frowned incredulously at the unexpected question voiced so softly. "What?"

"The money in Arizona. Is it actually there, or was that just one more of your lies?"

"Oh, it's there. It's there, all right. I don't lie about money."

"Where is it?"

"Shit, you think I'm gonna tell you and let you—?"

"Even if you drew me a detailed map, Mr. Savidge, I couldn't make it on my own." Josephina jerked her head toward the hill once more, as another report sounded. Her heart thudded heavily, desperately. "I've never been out of Brule County, much less the territory. Even if I knew where Arizona was, I'd never make it there without help. A man's help, unfortunately."

Savidge studied her. It was his turn to be suspicious. "It's outside of a little mining town south of Tucson. Gila Gulch, it's called. I've stowed it down in a dry well behind a mining shaft and an old stone Mexican shack. That's all I'm gonna say. I'll show you where it is, but that's all I'm gonna say."

"If I turn you loose, do you promise to take me to it . . . and to give me a quarter of it?"

"Just a quarter?"

"A quarter of fifty thousand dollars is all I'd need to make a fresh start. Besides, I doubt you'd give me half. If I insisted on half, I'd probably never make it out of Dakota Territory."

There was another blasting report. Josephina's heart skipped a beat, then continued chugging.

"Why, sure, sure. I'll give you a quarter."

Josephina rose with her blankets and walked over to Savidge. She dropped to her knees before him. She studied him for a time. He studied her in return, skeptically. There was another gunshot in the north. Josephina merely twitched a little now as she let the blankets fall to the ground, and unbuttoned her coat.

Shivering, she shrugged out of her coat and then unbuttoned her blouse.

"What're you . . . what're you . . . doin' . . . ?"

Josephina opened her blouse and lifted the long-sleeved men's undershirt and chemise that she wore beneath it. She raised the wash-worn garments to her neck, giving Savidge a good look at her breasts, which were covered in chicken flesh.

Her teeth chattering softly, Josephina said, "My husband never told me what he thought of my body, Mr. Savidge, but I've seen it in the mirror often enough to know that I am not ugly. And judging by his reactions when . . . when we were together . . . he was right pleased. Until he got tired of the same woman's body every night and drifted down to the woodcutters' camp." Her voice had hardened on this last.

"No, no . . . hell," Savidge chuckled. He swallowed as he glowered lustily at her exposed bosoms. "You ain't ugly one bit, Miss Josephina. I reckon you could please a man just fine. You'd never see me drifting down to no woodcutters' camp."

He snorted a lusty chuckle.

"If you promise to take me down to Arizona Territory and share your money with me, you can have me whenever you want. Just you. No one else. I will not sell myself to anyone else. Not ever. Only you . . . for the money and a fresh start. I would wager that freeing you from those chains and making my body available to you whenever you have the urge for it is worth one quarter of fifty thousand dollars—wouldn't you agree?"

"Hell, yeah." Savidge swallowed. "Hell, yeah."

"If you've grown tired of me by the time we reach the money, you can kick me loose. I know how men are. But you must promise right here and now not to double-cross me. You must promise me that your word is good, Mr. Savidge."

"I promise, Miss Josephina. I promise!" Savidge turned toward where another rocketing rifle report echoed. "What more can I do but promise? You're a purty girl, right man-pleasin', no doubt, and I'd be crazy not to take a deal like that! Now, you'd best free me before we get caught in one awful nasty whipsaw out here!"

Josephina knew that by trusting a man like Savidge, she was probably making an awful mistake. But desperation tugged hard inside her. She could see no other way to save herself. She certainly couldn't return to the ranch. She had to leave the territory. And she had to have money to make a fresh start for herself.

The heavy, cannon-like thunder peels minus the reports of any answering shots kept telling her that Prophet would soon be dead, and so would Miss Bonaventure, and she would be left to the mercy of the men after Savidge.

Men who doubtless knew nothing about mercy whatever.

She was taking a risk by trusting this known rapist and killer. But what other chance did she have of making it out of the territory?

She lowered her shirts, buttoned her dress, draped her blankets over her shoulders again, and walked over to where Miss Bonaventure's gear was piled. She'd seen Louisa place her set of keys to Savidge's handcuffs and leg shackles inside a small pouch inside her saddlebags. Josephina wasn't sure why she'd noted that, but she had.

She dropped to a knee and rummaged around until she found the pouch and spilled its contents into her hand.

A brass ring containing two keys dropped out—one relatively small key and one finger-sized key.

Josephina dropped the empty pouch on the ground and turned to Savidge.

"That's it," he said, and grinned. "Arizona, here we come!"

CHAPTER FOURTEEN

Prophet cursed as another slug hammered the ground about eight inches up the slight hollow in which he cowered flat on his back against a bed of cold leaves and dirt. The slug threw loam and gravel on him, showering his face.

He spat it from his lips, blew it out his nose, tried to blink it from his eyes. He didn't get all of it out of his eyes, which burned. He didn't want to lift his hands to brush it away. The shooter would key on the movement.

He tried to quell his crazy breathing, but that was no easy task. He hadn't been in a fix like this since the war, when he'd once been pinned down by Union sharpshooters behind enemy lines, when he'd tried to rescue his cousin, Melvin Prophet, from the farmhouse he'd holed up in after he and Lou had gotten separated from their regiment after the Battle of Kennesaw Mountain. Melvin had taken a bullet in the belly, and Prophet had slipped away from the badly shelled farmhouse to find supplies with which to tend him—to no avail.

Because of the snipers who'd kept him pinned down for most of a rainy night, by the time he finally reached Melvin, his cousin merely stared up at him, glassy-eyed in death.

Prophet pressed his back harder against the bottom of the hollow here in Dakota Territory. He'd found the depression when he'd been frantically scrounging for cover from that infernal cannon hammering away at him from a tree nearly directly north, maybe fifty yards away.

The hollow had been formed by the uprooting of a large cottonwood, and the roots of the cottonwood dangled over him now, though several of the thick, snake-like tendrils had been blasted away by the Sharps.

The infernal Sharps.

He held the Richards against his chest. The barn blaster was of no use at this range. His pistol was still in the holster strapped to his thigh, but the Peacemaker wouldn't do him any good from this distance, either.

Another bullet thumped into the ground a few feet away, blowing more dirt on Prophet. It was only a matter of time, he knew, before the shooter found his mark. At the moment, he was probing a haystack with a pitchfork. A couple more pokes, and . . .

A rifle barked somewhere behind Prophet. It barked again, and again. He recognized the ripping bark of a Winchester carbine.

Prophet lifted his head slightly and saw the rifle's flash about thirty yards away through the trees. Louisa. Had to be her. She was firing steadily, one shot after another, in the direction of the Sharps, which had suddenly fallen silent.

Prophet's heart quickened even more than before. It quickened with relief. He'd been no more than a minute away from becoming wolf bait.

Prophet counted out Louisa's nine shots. Her rifle fell silent.

Prophet stayed where he was, back pressed flat against the ground. He pricked his ears, listening, cold sweat streaking the dirt and bits of shredded leaves on his cheeks. He thought he heard brush crunching in the direction that the Sharps had been blasting from, but he couldn't be sure.

His ears were ringing from the reports and from the adrenaline coursing through his veins. His heart hammered out a rhythm in time with the ringing. It sounded like a powwow, as though nasty little Indians were dancing around inside him.

He resisted the urge to lift his head at the risk of getting it shot off.

Then he heard the distance-muffled, crunching thuds of a horse galloping through brush, the sounds retreating quickly into the northern distance.

Louisa's voice came to him like a buoy in choppy seas. "Lou?"

Prophet tried to answer but found his throat constricted.

Louder, she said, "Lou, are you out here?" Her voice trilled with worry.

Prophet lifted his head, wincing against the pain that had left him for a time, drowned by other concerns. But it was back now with a vengeance, kicking up a fierce rhythm in his leg and cheek, two more companion instruments joining the violent symphony in his ears.

He hacked phlegm from his throat, and spat.

"Here."

Louisa's soft, careful footsteps sounded to his right. "Where?"

Prophet waved an arm. "Over here, damnit!"

He sat up, brought a hand to his stinging cheek, and felt the dirt mixed with the blood there. He felt the ache of the bullet burn all across his face. The graze across his left thigh felt like a continuous lash of a willow switch, a sensation he'd been all too familiar with, growing up in Ma Prophet's house in Cobb County, Georgia. If Ma wasn't up to the all-too-frequent and all-too-deserved punishment, Pa unfailingly was.

But young Prophet had never been strapped this hard.

Louisa walked up out of the woods, her breath frosting in the air around her head.

"How bad, Lou?"

"Grazes, both."

She dropped to a knee and leaned her rifle against a tree

root. She sucked a sharp breath when she saw the cut on his cheek.

"You think it's gonna leave a scar?" Prophet asked her, ironically.

"A nasty one, but don't worry, Lou—your face has never been your strong suit."

"Thanks . . . I think."

Prophet removed his bandanna from around his neck and started to tie it around the bullet burn on his upper left thigh. Louisa snatched the cloth out of his hands, and performed the task herself, tying it tightly to stem the blood flow.

"We'll get you cleaned up when we get back to camp," she said.

"Hey, wait a minute," Prophet said, scowling at her. "What're you doing here? Who's watching Savidge?"

"No one. I heard the report of that big-caliber gun, and . . . come on—let's get you to your feet."

Louisa wrapped Prophet's left arm around her neck and helped the big man up off the ground. He grunted as he rose, his cheek burning as though a hot iron were pressed against it. At the same time, the blood was cold. An oddly uncomfortable combination.

"You shouldn't have come, girl."

"If I hadn't come, you'd be dead by now."

"There you go again—thinkin' with your heart instead of your head."

"I'll work on it sometime. For now, shut up!"

"Hold on," Prophet said, moving into the camp where the two dead men lay in dark, unmoving mounds. "Gotta fetch my rifle."

He picked up the Winchester and brushed it off. He looked into the darkness to the north, listening in case the gunman had turned back around. Prophet heard nothing but the scratching

345

of barren branches.

"Did you get a look at him?" Louisa said, coming up beside Prophet.

"No. Got no idea who he is. Doubt he's the man I shot back at the ranch. All I know is he's wielding a Big Fifty, and I don't ever care to be on the wrong end of a gun like that again!"

Prophet started moving through the trees, dragging his stiff left leg back in the direction from which he'd come. "That bastard's liable to get back to camp before we do, and cut Savidge's head off. Damnit, Louisa!"

"It's this way!" she said, tugging on his arm and adjusting his halting course.

It took them nearly an hour to get back to the rise north of the camp. Even at that rate, they were lucky, for they had no fire to aim for. Only Louisa's keen sense of direction led them on nearly an as-the-crow-flies course up and over the rise and into the camp.

At camp's edge, they stopped and stood side by side, looking around.

Prophet racked a cartridge into his Winchester's breech and aimed the rifle into the darkness before him. Into the vacant darkness where only his and Louisa's gear remained.

"Hmm," Prophet said, pitching his voice wryly. "Chaz? Where are you, Chaz? Oh, Chaz?"

Louisa strode quickly forward, gazing down at the tree she'd left Savidge leaning against, as though maybe he were only concealed by the darkness. Nope. Their prisoner wasn't where she'd left him.

Louisa kicked the shackles, which, along with the handcuffs, were all that remained of Chaz Savidge's presence here. The shackles clanked as they flew several feet away. Louisa strode around the camp quickly, anxiously, turning this way and that, aiming her rifle, her breath rising, frosting in short bursts around her head.

"Miss Hawkins is gone, too," she said.

Prophet was moving stiffly around, as well. "Done made note of that, partner." He dragged his burning left leg into the darkness east of the camp, and stopped dead in his tracks, staring. "Horses are gone, too," he said, feeling a cold stone drop in his belly.

Louisa chewed out an uncustomary curse, and stomped off into the darkness. She disappeared for a while, but Prophet could hear her kicking around as though maybe Savidge and the girl were hiding out there somewhere. When Louisa returned to the camp, Prophet was sitting on a log and pouring whiskey onto the dirty bullet graze on his leg, sucking a sharp breath as he did.

The bottle had belonged to Ben Ryder. The poacher had packed two. He'd been good for something.

Prophet raised the bottle to Louisa. "They might've took the horses but at least they left the whiskey."

He set the bottle down and began cleaning the wound with a handkerchief.

Louisa stood stiffly on the other side of the dead fire. "The shooter? You think he took them?"

"Nah," Prophet said, his casual tone belying his concern for their dire situation—alone out here without their horses, the man with the Big Fifty likely on the lurk nearby. "He'd have taken longer to find our camp without a fire to lead him in. And there'd have been a commotion. I'd say ole Savidge sweet-talked that young gal into turning him loose. You must have left your keys layin' around, like a damn tinhorn."

"I wasn't thinking," Louisa said, her voice trembling as she tried to keep her emotions on a short leash. "I heard the reports of that big-caliber gun, and . . . I knew you were out there, and

. . ." She swung around quickly and said in exasperation, "How did she know I kept my keys in my saddlebags!"

"A right observant girl."

"I didn't take her for a fool," Louisa said.

"She was likely scared. Heard that Big Fifty. Savidge likely convinced her that you and me were wolf bait. So she squirreled your keys out of your bags and turned him loose. They rode off and took our horses so we couldn't follow 'em. That was likely Savidge's idea, because he probably knew there was only a fifty-fifty chance that Big Fifty would cut us both down."

Prophet shook his head slowly as he scrubbed at the burn, both wincing and grinning. "But that girl, Josephina—she's been through a lot. Fear was talkin' to her. Fear's got a loud voice. It clouds clear thinkin'. I learned that in the war."

"I suppose you'd like to shoot me," Louisa said. "I'd shoot you, if you did something this stupid."

Prophet chuckled. "Hell, I'd want you to."

Louisa stared at him. She was a slender, straight-backed silhouette in the darkness, starlight glistening faintly off the brim of her hat. "How can you be so calm about this, Lou? Savidge is gone!"

Prophet scooped the bottle off the ground. "Because we're gonna get him back. No one hornswoggles ole Lou Prophet and the Vengeance Queen an' gets away with it. Especially a killer with a three-thousand-dollar bounty on his head. Especially when he took off with my hoss! Not that that cayuse wasn't headed for the glue factory, but . . ."

He poured more whiskey on his leg and sucked a sharp breath through gritted teeth.

"We'll catch up to him sooner or later," he said. "Hopefully sooner rather than later, but I reckon we'll see." He took a swig of the whiskey. "Thanks, partner."

Louisa scowled at him. "For what?"

"For savin' this worthless old hide." Prophet took another pull from the bottle and then splashed some of the whiskey on his face, and cursed a blue streak for a good ten seconds.

He shook his head as though to clear the burning misery, and corked the bottle. "Now, why don't you get your sewin' kit out and close up this cheek before I got no more blood left in my head?"

Something warm and bristly scratched at Prophet's injured cheek.

Deep asleep and leaning back against a log, cradling his Winchester in his arms, he waved the bristly thing away.

Again, the hot, bristled thing scratched at his cheek.

"Ow," Prophet heard himself mutter. It was like hearing someone else's voice from the bottom of a deep well, far away.

Prophet settled back against the log, wanting only to return to the cradle of sleep, away from the aches and burns in his battered body. A faint warning sounded in his ears, but the warm darkness cradling him away from his pain was more alluring.

He succumbed to it.

The bristled thing blew hot, fetid air against his cheek.

Then there was a sharp, burning sting. That plucked Prophet out of his cradle like a child scooped from a baptismal font into the cold, aching air of reality. The bounty hunter gave a grunt and raised his rifle but eased the tension in his trigger finger when he saw Mean and Ugly pull his bristled lips away from his rider's face.

The horse nickered and sidestepped, rolling his customarily jeering eyes.

"Goddamnit, Mean!" the bounty hunter said, brushing a hand across the cheek rough with the sutures that Louisa had used to close the wound. The fresh, aching burn told him that the horse had been nibbling at the stitches. "You cussed beast.

What I told you about that glue factory must not have . . . !"

Prophet let his voice trail off. He stared, dumbfounded, half wondering if he were still asleep and dreaming.

Mean and Ugly.

"Holy shit!" Prophet exclaimed, shrugging out of his blankets and climbing to his feet too fast and staggering as the ground cloaked in the gray light of dawn pitched around him.

"What is it?" Louisa was instantly awake, pumping a cartridge into her Winchester's breech as she shrugged out of her own blankets near Prophet.

"It's Mean, the old cayuse, returned to his poppa!" Prophet staggered over to the mount and wrapped his thick arms around the dun's stout neck. "My beautiful Mean and Ugly! He came back to bedevil his rider some more!" He patted the horse's wither. "Goddamnit, Mean—some habits die hard, don't they?"

He laughed and then laughed again when he saw Louisa's brown and white pinto grazing nearby.

"Girl," Prophet said, "I think we're back on that killer's trail!"

Louisa glanced around, still groggy. She looked at Mean and Prophet, reunited like old lovers. She blinked and lowered the Winchester. "I thought for sure we'd find them both dead . . . if we found either one at all."

"Savidge must've led 'em a ways off and then let 'em go, not thinking they'd make it back to us." Prophet looked at Louisa. "Don't look a gift horse—"

"No, Lou," said the Vengeance Queen, scowling her distaste for the big man's jokes. "It's too early." She donned her hat, picked up her saddle, and strode to the pinto. "Let's ride!"

CHAPTER FIFTEEN

One month later . . .

It was cold at night in December in southern Arizona.

The days were warm. Unseasonably warm, in Prophet's experience of that vast, rugged territory in winter.

Now the sun hammered down at him, clear as a lens, out of a broad vault of cerulean sky. He rode Mean and Ugly out between two pale stone escarpments and into a large, hard-packed yard where several corrals of woven ocotillo branches surrounded a two-story, mud-brick building with a brush-roofed front gallery.

Under the gallery, an *olla* swayed from its braided leather thong in the dry breeze.

A dark-haired girl sat on a rope-bottomed chair on the gallery, crouched over a mandolin. As Prophet gigged Mean into the yard, holding the horse to a slow walk while he gained a lay of the land, the girl looked up from watching her brown fingers caressing the mandolin's strings.

She had an Indian-dark face with long, raven hair tumbling about her shoulders. She was plump and large-boned, but the bones were nicely rounded and turned. Her severely featured face was made pretty by a long, straight nose and by soulful, coal-colored eyes.

She wore a cotton, Mexican-style dress, one strap hanging down off her brown shoulder. Her legs were tightly crossed and her bare feet rested, one atop the other, beneath the chair.

Now as the girl gazed toward Prophet, she absently reached over and pulled the strap of her dress back up on her shoulder, but as soon as she returned her hand to the mandolin, the strap slid off her shoulder once more. She left it there, though the dress hung down to just above the nipple of her small, brown left breast.

She continued to strum the mandolin very softly as Prophet reined the dun up in front of a hitch rack, and swung down from the saddle. A half-dozen other horses, all dusty, desert-bred mustangs, slouched at the two hitch racks fronting the place.

Prophet studied the shabby, sun- and heat-blasted building carefully. Its warped windows were darkly opaque.

This was border country, and no place here was safe, not that anyplace anywhere was safe for a man who'd been collecting bounties on outlaws for the past twelve years. Prophet had many enemies across the frontier, but especially in the southwest, to which men with bounties on their heads tended to gravitate.

Especially in the wintertime.

A slight breeze lifted dust from the ground at the base of the *cantina's* stone steps, swirled it, and hurled it against the front wall with a soft *whoosh* and with light, breathy ticking sounds as the dust met the windows.

Much of the dust disappeared over and under the batwing doors to the right of the girl, causing the doors to swing back and forth, as though a ghost had passed through them. The hinges squawked.

Prophet adjusted the coach gun's sling on his shoulder and slowly climbed the gallery's steps. He pinched his hat brim to the girl, offering a sunburned smile. The girl did not return the smile, but she removed her hands from the mandolin to let her dark eyes crawl up and down the big, tall man before her.

"You want Mexican girl or *gringa*?" she said in a thick Spanish accent. "I am Abella." She quirked her mouth corners with a flirtatious smile. "I make you feel good, *senor.* The charge is only three *pesos* for me, and that includes a bath and a glass of *cerveza.* I am good. Better than any *gringa.*"

"That's a damn steal, *chiquita,*" Prophet said, scowling as though deeply offended for her. "Three *pesos* for a pretty girl *and* a bath *and* a glass of *cerveza?* Why, you're worth six, seven times that alone—never mind that bath and the beer!"

She smiled curiously, skeptically, at the big, dusty rider before her. Prophet went to the *olla* and used the wooden ladle to dipper water out of the clay pot, and to take a cool, refreshing drink. As he did, he saw the girl studying him. The cut on Prophet's cheek had only partly healed, but he'd plucked the stiches out while drinking whiskey one night around his and Louisa's cook fire.

As he drank, the Mexican girl canted her head to one side, studying him as though trying to puzzle him out. She'd likely never run into a *gringo* like this one before—concerned about a *puta's* well-being.

Prophet and Louisa had been in Arizona for the past two weeks, hunting Savidge. That was long enough for even the winter sun to have turned him an Indian-like reddish bronze, and for his light-blue eyes to stand out in sharp contrast against it.

He and Louisa had forked trails just after leaving the railroad at Belen, New Mexico Territory, each investigating possible routes that, based on only slightly conflicting accounts of a rancher and a whiskey drummer, a man and a young woman fitting the descriptions of Savidge and Josephina Hawkins might have taken.

Prophet and Louisa had picked up the pair's trail in Denver nearly two weeks after losing them in Dakota Territory. They'd learned from several witnesses that the two had spent five days in that dusty cow town nestled at the base of the Front Range, while Savidge had played poker for several long nights in a row, apparently building a stake for himself.

A traveling stake.

Prophet had inquired at Union Station for them one day after he'd learned from a ticket agent that they'd hopped an Atchison, Topeka, & Santa Fe flier for the sun-blasted south.

Why? Was the killer just hoping to cool his heels in the land of sunshine and Gila monsters, like so many others of his ilk?

What was he still doing with the girl? Prophet was surprised he hadn't found Josephina's body along the trail. Had Savidge's story about his "retirement" treasure been more than a story, after all? Was he really intending on sharing it with Josephina?

Or was he just enjoying the nice-looking girl's company for as long as she sated his desires, stringing her along to amuse himself?

Prophet feared the latter. He doubted that Savidge could be amused by the same girl for long.

In Denver, the bounty hunters had built small stakes of their own—Louisa by riding a hotel desk for a few nights, and Prophet by swamping out the Larimer Street Saloon by day and bouncing at night.

A hornswoggled bounty hunter had to earn a living one way or another.

To the *puta* now, Prophet pinched his hat brim and said, "Maybe I'll take you up on your offer later. For now, I got business inside. In fact, maybe you can help me."

"*Si*, of course."

"Have you seen an ugly *gringo* around here lately, maybe stopping for a drink? Besides myself, I'm sayin." Prophet grinned, fingering the stiches on his cheek. "This *hombre* might have taken a poke. Or not. He's got a girl with him—a brown-eyed, brown-haired girl with a round, pretty face. When I say ugly, I mean this fellow is ugly as last year's sin. *Feo!*"

The girl flushed behind her natural dark complexion, and lowered her eyes to her mandolin. She started strumming the instrument once more as she shook her head quickly, her hair tumbling down to hide her face. "No, no, *senor.* I don't know about . . . anything like that."

Prophet studied her, puzzled by her reaction. Had she seen Savidge and just didn't want to speak about him, knowing he was dangerous? Or had she learned—probably wisely so—not to relay information about anyone to anyone, lest she wanted her tongue cut out?

Prophet felt bad about having asked her the question. He should have known you didn't ask whores questions like that, especially when someone might have overheard her response and taken umbrage.

"I beg your pardon, *senorita,*" he said, pinching his hat brim again.

He pushed through the batwings and stopped just inside the *cantina.*

It was a crude, smelly layout, a plank-board bar to the right. Crude shelves lined the wall behind the bar, around a four-by-four, fly-stained mirror that had a long, jagged crack running through it.

There were ten or so tables to the left of the bar. Only two were occupied, by men as rough-hewn as their surroundings— dirty, long-haired, raggedly dressed *hombres,* most sporting several shooting irons apiece. Four of the men were Mexican. Two were *gringos* less colorfully but just as roughly attired as the Mexicans.

Another, small Mexican sat at a table against the wall to Prophet's right, near the end of the makeshift bar. He had a crock jug on the table before him. A matchstick protruded from between his thick, blistered lips.

He was sharpening more matchsticks with a knife three times

larger than needed for the job, and setting the sharpened sticks in a neat pile beside a stone ashtray in which a half-smoked, cornhusk quirley smoldered. A fat, black cat lay on the other side of the table from the man, its green eyes riveted on Prophet.

The cat curled and uncurled the end of its tail. An empty tin plate lay just beyond its white-tipped front paws.

All eyes in the room had turned to Prophet, lingering on him. The two *gringos* shifted slightly in their chairs. The Mexicans muttered things Prophet couldn't hear. The air was rife with tobacco smoke and the smell of rotgut tequila or mescal.

Prophet turned to the lone Mexican, who just then poked his right index finger through the handle of the jug and lifted the jug to his mouth, hooking it over his right shoulder and taking two sizeable pulls. Some of the tangle-leg dribbled down the corners of his mouth, soaking his brushy mustache that had a white line, like a lightning bolt, running through it.

The little Mexican sighed as he set the bottle back down on the table. He said loudly, slurring his words liberally, "Come in, *senor.* Take a load off. Have a drink." He glanced at a table where the other Mexicans in the room were playing cards. "Play some poker, if you like. If you need to bleed off your loins, Abella is at your service."

"So I heard," Prophet said, walking over to the little Mexican's table. He glanced at the others in the room, cautiously, and hiked a boot onto an empty chair.

He patted the cat, which continued to curl its tail, and asked, "I'm looking for an ugly son of a bitch who might have rode through here with a pretty, brown-haired girl. They're both *gringos.*"

The little Mexican glanced at the others and then hiked a shoulder. "Many men ride through here, amigo. Many *Mejicanos,* many *gringos.* I had a *Negro* ride through here last week, and a fat *hombre* in a very nice suit. A city suit. The kind you

356

buy in a store. He was from back east somewhere, I think."

He shook his head slowly, smiling. "But I see damn few *gringos* ride through here with women. The reason they stop here is because they don't *have* a woman."

"You sure?" Prophet asked him pointedly.

"*Si, si, senor,*" the Mexican said, nodding and pooching out his lips. "I am sure. I do apologize. How 'bout if I make it up to you with a drink on the house, huh?"

Prophet studied the man. He glanced at the others. Only a few sets of eyes were on him now, but the other eyes were too busily trying to avoid him.

Why?

Apprehension tugged at the ends of Prophet's nerves.

With a slow sigh and a nod, Prophet said, "Sure I'll take a drink. I could use one."

CHAPTER SIXTEEN

Prophet tramped over to a table near the barman's, kicked a chair out, and doffed his hat. Giving a quick, furtive study of the others in the room—one *gringo* looked vaguely familiar—he ran his elbow around inside his hat, soaking up the sweat from the band with his sleeve.

As the Mexican came out with a jug and a filmy shot glass, Prophet tossed his hat onto the table, hooked the Richards over the table's near right corner, within easy reach, and slacked into his chair. By his own design, the batwings were not directly behind him but sort of off his left shoulder, seven feet away.

He faced all of the other customers in the *cantina*. The barman's table was six feet away on his right.

The cat still studied Prophet but it was no longer curling its tail. More even than the others, the cat was making Prophet feel self-conscious.

The Mexican set the shot glass on the table. His quirley drooped between his lips, and he blinked against the smoke wandering up into his eyes as he filled the glass with unfiltered mescal. The aroma of the astringent liquor itself was intoxicating, as it wafted up against Prophet's nose.

The Mexican glanced at the Richards, then twisted the cork into the jug's lip as he turned toward the bar.

"Leave it," Prophet said. "I'm a might thirsty."

"Come far, *senor*? Not that it's any of my business, but . . ."

"We all got a curious streak," Prophet said. "Yeah, you could say I've come far. Boy, it was cold up in Dakota. I'd hate to get stuck up there all winter!"

He chuckled and glanced around the room, but no one else seemed to find the comment in the least bit amusing. Maybe they'd never spent a winter in Dakota Territory. Or maybe their thoughts were elsewhere.

The *gringo* he thought he'd recognized sat about ten feet ahead and right, near the bar. Long, dark-red hair hung to his shoulders. He had a thin, scraggly beard and long mustaches damp from the forty-rod he was drinking. The top of his bulbous head was nearly bald, but Prophet judged he was only twenty-six, twenty-seven.

He was damned familiar, all right. Most likely, Prophet had seen that ugly visage on a wanted dodger or two . . .

He faced Prophet and kept casting owlish glances over the left shoulder of the man he shared his table with, whose back faced the bounty hunter.

The Mexican set the jug down on the table, on the Richards's wide leather lanyard. He blinked sleepily down at Prophet once more, then removed the quirley from between his lips, blew smoke out his mouth and nostrils, and strode back over to his own table, where the cat was now washing itself.

Prophet nudged the jug off the lanyard. He picked up the shot glass and studied the cloudy liquid through the filmy glass, then tossed back half the shot, stretching his lips back from his teeth and raking out a heavy sigh as the mescal stoked a frenzied fire inside him.

His eyes watered.

Whenever he drank mescal down here in the southwestern territories, he felt like a kid partaking for the first time of his old man's skull pop.

It usually took him a shot or two to get used to the vigor of the tangle-leg all over again.

He looked up quickly and caught the *gringo* glaring at him again over his friend's left shoulder. The *gringo* averted his gaze quickly, and his mouth moved as he said something to the man across from him. The Mexicans gathered around the table to the *gringo's* left, against the left wall, weren't saying anything. They were busily keeping their eyes off of Prophet.

Occasionally, they cut their eyes over to the fidgety *gringo.*

They were a surly bunch—the whole lot of them. There was no denying it. They likely never did much singing and dancing, but was there some particular reason they were looking so sullen just now?

Did they know something about Savidge, or did they know who Prophet was and were taking umbrage about his possible past transgressions against them or against those they knew? Prophet had done plenty of work down here in the past, so he wouldn't doubt that his reputation preceded him.

The Richards marked him as a bounty hunter, of course. And the nasty gash on his rough-hewn cheek likely told them he wasn't a deacon in the Lutheran church. Maybe they just didn't like bounty hunters. Maybe they all had prices on their heads and they were just naturally skittish about sharing a *cantina* with a man who made his living running their kind to ground.

In that case, their demeanors would be entirely reasonable and understandable.

Prophet threw back the rest of the mescal in his glass, and splashed out more from the jug. Damned good stuff. Really took the edge off a hard ride and a less than friendly situation. He knew from experience to go easy, though, for mescal would start going down like water after the third or four shot.

Over the next half a bottle you'd swear you were stone-cold sober, and could even win a few rounds of stud or 'jack, or take a girl to bed and enjoy yourself. But then it would slap you as hard as a deeply offended *puta* when you least expected, and send you crawling toward the nearest slop bucket with your eyes swimming and your guts on fire.

Prophet took only a small sip of the second shot, and then dug out his makings sack and began building a quirley.

He'd fired the quirley and was sitting back in his chair, smoking and conservatively sipping the mescal, enjoying himself for a short while before he'd hit the trail again, when the man sitting across from the familiar-looking *gringo* slid his chair back from their table, stood, stretched, and said with a laugh, "Time to shake the dew from my lily."

He did not turn toward Prophet but merely gave him his profile as he moved out away from the table before turning to tramp into the shadows at the back of the *cantina*—a broad-shouldered *hombre* in a sheepskin vest over a dark calico shirt. He also wore a necklace of what appeared dyed grizzly teeth—something he'd likely taken in trade from an Indian.

He had two cartridge belts crisscrossed on his waist, with one hogleg in a beaded holster thonged on his right thigh. When he'd gained his feet and turned away from his table, Prophet had glimpsed another pistol riding in a belly holster. Walking with an ever-so-slight limp, he pushed through the plank-board door at the back of the room, slipped out into the brassy sunlight, and closed the door behind him.

Before the door had closed, Prophet had glimpsed a privy leaning back there behind the *cantina.*

Now there was no one to obscure the nervous *gringo* facing Prophet. The man glanced up at Prophet briefly, furtively, then casually puffed his cheeks out and began rolling a quirley of his own. He and his friend had been playing red dog, and two decks of cards and a few coins were scattered on the table before him, around an earthen jug like Prophet's.

The mescal had oiled the bounty hunter's brain enough that

the man's name slipped out like fresh plop from under a cow's arched tail:

Buck Stinson.

A small-fry criminal wanted in several territories for mostly petty crimes including saloon robberies and stock and hay thievery. He may or may not have been involved in a range war up in Nevada, but he was wanted for questioning by the marshals up there. Prophet thought the price on his head wasn't worth trifling over.

Stinson licked his quirley closed and glanced fleetingly at Prophet once more.

Prophet raised his shot glass to him. "Hidy, Buck."

Stinson stared at him, hairy-eyed.

Prophet shook his head. "Pull your horns in. I ain't here for you." He glanced at the Mexicans. "Or any of these other *hombres*. I'm lookin' for another fellow, Chaz Savidge. Nasty bastard. Makes you look like an aged nun, Buck. Just now, however, I'm enjoyin' this here—"

He stopped talking suddenly.

The hair at the back of his neck was flicking around like an entire field of wheat in a prairie wind.

A shadow slid across the floor off his right shoulder. He dropped his shot glass onto the table, spilling mescal, and grabbed the Richards as he threw himself hard right from his chair. Just before he hit the floor, a pistol barked and there was a loud, shrill scream of breaking glass.

The pistol kept barking and the glass kept shattering.

Prophet hit the floor on his right shoulder, rolled twice, then twisted back onto his butt, spun, and looked behind him and through a window to see a man firing two pistols from out front of the *cantina*. Stinson's red dog partner was firing through a large patch of jagged-edged window he'd broken out with his first few shots.

Glass flew in all directions. Powder smoke wafted in the sunshine. Stinson's partner was bellowing and laughing as he fired each pistol in turn through the window.

The Mexicans were screaming as they dove for cover, and so was Buck Stinson, cursing loudly. "Hold it, Powell, you crazy bastard—you're killin' everybody but Prophet!"

Prophet raised the Richards up off the floor, clicked the left rabbit ear hammer back, and squeezed the corresponding trigger.

A much larger patch of glass was blown out of the window, the shattering noises drowned by the ten-gauge's booming thunder. Powell screamed as he disappeared in the rain of flying glass.

Behind Prophet, Stinson bellowed incoherently. Boots thumped loudly. Prophet swung around in time to see the small-fry owlhoot staggering toward him, blood oozing from his right, shredded ear.

Stinson's eyes were bright with fury as he raised both of his own Schofield revolvers. He got one shot off before Prophet tripped the Richards's second trigger and watched Stinson get blown straight back as though by a sudden cyclone ripping through the saloon.

Stinson landed on a table and rolled heels-over-jaw down the other side and out of sight, landing with a raucous thump.

One of the Mexicans had been hit in the mescal-inspired barrage by Powell, and the others were stumbling around, yelling in Spanish and pulling six-shooters. Since there was no one else in the room to shoot at, they began swinging their hoglegs toward Prophet, who tossed away the smoking Richards and palmed his .45.

Bang! Bang! Bang-Bang-Bang!

Only two of the Mexicans managed to squeeze off shots in Prophet's general direction, the bullets plunking into the floor wide of him, before the bounty hunter's bullets sent them pirouetting into the wall and over tables and chairs, screaming as they died. One hit the floor and tried raising his pearl-gripped Bisley, bellowing a less than polite insult against Prophet's mother.

The bounty hunter aimed carefully, knowing he had only one more round left in the Peacemaker, and drilled a blue, puckered hole in the raging Mex's forehead, just above the bridge of his nose.

Movement to Prophet's right.

He swung in that direction to see the barman aiming an ancient, double-barreled shotgun at him from over the bar.

"Oh, shit!" Prophet muttered to himself, automatically swinging his empty Colt at the snarling barkeep.

Seeing the big Colt aimed in his direction, the Mexican dropped the shotgun atop the bar, screaming, "No, *por favor*—you're too much killer for me, *amigo!*"

He swung around and, holding his arms over his head, ran through a door behind the bar, leaving the door open behind him. He obviously hadn't counted Prophet's shots. The cat, which must have taken cover under the barkeep's table, gave an indignant meow from somewhere behind the bar.

A few seconds later, Prophet saw the cat running tail-up after its master beyond the open door, both man and cat running toward a fringe of dusty willows and palo verdes some distance away.

Prophet rose, blinking against the wafting powder smoke. He looked around quickly, then, shaking the spent cartridges out of his Colt and replacing them with fresh from his cartridge belt, walked to the broken window.

Powell lay outside on his back. He looked as though his head and upper torso had been doused with red paint from which bits of window glass protruded. His eyes were gone.

Prophet strode back through the saloon.

None of the Mexicans were moving. He turned to Stinson, whose chest was rising and falling shallowly where he lay on his back, on the other side of the table he'd tumbled over. The buckshot had taken him in the upper chest, but somehow he was still breathing. Buckshot peppered his lower face and his neck, as well. Blood dribbled from the small wounds.

He stared straight up at the ceiling, blinking.

Prophet crouched over the outlaw. "Now, what the hell was that all about? I told you I wasn't after you."

"Wish you woulda told Powell," Stinson said, and chuckled briefly. Then he stretched his lips back from his teeth as pain lanced him. "We . . . thought you was gonna take . . . the girl. We was . . . havin' fun . . . with her."

Prophet frowned. "What girl?"

Stinson swallowed. He was sucking air now like a landed fish, his eyes growing wider as he clung more desperately to the life that was fast leaving him. "The . . . one . . . upstairs. Savidge— he's pimpin' her out up there . . . buildin' a stake."

Outside, hoof thuds rose.

"*Hy-ahhh!*" a man shouted as the thudding grew louder.

Prophet turned to a dust-streaked window in time to see a rider galloping away from a small *adobe* stable on the other side of the yard. Chaz Savidge whipped his rein ends across his dappled gray's right wither and shouted, "*Hy-ahhh,* you cayuse. *Hy-ahhhh!*"

Horse and rider galloped across the yard, passing from Prophet's left to his right, and then swinging around the ocotillo corral and heading west.

"Shit!"

Prophet ran to the front of the saloon and out the batwing doors. He shucked his Winchester from his saddle boot, racked a shell into the chamber, and planted a bead on Savidge's jos-

365

tling back as horse and rider galloped straight out away from the *cantina*.

Prophet fired three quick rounds. He cursed again as his bullets plumed dust to either side of the fleeing killer. He aimed once more, carefully, but held fire when the outlaw gave a wild, victorious whoop and dashed around a bend in the trail, the bristling desert swallowing him.

"Goddamnit!" Prophet shouted.

He was tempted to mount Mean and Ugly and give chase. But Savidge would keep. His trail was fresh.

The girl . . .

CHAPTER SEVENTEEN

"What room's she in?" Prophet asked Stinson as he ran toward the back of the *cantina*.

But a single glance showed him Stinson lying still in death now, gazing heavy-lidded, mouth slack, at the ceiling. Prophet took the stairs three steps at a time, turned at the top, and ran down a dingy, musty hall.

There were three curtained doorways on each side. Prophet pulled the first curtain on the left aside, peered into the room, and then turned to the opposite curtain.

He pulled that aside, as well, and then continued to the next curtain on the hall's right side.

He swept it away, and froze.

"No," a small voice said. "Please . . . no more."

Prophet moved slowly, haltingly into the room.

Josephina Hawkins lay on a small, low bed with a green wooden frame. The bottom middle of the bed sagged nearly to the floor. The room smelled of slop buckets, tobacco, and whiskey. Josephina lay naked spread-eagled on the bed, her wrists and ankles tied with ropes to frame posts. Her mussed hair screened her eyes. Her lower lip was split and one eye was discolored.

"Please," she begged in that same small voice. "No . . . more." Her voiced pinched off with a sob.

Prophet unsheathed his bowie, and cut the rope tying her right ankle to a bedpost. "It's Prophet." He walked over and cut

367

the rope lashing her other ankle to another bedpost.

As he walked up the side of the bed to cut the rope securing Josephina's right wrist, she opened her eyes to stare up at him through the screen of her brown hair. She didn't say anything. She just watched him cut her wrist free and then lean over the bed to cut the other one free.

Tears rolled down her cheeks.

Prophet straightened as he sheathed the bowie, and stared down at her. "Everything's going to be all right."

Josephina shook her head slightly and then rolled onto her side, facing away from him, raising her knees and crossing her arms to cover her breasts. Her voice sounded thin and far away. "There was no cache, like Savidge said."

"I don't doubt it."

Prophet harbored no ill will toward the girl. Desperate folks did desperate things. He walked to the door, stopped, and glanced back at her. She lay staring at the stained mattress.

"I'll get him," he said.

He moved out into the hall and stopped suddenly. He started to raise the Winchester but lowered it when he saw the young *puta* standing at the far end of the hall, near the top of the stairs. Lines cut across her dark forehead with fear and chagrin.

"They pay more for *gringo putas* here," she said softly, shaking her hair back out of her eyes. "*Senor* Stinson was going to buy her from the ugly gringo, Savidge, and take her down to Mexico."

"Yeah, I bet she'd make even more down there." Prophet moved to the girl, placing a hand on her shoulder. "See to her, will you, *senorita*?"

The girl nodded. Prophet shouldered the Winchester, dropped quickly down the stairs, and strode across the saloon. He scooped up the Richards and pushed through the batwings, stopping suddenly on the gallery and gazing east. Again, he started to bring the rifle to bear, but left it on his shoulder.

Louisa rode her brown and white pinto into the yard, the pinto's hooves lifting small puffs of dust as it cantered toward the *cantina*. Prophet stepped down off the gallery, slid his Winchester into its saddle sheath, and broke open the Richards.

Louisa rode up beside him, staring curiously down at him. He didn't look at her as he plucked the spent wads from the shotgun's barrels and replaced them with fresh shells from his cartridge belt.

"I didn't have any luck," Louisa said. "I assume you did?"

"If you could call it that." Prophet snapped the shotgun closed and slung it over his right shoulder. He stepped up onto Mean's back, and glanced at Louisa. "Josephina's inside. She's beat up. The bastard was pimping her. Check in on her, will you?"

"You're going after him, I take it?"

"You got that right."

"I should go with you."

"No." Prophet shook his head. "I wanna do it this way." He glanced at the *cantina*. "Stay with her. She's in a bad way."

He reined Mean around, touched spurs to the gelding's flanks, and bounded off in a ground-eating gallop, following Savidge's fresh tracks across the dusty yard and into the desert beyond. The man's tracks followed no trail but headed cross-country, weaving through the chaparral. They seemed to be leading toward a red, stone ridge wall looming in the northwest.

Prophet pushed Mean hard, slowing only now and then to make sure he was still on Savidge's trail. He wasn't going to lose the killer again.

When he'd ridden for a good fifteen minutes, he reined Mean to a sudden, skidding stop, and stared at the ground, frowning.

"What the hell?"

Another set of horse tracks angled in from the south, from

between two dusty mesquites. They overlaid Savidge's tracks. Another rider was now on Savidge's trail.

Thunder rumbled in the northern distance.

Prophet jerked his head up. He looked at the sky over the tall, craggy ridge. Not a cloud in that massive Arizona vault.

The thunder could be only one thing.

"Shit!"

Prophet spurred Mean into another instant, ground-chewing gallop. Horse and rider weaved through the chaparral and around cabin-sized boulders that had long ago tumbled from the northern ridge. The ridge itself grew larger and taller before Prophet, so that he could soon see every cleft and fissure, every pale splash of bird shit, every shadow. A gap opened in the massive wall. The two sets of tracks that Prophet was following led toward the gap.

Prophet galloped around a one-armed saguaro, and reined Mean to another skidding stop. The ridge wall bulged on his right. The gap was nearly straight ahead and slightly left. It was the mouth of a narrow canyon. The two sets of horse tracks led into the canyon.

Prophet swung down from Mean's back, and dropped the reins. Securing the Richards on his right shoulder, he slid his Winchester out of the saddle sheath, and pumped a cartridge into the chamber.

Slowly, he strode around the bulge in the ridge wall and into the twenty-foot gap that was the canyon's mouth. The wall still bulged out from his right, so he couldn't see more than a few feet ahead of him.

He took another two slow, careful steps, wary of an ambush. Something shiny lay on the red caliche before him, just beyond the bulge in the ridge. Prophet stooped and plucked the empty cartridge casing off the ground. He held it up between his thumb and index finger.

The three-inch .50-90 Sharps black powder cartridge glinted in the sun washing off the ridge. The brass was still warm.

Prophet tossed the cartridge down and walked farther but even more slowly into the canyon, his heart beating insistently against his breastbone. The bulge started pulling back away from him, revealing more of the narrow canyon beyond. The cleft was littered with rocks and driftwood likely deposited by monsoon rains, for the canyon was probably a creek bed in the wet seasons. Occasional clumps of brown grass and cactus grew between the rocks.

Prophet took four more slow steps, his spurs ringing faintly, and stopped once more. He looked down, grimacing.

A man lay belly down before him. The man wore faded denims with ragged cuffs, a brown leather vest over a striped shirt, and a cartridge belt. Two pistols were holstered on his hips. Two knives were sheathed at the back of his shell belt, the Spanish-style obsidian, silver-capped handles jutting over each kidney. His hands lay on the ground near where his ears would have been if he'd still had ears, which he didn't.

In fact, the man didn't even have a head.

Only ragged bits of bone and blood marked where the man's head had been hastily chopped off, likely with a hatchet. A hole the size of a silver dollar had been blown through the middle of his back between his shoulder blades.

Blood puddled the ground all around where the head would have been, atop Chaz Savidge's shoulders. The killer had probably acquired those two stylish pig stickers from the Mexicans whom Prophet had beefed in the *cantina,* in return for romps with Josephina Hawkins. Prophet didn't know why that thought occurred to him just now, when he had more important things to think about, but it did.

He ground his teeth in fury but also in disappointment that he hadn't been the one to kill Savidge. But the killer had gotten what he'd deserved, just the same.

About thirty yards beyond Savidge's headless corpse, the killer's dappled gray gelding stood pulling at the galleta grass growing amongst the rocks on the canyon's left side. Chewing, the horse turned to look dully at Prophet. Its ears twitched a quarter second before the familiar screech of a heavy caliber bullet came flying down from the right ridge wall.

The slug slammed into the ground two feet to Prophet's left, leaving a hole the size of a man's fist and throwing dirt and gravel in all directions.

"Who in the hell *is* that son of a bitch?" Prophet spat as he ran out away from the right wall of the canyon. He crossed the canyon floor at a dead sprint and ran up the opposite, sloping wall, his boots slipping on talus as he tried to gain a finger of crenellated rock about fifty feet up from the canyon floor.

He gritted his teeth as he ran, knowing he had only about one more second before the son of a bitch with the Big Fifty reloaded and drew another bead on him. The clock in Prophet's head wound down, and he dove forward a wink before another large-caliber chunk of lead screeched through the air a foot behind him to hammer a boulder with a wicked, deafening *ka-thunk!*

Prophet hit the ground behind the jutting finger of sandstone, rolled to the far side, tossed his hat down, and snaked his Winchester around the side of the stone finger. Smoke was webbing thinly about three quarters up the opposite ridge from the canyon floor, amongst boulders littering the steep slope.

Prophet saw a man's hatted head move in a notch in the rocks.

The bounty hunter opened fire, knowing he was too far away for accurate shooting with the Winchester but hoping for a lucky shot or a lucky ricochet. When he'd fired six fast rounds, the echoes of his shots echoing around the canyon, he drew back behind his cover.

Another bullet glanced off the side of the finger with a shrill spang. It was followed closely by the cannon's thunder.

"Bastard," Prophet said, pressing his back to the finger and punching fresh shells into the Winchester's breech. "Bounty-poaching bastard!"

Prophet racked a fresh round into the Winchester's breech. Holding the rifle straight up and down before him, the butt resting on the ground between his spread legs, he waited for another thundering report.

None came.

A man's voice shouted from across the canyon, "He's all mine, Prophet. Chaz Savidge's head is all mine. Why not admit defeat and go on your bloody way, bucko? If you don't, you're gonna lose your own head to my good ole cannon here! You two met before, I think. You and my Big Fifty!"

"An Englishman," Prophet muttered, mentally perusing the short list of foreign bounty hunters he was aware of.

He knew a Norski named Igor Iverson; a German named Rolf Becker, who'd earned a reputation working for the railroad back in the '70s; a Pollack named Paul "Pig" Stravinksi; and a couple of Mexicans. Prophet couldn't remember having come across an English bounty hunter. Bounty hunting seemed a little too messy, too uncivilized for an Englishman.

Didn't they shave every day and stick out their pinky finger when they sipped their afternoon tea?

He'd known Englishmen who hunted game animals for trophies, but *men* for *bounties*? This man was obviously an aberration. A savage English aberration.

Not only did he hunt bounties, he poached them . . .

Prophet turned his head to one side. "Who in the hell are you, you bounty-poachin' son of a bitch?"

"Rutherford H.L. Chivington the Fifth . . . at your service,

Mr. Prophet." The man's lilting voice echoed. "Call me Squire. Most folks do!"

"How 'bout if I just call you a cowardly, back-shootin', ambushin', bounty-poachin', limey son of a bitch!" Prophet returned. "Because that's what you are! If you don't turn that head back over to me *pronto*, I'm gonna gut-shoot you and leave you howlin' the coyotes in!"

"All's fair in such a bloody trade, is my way of thinkin', Proph!" Chivington yelled. "Besides, I'm not the tracker I once was. I've become lazy in my later years, you see? And I prefer having other men do the dirty work *for* me!"

"Dirty work?" Prophet laughed in exasperation. "You're the one who chopped ole Savidge's head off!"

"I meant the long hours of tracking and then running the quarry to ground. You see, this right here is tedious to me, and far more effort than it's worth. I'd rather be soaking in a hot tub with a big-breasted Mexican whore. Unfortunately, my long-range shooting skills must have deteriorated slightly, along with my tracking skills. More's the pity! I never used to waste so much lead. I'll have to remedy that in the future by getting closer to the bounty hunters I ambush. Consider yourself a mistake I'm learning from, Mr. Prophet!"

The man bellowed a raucous laugh.

CHAPTER EIGHTEEN

Another bullet came screeching in from the opposite ridge, followed a quarter-second later by the Sharps's menacing thunder.

A rocky clattering rose from the slope flanking Prophet. He looked up to see several stones rolling down the ridge, bouncing and clacking. Then he saw Louisa moving down the slope, keeping to the shade of the large boulders on her left, which, angled as they were, shielded her from Chivington's view.

She moved lithely through the wedge-shaped shadows angling out from the boulders, hop-skipping from one rock to another, steadily descending.

Slowing her pace, she crouched and looked across the canyon as she drew within several yards of her partner, then took two bounding leaps and dropped to her haunches beside him.

Her suntanned cheeks were flushed beneath the shading brim of her Stetson. She held her Winchester in one hand.

"I thought I told you to stay with Josephina," Prophet scolded.

"The Mexican girl's with Josephina. You're gonna need help going up against that Big Fifty again, you fool."

"I thought you were finally starting to defer to my considerably more experience."

She wrinkled a nostril at him. "Really, Lou—how long did you think that was going to last?"

Again, the Big Fifty roared as another heavy chunk of lead plowed into the side of the ridge near Prophet and his partner.

Prophet donned his hat, curling the brim to his liking. He

liked being able to see around the brim. "Well, as long as you're here, you might as well make yourself useful."

"All right," she said, giving an ironic quirk to her mouth corners. "How do you want to handle this?"

Prophet grinned. "Damn, I like the sound of that! Could you say it one more time, girl?"

She scowled at him.

"All right, all right," he said, edging a fleeting look around the rock toward Chivington's ridge. "You distract him while I work on across the slope. I'm gonna try and get across the canyon without him boring a train-sized tunnel through my brisket with that cannon of his, and then I'm gonna try and climb his slope and work around behind him. I want that head back, goddamnit. We've come too far, and it just ain't right. The man's got no honor!"

"Stop preaching to the choir, Lou."

"But be careful. You keep your pretty head down."

"Thanks for the compliment, but how am I supposed to keep my pretty head down and distract him at the same time?"

"You'll think of somethin'." Prophet ran the back of his hand through the long, blond hair trailing down over her left arm. "I sure would hate to see them pretty locks mussed."

"Will you get going?"

"All right, all right. We'll wait till he throws down on us again, and then you toss some lead at him, and I'll skin out."

They didn't have to wait long for Chivington's next shot.

When the dust from the bullet was still pluming, Louisa snaked her carbine around the right side of the stone finger, and cut loose. Prophet bolted out away from the left side of the covering stone, sprinting along the side of the slope, moving parallel with the canyon floor.

He ran hard, wincing, remembering the size of the hole that the Big Fifty had left in Chaz Savidge's back. The burn in his cheek and the ache in his left thigh were also reminders of the damage the buffalo gun could inflict.

Louisa kept working her Winchester—steady, even shots that, for the moment, were silencing Chivington's cannon. Prophet knew that as soon as Louisa had popped all nine of her caps, the Big Fifty would likely go back to work in earnest.

He counted the Vengeance Queen's shots as he ran, weaving around tufts of brush, cactus, and sandstone boulders. A rattle-snake gave a shrill, menacing rattle somewhere to his left.

"Shit!"

Prophet leaped high when out the corner of his eye he saw the granite-gray viper strike from a slice of shade by a small, square rock. The snake's flat head bounced off the heel of his left boot with a nerve-rattling nudge and a faint thump.

"Close one!" the bounty hunter wheezed out as, hearing Louisa's Winchester go quiet, he rammed his left shoulder up against a boulder roughly the size of a small farm wagon.

Across the canyon, the Big Fifty roared, its echoes rocketing around the chasm, dwindling quickly to eerie silence. Prophet didn't hear the bullets strike. He wondered if Chivington knew he was on the run, or did the poacher think Prophet was the one who'd been throwing .44 caliber bullets at him?

He hoped so. He'd like to give the limey, bounty-poaching, head-thieving bastard the surprise of his life.

When Louisa went back to work with her Winchester, Prophet ran out from behind the rock, running generally downslope now toward the canyon floor.

He traced a serpentine path of least resistance around barrel cacti and saguaros and wicked-looking patches of prickly pear. He holed up again when Louisa's Winchester fell silent and was curious when he did not hear the Big Fifty roar in reply to the Vengeance Queen's fusillade.

He would have liked to hear the blast, because then he'd

have a better idea, judging by where the .50-90 bullet was placed, if Chivington knew Prophet was trying to work around him. Prophet wanted to be the one to surprise Chivington. Not the other way around.

When Louisa's Winchester began speaking again from behind and above him now and a good ways off to his left, he sprinted across the canyon floor and up the opposite slope. He angled back in the direction of where he figured Chivington was still holed up in his nest of rocks.

Anxiety was a heavy weight in his lower belly. His left thigh was mostly healed, but it burned now as he ran.

Louisa had only so many rounds to feed Chivington. This batch she was triggering now was likely close to the last of what she'd had in her Winchester to begin with and what she'd been toting on her cartridge belt.

Should've given her a few of mine, Prophet thought as he climbed, his feet burning and swelling inside his boots as he trudged heavily up the incline. Boots were made for riding not running, just as Prophet himself had been.

When he was halfway up the slope and among slab-sided boulders larger than most prospectors' cabins, Louisa's shots quit.

The last one's echo spiraled quickly skyward. The echo hadn't died when the Big Fifty's roar assaulted Prophet's ears. He glimpsed the large frame of the shooter standing sixty feet up the slope from him now, aiming the cannon straight out from his right shoulder.

Prophet threw himself hard left as the slug scalded the air off his right ear and plunked into the ragged arm of a saguaro behind him.

"Another close one!" the bounty hunter told himself, pressing his back up against the side of a boulder facing the downslope.

Sweat bathed his face and his back. His shirt clung to him. His mouth was dry. He tried to spit dirt from his lips but he had no saliva.

Chivington called from upslope, from the other end of the boulder, "Your partner joined you, I see, Prophet. Always nice to have a partner. Especially one so beautiful."

"Chivington, have we met?"

"We've run into each other, a time or two. Here and there. Your reputation precedes you, Prophet, so I knew who you were but since my reputation is still chasing its own shadow, you didn't know who I was."

"Keep poachin' the bounties of honest, hard-working hunters, and you'll gain a reputation, all right."

"Come out of there, and let's introduce ourselves to each other right and proper. I think your partner has come to the end of her ammunition."

"I'm going to introduce myself to you with a forty-four round, you son of a bitch!"

"The head's mine, Lou," Chivington said. "Times change. People change. *Professions* change. It's a dog-eat-dog world."

"This dog bites back."

Prophet was making his way around the left side of the boulder, climbing the slope nearly straight up toward the top. Chivington was somewhere in the rocks around the boulder's far end, keeping to the high ground.

"Where are you, Lou?" the Englishman asked. "Are you on the move, prolonging the inevitable?"

Prophet didn't answer.

Setting each boot down carefully, he moved upslope along the side of the boulder. He held the Winchester out from his right side, dragging that shoulder lightly along the side of the rock. Occasionally, he glanced behind him to see if the poacher was circling.

Chivington had also fallen silent, not wanting to give away his position.

Prophet's heart beat slowly but harshly in his ears.

His throat was so dry he wanted to cough but resisted the urge.

That Big Fifty could do a lot of damage. From close up, especially . . .

He doffed his hat, and, holding it down by his left thigh, edged a look around the backside of the boulder.

Nothing. Only the slab sides and severe angles of more boulders—a geometric patchwork of copper-colored sunlight and purple shadows. The breeze whispered softly against the sides of the rocks. It whistled mournfully through the narrow gaps between them.

Those were the only sounds.

Prophet kept anticipating another thundering report of the Big Fifty blowing the silence to pieces.

Blowing *him* to pieces . . .

He looked behind. All clear.

He stepped around the front corner of the boulder and made his slow, silent way to the far side. When he came to the far corner, he stopped and cast another slow, cautious look along the downslope side.

Something clattered to his left. He swung the Winchester toward it.

It was only a flat rock just then coming to rest among other stones. Someone had tossed it from the opposite direction. A shadow moved in the corner of Prophet's right eye. He whipped his head back in that direction to see a tall man in fringed buckskins and long, yellow hair streaked with brown and gray whipping down around his shoulders and thick, tangled beard in the breeze. The Englishman wore a broad-brimmed leather hat.

Chivington was aiming the Sharps straight out from his right shoulder at Prophet, narrowing one eye as he gazed down the barrel. The Big Fifty's octagonal maw yawned wide. Prophet's heart thudded for what he was sure would be the last time as he brought his own rifle to bear too late.

The thrown rock had distracted him for a quarter of a second too long.

The Sharps's heavy hammer dropped . . . but with a clang instead of a burst of smoke and fire. There was a muffled crack and a hiss.

Chivington stared down in horror at the Sharps's heavy hammer shaped like a curled thumb against the firing pin. At the same time, Prophet finished his motion of aiming and firing the Winchester, which barked loudly in the narrow gap between the boulders.

Chivington grunted as he jerked his head up. The Sharps sagged in his arms. He took two shambling steps straight backward, dragging his heels and his spurs.

"Oh," he said, making a face. "Oh . . . bloody hell!"

Prophet moved forward, pumping another round into the Winchester's breech. "That's the thing about them buffalo guns," he said in his slow, southern drawl. "When they get too hot, they'll jam on ya. That's why I've always celebrated the day ole Winchester brought out the '73. I can take down bounty poachers from dawn till dusk, slick as shit on a hot metal roof!"

He smiled and pumped another round into the Englishman's tall frame.

Chivington stumbled backward again, this time kicking a blood-stained croaker sack with the heel of his left, mule-eared boot. Something tumbled out of the mouth of the sack and rolled down the slope. As Chivington fell, dropping the Big Fifty, he twisted around and shouted, *"Noo!"*

He flung an arm out toward the head of Chaz Savidge rolling down the slope behind him.

The man's anguished plea echoed.

The head came to rest against the right ankle of Louisa Bonaventure, who stood about twenty yards down the slope below the writhing Chivington. Holding her carbine across her chest, Louisa looked down at the head, bald on top, with mild interest, and nudged it with her boot toe.

Prophet walked over to stare down at Chivington, who ground his back against the rocks and gravel, groaning. The man lay still as his eyes found Prophet. Fear glazed them.

Prophet lowered his rifle toward the man's head. "Maybe you can find an honest occupation in hell," the bounty hunter said.

The poacher screamed and lifted his hands to cover his face, but not before Prophet's Winchester finished him.

Chivington farted as his body relaxed against the ground.

Louisa looked up the slope at Prophet. "Lose something?" she asked, and glanced down at Savidge's head, the man's face snarling up at her.

"Nah," Prophet said, picking up the empty croaker sack.

He walked down to Louisa, picked up Chaz Savidge's head by the long, tangled hair dangling over the ears, and stuffed it into the sack. He shook the sack to settle the head and then tied a loose knot in the neck. "Savidge did."

He narrowed an eye at his partner. "How 'bout if we go back yonder and give this ole head to Miss Josephina? I think she's the one person in this whole, ugly frontier who could use it even more than we could . . . hungry as I am."

Louisa arched a brow. "How 'bout the doxies? You never know when you're gonna have two dimes to rub together again."

Prophet shrugged. "*I* can wait for *them*. The question is, can *they* wait for *me*?"

As he started down the slope toward the canyon floor, he set his rifle on his right shoulder and slung the head of Savidge over his left shoulder. "Let's take the head of Chaz Savidge to

Miss Josephina," he said. "And watch the girl's eyes flash in delight!"

He began singing an old Confederate military song.

Louisa fell into step behind him, shouldering her own rifle. "You're a romantic cuss, Lou Prophet," she said, giving her head a slow wag, smiling. "I'll give you that."

ABOUT THE AUTHOR

Bestselling western novelist **Peter Brandvold** has penned over seventy fast-action westerns under his own name and his penname, Frank Leslie. He is the author of the ever-popular .45-Caliber books featuring Cuno Massey as well as the Lou Prophet and Yakima Henry novels. Recently, under the Frank Leslie name, he started the Revenger series featuring Mike Sartain. Head honcho at "Mean Pete Publishing," publisher of lightning-fast western ebooks, he lives in western Minnesota with his dog. Visit his website at www.peterbrandvold.com. Follow his blog at: www.peterbrandvold.blogspot.com.

The employees of Five Star Publishing hope you have enjoyed this book.

Our Five Star novels explore little-known chapters from America's history, stories told from unique perspectives that will entertain a broad range of readers.

Other Five Star books are available at your local library, bookstore, all major book distributors, and directly from Five Star/Gale.

Connect with Five Star Publishing

Visit us on Facebook:
https://www.facebook.com/FiveStarCengage

Email:
FiveStar@cengage.com

For information about titles and placing orders:
(800) 223-1244
gale.orders@cengage.com

To share your comments, write to us:
Five Star Publishing
Attn: Publisher
10 Water St., Suite 310
Waterville, ME 04901